MISS CARTER'S WAR

SHEILA HANCOCK

BLOOMSBURY
LONDON · NEW DELHI · NEW YORK · SYDNEY

First published in Great Britain 2014
This paperback published 2015

Copyright © 2014 by Sheila Hancock

Bloomsbury Publishing Plc
50 Bedford Square
London
WC1B 3DP

www.bloomsbury.com

Bloomsbury is a trademark of Bloomsbury Publishing Plc

Bloomsbury Publishing, London, New Delhi, New York and Sydney

A CIP catalogue record for this book is available from the British Library

ISBN 978 1 4088 4360 4

10 9 8 7 6 5 4 3 2 1

Typeset by Hewer Text UK Ltd, Edinburgh
Printed and bound in Great Britain by CPI Group (UK) Ltd, Croydon CR0 4YY

For my teachers

Author's Note

This is a novel and a work of fiction, based upon real historical events.

The characters of Miss Fryer, Miss Tudor Craig, Mr Duane, Colonel Buckmaster, Dr Peter Chapple and Dr Patrick Woodcock are real, but all other characters, although inspired in some cases by real people, have been fictionalised for the purposes of this work and are not intended to represent any actual persons.

I believe in aristocracy . . . Not an aristocracy of power, based upon rank and influence, but an aristocracy of the sensitive, the considerate and the plucky. Its members are to be found in all nations and classes, and all through the ages, and there is a secret understanding between them when they meet. They represent the true human tradition, the one permanent victory of our queer race over cruelty and chaos.

E.M. Forster, *Two Cheers for Democracy*

Chapter 1

Marguerite looked at her reflection in the mirror and despaired. Even with no make-up she was too flashy. Too French. She moved the cameo brooch higher on the neck of her white blouse to hide any hint of cleavage. The dark grey worsted skirt she had made from a Butterwick pattern looked suitably schoolmistressy, ending as it did just below the knee, its semi-flare gliding flat over her bottom, but her bosom betrayed her. She buttoned up the grey cardigan she had knitted in simple purl-plain from the pattern in *Woman's Own* to further lessen the impact of her troublesome bust. Better. It made for a pretty depressing image but one that was suitable for Miss Carter, English teacher in the Home Counties. The grammar school demanded not just academic excellence from its staff but a respectable example to be given to the girls.

The year before the Mistress of Girton had given her a lesson on dressing appropriately for the occasion. The occasion in question had been momentous. On the 21st of October 1948 Marguerite was one of the small posse of women to first receive the grudging recognition of their worthiness to become full members of the venerable University of Cambridge, rather than being excluded from societies, the library, the Union, grants and scholarships. A few dons had hitherto allowed women students to slink into lectures, but pointedly still addressed the assembly as 'gentlemen'. Now they were to receive proper degrees, alongside the Queen, deemed a more appropriate recipient of an honorary award than any of the women who had fought for years for that belated right.

Marguerite had concocted an outfit that would have pleased her French mother, based on the very latest Christian Dior trend. When she turned up in the Girton common room to fit her gown and mortarboard, she felt jubilantly happy in her scarlet skirt 8 inches from the floor, pushed out by a stiff buckram petticoat showing a flash of lace edging. The waspie waist corset that reduced her 21 inches to 20 enhanced the curvaceousness she had inherited from her mother. What with the matching black patent-leather wide belt and tottering high heels, the final effect, she knew, was ravishing.

The Mistress of the College was aghast.

'What on earth are you wearing?'

'The New Look for a new era. D'you like it?'

'For a wedding, perhaps. But this is a solemn ceremony in the presence of Her Majesty and all the university and city dignitaries. An historic occasion.'

'I know. That's why I made an effort.'

'Marguerite, we have fought long and hard for this privilege. Hitherto we have been reluctantly tolerated as long as we didn't frighten the horses. We have had to convince the nervous nags of this establishment that we pose no threat, that we will not upend centuries of tradition and destroy their cosy world. Yet. By guile and subterfuge, we have convinced them we are harmless ladies. And I use that word advisedly. Now you come prancing in to take part in one of their beloved rituals looking like a latter-day Zuleika Dobson.'

'Who is she?'

'All the men in Oxford fell in love with her and committed suicide.'

'Well, this is Cambridge.'

'Yes, that is where she was heading at the end of the novel. They have been expecting her here ever since.'

'Well, I'm sorry. But we've never done it before. There is no precedent for what we wear.'

'Come with me.'

The Mistress took her to her rooms and gave her a black dress with a white collar and long sleeves.

'You can keep the red nail varnish but wear these gloves when you kneel and take your certificate. You look disappointed.'

'I am a bit. I wanted to say, "See – I got a First, you sad, old misogynist stick-in-the-muds. Look – I'm all woman and very, very clever."'

The Mistress laughed then took her hands.

'You know, Marguerite, the gown is the important thing. Wear it with pride. You deserve it. Your life so far has been exemplary. You had a good war—'

'I always find that a strange choice of word – good.'

She stands holding the small boy's hand, watching the man shoot the girl in the flowery dress. Then he shows the boy how to hold the gun and helps him pull the trigger. 'Good,' he smiles, and pats the boy's head. 'That's for your mother,' he says, as he pokes the body with his boot to check that it is properly dead.

'I apologise. It is a ludicrous anachronism especially applied to this last nightmare, but you know what I mean. I know you don't like it talked about, but a Croix de Guerre implies great courage. You have been an exceptional student. You know,

Marguerite, you could have done anything. The Foreign Office is opening up for women now, as long as you don't get married, and politics would have been a possibility. And obviously writing. Academic appointments will now be available to women here, but you have chosen to teach children. Why?'

'I want to change the world.'

'Oh, is that all?'

'And where best to start than with the children? I hope I don't sound too highfalutin.'

'No, my dear' – she touched her face sadly – 'just young.'

'I have no pride in my life so far.'

'That's a shame. Well, perhaps you can wear your gown in tribute to all those women who won this for you.'

So she did. The ill-fitting black frock notwithstanding, tipping her mortarboard at a jaunty angle and brushing up the fur trim on her hood, as she stood outside the Senate House after the ceremony, she made a silent vow to emulate their commitment and thereby justify the pain that her desertion had caused Marcel.

So many debts to so many people.

Now, here she was, about to start the noble quest she had dreamt of and worked for and she was worrying about her hair, for heaven's sake. It was too red, too curly, altogether too unladylike. Her hat, a grey felt beret, would flatten it or she could tuck it inside, but she couldn't keep her hat on all day. Eventually, she settled for scragging it back into a tight pleat and sticking down any stray wisps with soap. That worked. She was desexed, neutered, unthreatening. The Mistress would approve.

Her legs were a problem. She toyed with the idea of the gossamer nylon stockings nestling in the drawer, wrapped in tissue paper, but worried that their dubious black-market source would be suspect. So, instead, she stained the offending slim limbs with gravy browning and drew a pencil seam up the back, made slightly wiggly by her nervous hands. Sensible lace-up black shoes eliminated any risk of allure.

She allowed herself only one dash of chic. From the back of her underwear drawer she took a small Chanel box. Inside, wrapped in a piece of white silk, was a pair of black-leather gloves. The best ones, for special occasions. She caressed their softness as they lay in her hand and then held them against her cheek. Did she imagine a faint echo of Jean Patou Joy? One day, when she was about three years old, she had shuffled about the room, naked apart from her mother's high-heeled red shoes and these gloves. She flapped her hands in imitation of Maman's animated elegance. Maman laughed and clapped. 'Comme tu es belle, ma petite. Viens.' And she folded her in her arms. Soft, warm, fragrant.

Her hands were bigger now and had done terrible things, but Maman would understand and forgive. The fingers were too tight, so she took from the box the ivory stretchers with the silver A for Adrienne and gently eased them to allow her mother's gloves to grasp her hands. This was her special occasion. She suspected Maman would have preferred it to be a good marriage but her intellectual English father would surely have been proud of his Cambridge-educated teacher daughter.

When she pulled on her hat and belted her grey gabardine mac, the disguise was as effective as any she had used during the war. The small flat she had found herself was a ride away from the school with a pleasant walk to the bus stop. She made her way anonymously in the slight mist through Wilmington, nodding at the few people around so early in the morning. A road sweeper gathering autumn leaves doffed his cap at her and they exchanged 'Good morning's'. She took a short cut to the stop along a path through a copse of tangled trees and brambles where the bosky smell tickled her nose. She sneezed, causing a woman walking her dog to say 'Bless you'. She wanted to say, 'Yes, I am blessed. This is the first day of the rest of my life,' but she was momentarily downcast by the sight of some huts behind a high barbed-wire fence, a former prisoner-of-war camp. What hell had awaited those men when they returned home?

The bus was crowded. A boy sprang to his feet and offered her a seat.

The bus conductor looked at her as he clipped her ticket.

'All right, duck?'

'Bit nervous. New job.'

'Where?'

'The grammar school.'

'Oh la-di-da. Tuppence to talk to you then.'

The laughter in the bus was good-natured. Several people wished her good luck. Marguerite looked around at her fellow passengers as the bus rattled along. There were men in overalls, worn housewives with stroppy babies and string bags for shopping, two men in smart suits with bowler hats on their laps, a group of children quietly giggling over a comic, making the most of the last day of the holidays, jam jars and nets on sticks ready for tiddler fishing, three nurses, and a couple of men in RAF uniform. It occurred to her that one of the few benefits of war was the enforced breaking down of class barriers. These people had been evacuated, served in factories or the services, and had lived with and worked alongside those they would normally only have encountered superficially. She herself was destined for an upper-class leisured life until the German invasion of France had derailed that course. She could barely remember the rigid convent school, the piano and dance classes, the trips to the Comédie-Française and the Opéra.

Enthused by the good wishes, she alighted at Dartford Heath.

The landscape was just recovering from its use for Army manoeuvres. The tank tracks were grassing over and the sand-filled sacks for bayonet practice, hanging from gallow-like structures, were being used as swings. The mist had lifted now to show a blue sky devoid of swollen barrage balloons. Gone too were the big iron cylinders lining the road in readiness for making a smokescreen. On a patch of waste ground were abandoned three small concrete pyramids, fortunately never called upon to test their effectiveness in stopping an invading army in its tracks.

As she walked along past neglected semi-detached pebble-dashed houses she saw that the gaps made by bombs had been tidied up, the remaining rubble providing a good playground. The blasted walls revealed the wallpapers so carefully chosen from sample books, now flapping in the slight breeze. In one house a staircase remained, leading to a void which had been a bedroom where there had been love and respite. Possibly the owners had sheltered from the bombing in the cupboard beneath, in which case they may have survived, while their world was destroyed around them. Shattered lives everywhere, but now the mending process was underway and she was eager to be part of it. There, in front of her, was the arena for her impending challenge.

Chapter 2

Dartford County Grammar School for Girls had been built in 1912 in a not-quite-Gothic style. There were stone walls and a modest tower in the middle, but there was a regularity about the edifice that undermined the gesture towards the medieval. It was nevertheless imposing and suggested a seriousness of purpose. Marguerite was suddenly scared to death – she with the nerves of steel. There was a double-fronted main door, and as she approached along a path, through the garden which had seen better days, she realised she was holding her breath, and had to stand for a moment gulping in air to calm herself.

On the door was an iron knob which she assumed was a bell. She tried twisting it and pressing it to no avail. Panicking, she pulled it and it sprang back making a loud clanging noise. She forced a polite smile in anticipation as the heavy door creaked open. The smile froze when a huge woman was revealed.

'You should have gone round the side. We don't use this door. Miss Fryer, Headmistress.' The woman proffered a large hand.

Miss Fryer must have been 6ft 2 in her bare feet which no one, it was fair to assume, had ever caught a glimpse of. They were firmly encased in thick lisle stockings and lace-up Cuban-heeled shoes, presumably handmade, because no shop would ever stock that size. She could have bought a man's shoe, but the slight heel indicated she had womanly aspirations, or just enjoyed towering over people. It was certainly effective. Marguerite was reduced to babbling an apology as she bent her neck to look up at the face above her.

The headmistress had a surprisingly small head, with pepper-and-salt hair held back by a tight bun. Her head did not seem to match the extraordinary body. This was large, very large, but solid rather than fat. It was difficult to detect any shape, encased as it was in a peculiar costume with a jacket, tailored to betray no trace of gender, reaching below her hips, where it paired a matching skirt that stretched, featureless, to her lower calf. Marguerite was profoundly relieved that she was not standing in front of this monument in her New Look frou-frou. The monument now smiled down at her.

'You weren't to know. Come to my study. We'll have what will need to be a quick chat. Rather a busy day, I'm afraid.'

The study was wood-panelled with two walls lined with books. A bay window gave a panoramic view of the playground and playing field beyond. Miss Fryer seated herself behind a large mahogany desk and indicated for Marguerite to sit on a wooden chair placed in front.

After a few pleasantries about the weather and her journey, Miss Fryer said, 'I see from your records you served in the FANY during the war. I see also that you were awarded a medal. So I suspect that nursing was a cover for something a tad more dangerous.'

Marguerite hesitated, then said, 'I was in the SOE.'

'Ah, Special Operations Executive. Bit of a mad lot. We at Bletchley called you the Baker Street Irregulars.'

The sun is shining in Baker Street. Inside Colonel Buckmaster's office the curtains are drawn. The colonel, a tall man, surprisingly in casual sports jacket and flannels, rises to greet her. 'Ah, Carter. My minions are impressed with you. You stood up to their grilling. I do not have to tell you of the dangers you face if you join the Firm, your parents' deaths are evidence enough. We will send you for training but you will be on your own. From this moment on you can confide in no one. Everything you do is to be kept secret. You will be living a lie.'

'You worked at the code-breaking centre, Headmistress?'

'Yes.'

'Miss Fryer, forgive me, but I'd rather—'

'Miss Carter, there is no need to expand on what you did. Four years after the war is too soon to disclose all our goings-on. Not easy to sum up anyway. It is difficult, isn't it, to break the habit of secrecy? None of the staff know what I did during the war and there is no reason why they should know about your role either.'

'Thank you, I'd prefer that.'

'Understood. But in your new job as a teacher at this school it will be an advantage that you'll have experienced the horrors of war. You will understand your pupils better. They too have suffered. Ripped from their families, labelled and pushed on a train to be billeted with strangers, some of whom were cruel to them, physically and mentally. They have been bombed and machine-gunned, underfed and deprived of all the usual joys of childhood. Now they are having to adjust to men they scarcely know coming back from heaven knows what nightmares and taking over their homes. I see it as our major task to bring the order and discipline of education into their disrupted lives.'

'I will do my best, Headmistress.'

Miss Fryer came round the desk and shook Marguerite's hand.

'Thank you, and welcome. Now, come and meet the rest of the staff. They are in the tower.'

'Oh, what have they done?'

The raised eyebrow told her the joke was an old one, so, eschewing frivolity, Marguerite settled for silence as she followed the headmistress's purposeful stride along a classroom corridor. The smell of floor polish and the head's faint Parma violet perfume was pleasant as she went up a flight of stairs, through a small wooden door that led to a spiral staircase, and then another door, behind which she could hear chatter and laughter.

Miss Fryer tapped at the door and, giving an alarming wink to Marguerite, waited a moment for the noise to subside. After the faux pas of the tower joke Marguerite was too frightened to react. A wink back would surely be misplaced, so she smiled wanly.

'Good morning, ladies and gentleman.' Everyone leapt to their feet, apart from the one man in the room, who rose slowly, with a reluctance bordering on impertinence.

'Forgive the interruption. Here is our new recruit, Miss Carter. I know you will make her welcome. Will you please do the honours, Miss White? I must be elsewhere. Do please sit down, Mr Stansfield, don't mind me. Save your obviously waning strength for the term ahead.'

The staff room was a perfect square, as befits a tower, but that was the only regular thing about it. Compared with the impeccable order of the teaching area she had passed through, it was chaotic. There were battered armchairs over which, after the headmistress's exit, various women draped themselves; some had books, one knitted, another had a copy of *The Times*.

Miss White, Maths, a cheerful woman with Eton cropped iron-grey hair, introduced her to the teachers in the room, pointing out that others were round and about preparing for the start of term tomorrow, when all hell would break loose. Two middle-aged women were marking a pile of books on a small table, throwing the completed ones onto the floor. One, Miss Lewin, History, had brown hair plaited and twisted into ear-phones either side of her face, the other, Miss Haynes, Domestic Science, had blonde hair but her plaits were looped over the top of her head. Other than that they had few identifying features.

Miss Lewin lifted her reading glasses to squint at Marguerite.

'Oh God, you're young.'

'I'm twenty-four.'

'Exactly. Promise me you won't be earnest. I'm exhausted already and term hasn't even started.'

Miss Haynes, the other plaited one, rapped her hand with her marking pencil.

'Shut up, you old drear. What kind of welcome is that?'

She stood and shook hands with Marguerite.

'We are catching up with last term's exam marking. We give them the results tomorrow, poor things. Should have done them in the hols, but Miss Lewin and I went camping in France and tried to forget that we were teachers for a bit. I believe you're French, aren't you?'

Marguerite stiffened.

'Half French. My father was English. I left France when I was a child.'

'Oh I see. That accounts for your excellent English.'

'My accent is not perfect, I'm afraid.'

'Nonsense. It's hardly noticeable. It's charming. We were in the Vaucluse. Do you know it?'

A silence.

'Yes.'

'Beautiful, isn't it?'

'Yes.'

The sky is azure, the distant mountains sepia, the ravine clad in a palette of manifold greens, the verge is ablaze with red poppies, pink valerian, purple orchids, yellow gorse, chaste white daisies. On the road are strewn body parts and pools of crimson blood.

'But one is aware that there are scars. It is hard for us to imagine what it is like to be occupied.'

'Yes.'

Miss Lewin snorted.

'The Vaucluse was Vichy France. I should think they had a pretty cushy time, thank you very much.'

Miss Haynes hit her quite hard with the pencil.

'Will you shut up.'

Miss White tugged Marguerite towards a handsome woman, sitting on a hard-backed wooden chair and intent on a complicated-looking petit point picture on a wooden frame.

Miss Yates, Latin, gave a cursory nod of greeting.

'Sorry. Can't look up. Tricky bit.'

In the corner, an unkempt, wispy-haired woman, Miss Tudor-Craig, Music, was sitting legs akimbo, humming and chuckling to herself as she beat time with her hands.

When she felt Marguerite's eyes upon her she said, 'Want to join the choir, whoever you are?'

'Oh, well, my voice is not good, I'm afraid.'

'Nonsense. Do this. Doh ray me fah soh lah te doh.'

Marguerite tentatively did as she was bidden.

'Perfect. A soprano. Tuesday after school in the hall.'

Miss White squeezed her arm and pulled a face just as a youngish woman with lively blue eyes and a fresh complexion rushed into the staff room.

'Oh good. Marguerite, meet Mrs Conway, Hygiene.'

'You're married?'

Mrs Conway laughed.

'Yes, it's allowed. Marriage for teachers has been legal for five years now, you know. I don't think Miss Fryer really approves but she thought it better to have a married woman teaching reproduction.'

'Too late for me,' shouted Miss Trevelyan, Geography, who looked about sixty. 'No one'll have me now. Too late to procreate, so I make do with other people's children.'

'I'd have you any day,' the man piped up.

'You! Lawksamercy.' Miss Trevelyan raised her hands in mock horror. 'I don't want any reds under my bed.'

'Who said I'd be *under* it?'

Mr Stansfield, Sport, was obviously cock of the roost. Sprawled on the sofa, reading, his tie loose and shirt unbuttoned, he was handsome and knew it.

He stared at her with mocking blue eyes and ran a hand through his unruly hair as he said, 'You're far too young and pretty to join us sad sacks. Don't look so scared. We don't bite. Well, on rare occasions, some of us have been known to have a bit of a nibble.'

'Shut up, Tony, 'said Miss Haynes. 'You'll frighten her off and we badly need some fresh young blood.'

He licked his lips.

'Mmm, delicious.'

Marguerite had no idea how to respond so she opted yet again for a wan smile.

Miss White offered her a cup of tea and put a battered kettle on the gas ring.

'What did you think of Miss Fryer?'

'She looks a little odd. She's a giant, isn't she?'

Miss Yates rose to her feet, revealing that she too was over six foot but beanpole-thin. Folding her work into an embroidered cloth bag with wooden handles, she said, 'She is certainly a giant. In every sense. But only to pygmies.'

As she closed the door behind her, Miss White explained that Miss Yates and Miss Fryer shared a house, and she was her deputy, so was therefore somewhat biased, but the headmistress was indeed a fine woman.

Marguerite was mortified.

'I didn't mean to be rude. I'm not doing very well, am I? Shall I go out of the room and start again?'

One of the overworked plaited women reassured her that this room was their sanctuary to relax in; in the tower the staff were free to let their hair down and say whatever they liked, in contrast to the rest of the school where numerous rules had to be strictly observed by staff and pupils alike. They invited her to sit with her cup of tea while they briefed her on the protocol. No running in the corridors, no talking anywhere between classes, and then only when addressed by the teachers. Hats to be worn at all times outside the school when in uniform, skirt length just below the knee, lisle stockings in winter, white socks in summer, pupils to rise when staff entered the room and say 'Good morning' in unison and of course only ever use a teacher's surname prefixed by 'Miss'.

'My goodness,' said Marguerite. 'Is breathing allowed?'

The teachers explained that the school was run on fiercely competitive lines, end-of-term results being read out and put up on noticeboards in order of achievement. Any girl consistently near the bottom was given remedial classes and, if she didn't improve, asked to leave. On Speech Day, once a year, the staff wore their caps and gowns, which the girls judged by their relative prettiness, as opposed to the prestige of the college they represented, which none of them had heard of anyway.

'Why don't you be a devil and take your hat and coat off?'

Mr Stansfield, rose to help her.

'Mmm, racy gloves.'

Marguerite wondered at the daring innovation of allowing a man into this female stronghold, but surmised that there were few women highly qualified in sport and physical training and Miss Fryer wanted the best for her girls. He was heavily out-numbered and the headmistress would doubtless keep a strict eye out for any hanky-panky. Which, judging by the way he was stroking her leather-clad hands, she would need to.

Miss White slapped his wrist.

'Stop it, Mr Stansfield. Behave.'

Whereupon he threw his arms around the protesting Miss White.

'Oh do that again, you naughty teacher. I love it.'

Miss White extricated herself from his embrace and laugh-ingly told Marguerite to ignore him, he was incorrigible.

And full of himself, thought Marguerite. She had met his type at university. Men whose approach to women was monoto-nously sexual. But at least here, in this women's world, it was not threatening.

Miss White led her to a classroom and handed her over to her colleagues from the English department who were meeting to discuss the term's syllabus. An elderly woman with tightly crimped hair, wearing a maroon velvet frock, lightly dusted with chalk, was standing in front of the blackboard. She sported a pince-nez on a gold chain, and several strings of assorted beads. Her appearance suggested she had been here since the school was founded. She indicated for Marguerite to squash into one of the double desks with three other women.

'Welcome to the fold, Miss Carter. I am Miss Farringdon, head of English. I congratulate you on your degree. When I was up at Girton all I got was a certificate through the post with "Titular" scribbled on by hand. Was the ceremony impressive?'

'Very. And moving.'

'All those men must have enjoyed seeing you gals on your knees in front of them. I would have been tempted to do them a mischief while I was down there, but I suppose it would have been unseemly in front of Her Majesty.'

A barking laugh set her beads rattling.

'Now to work. Which is what really matters'

Miss Farringdon spread a lot of chalk on the board and herself as she illustrated her plans for the term.

'As you see there are five of us to cover grammar, literature, and composition.' The chalk squeaked as she drew a chart.

'You, Miss Carter, will be general dogsbody while you learn the ropes. Have you had any teaching practice?'

'No.'

'Since fees were abolished I am afraid we have taken on board some dodgy customers, even worse than the scholarship girls, so you need your wits about you. Watch out for a scabby girl called Elsie Miller, for example.'

Miss Farringdon went on to explain that she had little time for the new emphasis on 'creativity', believing that could only come when you knew the basics. Her staff were to focus on grammar, spelling, handwriting, and vocabulary.

'"Nice" and "lovely" are strictly verboten.'

These rules would apply to composition and dictation where marks would be deducted for mistakes, however clever the ideas. She had been shocked by a slovenly letter of thanks from one of the girls who left last term. In fact she had corrected it and sent it back. Girls would never make their way in life if they could not write a good letter. Marguerite's mind wandered to Dr Leavis who took Cambridge by storm with his thrilling lectures on the glory of novels and poetry. He even cycled the two miles to Girton to speak to the women and enthused them about the value of language. His was a far cry from Miss Farringdon's approach. She finished by telling them that Miss Belcher was in charge of the timetable, and would give them their instructions tomorrow.

Marguerite felt dispirited as she walked down the corridor. The staff were not what she had expected. Some seemed jaded, even though term had not started. Then it occurred to her that several had lived through two world wars. Difficult to survive all that with much joie de vivre.

Suddenly Miss Belcher swooped on her and proved her wrong. She was fiftyish, cheerful, verging on hysterical. A permanent smile wreathed her pretty face, but as her upper lip did not move when she spoke, the effect was of a ventriloquist's dummy. Her voice too was reminiscent of Archie Andrews', when she welcomed Marguerite effusively, linking arms with her, and begging her not to be discouraged by Miss Farringdon, who was a funny old stick, but loved her subject. Would she like to start tomorrow by having a go at the gorgeous Shakespeare sonnets with 2a? It would all be the most tremendous fun, and the girls were smashing, and weren't they lucky to be teaching such a super subject. Marguerite's stomach lurched at the thought of actually standing up in front of a class and teaching but she went with the gush.

'Oh, yes, lovely. Thank you so much. I can't wait.'

In her effort to get back her enthusiasm she seemed to have turned into Joyce Grenfell. She looked and sounded like a woman she didn't recognise as Marguerite. The old Marguerite was passé, thank goodness. She was now a teacher, Miss Carter, English. And Miss Carter, despite being filled with trepidation, was, as Miss Belcher would put it, thrilled to tiny bits.

Chapter 3

The next day Marguerite watched from a window in the tower as the girls of Dartford County Grammar School returned for their first day of term. They had shining morning faces, but you could not say of these schoolgirls that they were creeping like snails unwillingly to school; they were skipping, laughing, chattering, arms around each other. Dotted amongst the crowd, stepping more cautiously, were a few solitary white-faced girls, presumably new like her, who were engulfed in immaculate uniforms several sizes too large for them, bought to 'grow into'. The rest looked more comfortable. Some were already in their regulation navy-blue serge winter coats despite the soft autumn sunshine, others wore green blazers, with the school badge on the pocket, but they still wore three-pleat tunics with girdles at the waist, and the school's maroon-and-green ties in the collar of the long-sleeved cream blouses. Everyone of course wore a green beret, or black velour hat with a ribbon of school colours. The uniform could not suppress their youthful vigour and individuality. It was to Marguerite a wonderful sight.

The staff room was filling up with bustling teachers.

'Look at them – all bright-eyed and bushy-tailed.'

Mr Stansfield joined her at the window.

'We'll soon put a stop to all that. A hefty dose of Caesar's *Gallic Wars* is what they need. Eh, Miss Yates?'

Miss Yates gave him a withering look.

'Probably more fun than *Das Kapital*,' don't you think?'

Miss White clapped her hands.

'Now, now, girls and boy, enough badinage, we must take our places in assembly. Come with me, Miss Carter, and I will show you where to sit.'

The staff were stationed in chairs set against the wall in the echoey hall. As the various classes marched in in silence, a small girl whose feet barely reached the piano pedals haltingly played a selection of Chopin's sonatas. About thirty girls were seated on the stage on rows of benches, surreptitiously wiggling their fingers at friends in the body of the hall. Several glanced curiously at Marguerite, and nudged others to appraise the new teacher. She pushed back an errant wisp of hair and tried to look cool, calm and collected despite a thumping heart. The choir stood as Miss Tudor-Craig walked onto the platform. With her sturdy legs astride, her squat body swinging in ecstasy, eyes closed, she conducted them in a rousing song, her contralto voice booming above the choir's descant.

'"I vow to thee, my country, all earthly things above,
Entire and whole and perfect, the service of my love;
The love that asks no question, the love that stands the test,
That lays upon the altar the dearest and the best;
The love that never falters, the love that pays the price,
The love that makes undaunted the final sacrifice."'

The unequivocal message of the song made Marguerite uneasy, but the girls were probably more taken with the stirring tune than the sentiment of the words.

Miss Fryer stood in front of the lectern.

'Thank you, girls, that was beautifully sung. And thank you, Miss Tudor-Craig, I'm sure we shall be hearing more from your wonderful choirs during the term.'

'Not half,' shouted the music teacher. Even Miss Fryer laughed.

Everyone listened avidly to the headmistress's address. She spoke quietly with gentle sincerity, encouraging everyone to work hard and guard the reputation of their school. 'The world is struggling to recover from dark times. You are the future, and have a duty to rebuild your country, using the opportunities that you are lucky enough to be presented with here. We are now going to sing "Jerusalem" and let us really mean the words.'

Marguerite watched the girls' eager faces as they vowed to build Jerusalem in England's green and pleasant land. She believed with all her heart that they would.

As they filed out Mr Stansfield whispered in her ear, 'Not a dry eye in the house.'

She did not look at him as she wiped a tear from her chin.

Inspired by the assembly, Marguerite lost some of the nervousness about her teaching debut. She too would not cease from mental fight. She had spent the night before preparing her class, and was ready to test the water of her ability to enthuse girls with her love of Shakespeare.

As she entered the room twenty girls shot to their feet and said, to say, 'Good morning, Miss . . . er . . . er . . .'

'All right, sit, girls. I think some introductions are in order, don't you? I am Miss Carter, this is my first day as a teacher, and I'm very scared.'

The girls first looked astonished at her honesty, then a few laughed.

'I'm going to call the register and would you help me by standing up when you answer so that I can endeavour to put a face to the voice.'

As they answered she did her best to turn the amorphous olive green group into individuals. Pauline had pigtails and the new National Health steel-rimmed spectacles, Heather was scrawny and wriggly, and Julia looked peaky and had a steel caliper on her leg indicating a past ordeal with polio. Amongst the skinny youngsters, only the unusually plump Wendy gainsaid the meagre war-time rations to which they were still restricted, suggesting noble sacrifice by her parents, or, more likely, black-market savvy. Hazel was uncommonly beautiful with ash-blonde hair and green eyes, and gazing adoringly at her from the adjoining desk was Barbara, ablaze with acne. That was enough to take in on her first day. The others remained indeterminate. They were a motley crew. Marguerite wondered if the impression given by their delivery of 'Present' or 'Here' and by the way in which they rose to their feet and recited their names would prove, on further acquaintance, to be accurate. Bold, shy, showing off, serious, giggly, flirty – all twelve-year-old life was here.

One girl, with a pudding-basin haircut and Bambi eyes, couldn't say her name at all. As she obsessively twisted a strand of hair round a finger, she gasped like a dying fish in her attempt to talk.

Marguerite went up to her and placed a calming hand on the girl's back.

'Don't worry, there's no hurry.'

Her neighbour interpolated, 'She's Irene, miss. She's a bit shy.'

Marguerite examined the register. 'It's Irene Brown, is it?'

The class held their breath. After an agonised pause the girl muttered, 'Yes, miss.'

'Thank you, Irene. Well done. That's very helpful.'

Marguerite rejected the chair in favour of standing in front of her desk to address them.

'Right. Now we are going to look at one of Shakespeare's sonnets. I understand you all have a Shakespeare. Will you get it out, please.'

The lids banged open and the girls rummaged inside their desks. All except one.

This was Elsie Miller, 'the scabby girl'. Marguerite had no problem distinguishing her from the others as her face was bright purple from the gentian violet painted on it in an unsuccessful effort to ameliorate the disfiguring impetigo scabs. When Elsie had grudgingly risen to answer the register Marguerite had seen that her tunic was crumpled, and blouse grubby, unlike the rest of her first-day-of-term classmates. Her 'Here, miss' had been surly and her eyes downcast as she slumped back in her seat.

She was in the same position now. Alarm bells rang in Marguerite's head but she said, 'Elsie, have you lost your book?'

A snarl.

'I ent got one.'

Marguerite decided not to engage with the reason.

'Oh well, Pauline, will you please share with Elsie?'

Pauline reluctantly moved very slightly closer to her unsavoury neighbour. Elsie shoved her book away.

'Don't bother, four-eyes. I 'ate Shakespeare anyway. It's rubbish.'

The class began to shift and giggle. Even the affronted Pauline. Marguerite sensed that Elsie's behaviour was a regular diversion.

She steadied herself.

'Rubbish? D'you think so, Elsie? Why, exactly?'

'Because it's gobbledegook.'

'That's a wonderful word. I think Shakespeare would have liked it.'

Not to be appeased, Elsie shook her head violently, and waved her hands about in dramatic bewilderment.

'I don't know what he's on about.'

'Let's see if we can find out, shall we?'

Elsie gave an exaggerated shrug of indifference then, resting her chin on tightly clenched fists, she stared, eyebrows raised, at her teacher.

This, thought Marguerite, is my first challenge. Her heart was pounding but she feigned calm.

'Will anyone be very brave, and read Sonnet 29 out loud to the class?'

Three girls thrust up their hands while the rest hid their faces.

She remembered one of their names. 'Thank you, Brenda. Take your time.'

Brenda, who was small, buck-toothed and keen, struggled through the poem, murdering the meaning and rhythm.

'"When, in disgrace with fortune and men's eyes,
I all alone beweep my outcast state,
And trouble deaf heaven with my bootless cries,
And look upon myself and curse my fate,
Wishing me like to one more rich in hope,
Featur'd like him, like him with friends possess'd,
Desiring this man's art, and that man's scope,
With what I most enjoy contented least;
Yet in these thoughts myself almost despising,
Haply I think on thee, and then my state,
(Like to the lark at break of day arising
From sullen earth) sings hymns at heaven's gate;
   For thy sweet love remember'd such wealth brings
   That then I scorn to change my state with kings."'

When the girl had made it, red-faced, to the end, Marguerite asked, 'What do you think, class? Do you like it?'

There was little enthusiasm. Anyone showing signs of approval was silenced by a glare from Elsie. She was in danger of being more in control of the lesson than Marguerite. Perching on the desk to relieve her shaking legs Marguerite continued, 'Can anyone sum up what the poem means?'

Blank silence.

'I'll give you a clue. In a sonnet, which this is, often the last two lines tell you what it is about.' They all studied the page with furrowed brows, muttering or mouthing the lines.

Before anyone could answer, Elsie grabbed Pauline's book and piped up, 'Tarts make more money than kings.'

Unflinching, Marguerite assumed serious interest.

'But, Elsie, do you really think a prostitute would describe the sex she sells as "sweet love"?'

There was an intake of breath. This was not the sort of discussion that a teacher should engage in, or indeed anyone in polite society. Even Elsie, caught off balance by challenge rather than reprimand, was disconcerted. Taking advantage of this Marguerite swept on. Hoping that Miss Farringdon would not pop in to check on her, she decided to abandon any attempt to parse the poem and stick to interpretation.

They next discussed whether they had ever 'bewept their outcast state', After some coaxing from Marguerite, they came up with examples that laid bare their insecurity about the way they looked, exam results, shyness and unanimous envy of the ravishing Hazel, who, in turn, revealed her jealousy of the effortlessly brilliant Miranda. All told, they concluded the clever poet had got it about right. 'With what I most enjoy contented least' puzzled them, until Wendy described how the Crunchie bar, which she had queued for the day before, was her most favourite sweet in the world, but when she had finished it, and even while she was eating it, she felt a bit disappointed and miserable.

They had more of a problem relating to the second half of the poem. Although, after some argument, they accepted that the word 'sullen' was a bit odd, but nevertheless a fair description of, for instance, the playing field on a gloomy day, only two of them had seen and heard a lark 'arising' when they were evacuated to the country. They had some difficulty in finding comparative surges of ecstasy in their war-torn young lives. The upward swoop of the all-clear siren after a raid, a rainbow after rain, a father returning after four years' absence were all discussed, but eventually they settled for the robin that sometimes perched on the tennis net singing its heart out. Brenda preferred her budgerigar.

Throughout these revealingly honest exchanges Elsie was silent, although she didn't interrupt and Marguerite could see that her eyes were registering what was being said.

Marguerite risked engaging with her.

'Now, Elsie, with your classmates' help, is the poem any clearer to you? Is there anything about it that you can identify with? Does it at least make you think?'

'A bit.'

Marguerite sensed some progress.

'I thought about the day my brother got out of the shelter without his shoes on and started shaking his fists and jumping up and down shouting "Bugger off, bloody Bosch" at the jerry planes going over. But they didn't notice his bootless cries.'

The class sniggered, waiting for Marguerite's reaction to Elsie's shocking bad language. Yet again, Marguerite doggedly chose the option of deflecting Elsie's defiance by taking her seriously.

'Actually, Elsie, you have hit on something interesting there. Well done. Maybe Shakespeare chose the word "bootless" not only to mean useless, but also to have connotations of poverty. Not like your brother, who just forgot his shoes, but people who can't afford them. Just as he uses that funny word "haply" not only to mean "perhaps" but possibly also because it sounds a bit like "happily".' Elsie was glaring at her but said nothing. 'Words are such useful things. I have an idea, class. How many of you collect stamps?'

Several hands shot up.

'And cigarette cards?'

Many more.

'Autographs?'

Almost the whole class.

'How about instead of just collecting your friends' and teachers' signatures, you collect words instead? Have a notebook or even use your autograph albums and every new word you discover or like, write it down. Elsie's "gobbledegook" is a good one and there are several in the sonnet. Then you can find ways of using them in your compositions, perhaps in unusual ways, like Shakespeare's "sullen earth". Shall we try it with our robin? Chose some adjectives to describe him.'

First up was "lovely". Mindful of Miss Farringdon's briefing, from which she had strayed, Marguerite now toed the party line.

'But, Heather, "lovely" could refer to anything. The sun is lovely, so, to my mind, is this sonnet. You are lovely—'

A blush and a snort at this.

'We need a word that is specific to our robin.'

'Cheeky', 'Christmassy', 'wounded', 'brave', 'chirrupy', 'pushy', 'lovable' (whispered by Irene), 'obese' (from Wendy), 'bleeding' (this grunted by Elsie), the adjectives flowed out of them. Going with the tide, Marguerite decided the girls were sufficiently at ease with one another to return to the subject of 'sweet love', a subject potentially uncomfortable for pubescent girls. It was a dangerous area to explore. Sex was a totally forbidden subject in lessons except for a rudimentary look at the basics in Hygiene. Aware of the ticking time bomb of Elsie, Marguerite steered the subject firmly into the area of gentle loving. They came up with touching examples.

'My granny when I cry.'

'My mum when she plaits my hair.'

'When my dad holds my hand as we cross the road.'

'Yes, I like it when I go trainspotting with my dad. He doesn't shout.'

'My brother's nice when we go bird-nesting.'

Pets featured heavily in the list led by Brenda's budgerigar.

Anxious to include her, Marguerite crouched by Irene's desk.

'What about you, Irene? Is there someone you value more than anything in the world?'

Her reply was barely audible but definite.

'My baby brother.'

The ideas were flowing now, and the class were visibly enjoying themselves, their relationship with their teacher relaxed and cordial. So much so that Rosemary Lewis, wide-eyed and brainy, dared to ask, 'What about you, miss?'

'Well, let me see,' replied Marguerite. 'I remember being cuddled by my mother.'

Her arms holding very tight, the soft perfume, her cheek wet against hers. 'Don't worry, ma petite, Maman and Papa will see you again soon.'

Marguerite could sense they found the thought of this kind of physical parental love slightly embarrassing. Only one girl, Helen Hayes, with ringlets that spoke of time spent with curling

28

tongs, offered the observation, 'It's nice when my mum kisses me goodnight, before putting out the light,' and then, judging by the flush creeping up her neck, wished she hadn't.

Marguerite checked that she had neglected no one, so that they were all involved with the discussion. Even Irene was attentive and as engaged as was possible at this stage. The only remaining renegade was Elsie.

Marguerite decided to go for broke.

'And you, Elsie, what "sweet love" do you remember?'

It was a mistake. A grave mistake. There was no clever-Dick rejoinder from Elsie. That Marguerite could have dealt with. There was a look of bewilderment. The girl was struggling to find an effective riposte but there was just a stricken silence.

Marguerite's growing confidence had overreached itself and led her into deep water; she was aware of invading the girl's complex privacy. She, of all people, should have known better. She could think of nothing to say, except a muttered, 'I'm sorry, Elsie.' The girl looked up and examined Marguerite's face curiously, then shrugged and turned away.

Marguerite moved on swiftly.

'Now we have about five minutes before the bell. Brenda, would you be kind enough to read the sonnet again, bearing in mind the things we have discussed?'

It was a risk, but it worked. The girl gave a clear, sincere reading and when she finished the class applauded.

'That was beautiful, Brenda. Hands up, class, if you like the poem better now.'

A sea of waving hands restored her faith in her ability to teach. Daring to look at Elsie, she saw that she had her arm half up, although her face expressed nonchalance.

'I am so pleased. There goes the bell. Class dismissed. Don't forget to collect some new words. And 2a—'

They hesitated.

'Thank you all for making my first ever lesson so enjoyable.' As they passed Marguerite in single file to go to their next class, Hazel Evans said, 'You shouldn't be scared. You're a good teacher.' And there was a murmur of agreement. She caught Elsie's eye. The girl gave a slight, solemn nod.

Marguerite could not remember ever feeling so happy.

Chapter 4

'You're looking very pleased with yourself.'

Mr Stansfield, in his sports clothes, was crouched on the floor in the rabbitry, smoking a cigarette. Marguerite backed out of the wire cage.

'Sorry, I didn't realise there was anyone in here. I have a free period so I thought I'd explore.'

'I've just finished morning gym sessions and I've got a break too. Let me finish my fag and I'll give you a guided tour.'

Marguerite said, 'Haven't you read the latest scientific research? Smoking is almost definitely linked to lung cancer.'

'Well, I like to live dangerously. D'you want one?'

'Yes, please.'

'Why don't you sit down and join me for a chat. It's a bit smelly but we won't be disturbed till lunch break, when the monitors come to feed the beasts.'

He spread his hanky on the stone floor and she crouched down beside him. He took another cigarette from the packet, lit it from his, and put it between her lips.

'Sorry about that nonsense with Lewin yesterday. She's an offensive old cow, but she lost a fiancé at the Somme and spent this last lot in the ARP dragging bodies out of bomb sites, so she's a bit touchy about wartime service.'

'I wasn't offended.'

'You must get fed up with all that anti-French stuff. But you're only half French, aren't you? How strange. Which do you feel most, English or French?'

'Well, let's say I miss the smell of a Gauloises, but I am loving this Woodbine.'

'Where were you during the war?'

'I served as a nurse. The FANY. You?'

'Merchant Navy. Dodging torpedoes, mainly successfully. Anyway enough of that. Muddy water under a ruined bridge. What about today? How did it go?'

'Wonderful. I've only done one lesson so far. I was nervous but in the end I really enjoyed it. Some of the girls needed a bit of coaxing, and one I handled badly, but on the whole, I feel I have come home. This is what I was born to do.'

'Wow. So you're enjoying it so far then, Mrs Lincoln?'

'What's that supposed to mean?'

'I just can't understand what a pretty girl like you is doing teaching.'

'Don't patronise me.'

'I thought I was paying you a compliment.'

'Oh, not again.'

'What? I'm lost here.'

Marguerite slowly blew out some smoke.

'It's something that happened in my final term at Cambridge. I was selected as the only woman of a group of five undergraduates invited to attend a seminar in America. I prepared my dissertation. Then, a week before we were due to depart, I was informed that I had been dropped, in favour of a male student. I went to see the lecturer in charge of the trip and asked him what I'd done wrong. I'd worked damned hard to prepare.'

Mr Stansfield held out a cupped hand for her to flick ash into.

'What did he say?'

'He smirked at me, with one eyebrow raised, and said, "You've done nothing wrong except be too damned attractive." Then he winked and said, "One or two of the lads are worried you might be distracting, and to be honest I can't guarantee I wouldn't jump on you myself." Ouch.'

Mr Stansfield took her glowing cigarette stub from her fingers and crushed it out on his plimsoll.

'What did you say?'

'I couldn't believe it. I said, "Are you serious?" and he smirked even more and said, "Would you like me to be?"'

Mr Stansfield stifled a laugh. Marguerite leapt to her feet.

'It's not bloody funny.'

'I know. I'm sorry. What did you say to that?'

'I said, "Do you know what I would like? I would like to smash my fist into your self-satisfied, flabby, stupid face, you drivelling idiot."'

Marguerite strode up and down the rabbit cages shaking her fist.

'He must have been terrified.'

'Not at all. He was astonished. He thought I would be flattered. Otherwise why did I "go to so much trouble with my lipstick and fetching clothes". I threatened to report him and he just said, "You're a very silly, hysterical girlie. I will merely say you are unsuitable for academic reasons. It's my word against yours and I will win."'

Marguerite sat down beside Mr Stansfield and shrugged.

'And of course he would have done.'

Mr Stansfield shook his head.

'I see what you mean. It hadn't occurred to me how disparaging my remark sounded. I apologise.'

Marguerite touched his hand.

'Don't worry, Mr Stansfield. I am an English teacher, so I am oversensitive to language.'

'Tony, please.'

'And I am Marguerite.'

They smiled at each other.

'Right. Let's go for a look round the grounds.'

He rose and put their cigarette butts in the back pocket of his shorts.

'Get rid of the evidence.'

He offered her his hand, and pulled her to her feet. She noticed that his blue Aertex sports shirt exactly matched the colour of his eyes, and his slender well-shaped legs were golden brown.

She lands with a crash and the chute pulls her about 50 feet over the rough ground. She manages to detach it, sees beside her two muddy boots. Her eyes travel up the sturdy body to meet piercing eyes staring at her in the torchlight. The face is craggy, jaw sagging in surprise. 'Vous êtes une femme.' He bends to yank her to her feet. His body is hard and smells of sweat. He is very definitely un homme.

Tony introduced her to the eight rabbits in the hutches.

'My best friends here. They don't answer back. Unlike the beastly girls.'

They then circled the allotments, tended by a couple of young girls wearing Young Farmers' Club badges.

'They'd run a mile at the sight of a cow. This was all playing fields, until the school had to dig for victory.'

He pointed out the remaining hockey pitch, and netball courts, hard and soft tennis courts, and cricket pitch.

'Are the girls good at cricket?' asked Marguerite.

'My God, yes. They're super at batting. Maybe because if they hit the ball hard enough it goes over the fence to the boys' field next door, propelled by their rampant hormones.'

Marguerite stopped and looked him in the eye.

'You don't sound as though you like the girls or the school very much.'

He raised his eyebrows.

'You're a forthright little madam, aren't you? Actually I do like both of them, but your indiscriminate enthusiasm brings out the cynic in me.'

'Well, don't let it. I don't like it.'

'Yes, miss. I'm sorry, miss.'

'It makes you seem very flippant. Which I suspect you are not really. What about all that stuff in the staff room about Marx and reds. Are you a political animal?'

'To some of the staff I am a raging Communist, whereas, in fact, I am just a member of the Labour Party.'

'I was a member of the Socialist Club at university. It was one of the few clubs that allowed women to darken its doors.'

'Is that the only reason you joined?'

'No, of course not. I am totally behind all that this government is doing.'

'Great. So if you want them to stay in power you need to get active. There is an election looming. And the Tories are desperate to get back in.'

'They won't, though, will they?'

'They could very well. They are playing on the collective guilt about rejecting Churchill after the war. Times are hard, and he rescued them before. They are very persuasive. I tell you what, there is a Conservative campaign rally with the prospective candidate, and the deputy Party leader, Anthony Eden. Should be a good double act. Why don't you come? Test the temperature. Have a bit of a heckle.'

Marguerite demurred. She had a lot on her plate. She doubted if her life could encompass more commitment.

Tony said, 'What's wrong with you? I am offering you a glamorous date. Dartford football ground with a lot of rabid Tories. What more could you want?'

'Put like that, how can I resist?'

There was a convivial atmosphere as the crowd, wearing their Sunday best, poured into the football ground, to the sound of the Callender Company Works band. Tony greeted Marguerite at the turnstile, with obvious approval of her figure-hugging costume, and high heels, and especially her bouncing hair, released from its prim pleat.

'I knew there was a woman beneath that grey school mouse. You look lovely. Very chic. Very French.'

The event started with community singing of patriotic songs, to which everyone knew the words, 'Land Of Hope And Glory', 'Rule, Britannia!' 'There'll Be Bluebirds Over The White Cliffs Of Dover', ending with 'There'll Always Be An England':

> '"There'll always be an England,
> While there's a country lane,
> Wherever there's a cottage small
> Beside a field of grain."'

Tony hissed, 'Or a terraced house, with no bath, and one outside lav between four houses, like the one my mum and dad live in. Thanks to you. You Tory bastards.'

If Tony was surprised by her off-duty appearance, Marguerite was even more taken aback by the change in him. He revealed a profound rage that took away all traces of his usual jocularity.

The crowd sang the heartfelt last chorus:

'"There'll always be an England,
And England shall be free
If England means as much to you
As England means to me."'

To which Tony shouted loudly, 'Yes, free of you lot.'

There were a few desultory cheers from other hecklers, and much shushing and disapproving looks from the Party faithful.

Marguerite roared with laughter.

'I can't believe this. You are actually growling. Going grrh and baring your teeth.'

Tony didn't laugh,

'Well, I hate them. Look at them. Up there. Pompous idiots.'

On the platform, at the top of the field, about twenty men in dark suits, some with Homburgs and some with bowler hats, and sporting mayoral chains or various service medals, were settling onto the benches. They rose and doffed their hats when the willowy, moustached Anthony Eden arrived, courteously ushering before him the only woman in the group of notables. She was a frumpy blonde, young with a middle-aged walk, dowdily dressed, head down, as if afraid that people would notice her sex and throw her off the stage. She was introduced by a nervous branch chairman as the prospective Conservative MP for Dartford, Miss Margaret Roberts. Sensing not whole-hearted approval of this unmarried woman candidate, Eden started his speech by saying that he thought Miss Roberts would make a great name for herself. He then went on, with shouted interjections from Tony, to condemn the Labour government's handling of the economy with its wholesale nationalisation, urging Party members to fight hard for Miss Roberts' election. He worried that people were not aware of the dangers ahead.

'The working man is not a bad chap, but he is easily led astray.'

Tony let out an exasperated yell.

'What! How dare you patronise me. You supercilious Tory toff.'

To Marguerite's delight Tony was now actually jumping up and down with fury.

'We as a party are a barrier to Communism, we never toyed with that creed, we never sang "The Red Flag".'

'What's he talking about?' asked Marguerite.

'The Labour Party members sang it on the first day in the Commons after their landslide victory. Those that knew the words, that is. Let's give 'em a blast, shall we?'

There was no stopping Tony now. At the top of his voice he sang:

> '"Then raise the scarlet standard high,
> Within its shade we'll live and die,
> Though cowards flinch and traitors sneer,
> We'll keep the red flag flying here."'

Marguerite and a few brave souls in the crowd joined in, only to be drowned out by a counter-song sortie of 'God save the King'.

When order was restored, Margaret Roberts sweetly, if slightly squeakily, thanked the shaken Anthony Eden.

'Anthony Eden, our deputy leader, is a great man, great not only in our time, but great in all times.'

Marguerite made a mental note to discuss the misuse of hyperbole with her pupils.

There was then a more reverential rendering of the National Anthem, sung by the whole assembly, during which everyone on the platform stood, and all the men in the crowd took off their hats and caps, and many saluted, including, Marguerite noticed, a suddenly solemn Tony. As the crowd drifted away it began to rain. One or two people quietly congratulated Tony on his heckling. One man grasped his hand and shook it vigorously. 'I don't agree with your opinions, but my son died to give you the right to express them. Good luck, mate.'

Tony insisted on going on the bus with her to Wilmington. When they were huddled on the seat he opened up his coat.

'Here, get inside. You're all damp.'

Marguerite hesitated for a moment. Miss Fryer would not approve of such intimacy but damn it, she was cold. It was cosy nestling inside his duffel coat, against the warmth of his body. She had enjoyed herself. Tony was diverting company. He made her laugh a lot. It had stopped raining when they got off the bus. He walked her to her flat, or rather he danced along the road doing a reasonable impersonation of Fred Astaire, casting her and the odd lamp-post as Ginger Rogers. At the door, breathless, he pulled her close, stroked her hair, and planted a kiss on her forehead.

'See you on Monday, you lovely creature.'

She was glad that he didn't suggest coming in. It would be a step too far, too soon. Besides, she had not yet had time to make the flat into a home. It had a bedroom, bathroom, sitting room and kitchenette – the 'ette' meaning there was just a rudimentary Baby Belling cooker and larder – and little in the way of furniture. She sat on her one armchair, gazing at the rain through the window and wondering at the whirlwind of the last week. After the turmoil of the past it seemed her future was set fair. She was also aware that she was looking forward to seeing Tony the next day. She fell into a contented sleep, curled up in the armchair.

Chapter 5

Over the next few months Marguerite enjoyed making her flat into a comfortable refuge. Money was tight on her teacher's salary, but she overcame sentimentality, and sold some of her mother's jewellery that was too ostentatious for her to wear. She had visions of inviting guests to civilised dinners, where wine and conversation flowed, although wine was a rare commodity in the austerities of English shops. Also, she discovered that civilised dinners were not a form of recreation customary in post-war Dartford. After the conviviality of her childhood in Paris, where her father's job in the British Council necessitated entertaining visiting artistes and writers, and the fun and fierce exchange of ideas at Cambridge, this was difficult for her to adjust to. Everyone was friendly in a polite, distant sort of way but social gatherings did not seem to take place even amongst her colleagues at work. Anyway, to begin with, she had little time for leisure, what with lesson preparation, teaching, playground and dinner duty; and out-of-hours activity, the redoubtable Tudor-Craig's choir on Tuesdays, some French-conversation coaching to help out the French department, parents' evenings, staff meetings and the endless marking.

As she settled into a routine she had more free time, and this she began to spend with Tony. The rest of the staff were older than her, with established friendships, and she found Tony more fun to be with. He occasionally went away for the weekend to visit 'a friend', so Marguerite assumed he had a serious relationship with someone and she settled for merely enjoying his companionship. They were merry in each other's company. He lightened her life with laughter. As at the Tory rally, he had a knack of drawing attention to himself. At first she felt embarrassed by this, but she could see that people were amused by his extrovert behaviour. Having, of necessity, always inclined towards reticence, she found herself enjoying being on the sidelines of his escapades. He could turn an everyday occurrence into an event. For instance, shopping.

Miss Fryer had hinted that his apparel for Parents' Day – a pair of the newfangled blue-denim Levi's and a Fair Isle jumper – was unsuitably casual, so Marguerite dragged him to the local department store to buy something more appropriate, despite his protests that he was a PT teacher, not a bank clerk, and the jeans, as he called them, were the latest thing. The whole shop was brought to a standstill by his howls of horror at his reflection in the mirror now that he was wearing a dark grey-flannel suit, complete with waistcoat and stiff-collared shirt and tie.

'I can't move. Arggh! I'm choking. I feel done up like a dog's dinner. I wouldn't be seen dead in this.'

Marguerite encouraged the gathering group of laughing staff and customers to reassure him.

'You look very smart, son,' said the lady on the glove counter.

The 'A real gentleman' from a passing Brylcreemed customer in an identical suit didn't help, but the two saleswomen from corsetry did. The elderly one, her ramrod stiffness a credit to her department, ventured, 'You look like a film star.'

'Which one? Bela Lugosi?'

But it was her sweet blonde colleague, a walking endorsement of their uplift brassieres, with her brazen, 'I could fall head over heels for you in that,' that quietened Tony's wails. Pouncing on his hesitation, Marguerite wrested the money from his pocket, handed it to the manager of the store, who, on Marguerite's insistence, stuffed it quickly into a container, and sent it whizzing along the overhead wire towards the cash desk, to the applause of the onlookers, who had thoroughly enjoyed the diversion from the usual solemnity of mahogany and hushed voices in the sedate emporium.

Thenceforth, outings were classified 'suit' or 'non-suit'. Definitely 'suit' were staff meetings with Miss Fryer, trips to the theatre, apart from the Royal Court, where his maligned jeans were de rigueur, concerts at the Wigmore Hall, but not Promenade Concerts at the Albert Hall. He and Marguerite always went up to the top gallery, where they were allowed to sit or lie on the floor, blissfully drinking in the music for which they shared a mutual love. Also 'suit' was a visit to the doctor's surgery with his smoker's cough.

More 'non-suit' occasions were trips to the pub, and going up to town, wandering round the bomb-scarred city, usually ending up at Joe Lyons Corner House for an ice-cream sundae whilst listening to Ena Baga, resplendent in chiffon, playing popular tunes on the Hammond organ, to which Tony would sing along, sometimes joined by other customers, to the delight of the usually ignored Ena.

'Semi-non-suit' occasions were football and motorbike speedway races when the waistcoat and stiff collar were replaced by a pullover, and team scarves and rosettes permitted. Both sports were new to Marguerite but she loved watching the English abandon their reserve and sing and shout their support or good-humoured opposition.

All political events, especially door-to-door canvassing, were definitely 'suit', to add respectability to the Labour Party members in the light of the patrician, born-to-rule image of the leading members of the Conservative Party. Sadly Aneurin Bevan and Ernie Bevin in their shambolic suits were no competition, in the sartorial stakes, for the relaxed elegance of Eden and Macmillan, or Churchill's aristocratic eccentricity. Tony did his best with his flannel, but after a while it began to look the worse for wear. He flatly refused to buy a new suit, arguing that the leather patches he stuck on the frayed elbows of the jacket were a good example of 'make do and mend' that the working class would understand only too well. He did not talk much about his childhood, but the odd comment made it clear that his personal experience of deprivation was what fuelled his left-wing zeal and devotion to a party that seemed, with its construction of the Welfare State, to be doing something about it.

They were both bitterly disappointed when the Labour Party suffered a major decline in its majority in the 1950 election. Marguerite was torn in her allegiance, feeling a secret delight that Margaret Roberts seriously challenged the seat of the long-standing male socialist MP, despite her sex and inexperience. Both of them had to be careful to keep their political activity separate from their job. Many of the girls demonstrated passionate commitment to the parties they were representing in the permitted mock elections, but Miss Fryer was adamant that the staff should be apolitical within the school gates.

Thus it had to be in a hidden corner of the school field that Pauline, a member of the Labour League of Youth, and Hazel a Young Conservative, cornered her with a leaflet about a meeting they were organising in the boys' grammar school, united by their opposition to the hydrogen bomb. Marguerite identified with the two girls, having grown up listening to her parents' political rhetoric and participated in their activism. She understood the passion for a cause that can consume a child.

She promised that she and Mr Stansfield would attend. It was probably breaking the no-politics rule, but the cause was so crucial to her that she decided it was worth the risk. Marguerite had been horrified at the destruction of Hiroshima and Nagasaki by the Allies' atom bombs; this meeting, jammed full of concerned youngsters, brought home to her how fear for the future, indeed the likelihood of no future at all, overshadowed the lives of these war-weary children.

The diminutive Pauline, with pink-satin ribbons in her pigtails, opened the meeting by reading out in a shaky voice the constitution.

'"We, the representatives of our respective countries, believing that since wars begin in the minds of men, it is in the minds of men that the defences of peace must be constructed, and believing that the peace must be founded, if it is not to fail, upon the' – here the girl took a deep breath – 'intellectual and moral solidarity of all peoples, have resolved to combine our efforts to form an association of the peoples to be known as the World Federation of United Nations Associations."'

Having made it to the end, she beamed with pride.

'That's us. There's going to be lots of us all round the world. So that's good, isn't it?'

And she took her seat amongst the people on the stage. Above her chair was a plaque dedicated to the sixty young men from the school who had died in the two wars. Marguerite could see that the poignancy was not lost on Tony.

Then the politicians had their say. A bumbling aide introduced the town's Tory candidate as 'Margaret Roberts, now Margaret Thatcher after her marriage to the distinguished Major

Denis Thatcher who is in paints'. She was transformed by her recent triumph at the polls; she may not have won, but the number of votes she had secured was a remarkable result in a Labour stronghold. Being married to a rich man probably helped as well. Her hair was several shades lighter, and her frock, a vivid blue to match her eyes and her politics, was short enough to reveal shapely legs, enhanced by elegant shoes, the high heels of which improved her previous clomping walk. She spoke with vigour of the danger of unilateral disarmament at which Tony groaned only very quietly, so as not to disrupt the meeting so efficiently organised by the young activists.

As they left the hall, Tony linked arms with Marguerite and muttered, 'Dear God, what have we done to these children – we so-called grown-ups? What kind of future have we given them?'

She and Marcel creep through the lavender field, the perfume makes her head swim; or is it the fear? The house seems deserted but the door is wide open. They enter cautiously, guns at the ready. There is a whimpering sound. As they go into the parlour the little boy clings to his mother, lying dead on the floor in a lake of blood.

'Please don't hurt us,' he says.

'I think a stiff drink is in order.'

Several beers and whisky chasers later, Tony blamed his mood on a headache brought on by suppressing his natural instinct to shout at politicians in deference to Pauline and Hazel. And 'complications' in his personal life. Plus 'the slight worry that we may be about to blow our world out of the solar system'.

Marguerite offered him a Veganin, ignored the 'complications', and insisted that things would change for the better.

'The stakes are so high now – total annihilation – the world will have to come to its senses.'

'Give or take the odd bomb-owning lunatic that may not have any senses to come to.'

'They will be defeated. Good will prevail.'

'Ever the bloody optimist. Little Lizzie Dripping.'

'Who's she?'

'Dunno. It's what we people oop north call people we love.'

When he said things like that she sometimes wondered how much he meant it. She half hoped that their warm relationship would develop into something more serious if he sorted out his 'complications'. But she was content to leave things as they were. Her working life was all-consuming.

Her pupils were her raison d'être. They were the future. Forget about the past.

Yes, for pity's sake, forget that.

Chapter 6

From the window of the tower Marguerite would often feast her eyes on the girls' lithe bodies as they leapt around in their skimpy gym skirts doing PT outside in the sun. She earnestly hoped that their beauty would not be drained away, as it had been from the careworn mothers she met on Parents' Day, nor their bright eyes dimmed by disappointment with their lives, scarred by war and want. She did everything she could to build their confidence; if they achieved something or amused her with their giggly humour, she would give them a hug. It would be no exaggeration to say that she loved them. The more unprepossessing, verging on hopeless they were, the more she endeavoured to transform them. Her Messiah complex, Tony called it.

She was never bored. She relished the challenge of changing her teaching techniques according to age group. Her relatively stylish clothes and slight accent made her the target of many a schoolgirl crush, which she learned to handle with tact. She gave equal energy to all her classes but she could not help having a soft spot for her very first pupils.

Irene Brown perplexed her. In the class situation it was well nigh impossible to deal with chronic shyness, as drawing attention to it only made the sufferer more withdrawn. Because Irene never joined in discussions, it was difficult to get to the bottom of her problem. Marguerite could forge no bond with the girl. The breakthrough came of its own volition. It was not part of the syllabus, but after the United Nations Associations meeting, which many of them had attended, motivated by Pauline and Hazel, it seemed apposite for the girls to look at the war poets. She Roneoed copies for all of them of Rupert Brooke's 'The Soldier', and Siegfried Sassoon's 'Suicide in the Trenches'.

Rupert Brooke irked them. They all knew men who were buried in 'some corner of a foreign field' and for them, the bitter loss overrode the patriotism. The Sassoon spoke more to their understanding of the fate of 'a simple soldier boy'. As Hazel Evans read the final verse Marguerite noticed that Irene was trying to hide the fact that she was crying.

> '"You smug-faced crowds with kindling eye
> Who cheer when soldier lads march by,
> Sneak home and pray you'll never know
> The hell where youth and laughter go."'

It was Marguerite's custom to walk about between the desks during lessons to keep contact with the girls, rather than pontificate from the front. As she passed Irene, without comment, she handed her a handkerchief.

After the lesson, Irene lagged behind until the rest of the class had filed out. Marguerite did not rush the girl, but waited in silence, until she managed to blurt out, 'Thank you, miss, I'll take it home and wash it.'

'There's no need for that, Irene. It's a sad poem, isn't it?'

'Yes, miss, but so is war. He tells it so well.'

'I agree. It's a short poem, but we feel we know that young man, don't we? Someone who "slept soundly through the lonesome dark, and whistled early with the lark".'

'Yes, miss, and then, in the horrible trenches, he's "cowed and glum" and then it's so sad, when "none spoke of him again" after he shot himself.' The girl's eyes started to fill again.

'Here, Irene' – Marguerite flicked through her book – 'let's look at a more cheerful one.'

'This one was written when peace was declared in the First World War – the armistice. Will you read it for me? I've lost my glasses.'

Rapt, Irene forgot her timidity and read out the text of 'Everyone Sang'. When she finished the last two lines, 'O but Everyone/Was a bird; and the song was wordless; the singing will never be done', she looked confused.

'Does that mean there'll always be poetry?'

'Maybe, Irene, or maybe – that as well as dreadful times there will always be joy.'

'That's lovely, miss. Oops, sorry, not "lovely". Positive, thoughtful, comforting.' She handed Marguerite her hanky. 'Thank you, miss, I'm sorry if it's snotty.'

Marguerite laughed. 'You keep it, Irene. And the book as well.'

'Really, miss?'

'Yes, really. Now wipe your nose.'

Thereafter Marguerite came upon the girl in corners of the playground, or vacated classrooms, deep in contemplation of her precious book. She still said little in class but would seize opportunities before and after lessons or in the dining hall, if Marguerite was on duty, to catch her on her own, and discuss that, or other collections of poetry she had borrowed from the library.

★   ★   ★

One of Marguerite's other lame ducks was the dreaded Elsie Miller. From a family of three girls and two boys, she was not an attractive child. Her dirty clothing, along with her impetigo, made most of the other girls give her a wide berth. She was ill-mannered and rude to the teachers, always 'answering back', but Marguerite found that almost a relief from the oppressive rule-abiding ethos of the school.

'Elsie Miller, stop talking in the corridor.'

'What if I see an unexploded butterfly bomb, can't I tell people?'

Elsie once sat alone for a whole afternoon in the canteen when she was ordered not to leave the table until she ate her cabbage, which she swore was full of caterpillars, and come home time, 'accidentally on purpose' knocked it on the floor. Tony valued her skill on the hockey field, but had to constantly remind her she should whack the ball, not her opponents' shins. Marguerite was certain that underneath this ferocious exterior was a good mind waiting to develop. She had, after all, passed her eleven-plus and she occasionally produced brilliant, if sloppy, compositions. She took little obvious part in lessons, but the gradual improvement in her work showed that she was listening. Marguerite learnt not to praise her in front of the class, but showed her approval in comments written on her homework and the excellent grades she gave her. Whilst Elsie's constant cry of 'Why' when asked to obey some rule was wearing, the same curiosity was invaluable for the critique of a literary text.

But she was trouble. Her reputation was that of a bully, and bullies were not welcome at Dartford County Grammar. She had been warned and Miss Fryer's patience was nearly exhausted, so when Marguerite saw Elsie arrive at school minus her hat, and looking even more dishevelled than usual, she took her into an empty classroom to remonstrate with her.

'What's going on, Elsie?'

'I had a bit of a fight, miss.'

'What?'

'And the police came.'

'What on earth happened?'

'It was my hat, miss.'

'Your hat?'

'Yes, they nicked it.'

'Who?'

'The secondary modern lot. They used to be my friends at primary but now they think I'm toffee-nosed because I'm at the grammar. They're always chi-iking me. But this time they went too far.'

'What did they do?'

'They knocked my hat off and started throwing it around, miss. And I was worried because of the rule.'

'Which rule?'

'That we must always wear our hats in public.'

Marguerite had always thought this a pointless rule but didn't say so.

'They started poking fun at my tunic and my scabs.'

'It's a very nice tunic.'

'No it ent, miss. My mum boiled it and it shrunk. Then that Baker-Jones snob from our upper sixth joined in and told them some things about my mum, cos she's got a crush on one of the boys. So I hit her. And then I hit everyone I could. That shut them up. I'm a good fighter, miss.'

Lying behind a bush, heart thumping but the comforting sun on her back and Marcel by her side; they are flat on their stomachs, guns and grenades at the ready.

'This one's for Jacob and the lads,' whispers Marcel. And she feels a

rush of pride. There is a distant sound of engines. They grovel to the edge of the precipice. In the distance, three cars worm up the curving road. Gradually she can make out people in them. One man is standing in the first, which has the top down. He is scanning the area with binoculars.

'He's yours,' says Marcel. 'Arrogant swine.'

As he comes into focus she sees he has blue eyes. He is sternly handsome. Attractive. Aryan. Bastard. They round the last curve until they are nearly level. As she pulls the pin from the grenade he looks up and stares into her eyes in wonderment like a beautiful child. Then his head bursts open and splatters all over the other men in the car. Marcel fires at the cars with his Sten. From the other side of the road grenades and bullets are flying through the air.

'Right. That's it. Run.'

'OK, Elsie, I'll have a word with the head but I can't promise anything. That sort of behaviour won't do – you are supposed to uphold the reputation of the school. Remember our motto: "Quietness and Confidence". You must control your temper.'

'Thank you, miss. I'll try, miss.'

'Good.'

'Miss—'

'Yes, Elsie?'

'Pamela Baker-Jones is an arseho – um – a bumhole. Don't you agree?'

Miss Fryer had already heard from the police, and she was determined to expel Elsie.

'This is not her first offence. She has let the school down on other occasions. She is slovenly and a bully. I don't want girls like that at my school.'

Marguerite said, 'Don't you think her background is the problem?'

'Certainly on the one occasion her mother deigned to attend a parents' meeting she looked like a tart, which, rumour hath it, she is. Her father was aggressive with the teachers and smelled of alcohol. So there is little hope of them disciplining her.'

'So she is being set a bad example at home. Can't we try and do better here at school?'

'She is surrounded by girls who work hard and behave them selves. Many of them have horrendous stories to tell.'

Marguerite tried another tack.

'She is very bright. I seriously think she could get a State Scholarship and go to university.'

'Very difficult, without the support of the home. I fear there will be more trouble, Miss Carter.'

'She was provoked this time. The secondary modern girls were goading her.'

'That doesn't surprise me. They're rabble. We've had a lot of trouble from them.'

Miss Fryer's fingers drummed on her desk.

'Very well, Miss Carter. On your own head be it. I know you have a way with the girls. I'll give her one more chance.'

'Thank you so much.'

'Miss Carter, regarding another matter. We are here to teach. That is our job. It stops at the school gate. I understand you went to an anti-bomb meeting with some of the girls—'

'How did you—?

'I promise you nothing escapes my notice. Our task is to train their minds, and equip them to earn a living and to be well-informed, good wives, but we allow them to have their own opinions about how the world is run, with no influence from us. That we leave to others. Understood?'

There seemed little point in arguing so Marguerite nodded.

'And best to stick to the syllabus, Miss Carter. It is carefully thought out. The war poets are deemed too disturbing for sensitive girls.'

Marguerite inclined her head and bit her lip as she made for the door.

Miss Fryer stopped her with, 'Miss Carter—'

'Yes, Headmistress?'

'You really care, don't you? Not just about Elsie?'

'Yes, Miss Fryer, I do.'

'Well, believe it or not, even after all these years, so do I.'

As Marguerite opened the door Miss Fryer added, 'Oh, by the way, I would be grateful if you would find time to go and speak to the head of the secondary modern – Miss Scott is her name. See if we can't improve the situation between us.'

Elsie was sitting outside in the corridor.

'All right, Elsie, you have a reprieve. Now you go in and apologise, don't answer back, in fact only say yes and no and thank you. And come and see me later.'

When the relieved Elsie came and thanked Marguerite, a rare gesture from her, Marguerite told her she wanted a favour in return.

'You know Irene Brown is very shy, and I suspect she is sometimes bullied. Not physically but by being laughed at, or left out. I'd like you to keep an eye on her for me. Help her to stand up for herself.'

Elsie looked astonished at being given this responsibility. Marguerite knew that empathy was not naturally in her emotional make-up. The girl looked warily at Marguerite.

'I'll try. And thank you, miss.'

'Two thank yous. That's record. Now run along.'

'Oh, but I mustn't run in the corridor, miss, must I?'

Marguerite took her grubby hand and gently pretended to slap it.

Over time Miss Farringdon nervously entrusted Marguerite with more freedom, acknowledging her talent for developing the girls' imaginations in their written work. In her mission to improve their creativity Marguerite got permission from Miss Fryer to restart the school magazine that had lapsed during the war. She let it be known that, apart from the usual house and club reports, she wanted original pieces.

She was on playground duty, surrounded by the usual gaggle of chattering girls, when she saw Elsie fighting with Irene. Elsie was dragging the struggling girl towards her, elbowing others aside. 'Out of the way, you. Push off.'

She hurled Irene forward. 'Go on, Irene. Do as I told you.'

Marguerite was devastated that her clever plan to benefit both Irene and Elsie had gone so disastrously wrong.

'What on earth are you doing, Elsie?'

She was forcing Irene's hand up towards Marguerite. In it was a torn sheet of paper. Elsie shouted, 'It's a poem, miss, for the magazine. And don't you dare laugh, fatty.' She turned, fists raised, towards the rotund culprit.

Marguerite was relieved to see her walk away with her arm round Irene's shoulders, head bent sideways as if she were talking to a child, to which Irene responded with a smile.

Marguerite read the poem in the quiet of the tower staff room.

> Darkness covers the bay.
> The stars are cold and clear.
> The moon gazing down upon me.
> A breath grazes my cheek.

Grows to a sea breeze.
The rustling of the pine trees,
The grass shimmers with moon rays,
But it ends now.

The first pink blood of the sun bleeds the
horizon line.
Birds start chirping,
Night is over,
I take cover.

She asked Irene to stay behind after her next English lesson.
The girl was trembling.

'Where did this spring from, Irene? Do you know a place like
the one you describe?'

'No, I imagined it, like you told us to.'

'What about the last line? What are you taking cover from?'

'Dunno, miss. The raids? The day? My – I dunno.'

'Well, it's very good. It will definitely go into the magazine.'

'Thanks, miss.'

'Your parents will be pleased.'

'My mum will.'

'Not your father?'

'Dunno, miss.'

'Don't know?'

'He don't say much.'

'Oh?'

The girl hesitated for a moment, then abruptly turned and
left the classroom.

Chapter 7

Over a drink with Tony, Marguerite shared her growing frustration that they were battling against some of the girls' environments away from school.

'There is only so much you can do. Concentrate on that, for heaven's sake, or you'll burn out.'

'But, Tony, I can't bear the waste. For example, I know, with time and effort, Elsie and Irene can be something special. If I had my way, they'd be taken away from their useless parents.'

'Whoa, that is going down a very dangerous path. And anyway they love them, I'm afraid, even if you don't.'

'I want my girls to rule the world.'

He laughed.

'You've got your feet firmly placed in mid-air, and it's wonderful to watch.'

'I'm going to get those two girls to university if it kills me.'

'I love it when you're determined. You look like a juicy apple with your red cheeks and red hair. Go on, give us a smile.'

'Oh Tony. You're so good for me. You're my light relief. I know I get too serious.'

'Yes, you are in grave in danger of being dull, like brother Jack.'

'How d'you know he was her brother? There is nothing in the verse about Jack's relationship with Jill.'

'Are you suggesting that there is a sexual connotation in our well-loved nursery rhyme? That fetching a pail of water is a euphemism for a bit of how's yer father?'

'Could be.'

'Anyway, you dirty girl, that's not the Jack I'm referring to. I'm talking about the one who did all work and no play.'

'He didn't have a sister.'

'He may have done, you know-all English teacher you. It's probably his nasty sister that said it in the first place, about hard-working Jack.'

'And now you're saying it about me.'

'I am merely suggesting a bit of play would be good for you.'

'What kind of play?'

'What are you suggesting? Mind your tongue, you hussy. Don't you dare sully my innocent Lancashire mind with your mucky French ways. Do you want to hear about my treat, or not?'

'Go on.'

'When we take the fourth form to the Festival of Britain I have permission from the head for you and I to stay behind after we get them back to the coach.'

'Really? It's "you and me", by the way.'

'Yes, there's plenty of staff going, and then "me" has tickets for a concert at the new Royal Festival Hall.'

'Oh how wonderful. A day and night of glamour.'

In anticipation of the evening Marguerite secretly wore a daring chiffon blouse with her worsted skirt under her teacher's grey gabardine, and donned her nylons and 'racy' gloves. With her hair in an elaborate chignon, she braved Miss Fryer's raised eyebrow, in the hope of perhaps making inroads into Tony's 'complications'. The girls were enchanted by these small concessions to chic and fought to shield her hair with their umbrellas and offers of plastic pixie hoods.

Traipsing round the thirty acres of the Festival in drizzling rain with twenty at first overexcited then later wet and whingeing schoolgirls was not quite the uplifting experience Marguerite had hoped for. She wanted the girls to be as thrilled as she was. The Dome and various other exhibition halls were crammed with past and future scientific and industrial developments in Great Britain, but the scale of the information on offer overwhelmed them. Marguerite tried in vain to stir them to patriotic pride in the art and engineering on display, the panoply of brilliant design. The science teacher Dobbin, so called because she once told her class she was 'a little hoarse', led them to see the miraculous automated tortoises. She had devoted a lesson to the mechanics involved, to impress upon them that the reason for their visit was educational. These tortoises were the way forward. Or would have been if the display did not have an 'Out of Order' notice on it. The Henry Moores were deemed 'a bit lumpy' and the John Minton mural 'peculiar'. The pièce de résistance, the Skylon, balancing on a few cobwebby wires, reaching up to the sky like a V2 rocket about to be launched, was given a wide berth by the girls, used to similar-shaped objects trying to kill them.

Eventually the sun came out and at last they were thrilled – by eating their jam sandwiches in an open-air café. Marguerite told the girls it felt like the Champs-Elysées.

'It'll never catch on over here,' predicted Tony, 'not with this climate.'

There were squeals of laughter when Pauline dropped her paper bag on the ground and a voice came over the loudspeaker.

'This is your exhibition. Please help to keep it tidy.'

In time, the magic cast its spell on them. The citrus yellows, shocking pinks and reds that dominated the colour scheme cheered their beige wartime spirits. The waterfalls, the Thames beach with imported sand, putting on funny glasses to see a three-dimensional film, sending messages to the moon all thrilled them. They joined the crowds of women in their Sunday-best outfits and the men in demob suits on their highlight of the trip, a boat ride to the Battersea Festival Gardens. Marguerite noticed Irene's face, wreathed in smiles, tics almost obliterated, as she stared at Rowland Emett's crazy train. She was hand in hand with Elsie.

Miss Fryer actually let them all remove their school hats and have a go on the rotor, which Dobbin shouted was an example of centrifugal force, as she and the giggling girls were flattened against the revolving wall. Then they went on the helter-skelter. Miss Fryer turned pale as she watched them descend, serge tunic skirts blown up to reveal their green woollen school knickers. By this time, the girls were past obeying the blowing of the whistle around her neck and they whirled off to join a growing conga line that was weaving round the flower beds and rides.

The rule book was thrown away. It was as though they had been liberated from years in prison and had abandoned themselves to freedom. They had known so little joy in their young lives. They had almost forgotten how to have fun, or not to feel threatened. Now this glorious place, created with skill and love for pleasure, had touched their damaged spirits, and they let go of restraint and fear, wallowing in the gaudy jingoism. Yep, we won the war and look at us now. We may be bankrupt, but aren't we clever? Marguerite and Tony squeezed each other's hands with delight as they watched the capering youngsters. Even Miss Fryer smiled, albeit rather nervously.

Tiredness overcame the girls. Food rations did not provide fuel for sustained exertion. On the boat back to the South Bank site, they were subdued but happy. They took it in turns to sit next to the teachers, there being quite a battle to claim closeness to Mr Stansfield, who laughed loudly at their 'what was best' choices. Top of the list was seeing Dobbin's suspenders and bloomers when she was on the rotor.

Tony agreed there had been a lot of underwear on display.

'The brass band.'

'The coalmine.'

'The lovely, sorry, not "lovely", er festive flowers.'

'The tree walk.'

'The funny clock.'

And, 'Being here with you, sir.'

Marguerite saw the pleasure on Tony's face at this remark. For all his frivolity he was a dedicated teacher, and as fond of his pupils as she was.

When the girls discovered that Marguerite and Tony were staying behind, there were some yearning looks directed at them as the coach departed. It had been exhausting coping with the myriad questions that arose about the exhibits and artwork, so the comfortable seats inside the huge modernist concert hall, with its protruding ashtray-like boxes, were very welcome. The music rounded off the patriotic day well with Elgar and Tippett. Marguerite found herself silently weeping, reflecting how her British father would have relished the event.

Tony took her hand and she saw his eyes were brimming too.

'Not a dry eye in the house, eh?' she muttered.

After the concert they joined the crowd dancing to Geraldo's band. They danced elegantly together. Some of the people applauded their quickstep. Then they leant on the river wall, and gazed in silence at the floodlit buildings on the other side of the river. There were some gaps where the bombs had destroyed buildings, but the city looked proud and defiant, as it had when lit by the fires of the Blitz.

Oxford Street is deserted. Broken glass is strewn on the road. Just a few people are picking their way through the debris. He is in an RAF uniform. As he approaches she can see he is darkly handsome. She winks and he laughs and grabs hold of her. They waltz down the middle of the road, laughing, not saying a word. He is strong and young and reckless. One of 'the few', he eventually tells her. He has a night off, his wife is in Wales. She is about to go into training for an operation in occupied France. They have nothing to lose. Well, actually she does. And is delighted to do so. Chastity does not seem relevant when death could be just around the corner. They cling to each other in the tatty hotel room as the Blitz crashes and flashes outside. They give themselves to one another with passion and tenderness. The next morning they both go their own way with a gentle kiss, knowing full well they will never see each other again.

'I love being here with you, Tony. Are you glad you are with me?'

He put his arm round her and nodded.

'My goodness. What a wonderful day. It feels like the end of a ghastly nightmare and we're waking up to a world full of hope. I feel so excited about the future.'

Hugging each other, they watched the crowds still dancing under the stars, the lighted Skylon floating above them. The band upped the tempo. They were doing the jitterbug now, whirling and leaping, pale faces wreathed in smiles. Tony and Marguerite laughed and applauded.

She shouted above the band, 'Look at them. Just think what they've been through. "O brave new world, That has such people in't." We are so lucky, what a wonderful time to be alive. Isn't it?'

She held her face up to him. He put a finger gently on her lips and said solemnly, 'Yes, my dear one, it is.'

She waited.

'We must leave soon, Cinders, or we'll miss the last train.'

The moment was lost.

Chapter 8

Marguerite had never seen the secondary modern school on the outskirts of town. The building was ugly, thrown up in a hurry, just after the war. There were huts in the back to accommodate the overflow for which the main building was too small, and one scrubby grass field, marked faintly for both hockey and football together, which must have been confusing for the players.

The headmistress, Miss Scott, was surprisingly young and attractive. She wore a pencil skirt and white blouse, nylon stockings and high-heeled shoes. Her short black hair was bobbed, revealing pearl earrings. When Marguerite broached the reason for her visit, she soon realised the feminine appearance hid a steely determination. She was subjected to a diatribe, delivered in cool measured tones that belied their content.

'I don't think you are aware of what we are up against here, Miss Carter. You have clever pupils with supportive parents.'

'Not all of them—'

'Maybe, but the vast majority. We are left with the rejects.'

'Surely—'

'I'm sure you are going to say that with the right guidance they could improve. Too true. With the right teachers. But who would want to work here? Not you, for one. Lousy facilities, rotten pay and a school full of children who at eleven have been branded failures.'

'I can't believe that—'

'Come with me.'

The headmistress led Marguerite down a grubby corridor towards a cacophony of shrieks and raucous laughter. Looking through the glass panel of the classroom door Marguerite saw a chaotic scene. There were about fifty youngsters running amok. Two boys were fighting viciously on the floor, others were banging their desks in rhythm to bloodthirsty chants, and girls and boys were bellowing with excitement.

'Right. Fancy taking this lesson? It's English. The teacher has no doubt gone to vomit in the toilet, which is probably preferable to confronting 5c. Be my guest.'

'No I—'

'Bit different from your grammar school girls, eh? Sitting with their hands in their laps, avid to learn.'

It certainly was different. Marguerite had never in her life seen children so out of control. She had come across wild individuals like Elsie, who, it was her professional credo, could be tamed, but this was a roomful of unrestrained children running riot. The sight of such chaos appalled her. The latent wartime fright that she was learning to master, with its dry mouth, lurching stomach and shaking legs, surged up inside her so that she feared she might faint. Her instinct was to retreat, run away, but she heard Miss Scott's voice.

'Right. Once more into the breach.'

Taking a deep breath, Miss Scott entered. The room quietened slightly until, as Marguerite followed her in, one boy wolf-whistled. He was reinforced by other cat-callers. With sergeant-major-like strength Miss Scott shouted, 'Sit', whereupon one lad jumped to attention and started goose-stepping with a finger under his nose.

'Ja, mein Führer. Achtung. Sieg Heil.' Some of the others joined in.

The shrill commands. The clanging of boots on the cobbles. Through a crack in the shutter, the girl watches the three uniformed men stride down the street. The one in front has a clipboard and is checking the numbers. They stop outside Rachel's apartment and hammer on the door. They shout up at the windows.

'Be quiet. Shut up, shut up.' Marguerite was shaking. 'How dare you make a joke of it. The horror.'

Coming to her senses, Marguerite was aware that she must have spoken. The children in the classroom were staring at this demented stranger. Miss Scott too was looking at her. Quick, take command of the situation. Control was essential. She wrenched herself into teacher mode, turning it into a learning opportunity.

'Do you know how many people died in the war that you find so funny?'

Silence.

'Come along now. How many? D'you mind, Miss Scott?'

'No, please go ahead.'

The room was now quite still.

'Come on, you were making enough noise just now. Cat got your tongues? How many?'

A girl's voice, quietly:

'Three in our road.'

A few sniggers.

'It was a landmine, miss.'

A hand went up. 'My dad.'

Another hand.

'And mine.'

And another. Three fathers in all, and two brothers. Marguerite came out of her whirlwind of fury and saw the pinched, sober faces trying to work out how to deal with such an outburst, from what was presumably a teacher.

Marguerite herself was bewildered.

'I'm sorry. I'm so sorry.'

This was even more alarming. A teacher apologising to them. Although they were not sure for what.

An eager-to-please child, with unkempt hair, was thrusting her hand in the air.

'That's eight, miss. That's right isn't it, miss? Three, plus two, plus three. How many do you make it, miss?'

'Yes, that is correct, dear.' Marguerite hesitated. 'I was going to say 51 million, but three friends, three fathers and two brothers is much worse. I'm so sorry.'

And now they saw a teacher's tears.

Marguerite felt a cool hand on her arm. The head indicated the door, where a frail, youngish woman was apologising for her absence.

'Never mind, Miss Wilberforce. 5c, Miss Wilberforce is back now, get out your books and get down to work.'

As they walked back to her room, the headmistress sighed as the noise-level rose again behind them.

'She won't last the week.'

Over a cup of tea Marguerite apologised for her unprofessional behaviour. She was embarrassed by her outburst. Miss Scott was sympathetic.

'I deal with this on a day-to-day basis. I have grown accustomed to it, but I remember when I first came to this school, after the wonderful theories of teaching I learnt at college, and then a post in a civilised little Direct Grant school in leafy Surrey, I too couldn't believe it, but now I know it's true and I have to get on with it.'

Marguerite was dumbfounded.

'How on earth do you cope?'

'I suppose because I care about them – if that doesn't sound too wishy-washy. As you found out, those kids have suffered. Bombing, evacuation, fractured families. And now, when they expected peace to be wonderful, it isn't. There's dreariness everywhere. Only bomb sites to play in, rationing, and prefabs to live in.'

Marguerite said feebly, 'Well, there's the National Health.'

'True, their teeth will improve, but the education they're getting is lamentable. We've let them down.'

'But their behaviour towards you—'

'They're youngsters with no hope, no self-respect. So why should they show it to others? They have sat in their primary school class and heard the names read out of the successful with grammar school places, and realised that they were going to be dumped in a secondary modern or a tech. Herded together with all the other failures.'

'I hadn't realised.'

'If I didn't have fifty in a class, and teachers like that poor mouse, I could turn their lives around, but they have been branded as rubbish at eleven, so that is what they will be. We are producing a lost generation here.'

'But things have improved. Girls at my school have been lifted out of their backgrounds to be given a tiptop education.'

'But are they comfortable there?'

'Yes, I'm sure they are.'

Then she thought of Elsie and Irene. Miss Scott raised a plucked eyebrow.

'I hope so. I do so hope so.'

Marguerite recognised in the headmistress the same reforming zeal as she herself had, but in Miss Scott it was swamped by exhaustion. Closeted in her safe little world Marguerite had had no idea such schools existed. She was so privileged to be at a grammar school, for all its sometimes irksome rigidity.

When she reported back on her visit, Miss Fryer's reaction was in accord with that strict ethos.

'They are given too much freedom at that school, admittedly partly to do with overcrowding. You see, Miss Carter, during the war children ran wild. They must be tamed. They need tactful discipline from teachers and, essentially, parents too, with clear standards. Too much freedom breeds selfishness, vandalism and ultimately personal unhappiness. As you have witnessed at the secondary modern.'

Marguerite wanted to dispute this opinion, but she would be challenging a woman who ran a successful school, liked by parents and pupils, from the standpoint of a teacher of a mere two years' experience. Instead she arranged to meet Tony in the pub and bombarded him with her confusion. He was an invaluable safety valve.

'Of course you can't leave the grammar and go and teach there. It's a dump. You would be wasted. Miss Scott is an excellent head, but she can't turn it round. It's the tripartite system. Grading them as successes or failures at eleven is absurd. It stinks.'

'Well what can we do?'

'Keep on doing the good job you are doing here. You are transforming lives because you are a brilliant teacher. Stick to what is possible.'

'I can't get those kids out of my mind. It's so unfair. I'm really upset, Tony. Come back to my place, please. I need you.'

Up to now they had met in public, but seldom had any

privacy. She knew that he was frightened of compromising her reputation, and therefore her job, by letting their friendship become too intimate; Miss Fryer would never tolerate that sort of carry-on between staff members. Then there were his week-ends away, which she presumed involved a woman, maybe married, but certainly 'complicated'. Marguerite was not even sure what she wanted from Tony but, of late, she was feeling the need for a deeper understanding between them. Her Catholic guilt had always prevented her from having the sort of promis-cuous sex life her fellow university students had had. In any case the bond with Marcel was difficult to break. She had been his, body and soul, in tempestuous circumstances, and no trivial affaire de coeur could compete with that. Other than the one fleeting episode when she lost her virginity, before she met Marcel, he had been her only sexual partner. At twenty-seven she was beginning to wonder if she would suffer the fate so dreaded by her age group of being 'on the shelf'. She was pan-icked by a statistic in *The Times*: 96 per cent of adult women were married. But her work did not bring her into contact with, or allow her much time to meet, available men. Her colleagues seemed content to sublimate any urges by pouring their energy into their work. Maybe that would be enough for her too.

But Tony unsettled her. Occasionally she felt the need for more than fun and chat with him. Dancing close to him at the Festival of Britain she had felt a surge of desire, which she sus-pected was mutual, but he had insisted that they get the last train home. In retrospect she was grateful that he saved her from the squalid business of a borrowed wedding ring and signing a hotel register as 'Mr and Mrs'; that would have been no way to start a romance. Since then, she had got pleasure from the sight of him, brown and lithe and tousle-haired, playing tennis with the girls. She wondered what it would be like if their chummy hugs turned into something more satisfying. As for the scandal, with her need for comfort, Marguerite was past caring.

She grasped his hand.

'Please, Tony, come back with me.'

He stared at her long and hard. He didn't reply. The chatter and clink of glasses in the bar were the only sounds.

'Best not, lovey.'

Then he said, 'But I tell you what, we'll have one of our treats. Next week, Judy is appearing at the Palladium. I've got two tickets.'

'Judy?'

'Garland, woman. The one and only. It'll be a night to remember.'

Chapter 9

On the night they went to the West End of London there was a pea-souper of a fog, which made it difficult to see more than a few feet in front of them. Even inside the theatre it was faintly misty, and people were coughing and wiping their eyes. There was an atmosphere of excitement. Marguerite was surprised at how many of the mainly male audience knew Tony, and greeted him effusively. One blond young man ruffled his hair.

'Oh vade the bona riah,' he said. Then he cast a glance at Marguerite.

'Who's the palone? Lovely lallies,' the young man said, sizing her up.

When he'd gone she grabbed Tony's arm.

'What's going on? What's he talking about?'

'Oh that's Polari. Our secret language.'

'Our? Whose? What do you mean?'

He avoided her eyes.

'Come on, there's the bell. Mind you, she's bound to be late.'

The red plush of the Palladium was tatty, and the gilt tarnished. The star was indeed late. About half an hour late. During which time the excitement in the auditorium rose to fever pitch, so that when, at last, the tiny woman in a sequinned jacket and black tights on exquisite legs came onto the stage, there was a great roar of welcome, then a gasp when she seemed to stumble. The whole performance was nerve-racking for Marguerite. Garland forgot the words of one song, and ordered the conductor to start again. The audience were now at her feet, and even though her voice was cracking, and every now and then she stood stock-still as if she wasn't sure where she was, they lapped up every moment. Occasionally she would take a number at breakneck speed, frantically striding the stage, and batting her arms about as though to thrash the song out of herself. It was disturbing to Marguerite, but the audience seemed in seventh heaven. She was conscious of Tony watching her reaction. When this big-eyed waif sat on the edge of the stage, legs dangling into the orchestra pit, tremulously singing 'Over The Rainbow', it had even Marguerite gulping back a sob.

After the tumultuous reception, during which Judy threw kisses, and picked up the flowers thrown onto the stage, Tony insisted on following the crowd of shrieking people to the dingy stage door. When, after a long wait, Garland ventured out of the theatre, to whoops from the crowd, she looked genuinely surprised and delighted, although presumably it happened every night. Her tiny frame was cocooned in white fur, and diamonds flashed from head and wrists. She seemed supernatural, insubstantial, as though her quivering white face might melt into nothing. She grasped hands and laughed and joked hysterically, devouring the devotion. Tony was in the thick of it. Marguerite had noticed, through the smog, a group of policemen surveying the scene, disgust etched on their faces. When eventually the adored diva had been manoeuvred into her Rolls-Royce and had departed, waving, several men, including Tony, hugged each other and Marguerite saw a policeman ostentatiously write something in a notebook.

One of the them gave a warning.

'Vade lilly law, boys.'

And the crowd quickly dispersed.

Tony came towards her. They stood silently facing each other, the fog swirling round them.

'Now you know.'

'My God, Tony. Why didn't you tell me?'

'The clues were there.'

There were no buses or taxis running, but they groped their way on foot to Charing Cross Station. Neither spoke, except to warn the other of a kerb or an obstacle. They kept their distance. There was a long, silent wait for the train and it drew away very slowly. They managed to find a compartment to themselves. Tony yanked at the strap of the window to close a small chink and closed the door to the corridor, before sitting opposite her.

'Why didn't you tell me?'

'I thought – hoped – you'd realise. You've seen life. You went through the war, for heaven's sake.'

'That doesn't make me an expert in sexual deviance.'

Tony flinched.

'Why didn't you tell me straight out?'

'I was terrified.'

'Of what?'

'Everything.'

He looked terrified, quite unlike the exuberant man she was used to. He seemed to have shrunk, huddled into his duffel coat, scarf around his chin, hands deep in his pockets, slumped down in the seat.

'You should have told me before.'

'I didn't dare.'

'But you could have trusted me.'

'I don't trust anyone. I can't. The punishment for being what I am is too great.'

'You're being melodramatic.'

'You think so? Have you not read all the stuff about Guy Burgess? Everyone is much more concerned about his being homosexual than about his giving away state secrets. Did you see the *Sunday Mirror* this week? A warning to avoid "these evil men", with a handy guide – "How to Spot a Homo"?'

'Please stop. I don't know what to say. I'm lost.'

The ticket collector slid the door across and Tony sat up straight and showed him his ticket, saying chirpily, 'All right, mate? Awful weather.'

The man left, and Tony again pushed the door tight.

He lowered his voice. 'I can't risk telling anyone outright. Even you. My whole life and my job are in jeopardy.'

'Does Miss Fryer know?'

'She's probably guessed, but doesn't discuss it openly, apart from saying occasionally, "Take care." She's a good woman, and knows her own living arrangements could be questioned, although I'm sure nothing much happens between her and Miss Yates. The police and the Home Office are flummoxed by lesbians anyway. And homosexuality, come to that.'

'Me too.'

'Exactly. That's why I didn't want to tell you.'

Marguerite felt sullied by his news. Tony was suddenly a stranger, who had a secret life that she didn't dare to think about. She felt foolish, and revolted by his prancing friends at the Palladium.

'Have you been using me as a cover?'

'I swear to you on my mother's life that I haven't. I love you with all my heart.'

Marguerite began to cry.

'How can you say that? You're a homosexual.'

'My being homosexual does not in any way alter what I feel

for you. In fact it makes it more important, because I'm not permitted to have the sort of relationship I should have. That's probably why I was so frightened to tell you. You are everything to me.'

'Except for sex.'

'Sadly, yes. It's my huge loss.'

'And mine. Oh Tony, and mine.'

He crossed to her seat.

'May I?' he said.

She nodded and he folded her in his arms, where she sobbed into his Fair Isle jumper saying, 'We'll be all right, my darling. You'll see, we'll be all right.'

The ticket collector tapped on the window.

'All right, miss?'

She turned her tear-stained face towards him.

'He's just told me—'

She felt Tony stiffen.

'That I don't understand him.'

'That's what they all say, miss. You watch out.'

Chapter 10

After Tony's revelation Marguerite felt foolish and bereft. Foolish that she had thrown herself at him, foolish that she had beguiled herself into believing that they could have a proper relationship, and bereft at the possibility that they would now have no relationship at all, for to do so would necessitate her accommodating to a world she preferred not to acknowledge.

She was vaguely aware that such perversion went on, but it was not discussed. Even in France, when she and her group of résistants were forced to live closeted together in hiding for months on end, the bawdy talk she overheard was always about women. When she was at Cambridge, there was a group of epicene students who affected devotion to Greek male love, but most of them were now respectably married. She had once been deeply embarrassed by an Army officer friend, in a pub, expressing loud disgust that a couple of men in his regiment were 'poofs', 'pansies', 'queers', but until now it was not a subject she had dwelt on. Marguerite could not get out of her head the overexcited squealing men at the Palladium. She could not adjust her version of Tony as a strong amusing partner, and, yes, potential lover, to fit that image.

For Marguerite, sex was something that came from love

between a man and a woman, which ideally led to marriage. She was brought up as a Catholic to believe that you remained a virgin till your wedding night. She had sinned, but war had turned the old morality upside down – not without risk for women, who were still cast out of respectable society should they fall pregnant. Fear was a woman's bedfellow. But during the war, another fear took precedence. Fear of loss and death. In those dramatic years passion ran rampant. Love could be dangerous, if wrongly bestowed.

The roaring mob manhandles the girl down the narrow, ancient road, her head brutally shaved, a swastika carved, bloody, on her naked breast. They pass the church. The screams of hatred disturb the congregation's celebration of the Stations of the Cross.

How could she relate to this new Tony who had lied to her by omission about something so pivotal to their lives? Fortunately Tony, whether from fear or resignation, kept his distance. There was no need for their paths to cross except in the staff room, where they had always downplayed their closeness to avoid gossip. So the change in their relationship was not noticed. Marguerite decided to take on even more responsibilities at school to occupy her mind, and drive out any necessity for a private life. She wanted no more emotional complications. That way disorder lay. She considered contacting Miss Scott to strike up a friendship with a like-minded woman but decided even that would be a distraction. Her work was all she needed.

Elsie and Irene and their contemporaries had just finished their General Certificate of Education exams. Most had done well, with many getting distinctions in English. Marguerite allowed herself some pride, but was immediately focused on pushing them to achieve top A level results at eighteen, which could gain them entry to university.

She was shocked when Miss Fryer announced at a staff meeting after the exam results that eight girls would be dropping out of school, one of whom was Irene Brown.

She protested, 'But the girl is brilliant. She must go to university.'

Miss Fryer smiled.

'I'm afraid it is not your decision, Miss Carter. It is her parents'.'

'No, it is Irene's. Surely?'

'I have spoken to Irene and she intends to leave.'

Irene was sitting in the corner of the hockey field with Elsie.

'Can I join you, girls?'

Marguerite sat on the sweet-smelling newly cut grass. Elsie offered her a piece of the sliced Mars bar they were sharing.

'No, I won't take of your ration. I want to talk to you.'

Irene concentrated on the daisy chain she was making, cutting a slot in the stem with her fingernail, and threading through the next flower.

'Is it true you want to leave at the end of term, Irene?'

'Yes, miss.'

'Why, for heaven's sake? You're doing so well at school.'

'I want to get a job.'

'But you'd get a better job if you'd got a university degree.'

'I'm sick of school.'

'University is not like school, Irene.'

Marguerite tried to explain the freedom, the fun, the excitement of her experience at Cambridge, but it was a losing battle with someone who knew no one apart from her teachers who had experienced it. She contemplated taking Irene on a trip to

Oxford or Cambridge, but decided that could overwhelm a girl who she knew had never set foot outside Dartford except for her trip to the Festival of Britain.

'What about your parents?'

Irene shrugged.

'My mum wants me to leave.'

'She can't understand what it would mean for you, or she would want you to go to university. Like Elsie's parents.'

Elsie laughed.

'Oh, mine couldn't care less, miss. I didn't even discuss it with them. I might as well stay on. But I won't get into any university. I'm not posh like you and the other teachers.'

'Nonsense. You can do anything if you set your mind to it. Both of you. I'm disappointed in you, Irene.'

Marguerite went to rise from the ground. Irene stopped her and, kneeling in front of her, put the daisy chain around her neck.

'I'm so sorry, miss.'

Seeing Irene's defeated expression made Marguerite determined not to give up.

After lessons, knowing that Irene would be staying for Poetry Club, Marguerite made her way to the girl's home. She knew that this engagement with pupils beyond the school gate was frowned on by Miss Fryer, but her belief in Irene's talent overrode her qualms. She could not believe that the parents would not want the best for their daughter and was sure that, given the facts, they would encourage her to improve her prospects.

This was even more obvious to her when she saw where they lived. The council estate sprawled over several acres, and consisted of identical red-brick two-storey terraced houses. In front were tidy gardens, mainly monotonously composed of neatly mown lawns, with privet hedges behind the low garden walls. There were few flowers, but the houses were well maintained. Except for No. 210. The garden in front of this house was littered with bicycles in various states of repair. A clothes horse had blown over, scattering a load of washing over the neglected grass. Marguerite noted that the curtains were drawn over the front-room windows.

She started to pick up the washing, when the front door flew open.

'What the bloody hell are you doing? Get out.'

A scarecrow of a man stood in the doorway. As she approached slowly to explain, he went inside, slamming the door behind him.

A man appeared in the next-door garden.

'Take no notice of him. He can't help it, poor soul. He won't hurt you. What did you want?'

'I am Irene's teacher. I want to talk to her parents about something.'

'I'll go round the back and tell his wife.'

The man went through an archway between the houses.

Marguerite stood her ground, and a few minutes later, a woman in an overall came to the door, holding a baby in her arms. Clinging to her skirt was a small child, who Marguerite guessed was the baby Irene had mentioned in that first sonnet class.

The woman looked terrified.

'What is it? Is Irene in trouble? Has something happened? Has she done something wrong?'

Marguerite assured her that the opposite was true. After a lot of reassurance, the woman reluctantly let her into the house.

In the living room was a scrubbed table with two wooden chairs pushed beneath. A battered armchair stood by an unlighted single-bar electric fire and an old pram was pushed into a corner, where Irene's mother now laid the screaming baby and rocked it to quieten its cries. And that was it. No orna-ments, no rugs on the cracked lino floor, no signs of comfort, apart from a bottle of HP sauce on the table. The half-shut curtains were made of blackout material. Marguerite wondered where on earth Irene had managed to do her homework. Presumably at the table, where the man who shouted at her was now poring over a football coupon. When he saw Marguerite, he snatched it up, and rushed into the scullery.

'I'm sorry. You scared him. He thought you were from the council. Come about the state of the garden or something. They're always round here.'

'I'm so sorry. I didn't mean to upset you.'

Marguerite waited as the woman rocked the pram until the baby's weeping subsided, and there being no obvious place to sit she stood talking to the woman, loud enough for the man to hear. She could see him clinging to the handle of the back door, staring at her. He was wretchedly thin and wild-eyed.

Marguerite explained why she had come. How clever Irene was, what a future lay ahead of her if she persevered with her education. How it was possible to get a State Scholarship that would pay her university fees, and something towards her maintenance.

'Will she have to go away then?'

'Well, yes, of course.'

'But I need her here. I'd be at my wits' end coping with the two kids and him on my own. And I need help with the rent and everything. When she gets a job.'

'But that shouldn't be Irene's responsibility, surely? What about your husband?'

The woman lowered her voice.

'He can't do anything. He was in a Japanese camp, worked on the Burma Railway. Didn't speak for a year after he returned. His mind is hurt. He tries. He takes in bikes to repair, but he can't concentrate.'

Marguerite looked through at the man, who was staring into the room. She could understand why Irene had been so distressed by the Siegfried Sassoon poem. There, in her father's eyes, was 'the hell where youth and laughter go'.

Suddenly his face lit up. He rushed into the room to embrace Irene, who had come in behind Marguerite.

'Don't leave me, girl, don't let them take you away. Let me keep you safe.'

'Don't worry, Dad, I'm not going anywhere.' She took his shaking hands firmly in hers.

Over his head, she looked at Marguerite.

'You shouldn't have come here, Miss Carter. But perhaps it's just as well. Now you see why I have to stay. There are more important things than education, miss. There's real life. This is mine.'

Marguerite could think of nothing to say. The hopelessness of the trap that the girl was in silenced her; the trap of poverty and other people's weakness. How could a young girl survive in this hell-hole? Marguerite had seen rural poverty in France, but it had seemed beautiful, even in wartime, with the smell of the ever-present stockpot on the black stove, the warmth of the sun, the chickens and dogs. She was shocked that anyone should have to live in this barren place with its miasma of want, least of all Irene, with her burgeoning imagination. On the walk back to school, she racked her brain to find a way of releasing the girl from her prison. She longed to discuss it with Tony. Or rather the old Tony she had known.

★　　　★　　　★

When the news of Marguerite's visit reached Miss Fryer, she was summoned to her study.

'You have overstepped your authority, Miss Carter. You are not a social worker, you are a teacher.'

'But surely I have a responsibility towards my pupils?'

Miss Fryer sighed.

'Sadly, as I have pointed out many times, the most important influence on a girl's future is her background. Without parental support she will seldom succeed. But – and this is the salient point, Miss Carter – *we* cannot change that background. Despite what the Labour government may have thought, the schools cannot bring about a classless society. It is not our task to socially engineer equality. It is other people's duty to ensure everyone has decent housing, stable jobs, good health, so they are ready to seize their right to the equal opportunities – very different from equality – offered to them and their offspring.'

'But in the meantime, until we have Utopia, Irene is thrown on the rubbish heap? It didn't happen to her at eleven. It was just postponed till she was sixteen.'

'I think that is a preposterous insult to Irene. She now has a good grounding. Who knows what she will make of herself? Or, and this is perhaps more important, her children? The next generation. At the very least, I doubt, thanks to you, that their home will be devoid of books, as their mother's has been.'

'But Irene—'

'No more, Miss Carter, We must get back to our work, which I will allow is vital.'

Miss Fryer gave one of her rare smiles.

'You are now learning one of the hardest lessons for a teacher. We have to let the fledglings fly the nest. You must let go, even of your favourites – and every teacher has them. They are free to make their way in the world, well or badly. Your job is done.'

It was impossible for Marguerite to accept Miss Fryer's sanguine attitude to the girls' destinies. Her whole method of teaching was to engage with their psyche; to bring it into their study of literature. She wanted to inspire them, to nurture them, to love them. Anything less seemed cold and insufficient. She regarded the Irene incident as an abject failure on her part. She did not want to adjust her approach to Miss Fryer's more detached formula.

This deep disappointment, without the old solace of her companionship with Tony, made life very difficult for a while, but then her natural 'bloody optimism' returned, and she decided to focus her talent to transform on Elsie.

Chapter 11

Elsie's parents were easier to circumvent than Irene's, as they took little or no interest in their daughter. In the past the welfare people had investigated them, and decided there was no actual physical cruelty towards the children, just casual neglect, with which the girl and her siblings were apparently coping. Their family life was chaotic. The neighbours reported that the father, when drunk, was violent towards his wife, but nothing could be proved, and each incident was deemed by the police to be a 'domestic'. Unlike Irene, Elsie had no household duties – they were just not done. As her parents did not care what time she came home, her habit was to do her homework in the local public library after school. The girl was self-sufficient, relying on free school dinners, where her gluttonous table manners were a source of distaste to her fellow pupils. She would eat anything, including the vile frogspawn tapioca they all loathed. She cleared the other girls' plates into a tin she kept for the purpose, to take home for her tea. Breakfast was unknown to her.

The girl was a fighter, a survivor. There was no softness in her personality. Her eyes blazed and her tongue lashed out, as did her fists, if she deemed it necessary. The rest of the staff recognised that she had an exceptional mind, she excelled in

Maths and Science as well as English, but they could not warm to her constantly challenging personality. Marguerite went out of her way to encourage the girl, but her compliments were always shrugged off or ignored. Although she was disruptive in other teachers' lessons, she did not cause trouble in hers, but maintained a brooding silence, despite which her written work was consistently brilliant. After Irene left Elsie drifted around the school on her own, isolated by the loss of her only real friend. Then came an unexpected breakthrough.

In the course of a lesson on Tennyson they were looking at his 'The Charge of the Light Brigade'. Elsie started groaning and laughing in turn. When Marguerite asked her if she felt ill, she replied, 'Yes, this poem is making me feel sick.'

'Perhaps you could elucidate your criticism,' replied Marguerite, whereupon Elsie took from her satchel the book of war poetry that Marguerite had given to Irene, who presumably had handed it on to Elsie, thinking that her academic friend would have more need of it than she.

'I think Tennyson's poem is patriotic bull. Now this is a real description of battle, from someone who was actually there.'

Chancing Miss Fryer's disapproval, Marguerite was not going to pass on the opportunity of getting Elsie's active participation in a lesson, so she did not stop her reading out Wilfred Owen's 'Dulce et Decorum Est'. Elsie gave the description of a First World War gas attack a searing clarity, and snarled out the final sardonic challenge:

'"If you could hear, at every jolt, the blood
Come gargling from the froth-corrupted lungs,
Obscene as cancer, bitter as the cud
Of vile, incurable sores on innocent tongues,
My friend, you would not tell with such high zest

To children ardent for some desperate glory,
The old Lie; Dulce et Decorum est
Pro patria mori."'

The class was silent. Marguerite waited. Then she said, 'Yes,
Elsie, perhaps that poem speaks to us, these days, more than
Tennyson,' and as she looked at their youthful faces, it agonised
her that it was so.

Then Pauline, never one to miss a campaigning opportunity,
piped up, 'And that was what it was like in Hiroshima, so
bloomin' well join the World Federation of United Nations
Associations, all of you.'

Having once broken the ice, Elsie started to read pieces out
to the class, frequently asked to by the girls themselves. When
absorbed in a poem or piece of Shakespeare, her usual aggres-
siveness disappeared, and a dormant sensitivity revealed itself.
Marguerite had toyed with the idea of producing a school play
so, seizing on the chance to engage Elsie, she chose George
Bernard Shaw's *Saint Joan*. Saint Joan seemed an ideal role for
the girl – a pugnacious, outspoken, brave young woman. There
was only one other female role in the play and, as Marguerite's
request that the boys from the grammar school should be
involved was flatly rejected as too risky, the play was a somewhat
perverse choice for a girls' school, but Marguerite's obsession
with encouraging Elsie overrode any misgivings she might have
had. In any case, the other girls seemed to relish portraying male
authority and power.

Her belief in Elsie's ability was justified in the rehearsals. She
was soon word-perfect, not only with regard to her own role,
but everyone else's. One day she started playing the part with a
Somerset accent. She explained that, as Joan was a country girl,
she would use the voice of the man she was billeted with as an

evacuee. She doubtless also used the abject dread she had felt as a three-year-old child, at the mercy of the sixty-year-old predatory widower, in the scene where Joan loses her nerve in the face of the male hierarchy that tries to destroy her.

Marguerite was astonished at the range of the girl's emotions and her ability to express them. As rehearsals progressed, the other girls acknowledged her superior talent, and deferred to her opinion as to how a scene should be played, never minding that Miss Carter set the moves in such a way that Elsie was always centre stage. Two of the younger girls developed a crush on her, and would bring in hard-to-find sherbet fountains for their star.

Such gestures were rejected gracelessly by Elsie.

'Don't be stupid. You had to queue for that. Keep it.'

But when Julia, who had a bad limp as a result of her polio, brought her a bunch of wild violets she had laboriously gathered, Elsie managed a muffled, 'Thanks. Nice smell.' And Marguerite saw her walking home later, carefully balancing the flowers in a jam jar of water.

Finding herself the object of admiration had a salutary effect on her personal hygiene. Her clothes were occasionally washed, although the concept of ironing was foreign to her, so she still appeared fairly crumpled, a look which some of the juniors began to emulate, by rolling their nicely pressed blouses into a ball when they got to school. Even her impetigo began to improve, probably because her fellow thespians shared their healthy packed teas, provided by loving mothers to tide their daughters over their after-school rehearsals. Marguerite persuaded her that she could use less gentian violet on her face.

'Perhaps the audience'll think it's woad, miss.'

'That might confuse them, Elsie. She's French, not an ancient Briton.'

Marguerite had to enlist Tony's help in staging a sword fight that would look effective without causing damage, especially as Elsie, not known for her reticence in battle, was one of the protagonists. He was happy to help. She watched him carefully drilling their moves with admiration for his gentle handling, in particular of Elsie. All thoughts of their shared secret were pushed out of her mind. It was a relief that they could relate in a professional manner. They were polite and respectful to one another, whilst avoiding eye contact.

The performance of the play was open to staff and pupils from their school as well as, great excitement this, from the adjacent boys' grammar school. And, of course, the parents. After the first performance there would be a party, to which each child was allowed to take two guests, whose names were to be submitted to Miss Carter. When, a week before the show, Elsie had still presented no names, Marguerite reminded her that time was running out.

'I don't want no one to come.'

'Why on earth not? You're going to be wonderful. Don't you want people to see that? What about your parents?'

'It's not really their cup of tea. Plays and that.'

'Did you ask them?'

'My mum said she'd try, but she's very busy.'

'Doing what?'

'Things.'

Marguerite dared not pursue it further. On the evening of the first performance she went onto the stage before curtain-up to check that the rudimentary set for the first scene, a wooden cut-out tree, made by the art department, was in place. She found Elsie peering round the edge of the stage curtain, scanning the buzzing audience. She gently said the girl's name. Taken by surprise, Elsie wiped her hand across her eyes.

'This stupid make-up makes my eyes water.'

Marguerite dabbed at her eyes with her hanky.

'Do it for yourself, Elsie.'

'No, I'll do it for Irene. She's coming. And you, miss.'

Whatever motivation it was that propelled her performance it was effective. Whilst the rest of the cast were never anything more than schoolgirls dressed up, reciting lines, she simply became Joan. Only once did Elsie's own anger take over. The girl playing the Dauphin forgot her lines. After an endless pause, Elsie grabbed the girl and shook her violently, managing to make it look as if it was Joan's rage that prompted the action, as she said, 'I know what you're going to say,' and did the quaking girl's lines for her. The audience were convinced it was part of the scene, and continued to be enthralled. Parents who had come to cluck over their daughters found themselves caught up in the story, and profoundly moved by the dedicated, mistreated young Frenchwoman. Elsie's fellow pupils stopped giggling at the boys in the audience, and their friends' baggy tights and homemade doublets, and willed Joan to save herself from her appalling death.

As the light faded on Elsie saying Joan's last line, '"O God that madest this beautiful earth, when will it be ready to receive Thy saints? How long, O Lord, how long?"' there was a silence before the applause started.

Marguerite looked around and realised something very special had taken place. Tony was shaking his head in amazement and gave a solemn thumbs-up sign as he caught her glance. The applause was tumultuous, there was even the odd 'Bravo', despite the august presence of Miss Fryer in her academic gown. She nodded her head, and smiled appreciatively at Marguerite. As for Elsie, she at first seemed startled at the acclamation as the rest of the cast generously pushed her forward for a solo bow, then her face lit up, radiant: for the first time in her life she was appreciated and admired. At the party afterwards she had a look of shy disbelief as people patted and praised her. Marguerite was particularly pleased to observe that the head boy of the boys' school, the focus of all the girls' fancy, shook her hand, and talked to her for some time. Although he did most of the talking.

The very next day, Marguerite extricated Elsie from an admiring flock of chattering girls in the playground, and struck whilst the iron was hot. Irene had got herself a job in a local solicitor's office, and Marguerite realised that the lure of a regular salary, however paltry, would be tempting to her friend, not to mention Elsie's parents. Marguerite led the girl into a classroom and sat her down.

'Well – I hope you're feeling proud of yourself, Elsie.'

A shrug. Marguerite remembered the Mistress of Girton's advice to her.

'Elsie, stop that. Allow yourself to enjoy what you have achieved. Relish the feeling of a job well done.'

'I can't, miss.'

'Why ever not?'

'I don't know how.'

'Well, you must learn. Because this is the beginning of a very exciting professional life.'

'But what use is it? I can't be an actress.'

'You could. But you don't have to be. It's too early to decide that. At university you will be able to join drama societies and see what that leads to, but whatever degree you do, English or one of the sciences, there will be all sorts of jobs open to you. The world is your oyster.'

The girl's eyes were beginning to show interest.

'You are exceptional, Elsie. Last night proved that. You

brought intelligence and understanding to your role and showed an amazing ability to reach out to people. Those qualities could take you far. Why, you could be our first lady prime minister.'

Elsie roared with laughter.

'No, don't laugh. Women are getting into politics.'

Marguerite could see that a chink of light was breaking into the girl's gloomy expectations for herself.

'See how the girls admire you? And I understand Miss Fryer saw you this morning to congratulate you.'

'And the head boy of the grammar school asked me to their school dance.'

'Well there you are. Fame indeed. What more could you want?'

'I can't believe it, miss. Will you show me how to put that make-up on my scabs?'

'I will, Elsie, I will. If you will promise me to work hard for your A levels so we can get you a state scholarship and you can go to university. Bargain?'

'Bargain, miss.'

And she was as good as her word. The staff universally enjoyed teaching the crème de la crème that made it through to the upper school. They regretted the loss of those bright girls, like Irene, who were forced to leave by circumstance, but, on the whole, the girls that survived were the cleverest and a joy to lead forward to greater heights of knowledge. This was the reward for their teachers' diligence and dedication. They all agreed that Elsie had changed radically, and her colleagues were generous in their praise of Marguerite's tenacity with her, and only too willing to join in the mission to push this exceptional girl to her limits.

Now it seemed that Marguerite's entire life revolved around

school. She had tried attending a few concerts and plays on her own, but she missed discussing them with Tony. Watching him work on the fights for *Saint Joan*, laughing and joking with the girls, reminded her of what fun he was and how much she missed him. But Elsie's progress was her compensation for any loneliness.

The seniors had the use of a room in the tower to read and study, as their syllabus involved more coursework. Leaving the staff room at the end of the day, Marguerite would see Elsie hard at work in the room below. She was producing essays of startling originality, and Marguerite found herself challenged by the freshness of the girl's approach to criticism of standard classics. She had no shadow of a doubt that Elsie could get into an Oxbridge college. The interview would be the only stumbling block. Her grammar had improved, but not her Dartford accent, and she was still prone to allow her inferiority complex to render her inarticulate, making her seem sulky and introvert. Marguerite organised weekly conversation-practice sessions with Elsie, and some of the other aspirants, to help them towards the self-confidence of the privately educated girls against whom they would be competing.

It was during these sessions that Marguerite noticed Elsie was not as focused as she had been earlier. She was reverting to her old truculent manner, and her work was sometimes slovenly and ill-thought-out. Marguerite brought up her worries at a staff meeting, and several others agreed that her work had deteriorated. Miss Fryer maintained that she lacked stamina, and her burst of enthusiasm after the success in the school play was unsustainable without family support. Marguerite was delegated to give her a pep talk.

She invited her into the holy of holies – the staff room – after lunch, when the rest were all teaching. She offered Elsie a cup of tea, which she accepted, but she rejected a chocolate biscuit, because she said she felt sick.

A surge of fear gripped Marguerite.

'Are you ill?'

'Not really, miss. I'm just up the duff.'

Chapter 12

'Oh no.'

Marguerite abandoned the tea-making and sat beside Elsie. She took her hand.

'How far gone are you?'

'Three months.'

'Who's the father?'

'Jeremy Addison.'

'The grammar head boy?'

'Yes.'

'Why on earth did you let this happen?'

'He said it was safe if we did it standing up.'

Marguerite was dumbfounded.

'How could you be so stupid?'

'I didn't know, did I?'

'But you must have heard about birth control?'

'Yes, I heard about it, so when he wanted to go all the way, I went to my doctor for his help, and he said he'd tell my mother if I did it, and I'd better behave myself or he'd also tell the police. I went to the council offices to see if there was a family planning clinic and they said Kent County Council doesn't have one as they consider they lead to loose morals. Then I saw that newsreel with that important man opening some clinic in London. Bloke with the glasses and a funny hat. I wrote down where they said it was, and got a train to London, and found it. I hung about outside for a long time trying to pluck up courage to go in. I shouldn't have bothered.'

'Why not?'

'They said I had to go with my fiancé, and have a letter from my vicar saying we were getting married, and then they would give us something four weeks before the wedding. Well, there is no wedding. There's not even an engagement.'

'Have you told Jeremy Addison about the baby?'

'No, he'd go off me. He read somewhere about the standing-up thing – knee trembling, it's called – so that's what we did. We'd only done it twice. It's my fault. But nobody ever told me anything. My friends didn't know either. Mrs Conway in Hygiene just talks about reproduction in frogs and rabbits, and Miss Lewin in Science talks about dogfish doing it.'

Marguerite was dismayed but she tried not to show her panic.

'Elsie, I am so sorry. Everyone's let you down. Do you love Jeremy?'

'I don't know, miss. He was nice to me after the play and at the school dance he said he was proud I was with him. He thinks I am pretty and clever. I can't believe it. I don't want to spoil it.'

'But, Elsie, be sensible. What's going to happen to your future? You can't go to university with a child. What will you do?'

'I don't know, miss.' Elsie's face crumpled.

Marguerite held her tightly, desperately trying to think of a solution.

She ventured, 'I know this is awful but have you thought about an abortion?'

'I tried that, miss. My doctor said they were only allowed for medical reasons. Not social ones. Didn't feel very social. Being crushed against a pebble-dashed wall.'

'Your doctor doesn't sound very helpful.'

'He isn't. He told my mum, and she told me my dad will throw me out when he finds out. He probably won't notice anyway. He's always drunk as a lord.'

'There must be something we can do. We can't let this ruin your life.'

'It won't, miss. I'll survive somehow.'

The girl looked lost.

'It's a pity though, ent it, miss?'

The next day Marguerite took the news to Miss Fryer, who insisted there was no alternative but for Elsie to leave school before the pregnancy began to show. The rest of the school must not know about it, partly for her sake, and partly because of the bad example it would set.

'But what about her education?'

'There are correspondence courses. Perhaps she can do one in shorthand and typing. There are good secretarial posts.'

'But she's better than that. She could have a brilliant career.'

'Well, she should have thought of that before she went astray. This time I will not be persuaded, Miss Carter. She is a wayward girl and a not a good influence – as soon as possible she must disappear.'

Marguerite knew it was useless to plead for understanding. Women who succumbed to desire must be punished. Banished to mental homes, convents, or just a life of drudgery, which was probably now Elsie's destiny.

The two women cling to their crying babies as the crowd manhandles them out of the village into the waste land beyond. An old woman shouts after them, 'What are the bastards? German or American?'

98

Elsie had only two choices. Either to have the child and drag it up, supported by whatever menial job she could fit in with caring for it, or she could have the baby adopted at birth, a heart-rending sacrifice that Marguerite could not imagine the love-starved Elsie being able to make. She would not be able to find a husband with an illegitimate child, and Jeremy Addison's respectable middle-class family would move heaven and earth to deny their son's responsibility, should she decide to tell him.

Distraught, Marguerite asked Miss Belcher to cover for her for the rest of the afternoon, and went for a walk in the playing field. The rain started to teem down so she took shelter in the rabbitry. She slid down the wall and crouched on her haunches in the corner, in despair at her impotence to deal with the situation. First Irene, now Elsie. The rabbits snuffled in sympathy as she looked at them, pressing their twitchy noses through the wire of their hutches. On an impulse she rose to her feet and started to undo the doors of the cages to set them free. Three of them were hopping in confusion on the ground, when Tony appeared at the door.

'They won't survive in the wild. They're too tame.'

He started to pick them up by their ears, supporting them gently underneath, and to put them back in their cages.

'But Elsie will – she's tough.'

'You know?'

'Belcher told me.'

'Oh Tony. Everything's gone wrong. It's such a mess.'

He took one of her hands, tentatively, gently.

'D'you mind?'

She shook her head.

'It's life, my dear girl. It just happens.'

'I feel so sad. And useless. And disappointed.'

'You can't force people to be as you want them to be. It's

called free will. Unless you put them in a cage like these poor creatures.'

'But it's not just Elsie. There's Irene. You and me. Life. I had such high hopes of everything. I believed anything was possible. Remember that night at the Festival?'

'I'll never forget it.'

'But even that ended in tears. The bloody Tories destroyed it immediately they took over. That lovely, silly Skylon we danced under was chucked in the Thames, or somewhere.'

'Well, it would only have gone rusty. It was fun while it lasted. We carpe-ed the diem. That's what you have to do.'

He kissed her hand.

'It was one of our treats.'

'Oh Tony, our lovely treats. I miss them so much. I miss you so much.'

'I tell you what—'

He looked at her nervously.

'Why don't we have one now, to cheer us up?'

'Have what?'

'A treat. I've got a new snazzy motorbike. It's stopped raining. I'll take you for a ride.'

She wiped her eyes on his shirt.

'Hey watch it, that's clean on. Here, blow.'

He held his hanky for her to blow her nose, then gently took a corner of it to wipe her face.

Looking into his eyes for the first time in months, she said, 'If I promise not to flirt with you, will you please come back to my place for supper? We could call in at the butcher, and I will use my womanly wiles to get some rabbit out of him.'

Tony covered her mouth with his hand. 'Ssh.' He looked at the cages. 'Don't worry, no one you know.'

He led her out of the rabbitry.

'By the way, if you mean the butcher on Shepherd's Lane, he's more likely to respond to my wiles than yours.'

'What? He's married.'

'Oh, my lovely innocent. Meet you at the bike shed.'

The motorbike was a vision of shining silver and black, polished within an inch of its life. Tony now sported a leather jacket and a white silk scarf with his respectable teacher's grey flannels. She mounted the pillion, and put her arms round his waist, laying her head against the cool leather, drinking in its smell and that of the diesel. He did a detour to the Heath, where the hillocks made for tank-training exercises still existed. He roared up and down them, sometimes propelling the bike off the top of a lump, both wheels in the air, landing with a wallop and roar. Marguerite found herself suspended off the saddle, with her bottom and legs afloat, and only her arms round his neck restoring her to her seat. She screamed with delight, the speed and manoeuvring making her heart pound, and taking her breath away.

He shuddered to a halt and turned to look at her.

'Better? Blown the dirty cobwebs away?'

'Oh Tony, yes, thank you. I'd clean forgotten about laughter.'

Windblown and dusty, they stopped at the shop, where she watched Tony charm both the butcher and his wife into producing a rabbit from behind the empty counter. Seeing Marguerite's baffled face as he put the rabbit into the saddle bag he laughed.

'I know, I'm a shameless hussy. But if you've got it, flaunt it, I say.'

'But the butcher, is he—?'

'No he's not a poof. He's a bit of a closet queen, plays rugby with the local team and enjoys a frolic in the showers after, but he wouldn't really do anything. He's neither Arthur nor Martha. There's a lot of men like him. Especially after being in the services during the war. Stuck in a ship for months on end in the Navy I had a ball, I can tell you. He does no harm, poor sod.'

Once in the flat, Marguerite busied herself in the kitchenette, making a rabbit pie, whilst Tony looked around.

'Nice view.'

'Yes, they play cricket out there in the summer. I love watching it. It's very English.'

'But you're French.'

'Only half, remember. My father was English.'

'Was?'

'Yes, they're both dead. I told you.'

'Where did they die? You never told me that.'

'Paris. I think.'

'You think?'

'Yes. Do your parents still live in Oldham?'

'Yes. We don't know much about one another, do we?'

Marguerite realised that was true. Their relationship before had been fun but necessarily superficial because, she now knew, both of them had a lot to hide. Marguerite opened a bottle of wine that she had kept for a special occasion. He poured them a glass.

He leant on the door and watched her chopping and rolling, occasionally tasting or smelling an ingredient.

'You're good. Do you like cooking?'

'Not for myself. But I enjoy cooking for others.'

'Perhaps you should stop doing so much for others. Don't risk all your eggs in other people's baskets.'

'You mean Elsie?'

'And that other girl.'

'Irene?'

'Yes.'

'I meant to help them.'

'And you did. But you can't dictate what they do with your help.'

'But I am a teacher. My job is changing children's lives.'

'No. It's to teach them English, French, Sport, whatever. Their lives are their own. Take me. I was in a slum school, and a teacher moved heaven and earth to get me to physical-training college. If it hadn't been for him I'd be sweeping streets now. Mind you, they'd look bona if I did. He rescued me but, try as he would, he couldn't stop me being queer.'

Marguerite was embarrassed.

'Are you sure you are? Maybe you're like the butcher.'

''Fraid not, poppet. My teacher made me go to a doctor to be "cured". He looked at me with revulsion and said, "You do know you're breaking the law?" and prescribed aversion therapy, electric shocks, hormone injections, the lot. I refused all of it, but agreed to try therapy, and ended up making a pass at my butch psychiatrist.'

Marguerite laughed on cue but hid her face as she put the pie in the oven. Tony chattered merrily whilst looking through her LP records stacked on the floor, a mixture of classical and jazz, like the George Melly and the Humphrey Lyttelton they had bought together after hearing them play in clubs. He held up the Judy Garland LP that they got after the concert at the Palladium.

'Fancy a bit of Judy to celebrate what I hope is our reunion?' He looked at her anxiously.

'Yes, I'd love that.'

As the familiar throbbing voice started, Marguerite remembered.

'Those men that night. Were they your friends?'

'Ships that pass in the night.'

'What does that mean?'

He paused, looking out of the window, then turned to face her.

'Marguerite this is difficult for me. I want to be honest with you, but I tread a dangerous path. Can I trust you?'

Marguerite felt battered by the complexities of other people's lives, but knew that to reject Tony's offer of openness would sever any bond they might have.

'Yes, Tony, you can trust me.'

'Do you know where it's from, that quotation? "Ships that pass in the night"?'

'Yes, it's Longfellow.'

'An old actor laddie, a sad old queen, taught me it. I know it by heart:

'"Ships that pass in the night, and speak each other in
    passing;
Only a signal shown and a distant voice in the darkness;
So on the ocean of life we pass and speak one another,
Only a look and a voice; then darkness again and a
    silence."'

Marguerite waited for him to say more. Eventually he took a deep breath.

'I have this secret life, you see, and that describes it perfectly, if somewhat more poetically than it merits.'

'It sounds so lonely.'

'It has to be. I dream of meeting the love of my life, but it is not allowed. So I make do with hanging around Hyde Park looking for guardsmen who want to earn a few bob, or lurking around shop windows in Piccadilly till someone asks me for a light, and we go and spend the night in the Savoy Turkish Baths on Jermyn Street. Or I find a bit of rough in Trafalgar Square.'

Marguerite wanted him to stop. She felt sickened.

'Yes, it sounds squalid, I know. Just sex really. But we have some jolly times together too. There's all sorts of clubs, pubs where we meet and shock the natives with our camping about, before we go back to our schools, banks, hospitals, whatever, and become respectable citizens again.'

Marguerite tried to equate this new image with the Tony she thought she knew.

'Does it make you happy?'

He laughed.

'God, no. But it's a relief not to have to pretend all the time. We cling together, us poofs. We belong to a Masonic society with its own language and rules. And some of it is more elegant. There is a famous theatrical producer who has parties with all the stars that I go to as decoration, and a very clever art historian who has fabulous parties in a flat on the top of the Courtauld Gallery. The conversation is slightly more superior than the average orgy. He's very left wing, and we are delightfully class-less, we pansies. Intellectuals, the odd Tory MP, bank clerks, politicians, actors, judges, soldiers, sailors, navvies, anyone is welcome, especially if they've got a bona bod.'

'What if you get caught?'

'Well, the game's up. My proper life, the one I'm proud of, my work, my place in society, will be destroyed. No room for queers. It would kill my mum and dad. I'm the one bright spot of their lives – their son, the teacher. Two world wars, and a lifetime of drudgery. They don't deserve a pervert for a son.'

'Oh Tony, don't, please. Don't talk of yourself like that.'

He looked straight at her.

'Well, they are not "experts in sexual deviation".'

She closed her eyes.

'I am so very, very sorry I said that.'

'Don't worry, it's normal. Unlike me.'

'Don't—'

'No, let's face it, we are pariahs and they're out to get us. Anyone caught is used as an example by our erudite press. Especially if they're important and clever people, as many queers are. Like poor John Gielgud. You, and the great British public, would be amazed if I told you how many of the people you admire are pansies.'

'Oh Lord. Why does sex, love, whatever you call it, have to be so furtive? Same with Elsie. Full of guilt and fear.'

'Well now you know about me, I'm in your power. You could blackmail me, which is another of our little worries.'

'Don't be silly, Tony. But I'm now very scared for you.'

'I'm Lady Luck, don't worry. Last week I was in a club in Soho, full of screamers, and Lilly Law raided it and started taking everyone's names. The young copper who came up to me had a northern accent so I reverted to my Oldham lingo that my mum tried so hard to get rid of. He said, "Where are you from?" and when I told him it turned out he grew up a few streets away from me, so he let me nip out the back way, and pinched my bottom as I left.'

'Thank God.'

Tony helped Marguerite lay the knives and forks on her yellow Formica table, and she brought the welcome distraction of the rabbit pie from the oven. As they ate, she with some difficulty, he looked at her across the table.

'You asked about happiness. I'm happy now. Here with you. Bona mangarie and Judy singing. What more could a girl want?'

'But where do I fit in?'

'You're everything I want. Companionship, beauty, style, shared tastes, shared ideals. I love you. You are the relationship of my dreams.'

'But you don't desire me.'

'I don't want to possess you. I don't need to own you. I just would like to be part of your life for as long as you want me or need me. But I'll quite understand if you prefer to back off, after what I've just told you.'

She just shook her head, not knowing what to say to such a strange proposal. Of what? Not marriage obviously. And not a normal friendship. It was definitely not a normal situation. There was a long pause.

Then, as though at a polite dinner party, Tony said, 'This is delicious.'

'It was my mother's recipe. I used to have it as a child.'

He nodded and concentrated on his plate.

'*Thank you, Maman, that was delicious.*'

Why are they so solemn, why aren't they talking like they usually do over supper? Why are there long pauses?

'*Marguerite, we are going away.*'

'*What?*'

'*And you are going to stay with Henri and Anne.*'

'*Why? When?*'

'*After supper I'm taking you there. I have packed your bag.*'

'*I don't want to go and stay with them. What about the leaflets? Who will deliver them?*'

'*Marguerite. You must forget all that. Never tell anyone what you have been doing.*'

'*Why aren't you coming?*'

'*The work needs to go on. But you must go tonight.*'

Tony was looking at her anxiously.

'I'm sorry I've upset you so.'

'It's not you. I was just remembering something.'

'About your parents?'

'Yes. Temps perdu. It's the taste of the rabbit. It's my madeleine. We had this pie the last night I saw them. A week later they were killed. For distributing anti-Nazi propaganda. They and a group of like-minded intellectuals produced a newspaper and posters and stickers attacking the occupation. I used to deliver some of them. I took them round Paris hidden in the frame of my bike, or in my satchel or music case. They suspected they had been betrayed and planned to get me away before they were arrested.'

'Did you know at the time they had been killed?'

'Not until I got to England and joined the SOE and they found out for me that they had been taken to Fresnes Prison. My beautiful mother was tortured to death and my father was shot.'

'God, you've never told me any of that before.'

'No, I don't talk about it. It's bloody Judy Garland, she's lowered my defences. Forget it.'

'But you worked in the Resistance—?'

'Please. Enough. It's all in the past. I can't talk about it.'

She genuinely couldn't; she did not know how to gather the fragments into a whole that could be voiced out loud. It was buried deep in her mind, where she did her best to keep it.

'Fair's fair,' Tony persisted, 'I've been honest with you. It's confession time. How did you get to England?'

'OK, but no more after this. I was fine. My parents had organised my escape through France to Spain and eventually to England.'

'On your own?'

'Yes.'

'How old were you?'

'Fifteen.'

'Christ. Younger than Elsie and Irene.'

'Yes.'

'See? And look at you now. You survived all that.'

'Only just. Many didn't. My best friend Rachel and her sister were taken away, with many of our Jewish friends. I discovered later that she spent six days shut up in a sports stadium called the Vélodrome d'Hiver.'

Marguerite was now fighting to block the memory but the words forced their way out.

'Six thousand of them, six days in the blistering heat. No shelter, no food, no water, no lavatories. Those that didn't die there were carted off in cattle trucks, where more died. She was thirteen, her sister was four years old, crouched on the floor amongst the shit and corpses for days, only to be stripped, gassed and incinerated at Auschwitz.'

Tony had his head in his hands.

'Oh my God.'

'And from my bedroom window I watched them taking her away. And did nothing. Which is why I can't do nothing ever again.'

Tony hurried round the table, lifted her to her feet, and wrapped his arms around her.

'My valiant little love, I'm back now. You've got me. We'll "not do nothing" together.'

Chapter 13

After the night of the sharing of demons, Marguerite and Tony moved into a deeper relationship. She stopped trying to define it; they were more than friends, yet less than lovers, was the best that she could achieve. But was it really less? Life was a damn sight more pleasant with him than without him, she knew that.

She found out, through Pauline, that Irene had settled into her job, and that Elsie was going to have the baby, although she did not know whether Elsie intended to give it up for adoption. On Tony's insistence, she did not pursue the matter further and jeopardise her job by defying Miss Fryer. As she had already learnt, it was pointless anyway; there was nothing she could do to help the girl. Best move on. Put it behind her.

Having discovered the other's vulnerability, Marguerite and Tony were solicitous of each other. One of the ways this was expressed was through their mutual love of cooking, which Tony had been nervous of sharing with her before, lest she should think him effeminate; it was true he was the only man she had ever met who would set foot in a kitchen, or undertake any household chore. Judging that it was now safe to visit her flat without there being any sexual expectations he could not fulfil, he would don her pinny, and, Elizabeth David's *French*

Country Cooking in hand, conjure up fragrant dishes reminiscent of her childhood family holidays in Provence. His pièce de résistance was David's coq au vin, which was produced on the few occasions they entertained. The nature of their relationship was never discussed, as everyone at school seemed to have unconventional partnerships, the definition of which was irrelevant. Their usual guests were Miss Lewin, History, and Miss Haynes, Domestic Science, 'the plaited ones' as they became, who holidayed together, and Miss Belcher and Miss Farringdon, English, who argued like an old married couple, but it was hard to put a label on exactly what they were to each other.

For the coq au vin they took it in turns to chat up the butcher for a chicken. They had to save up several weeks of their 6-ounce butter ration. The other ingredients were still difficult to obtain. The only olive oil available was a nasty, yellow medicinal version from Boots, and when asked for basil, the local greengrocer said he knew no one of that name. A trip to Soho was the only answer. With the help of some of the many women plying their trade from doorways, they located small shops that miraculously stocked Italian olive oil, fresh mushrooms, lemons, basil and a fine Châteauneuf du Pape red wine that Elizabeth David insisted was essential.

Marguerite could hardly bear to watch as a whole bottle was poured into the pot, especially as it followed a glass of fine brandy that had been used to set on fire the scraggy little bird. On top of the hunter-gathering, the actual cooking took hours, with a lot of flamboyant flambéing, glazing, and sautéing, whilst Marguerite rushed around washing the many utensils Tony used and generally acting as his commis chef.

Tony seemed to enjoy cooking in Marguerite's kitchenette, even with the restrictions of the Baby Belling, with its tiny oven and hotplate. He bought her a pressure cooker, but she was much too frightened to use it lest it explode. Their fare was less ambitious when they cooked for themselves alone, Tony's specialities being shepherd's pie and bangers and mash and Marguerite's her omelette and her mother's cassoulet, with the occasional foray into a novel spaghetti bolognese; more appetising than had been the wartime whale meat and Spam fritters and in France an excess of wild boar, rabbit, even, one desperate time, mule.

Marguerite and Tony's joint quest 'not to do nothing' led to occasional suppers with anti-bomb campaigners and other political activists. Coq au vin was not on the menu on these occasions, lest it be deemed too bourgeois. They usually settled for fish and chips from the shop round the corner, eaten on the knees, out of the newspaper wrapping and salted and vinegared in the shop – Tony did however add a northern flourish with his mushy peas concocted out of the newfangled frozen peas.

The discussions were intense; more so now the Labour Party was in opposition, the country having voted back the aged Churchill. Opposition suited them both, unleashing their aggressive instincts in the face of the foe. They both did their level best to show the electorate the error of their ways. They sought out any public meeting held by Margaret Thatcher, who popped up everywhere in her quest for political office. Another victim of their heckling was Edward Heath, the newly elected MP for Bexley. He was a bumbling young man who could very easily be reduced to satisfying red-faced rage. Whilst Tony went easy on Heath because of the constant jibes at his unmarried state, Marguerite felt a sneaking regard for Thatcher. She pointed out to Tony that the woman had managed to qualify for the bar four months after the birth of her twin children and written a series of articles headed 'Wake Up, Women' for the *Sunday Graphic*, about women being permitted to work. 'Why not a woman Chancellor – or Foreign Secretary?' Mrs Thatcher had posited, somewhat optimistically.

'Anyway. We will soon have a woman in the top job after Elizabeth is crowned.'

Marguerite knew that mention of the planned coronation riled Tony.

'All that campery. We can't afford it.'

'Oh shut up, Tony. You'll love it more than anyone.'

'You're probably right. I can't resist nice frocks and a bit of jewellery. Not to mention trumpets. I cherish a well-blown trumpet.'

On Marguerite's insistence Tony rented a television set so they could watch the big event in his digs.

Tony lived in a boarding house run by a German. He liked and respected Mrs Schneider. When he told Marguerite the woman's story, despite her instinctive reservations regarding all things German, she could understand why. Mrs Schneider had left Germany with her husband and two sons in 1937, when the children, who had been forced by their school to join Hitler Youth, were cross-examined about their Communist parents. They were not Jewish, and Mr Schneider was an eminent surgeon, but they could not bear to stay in a country that was in the hands of what they considered to be criminal lunatics, who were polluting their sons' minds with Master Race claptrap. The summer camps, the rallies, the uniforms, the dedication to Aryan purity, the vows of loyalty to Hitler and the flag were exciting to young minds and the children did not want to leave their country. By forcing them to do so their parents saved their lives, for the indoctrinated members of Hitler Youth were being turned into fierce fighters, many of whom were decimated once the war began. A few of the survivors remained loyal to their vow, even when Hitler and his thugs were cowering in his bunker, before escaping through suicide or flight, leaving the children to be slaughtered by the invading Russians.

At the start of the war the Schneiders were interned in England. Mrs Schneider was released, but Mr Schneider was held at a camp for aliens near Liverpool where the appalling conditions contributed to his death. Mrs Schneider was left to bring up and support her sons alone. A wise and compassionate woman, she rented a big house and took four paying guests under her sheltering wing. Tony had told her about his sexuality and she was fiercely protective of him. In return he endeavoured to provide the boys with a father figure.

The tenants were a motley crew. Tony, for once, felt he was not the motliest. The others at 112 Blomfield Road seemed to have little contact with the real world. Miss Allum went once a week to have a shampoo and rigid set, with the occasional trim, at the local hairdresser, but as it was always exactly the same style, no words were exchanged with the lady in the shop other than 'Good afternoon' and 'Thank you'. A cheery new girl once tried to engage her in the usual, 'And what are you doing for Easter, madam?' only to be silenced with a firm, 'Nothing.' Which was almost certainly true. The highlight of her day was settling in the one armchair in her room, a tray with a pot of Earl Grey tea, milk, sugar and two Garibaldi biscuits on the table beside her, to do the *Telegraph* crossword. No one knew or dared to ask what she had done with the previous, at a guess, sixty years of her life, the only clue being a small sapphire ring on her engagement finger.

Equally uncommunicative was Mr Humphreys. If addressed by anyone other than Mrs Schneider, whom he seemed to trust, he would mutter a reply and scuttle away like a threatened mouse. He always wore the same navy-blue three-piece suit, with a watch chain draped across the front, and a stiff-collared shirt and spotted bow tie, which would have been smart, but for the egg stains on the waistcoat and the button missing on the flies of his sagging trousers, which he constantly tried to conceal. Mrs Schneider once boldly offered to replace it, but he recoiled in horror at the thought of her handling his trousers. Every now and then, he shed the suit and appeared in a startling rambling outfit. Knee-length baggy shorts, Aran sweater and heavy boots with woolly socks. Where he rambled to no one knew, but it was almost certainly on his own. Every Monday night he went out somewhere, and Tony and Marguerite hoped he had a secret lover of either sex, but none but Mrs Schneider knew his destination.

The last, but in her own opinion certainly not the least, boarder was Moira Devine, the leading lady at the local repertory theatre. Rising above the tattiness of the company, Miss Devine was the epitome of glamour. In accord with the biggest stars of her profession, she believed it her duty never to let her public, in her case the residents of Dartford – or a few of them – see her less than perfectly groomed, with immaculate pancake make-up, coiffed red-gold hair with no black roots, pencil skirts or figure-hugging frocks and costumes, revealing nylon-clad perfect legs, with high-heeled, expensive court shoes. Her voice was attractively husky from the chain-smoking of the du Maurier cigarettes in an ivory holder that she wielded dramatically à la Bette Davis. They did a different play each week, rehearsing a new piece during the day whilst playing the current one at night. This demanded commitment which she gave selflessly for her 'art', and versatility, which was harder for her to come by.

She was more at home in sophisticated parts. Her only concession to characterisation of the lower classes would be a turban to hide her radiant hair and perhaps a pretty apron. The make-up and the voice remained the same, whatever age or type she was called upon to portray. But this was what 'her public' expected of her. Her rather scruffy band of admirers came every week just to see her. One of the attractions was her clothes – it was part of her contract to provide them for herself, which she did by toiling over her Singer sewing machine with the current script propped up so she could learn her lines while she stitched. The Royal Shakespeare Company or West End of London had no more dedicated actress than Miss Moira Devine.

When they occasionally did a good play, as opposed to the succession of Agatha Christies and Whitehall farces, one could glimpse the actress she could have been, had she been in the right place at the right time for that lucky break. In Noël Coward's *Private Lives*, albeit with only one week's rehearsal, she gave a performance of skill and enchantment. The critic on the local paper, who always gave her good reviews, on this occasion reached for superlatives, declaring her 'one of the best actresses on the English stage, with whom the whole world will, one day, fall in love'.

She did not notice when she proudly read it out to Tony and Mrs Schneider that Mr Humphreys blushed and backed out of the room. One person at least was already in love with her, for, as only Mrs Schneider knew, Mr Humphreys was himself the unlikely theatre critic of the *Dartford Messenger*. The job suited him, as it was incumbent upon him to keep himself to himself so as not to let others' opinions influence his reviews. He could therefore sit in the darkened theatre every Monday, doting on his idol, and that night, back in the privacy of his bare room, do his best to write something that would, over breakfast, light up Moira's lovely face with happiness.

This was the little group of Her Majesty's subjects who sat in front of the 14-inch black-and-white television that miraculously relayed the splendid crowning of their Queen to them and 27 million other awestruck commoners.

They all dressed up for the occasion. Even Tony dug out his suit and Moira was gloriously attired in a long white satin dress and diamond tiara that she had worn as the dowager empress in the play *Anastasia*. Miss Allum wore a lacy number that smelled of mothballs, and Marguerite looked, according to Tony, 'fantabulosa' in a red-satin sheath cocktail dress with a white-and-blue-feathered hat.

Mrs Schneider provided schnapps, and made a stollen cake, with ingredients she had been saving up for months, Miss Allum produced a bottle of sherry, Tony and Marguerite a bottle of champagne, and Moira, crème de menthe liqueur. Mr Humphreys presented a box of slightly grubby marzipan sweets, which he had made himself, with Mrs Schneider's help.

To begin with the conversation was stilted, it not being something the residents were used to, but once the programme started, with the help of the eclectic mixture of drinks, the atmosphere became more relaxed.

The obligatory British rain poured down on all the nobility in their splendid horse-drawn carriages, and the thousands of ordinary citizens, many of whom had slept on the pavements overnight for a good view. The armed forces marched impeccably to their regimental bands, or lined the route in full dress uniform, putting behind them the horrors that many of them had seen in the war.

When the absurdly ornate golden coach appeared, drawn by eight grey feather-bedecked horses, Tony gasped.

'Those horses have gone a bit over the top with their outfits, haven't they?'

The others shushed him as they caught their first glimpse of the young Queen, sparkling with diamonds, peeping through the window at the ecstatic crowd waving hankies, doffing their caps, raising Union Jacks and roaring their approval, their gratitude, that something good was happening, a great wave of love flooding over the country, that even lapped at the toes of Tony.

'It's a terrible waste of money, but we do do these things bloody well,' he conceded.

Moira was full of admiration for the handling by the maids in waiting of the Queen's voluminous gown and long train as she alighted from the rickety steps of the carriage.

'My God, they must have rehearsed that over and over again.'

When the young woman began the long walk, hands clasped demurely in front of her, down the aisle towards the altar, to spine-tingling shouts of 'Vivat Regina!', Miss Allum added her reedy underused voice to the acclaim. 'Yes, yes, "vivat", indeed.'

Moira stood and applauded.

'I couldn't have done it better myself. Look at that – she's perfect in the part. Think how terrifying it is. The first time something like this has been seen by millions of us riff-raff.'

It was only afterwards that they discovered that some idiot had laid the carpet back to front, so that the plush pulled back her gown and train, making it doubly difficult to negotiate.

The complicated mysterious rituals were performed, with the solemn young woman at the centre of everything. She was handed an orb, followed by a sword of equity, and then a sceptre. The picture was not clear enough to see quite what happened to the orb, which caused Tony some consternation.

'Has she got three royal hands, or has she dropped it?'

Mr Humphreys' voice was surprisingly strong.

'That's enough, young man. Show some respect.'

'Sorry, Mr Humphreys, but I find all this a bit odd in this day and age.'

Marguerite kicked him and whispered, 'Don't spoil it.'

He whispered back, 'I'm surprised at you, Marguerite. The

only women involved are glorified dressers, with all the men in frocks and tights doing the important stuff.'

'OK, but a woman is the boss. She could have their heads chopped off.'

'Er, I don't think you have quite grasped the finer points of the English Constitution, you little Froggy person.'

As the Queen was draped in a cloth-of-gold coat, Moira shook her head in wonder.

'God, the cossies are magnificent.'

But to Marguerite the most moving moment was when the Queen, stripped of her coronet and jewels, her beautiful embroidered satin dress covered by a simple cotton one, sat in solemn stillness as a canopy was pulled over her head under which she was anointed with oil by the Archbishop. So affecting was the ritual that Marguerite momentarily regretted that she was half republican.

When the crown was lowered onto Elizabeth's head, all six of them rose to their feet and joined in the 'God save the Queen's, toasting the television set with their glasses.

'God bless her, I say. So there!' shouted Miss Allum, slopping sherry on her lace.

Mr Humphreys, too, was surprisingly loud.

'Yes indeed – long live the Queen.'

'These things weigh a ton, you know,' commented Moira. 'I had to wear one as the Queen of Spades in panto once, and it nearly broke my neck.'

Moira, by this time carried away by the whole thing, dropped an expert, if slightly wobbly, low curtsy to the television. Mr Humphreys, wide-eyed, offered her a trembling hand when she had slight difficulty getting up. Marguerite realised that Tony was right. The Queen was surrounded by men, ladening her with orb, sword and sceptre, and making vows of allegiance, but the young woman seemed utterly alone. She sat on the uncomfortable Coronation throne, weighed down with the enormous crown, the heavy regalia balanced precariously on her knees, men all round her, and none of them so much as glanced at her to see if she was all right, so intent were they on bowing and scraping and walking backwards.

Marguerite by this stage was just capable of a sniffled, 'Poor her, she's so young.' Even Tony managed a, 'Bless her little cotton socks.'

Only Mrs Schneider was quiet. When Marguerite asked if she was all right, she replied, 'I have been remembering mass events in my country. Ugly, manipulative, full of hatred, centred on a vile man. To you, Tony, my dear, this is, how d'you say, anachronistic, I know, but to me this piece of history, with lovely music and pageantry, for what seems to be a good woman, is quite beautiful. You should be proud.'

Looking round, Marguerite could see that this little bunch of disparate loyal subjects, including even Tony at that moment, were. Proud.

Chapter 14

The Coronation affected everyone. Talk of a new Elizabethan age seemed to lighten the mood after the disappointing post-war austerity. The television helped with that. Mrs Schneider bought, on the hire purchase, the set that Tony had rented, for the enjoyment of her tenants. A quiz game, *Double Your Money*, and a talent contest, *Opportunity Knocks*, which allowed the viewers to send in votes for the winner – a process Miss Allum and Mr Humphreys took terribly seriously, never revealing their secret ballot – gave them endless pleasure. They would emerge from their rooms, yet not have to talk to one another, as they gazed in silence at the world outside, through the 14-inch window of 'the goggle box'.

Tony had a field day every time a politician of any persuasion appeared on the screen. Unlike his heckling at the old public meetings, where he frequently bested the speakers, he now sat in front of 'the box' and subjected them to a vicious stream of abuse, of which they were blissfully unaware. Miss Allum usually left the room. Once Churchill was out of the picture, the Tories were to provide Tony with a succession of glorious hate figures. Eden, Macmillan, and eventually Douglas Home. 'How can those morons be so sodding stupid as to vote in all these obsolete, tight-arsed, ossified, Eton-educated has-beens?'

In the meantime, Marguerite's disgust with Churchill's government was more restrained, but she too could not understand how such a progressive idealistic Labour government of eclectic rough diamonds could have been ousted by a lot of public-school Oxbridge gentlemen. When Tony moaned about the government, and the inevitability of 'tears before bedtime with all this profligacy' as he called its 'dash for growth', Marguerite responded with 'If you can't beat 'em join 'em', insisting on the two of them enjoying the fun while it lasted. And enjoy themselves they did.

Apart from occasional visits to the Embassy Ballroom in Welling to dance to John Dankworth and Ted Heath's bands, they spent most weekends visiting the West End. A new phenomenon was the coffee bar, a source of great satisfaction to Marguerite, who remembered the smell of the beans being ground by Maman and could now demonstrate to Tony why the bottles of Camp Coffee – revolting brown stuff – bore no resemblance to the real thing, despite his affection for the name.

Tony reluctantly accompanied her to these chrome-and-glass cafés.

'What's all this foreign muck? We're English, I tell you. What's wrong with a good old British cup of char,' he would say in his Colonel Blimp voice, shouting over the blaring juke box. Ignoring Johnnie Ray and Perry Como, he would insist on playing Patti Page singing:

How much is that doggie in the window (woof, woof),
The one with the waggy tail (woof, woof) . . .

Getting everyone to join in the 'woofs', he would then tell them that the combination of money and inanity made it a song for the times.

At weekends, and in the holidays, they started exploring England on the motorbike, using the new *Good Food Guide* to plan their routes. They stayed in the boarding houses and hotels the guide recommended, and duly sent in their critiques. They would book a double room under Judy's maiden name, Gumm, Marguerite as Mrs Gumm wearing a curtain ring on her wedding finger. All of the establishments were attempting to up their game, but they were on the whole not succeeding. Marguerite and Tony soon tired of the grapefruit segments and bright pink prawn cocktails, followed by overcooked paper-thin beef, with Bovril gravy, and the inevitable tinned fruit cocktail, but at least some of them were trying, and the infinite variety of the English landscape more than made up for the indifferent food.

Tony succumbed to the improvements in London restaurant cuisine. Instead of their old favourite Lyons Corner House, they both now preferred to eat in the Soup Kitchen, the brainchild of a young entrepreneur Terence Conran, with its earthenware pots, delicious selection of soups and crusty bread, followed by apple tart. They discovered that the exuberant if incompetent staff were mainly aspiring young actors and dancers – students or 'between jobs'. They persuaded Moira, who had a week off, to go there with them. When Marguerite told their waiter that Moira was a working actress, they all gathered round the table, agog for her advice, expecting some Stanislavsky-type gems. They were not sure whether they were meant to laugh at her 'Know your lines and don't bump into the furniture'.

When they went away Moira said, 'Lucky little buggers. They've all got grants to go to drama school. There was no such thing when I was young. Then, when I should have been establishing myself, there was the war. I missed the boat, I'm afraid.'

She stared wistfully at the youngsters by the counter, calling each other 'darling' and shrieking with laughter as they frothed the coffee machine, glancing out of the corner of their eyes to see who was watching.

'I wonder what I could have been, eh?'

Marguerite thought: I don't know a single person whose life has not been blighted in some way by that bloody war. But she said, 'Never mind could have been. You are. You are a very good actress.'

Moira laughed.

'Well, so Mr Humphreys thinks. That's an irony, isn't it? I took comfort that at least a critic thinks I'm good. And it turns out to be the pathetic Mr Humphreys. Mrs Schneider told me. Hardly Kenneth Tynan, is he?'

'No, but he . . .'

'Life can be pretty bloody sometimes, can't it?'

There seemed little point in arguing.

Tony took her hand.

'Yes, Moira, it can. And very unfair.'

'Oh bugger this for a lark.'

Out came her powder compact, bright red lipstick and the old panache returned.

'Let's go for a drink at the Salisbury.'

Here Moira was in her element again. In this flamboyant, if faded, Victorian pub on St Martin's Lane, she was kissed and hugged and greeted with cries of 'Darling, you look wonderful'. She told everyone she was helping out at a little rep for a while, before she started 'a biggy', which it would be unlucky to talk about. She hung on to Tony possessively, smiling shyly when someone asked if he was 'her latest'. 'Her latest' meantime was eyeing up a graceful young man who was playing a sailor in *South Pacific* at Drury Lane Theatre. When he disappeared, Marguerite knew that she and Moira would be going home alone. Although she had accepted the status quo of their relationship, Marguerite always felt a pang of regret when that happened.

Tony and Marguerite still went on their theatre jaunts together. On a Saturday they would rent a stool for the gallery queue in the morning, go for a walk or to a museum, and then, in the afternoon, return to sit on their stool, entertained by buskers and mad people. Then when the stools were collected, and the doors opened, they would charge up the endless stairs to the top of the theatre, where the show was watched as through the wrong end of a telescope. They judged actors by their ability to hold their head up so that the audience was afforded a glimpse of their face. And, of course, how well they projected their voice. Tony was one of the gallery regulars who would shout 'Speak up' if someone was too quiet. Marguerite didn't like the booing that was often decided on in the interval by the regulars, however well deserved. One Royal Opera House outing, to see *La Traviata*, ended in disaster, when the fog was so bad it infiltrated the auditorium until they couldn't see the stage at all, and the performance had to be cancelled.

They gave the super-romantic Ivor Novello musicals and boulevard comedies a miss, but became regulars at the Royal Court Theatre in Chelsea, and Theatre Workshop in Stratford East, where the kitchen sink drama spoke to their concerns about society. Tony was grateful to see the working-class world he knew portrayed on a stage. When they saw the angry, frustrated, venomous Jimmy Porter in *Look Back in Anger*, he was dumbfounded.

'That's me up there.'

'A bit butch for you,' suggested Marguerite.

'True. I wouldn't bother with the boring blonde if I were in a room with Alan Bates.'

At school too Marguerite was aware of changes. The girls were more forthcoming in lessons, the lisle stockings were replaced by nylons, and school hats were worn at daring angles, if at all. She was on break duty one lunchtime when she heard raised voices. It was a group of girls who were leaving at the end of term, whom she had cherished and worried over since she started as a teacher, contemporaries of the already departed Elsie and Irene. In the centre of the angry crowd were Pauline and Hazel, the United Nations zealots, having a violent row. Intending to instruct them that politics should be argued rationally, with due respect given to other people's opinions, she crossed the playground to intervene.

'What on earth are you talking about, you idiot?' Pauline was incandescent with rage, yelling at Helen Hayes.

'How can you possibly say that Tommy Steele is better than Elvis?'

Helen quailed but stood her ground.

'I think "Rock With The Caveman" is very with-it.'

'With *what*? Are you mad?' The ardent Hazel threw in her twopenn'orth. 'Have you actually heard "Heartbreak Hotel"? It's to die for.'

Anxious to join in, Wendy, her chubbiness having developed into voluptuousness, said, 'Well, I've got a pash on Bill Haley. He's smashing.'

This was greeted by a chorus of vomiting noises.

'That horrible kiss curl. How can you?'

Marguerite laughed.

'Well, girls, this is a truly erudite discussion you are having. I am glad that education has not been wasted on you and that you are going out into the world with your critical faculties well trained for cultural matters.'

'This is *our* culture, Miss Carter. It's an interesting phenomenon, don't you think?'

The brilliant Miranda was eager to demonstrate the academic approach that had won her a state scholarship to Cambridge.

'We have even got a sociological-group name – teenagers.'

'I think you'll find that word has been around for some time, Miranda.'

'But now it's used for commerce. Records, make-up, magazines – all for us teenagers.'

'Yes, well, we ancients buy records as well.'

'Yes, Beethoven and stuff.'

'I'll have you know I bought a Lonnie Donegan LP the other day.'

This was greeted by silence.

'Oh dear, does that make me old hat?'

'Well, a bit, but he's great too,' exclaimed Hazel and broke into a spirited rendering of:

> '"Now the Rock Island line
> She's a mighty good road . . ."'

Some were now jumping and clapping and jiving. Marguerite reflected on how they had all blossomed from the cowed girls they once had been, and how she wished Irene and Elsie were here to join in the fun.

Suddenly the dancing and singing stopped. Miss Fryer was standing by the entrance.

Marguerite blew her whistle.

'All right, girls, break is over. That was very entertaining. The grammar of the song leaves something to be desired, but I can see the attraction. Get in the queue now.'

Silently they formed into class formation, and filed back into the building. Helen Hayes' voice rang out, 'See you later, alligator.'

'In a while, crocodile,' a bold chorus replied.

As Marguerite walked down the corridor to the staff room, Miss Fryer appeared at her study door and asked to speak to her.

'Miss Carter, you are a teacher who is naturally gifted with children. Therefore I am curious as to why you allowed a situation to develop that caused such a rumpus that I was forced to come out of my office to investigate.'

'I'm sorry you were disturbed, Miss Fryer. They were only singing and dancing.'

'The break periods should be used for them to rest and gather their thoughts for the next session of study.'

'But they are young and exuberant, trapped behind their desks all day. Don't you think perhaps it does them good to let off steam?'

'Miss Carter, it is not all that long since the end of the war. The eighteen-year-olds who started this commotion in the playground, as far as I could see from my window, have had disrupted childhoods. The younger ones too. Many of them have been rendered dysfunctional by the instability they have had to cope with in their families. What these children need to be given is order.'

'But Hazel and Helen and Pauline and their friends are no longer children, they are young women.'

'And is that really how you think young women should behave?'

'But you make it sound as if they have done something dreadful. They were just having fun.'

'Fun? You may think I am an old dodo, Miss Carter, but I do keep up with what is going on in the world. I have heard this new music that is being sold to them. What about taste and judgement? Are those hip-swivelling ignorant creatures really worthy of their devotion?'

'Some of the lyrics are not entirely without merit – "Heartbreak Hotel" for instance. But popular music has, down the ages, always been banal.'

'Miss Carter, I have been a teacher for many years now, and I have never felt quite like this before. I am fearful of the future for my girls. The old order changeth, and I am not sure where the new one is heading.'

'Miss Fryer, I truly believe the world is becoming a much better place. You have to trust that good will prevail.'

'Sadly, I do not share your optimism. You see, and this will sound harsh, but I believe it to be true, I do not think children are naturally good. They have to be taught proper standards and values.' Marguerite thought uneasily of Mrs Schneider's sons. 'That to my mind is the duty of teachers, and above all parents. If we allow the wrong people, the merchants, the unprincipled, the ignorant, to set the standards, we are in for trouble. Mark my words.'

'I will think about what you say, Miss Fryer, and I'm sorry that the incident, which I thought was quite innocent, has so disturbed you.'

'I will be retiring soon, Miss Carter, and not before time. Truth be told, I am no longer relevant.'

Marguerite was saddened by this usually confident woman's declaration, because, in her heart, she knew it to be true.

Chapter 15

Something was stirring. By the late 1950s London was full of iron balls lunging into bomb-damaged buildings, which crashed down, making way for construction of the new. It felt exciting, although as they walked round the city not everything pleased Marguerite and Tony. They were upset when an ancient mews near Trafalgar Square with gas lights, and ghosts, was flattened to make way for a bland office block, and they were angry that the indestructible dome of St Paul's, that had been such a comfort during the Blitz, was gradually being hemmed in by buildings not worthy of it. After years of choking smogs they were delighted that the air was now cleaner, so that the buildings they had come to believe were black emerged revealing white stone, or in the case of the Natural History Museum, terracotta tiles in an amazing palette of various creams and pale blue, with sculpted animals and flowers.

Now that she had nearly ten years' experience behind her, Marguerite was confident she was a good teacher. All her pupils had done as well as they were able, and she was learning to accept that the circumstances that could hinder their progress were beyond her control. Her failure to persuade Elsie and Irene to fulfil their potential still pained her, but it taught her to resist being too emotionally involved in her pupils' lives. She gritted her teeth, and followed Miss Fryer's advice to allow them to 'fly the nest' unassisted, concentrating all her energy on making the most of the time she had with them. An increasing number of her girls were getting into universities and, gently prodded by her, considering a career rather than just any old job until they fulfilled their destiny as good wives. She once saw Irene, in the distance, walking along Bexleyheath Broadway, with three young children in tow. The rush of rage Marguerite felt towards the shiftless mother who had apparently landed her brilliant pupil with yet another debilitating burden made her turn and walk in the other direction, knowing that she would not be able to contain her frustration if she spoke to Irene; she would be tempted to say things that would only unsettle her.

She heard through Pauline that Elsie had a very good job in London, though she didn't know what it was, or what had happened to the baby. Pauline and Hazel had obtained coveted places at the London School of Economics, from where they inundated Marguerite with leaflets and invitations to various meetings. She was proud of her ex-pupils' continued activism and wanted to encourage them, especially now that she could no longer be accused by Miss Fryer of political influence. One meeting in particular she decided to attend.

Since the test explosion by the Americans of the hydrogen bomb, even more ferocious in destructive power than the two atom bombs that had destroyed Hiroshima and Nagasaki, Marguerite was convinced that this was the biggest issue of the age, probably the biggest since the start of civilisation. The human race was now capable of wiping itself out.

His head explodes. The blue eyes blown away. The three other men in the car sprawl grotesquely like her childhood dolls thrown into the toy box. Yet the grenade had fitted into the palm of her hand and all she had done was pull out the small pin and throw it like a ball.

Tony, too, who had been at that first anti-bomb meeting of the United Nations Association in Dartford, was deeply concerned about the legacy of this admittedly amazing scientific achievement. The two of them were in accord that the world must rid itself of these weapons, before it was too late. The problem was how. Tony had been for the unilateral option, particularly when he heard Margaret Thatcher opposing it, but when he came back from a Labour Party conference he told Marguerite how his idol Aneurin Bevan had made a typically brave speech, saying that, if the Party voted for Britain alone to ban the bomb regardless of other countries, they would be 'sending the next Foreign Secretary naked into the conference chamber'. He derided their idealism. 'I call it an emotional spasm.' Although he was outvoted, many people, including Tony, saw his point.

'If all the big boys have a bomb they're not going to listen to a little squirt with no weapons.'

'We are not "a little squirt". We are a much respected force in the world,' Marguerite argued.

'Marguerite, we are a tiny country that is losing its empire, and has already lost its credibility since the Suez nonsense.'

'We stood alone and virtually unarmed against the Nazis.'

'We were just lucky that Hitler didn't have the sense to cross the Channel.'

'But if he'd had a hydrogen bomb, don't you think he would have used it? You talk about having to negotiate from strength. You overlook the odd madmen that crash into history. You can't negotiate with them. Once they get one, we're done for.'

'Even madmen will realise that, if they drop one, they too will be annihilated. It will stop them.'

'It didn't stop the Americans.'

'That's just my point. It would have done, if Japan had had the bomb.'

'But it was wicked, wicked. We cannot be compliant in such criminal acts.'

'It is war. Appalling crimes always have and always will be committed in the name of "a just war".'

'Tony, I can't believe this is you saying these things. What's happened to you? What happened to us "not doing nothing"? We have to make a stand.'

'Oh, you mean like the people in Hungary? Slaughtered by Russian tanks? Khrushchev turns out to be as bad as Uncle Joe Stalin.'

'And, yes, imagine if he gets the bomb. We can change things, Tony. We can. Please come to this meeting at Westminster Hall. There are all sorts of people speaking who can put the case better than me.'

'No, my love—'

'Tony, please. This is so important for me. I can't bear not to have you with me.'

'Oh my dear little cockeyed optimist. When you look at me like that, all bright-eyed and bushy-tailed, I can't resist you. I'll be there.'

And there Tony was, among the four thousand others crowded into Central Hall and spilling over into three extra rooms, with a stage full of the great and the good from all walks of cultural, political and religious life. The atmosphere was electric to begin with, but some rather overlong speeches began to dampen the fervour and people started drifting away. Then the historian A.J.P. Taylor stood on the platform, gesturing only occasionally with relaxed hands, calmly describing in minute detail the hor-rifying injuries and agonising death caused by atomic radiation.

He ended by saying quietly, 'So now, which of you will press the button?'

Silence. 'Is there anyone here who would want to do this to another human being?'

Again silence.

Then for the first time in his speech, showing passion, he shouted, 'Then why are we making the damned thing?'

The crowd erupted into cheers.

Marguerite hugged Tony.

'Wasn't he wonderful?'

Tony looked solemn amidst the rejoicing.

'An emotional spasm, I fear.'

He did not go with Marguerite and her two protégées on the spontaneous march to 10 Downing Street after the meeting, and when they met the next day at school, he tried to explain his reticence.

'I'm truly frightened, Mags. These are perilous times that need pragmatism rather than idealism.'

Marguerite covered her ears.

'Don't, Tony, don't. I don't want to hear this from you. I would rather we were blown to smithereens than take part in this obscene arms race. We must do what is *right*. Never mind the consequences. Remember, "All that is necessary for the triumph of evil is that good men do nothing."'

'Well, I'm not particularly good, and it's a case of tactics, not doing nothing. Anyway I seem to remember in one of A.J.P. Taylor's television lectures he said Burke didn't actually say that. It's a misquote.'

★　　　★　　　★

When, the following Easter, a march of protest was organised from Trafalgar Square to Aldermaston, where nuclear warheads were being manufactured, Tony declined to accompany her, but the day before she left, he put a note in her letterbox.

Dear Maggie Pankhurst,
This is what good old Eddie Burke actually said. 'When bad men combine, the good must associate; else they will fall, one by one, an unpitied sacrifice in a contemptible struggle.' Not sure what it means, or who are the goodies and who the baddies, but take care of your pretty feet in 'this contemptible struggle'.
I love you.

Standing in Trafalgar Square with Pauline and Hazel and about two thousand other enthusiastic supporters, Marguerite missed Tony. It was the first time she had been at such an event without him by her side. Representatives of the new Campaign for Nuclear Disarmament, a pipe-smoking J.B. Priestley, a befrocked Canon Collins, a dishevelled Michael Foot, and a cerebral Bertrand Russell, made rousing speeches under an indifferent Nelson, and she would like to have heard Tony's wry take on the proceedings. When the march took off, through the deserted streets of London on this Good Friday morning, she needed his quick wit to respond to the occasional shouts of abuse.

'Go back to Moscow.'

'There's snow on your boots.'

She knew he would have enjoyed it when a car passed them in Knightsbridge with honking horn, and a woman in a fur coat leaned out, and with a cut-glass accent shouted from the window, 'Ostriches, ostriches.'

The whole thing was pretty haphazard. The ardent young organisers were running up and down the slowly moving line, issuing orders with loudhailers, handing out limp daffodils to wear, and home-made banners to carry. There was a lorry for rucksacks and tents, as it was not clear if there would be indoor accommodation for everyone before they reached Aldermaston on Easter Monday. As they passed through London the mood was very good-natured. At the Albert Memorial they stopped for a picnic, and someone played a guitar for a sing-song and dancing, until the police politely intervened. As they proceeded the only bone of contention was between some youngsters, who wanted to hear the accompanying bands, and the organisers, who insisted on silence, in respect for the religious sensitivities of participants observing the solemnity of Good Friday.

By the time they got to Hammersmith, the weather had changed for the worse. It was cold and it began to rain. Marguerite was glad that she had worn slacks and had her galoshes in her knapsack. Many of the great and the good had returned to their cosy beds, and only about two hundred stalwarts remained.

One bedraggled marcher came up to her.

'Excuse me, I've got blisters on my hands and feet, I am wet through, and suddenly I don't give a monkey's if the whole world goes up in smoke. Here, have this?' She thrust a banner with a strange emblem on it into Marguerite's arms.

'What does it mean?'

'Haven't the foggiest,' replied the young girl.

A male voice intervened.

'I think I can help you pretty ladies there.'

Marguerite turned. A thatch of neatly cut, naturally curly, light brown hair, piercing blue eyes, square jaw, tall, sheepskin-lined ex-RAF flying jacket and polo neck, with Paisley scarf nonchalantly draped. An archetypal dish. His mouth was set in a lopsided smile, while his eyes appraised her face and body, then looked deep into hers.

Marguerite stared him out, and his eyes faltered, darting momentarily to size up the alternative of the pretty erstwhile banner carrier, who hovered, simpering flirtily, then swivelled back to the challenge of Marguerite. The ex-banner bearer left in a disconsolate huff.

The Dish continued, 'Forgive me. I and my friend here'– he indicated a tall buck-toothed man, also in flying jacket – 'have been following behind you, and what a pleasure that has been, with you in those fetching slacks.' His friend snorted. 'And I couldn't help overhearing your question.'

'And?' said Marguerite.

'It is the semaphore for the letter N and D put together, standing for "Nuclear Disarmament". Show her, Stan,' he ordered.

His gangly friend suddenly stood to attention and made the two signs with his arms.

'Clever, don't you think?'

'Yes,' replied Marguerite.

'And rather lovely – like you, if you don't mind me saying so.'

Marguerite looked hard at the banner. 'It could also be some-one standing with his arms spread low in despair. Possibly at man's inhumanity to man.'

The Dish hesitated. 'Er – I hadn't thought of that.'

His debonair veneer faded momentarily, and he said, 'God knows it would be fitting.'

'Yes.' Marguerite fixed him with a steady gaze.

He reverted to his charm offensive.

'Has anyone told you that you have the most beautiful eyes?'

'Yes.'

'Oh really? You mean your boyfriend? Lucky bloke. Or husband perhaps?'

'Neither.'

'Who then?'

'You. Just now.'

'And your hair is the colour of—'

Marguerite interrupted, 'Oh please stop this nonsense. I feel like a drowned rat standing here, and we are dropping behind.'

The man dropped his jaunty façade.

'OK. I know when I'm beaten. Here, give us that. We'll carry it.'

And he and his friend hoisted the banner aloft and set off with Marguerite between them.

'Oh, by the way, I am Jimmy and he's Stan. Ex-RAF, now in Civvy Street, with nothing better to do than go for a freezing-cold walk to the country, carrying a banner that no one understands. You?'

'I'm – Marguerite.'

'Is that all?'

'A teacher. That's all.'

'Why are you here?'

'Because two of my ex-pupils asked me to come. And I want to rid the world of this evil thing. You?'

'Oh, we thought there might be a few laughs and some totty. It's proved to be a bit short of both.'

Stan chimed in, 'Up till now, Jim.'

'Shut up, you erk.' Boxing him round the ears Jimmy said, 'This is not totty, Stan.'

'But back there you said—'

The Dish interrupted, 'This is class, you useless animal. Forgive my friend. He's a bit short on the old social graces.'

Marguerite asked, 'Where did you serve?'

138

Jimmy looked into the distance.

'I think we're stopping. Where are we?'

Marguerite looked at a sign.

'It's called Turnham Green. Chiswick, I think.'

It was now pelting down with rain, and everyone stood around in depressed damp groups on a small area of sodden grass. Jimmy produced a military rain cape and draped it solicitously over Marguerite. Hazel came running up to tell them that there was shelter in a school round the corner; it turned out to be a primary school, so the tiny toilets and washbasins were not ideal. Eventually Hazel used the loudhailer to explain that men would sleep in the hall, and women and children in the classrooms round it. There were some mattresses and sleeping bags provided.

Stan climbed up on a table and turned a picture of the Queen round to face the wall.

'I can't take my trousers off in front of Her Majesty,' he announced.

Then Jimmy started to vamp pretty badly on an out-of-tune piano, and everyone sang. 'If I Had A Hammer', 'When The Saints Go Marching In' and of course 'Jerusalem'. Marguerite was relieved that Tony was not there to give his rendering of 'How Much Is That Doggie In The Window'. In fact, truth be told, she was just relieved that he was not there, with his ambivalent attitude to the cause.

When the party had broken up and she was preparing for sleep, she looked through the window of the classroom and saw Jimmy looking back at her. He blew her a kiss, and she curled up on the hard floor, chuckling to herself. It was a novel experience to be 'totty' – classy or otherwise. And she quite liked it.

Chapter 16

The next day it snowed. It was declared the coldest Easter in forty years. Chiswick sold out of Wellingtons. The local Quakers did a wonderful job rounding up boots and umbrellas for the remaining little band of valiant marchers. The rude comments from passers-by grew less dismissive as the marchers' dedication became evident. The worst they encountered was shaking heads, one sad-faced old man in a wheelchair, who could have been a veteran of both wars, holding up a scribbled notice saying, 'You march in vain.' Some of the children from the school brought them a colourful new placard reading, 'The human race, we could lose it.' And another was given to them by the local church reading, 'Love your enemies.' Uplifted by these kindnesses and fired by their absolute belief in the rightness of their cause, the walkers trudged on through the sleet. Jimmy and Stan acquired some beer, which lightened the mood no end. They were entertained by a jazz band and some skiffle groups, so the whole thing, despite the appalling weather and the blisters, became more fun.

At the next stop Jimmy, Stan and Marguerite were at the end of the column as Jimmy had insisted on their stopping off at a country pub for a drink or two, so there was no indoor accommodation left. The Co-op van that was travelling with them issued some heavy-duty tents, which a farmer allowed them to pitch in his field.

Jimmy was concerned for Marguerite.

'Will you be all right? It's going to be bloody cold. I suggest we throw propriety to the wind, and all share and snuggle up together. I'll protect you from Stan.'

'That's very gallant.'

'I don't like a lady having to sleep rough like this, but I'll take care of you.'

'Don't worry I've done it before.'

He raised a quizzical eyebrow.

'They won't find us here.'

The borie is in the corner of a field halfway up the Grand Luberon. The night is turned to daylight as the lightning flashes, thunder cracks and the rain thrashes the fields. He lies down on the earth floor inside the egg-shaped drystone shelter and enfolds her in his arms. The dank earth, the heat of his body protecting, exciting her. If they come and kill her in the morning she will have had this perfect night.

Jimmy was as good as his word. He had Stan gathering what little dry wood he could find and, the snow having at last stopped, they cleared a patch of sheltered ground, and with some difficulty got a blazing fire going. Marguerite enjoyed playing the wilting maiden while they inexpertly raised the tent, Stan doing most of the hammering in of pegs, and pulling of ropes, whilst Jimmy sat on a log and smoked a fag, issuing orders.

'I always do his dirty work,' moaned Stan.

'You're doing very well, Sergeant. Give that man a medal.'

'I'll have yours then.'

Marguerite interrupted, 'What medal?'

'The DFC, miss. He got the bloody DFC.'

Jimmy stood up and said firmly, 'Shut up, Stan. I'm going to that pub we saw, to get some of the hard stuff. Cook some of the sausages. And shut up,' he repeated firmly.

In the absence of any cooking utensils Marguerite demonstrated with Stan's penknife how to sharpen and shave sticks to pierce the sausages to grill over the fire.

'Where did you learn that?' Stan said.

'Girl Guides.'

As they sat, wrapped together in a rug that had been issued, and holding the sticks, Marguerite asked, 'So what about this medal?'

'I can't tell you. He'll kill me.'

Such was the man's pride in his friend, it took little persuasion to get the story out of him.

'We were coming back from an op and got hit by flack. We had to ditch into the North Sea. Which he did, although the plane was on fire – he's a wonderful pilot. Me and two of the others got out, the rest didn't make it. I can't swim but I clung on to a bit of debris. He stayed in the burning plane to get the dinghy. He had a broken leg, fractured skull and burns – he's still got the scars – but he managed to throw it out, inflate it and get us into it. By the time he struggled in himself he was spent. He was gurgling in the water at the bottom of the dinghy, too weak to lift his head, and I managed to get my foot under his chin, which was all I had the strength to do. We had no oars, but thank God we drifted away from the burning plane. Then, would you believe it, miss, he made us bloody well sing "Roll Out The Barrel" and tell jokes, all the sodding night, sprawled like dead fish, till a destroyer picked us up the next day. But he kept us alive. And there were other times . . . Shush, here he comes. Not a word, miss, please.'

'Stan, you don't have to call me miss.'

'But you're a lady, miss.'

'It's true I'm a woman, Stan, and privileged to be your friend. It's Marguerite.'

Jimmy was weaving between the tents, with his arms full of bottles of beer and whisky.

'This should set us up nicely. Bought some crisps to go with the sausages. A positive feast.'

Despite downing a large quantity of beer and whisky chasers, the men became talkative, in turns cheerful and maudlin, rather than roaring drunk. The anecdotes flowed from them, and it was obvious that Stan's fierce guardianship of Jimmy landed him in awkward situations. Marguerite learnt that, having been a budding welterweight boxer before the war, Stan was, on several occasions, forced to use his skills to protect his friend. Jimmy, devastatingly handsome in his uniform, was prone to make eyes at attractive women in the pubs they visited, using the technique that had singularly failed with Marguerite. Should the bewitched female respond with a quick snog in the corridor – or more – Stan was frequently left to deal with violently angry local men, after Jimmy had disappeared with or without the errant lass. Stan described how, on one occasion, he got his own back on Jimmy.

Finding their bombing targets was a chancy business. Especially at night. Frequently they got completely lost, sometimes even finding themselves in the wrong country. Trying to recognise a river or town from the map in the flares left by the pathfinders, was not easy. Thus, it was the rule not to release the bombs unless the targets were found; Jimmy more than most obeyed and returned to base with his bombs still on board. After several ops like this, and flying back with a damaged wing, he decided to lighten the plane for landing by letting go of the bombs harmlessly in the English Channel. After they landed, Jimmy went to take off the layers of clothing necessary in the freezing plane. He was down to his latest girlfriend's silk stockings, which he wore under his two pairs of trousers and flying boots for extra warmth, when Stan came in long-faced.

'You're for it now.'

'What are you talking about?'

'The bombs hit some of our bloody fishing boats.'

When Jimmy walked into the debriefing room, there was silence and glum faces all round. The squadron leader challenged him, 'Well, what have you got to say for yourself, Richardson?'

'I didn't want to risk killing civilians, sir.'

'Well, you may have saved a few jerry, but you've managed to wipe out some of ours instead.'

Stan and Jimmy were now roaring with laughter at this, though Marguerite was not.

'Don't worry. It was a jape. They were all in on it. Set up by this bastard. Gave me a fright, I can tell you.'

'It's not that—' Marguerite broke off.

'What?'

'How callous war makes us. It's all right to kill some people but not others. And we can laugh about it.'

Jimmy nodded.

'True. It's how you get through it. Sorry.'

'Don't be. It's not just you.'

The Milice burst into the barn as Marguerite and the men sleep. 'Traitres', shouts Jacob. They herd them to one end of the barn with two Milice on guard, talking and laughing about the meal they will be having that night and the women they will be seeing. Four at a time they push the men outside with their rifles, where a machine-gun burst is heard. Another Milice beckons through the door for the next batch to be dispatched.

As young Antoine, who is seventeen, is taken through, he says to his captor, 'Hello, Marc.'

'Do I know you?'

'Antoine. We went to school together.'

The man pushes him through the door, hitting him on the head with his rifle butt

'Well, now we're grown-up.'

'Anyway you're here. On the march. We're going to stop all that.'

'Yes.' He smiled at Marguerite, his charming wonky smile.

Stan stood up.

'I'm going for a slash. Pardon my French, Miss Marguerite.'

Jimmy took a swig from the whisky bottle.

'I'm not as callous as you think, old girl. All that stuff about coming for the totty wasn't altogether true. Fact is, I don't want any other poor bastard to do what I did. I used to go to the pub and get shot to ribbons. That's how I coped. Blot it out. My mucker, rear gunner, his flesh melted as I tried to smother the flames. It was carnage all round. I want it to stop. I want it to stop. I want it to stop. Oh Jesus. I've had too much to drink. I'm sorry. I'm a bit blotto.'

Marguerite took him in her arms. He looked surprised, and then clung to her for a while before kissing her on the mouth, long and hard. And she responded. Enjoying the sense of yielding to his strength. Or was it his need? Or hers? Whatever it was, it felt good. He ran a finger down her face.

'I suppose you know how beautiful you are? Lots of men must have told you. I just thought I'd mention it though. This time I'm not shooting a line. I mean it.'

Stan came back and tactfully picked up his sleeping bag and was about to leave the tent.

Jimmy stopped him.

'No, Stan. As you were. You are guarding this lovely lady from my lustful ways.' Then more quietly he said, 'This is different, Stan. Not my usual love 'em and leave 'em stuff.'

'I can see that, chief.'

As both men could hardly stand now, it was difficult to take this show of chivalry very seriously. Marguerite had drunk far less than them, so it fell to her to help them get out of their outer clothing, and into their sleeping bags. She got into hers, between the two cocooned men, who were instantly fast asleep, and lay for some time wondering at the novelty of her situation. From years of chastity to sleeping with not one, but two heterosexual men, both of whom were oblivious of her presence. Tony would have something to say about that. If she told him. For some reason that didn't seem a good idea. How would she describe Jimmy? Or what she had felt when they kissed? Lust? Desire? Alive? Whatever it was, she hadn't felt it for a long time. And she'd missed it.

The next day, Easter Monday, was supposed to be the triumphant culmination of their pilgrimage. Her two new friends were blindingly hungover and she had slept very little. The sun was attempting to shine, and as they made their way to Falcon Field for a final rally, they saw hundreds of new supporters had joined the demonstration. They drowned out the objectors, still bellowing through loudspeakers about Russian influence, with their cheers for a succession of rather dull speeches. Jimmy and Stan persuaded her into the Falcon Inn for 'the hair of the dog', and they were much more cheerful afterwards, but on the whole the event was an anti-climax.

On the coach back to London they said little. Marguerite was disturbed by the previous night's events. She felt achy and exhausted and desperate for a bath. They alighted from the coach at Trafalgar Square and the two men walked her to Charing Cross Station. They had a cup of tea in the snack bar, making awkward small talk as they waited for her train. Stan said he was going to wash his face in the Gents and when he had gone Jimmy handed her a piece of paper.

'It's my telephone number. I won't ask for yours because I don't want to be a pest. I don't suppose you'll want to contact an oik like me, but if you should, well, I would like that very much.'

She put it in her purse.

'Thanks, Jimmy. That's very kind. I have a pretty busy life but—'

'Yes, yes. I quite understand. Say no more. I'm an idiot. Why would you, for heaven's sake? But it's been a wizard jape. Thank you.'

Marguerite could think of nothing to say. She had thought of the events of the last few days as something peculiar that had happened in a heightened atmosphere, fuelled by alcohol, after which everyone would go their own way. And on the whole that seemed the sensible course.

'I think I'll go and wash some of the mud off my face and hands before I get on the train.'

Splashing her face and brushing her hair in the ornate Victorian washroom, only slightly spoilt by the warning notices about venereal disease, she steadied herself. As she came out, Stan was waiting.

'Miss – Marguerite, forgive me if this is rude. He doesn't usually talk like he did last night. Life's a bit tricky at the moment for him. The war, and all that. He took it all to heart too much. Now it's over, he's a bit at sea.'

Marguerite was embarrassed.

'I'm sure.'

He had tears in his eyes.

'Please don't hurt him.'

'I'll try not to.'

'I'll get off now. Leave you two alone.'

Marguerite was alarmed at the responsibility that appeared to be landing on her shoulders. When she got back to the cafe, Jimmy had gone.

Chapter 17

It was good to see Tony when she returned. With him she felt on firmer ground. He came to her flat and made some chicken soup.

'Good mangarie for chills – you poor little drowned rat. Tell all, did you get off with any bearded gentlemen? I hear there was folk dancing and Peter Seeger songs. You must help me to bear missing that.'

'Stop, Tony. It was very serious.'

'Bit middle class for me, by the sound of things.'

'It wasn't, there were all sorts of people. One at least was working class. He called me miss.'

'Not madam? I hope you put him in his place, you French intellectual aristocracy and all.'

'The French have no class structures, I'll have you know. We are a republic.'

'But when you're English you love a bit of curtsying and crowns, don't you, sweetie?'

'What have you been up to without me? No good, I'll be bound.'

'Well, yes, a bit of no good in Portsmouth, but I missed you. And worried about you.'

She opted not to tell him about Jimmy, lest he took it more seriously than it warranted.

'I was fine. It all feels a bit flat now though. What are we going to do with the rest of the holidays? Let's have some fun.'

'We could go somewhere on the bike.'

Marguerite decided this was the moment to broach a subject she had been mulling over for some time. With increases in both their salaries, plus Marguerite taking on private pupils for tutoring for the eleven-plus, and Tony teaching swimming at the local lido, they actually had a bit of spare cash.

Marguerite ventured, 'Tony, I'm over thirty, and a respected teacher at a grammar school. I think it may be a bit undignified to be still riding pillion on a motorbike.'

Tony looked shocked.

'You're not becoming *staid*, are you?'

He said the word as though it was a capital crime.

'Maybe, but' – and it came out in a rush – 'how about buying a car?'

He gulped.

'Well, you can't drive, for a start.'

'I can. I've been taking lessons and I passed my test.'

'Well, I'm blowed – not as often as I would like, mind you. You secretive little hussy.'

She described her examiner, who had been a wizened middle-aged man with the unfortunate name of Mr Worms. At the end of her test he put his hand on her knee and said, 'I am delighted to tell you you have passed, Miss Carter. How about a little drive to Brighton to practise?'

Tony gasped in mock horror.

'Well, that's shocking. You probably can't drive at all. You just seduced the examiner, whereas I—'

'What?'

'Well, actually, so did I. He was a big butch marine, who taught me to drive trucks. Irresistible.'

So it was that Gladys came into their lives. She was chubby and pea green. Marguerite had already seen her in the local garage. She was a convertible Morris 1000 and she was beautiful. They christened her Gladys to stop her getting above herself.

Marguerite had looked up the few cars in production, becoming quite expert on motor engineering in the process. In the showroom, she asked the slick young salesman, 'What is the petrol consumption?'

Looking at Tony, the salesman replied, 'About 36 miles per gallon, sir.'

She tried again.

'And the top speed?'

'It can do a staggering 65 miles per hour, sir.'

'What about the 60 seconds' acceleration?'

'Oh, an amazing 52 seconds, sir.'

Marguerite let rip.

'It may have escaped your notice, but I am wearing a skirt. And my anatomy differs from yours in the chest area. I am not a sir – I am a madam.'

The man was genuinely taken aback, fearful of losing a sale.

'I am so sorry. . . . The seats are very comfy, miss.'

Marguerite was now in schoolmistress mode.

'No, not miss – madam, to you, if you don't mind. Call me madam.'

Tony started humming 'You're Just In Love.' To which she snapped, 'And you can shut up too, you – you – man.'

Now feeling fairly stupid, Marguerite could not be bothered to quibble over the fact that the hire purchase agreement had to be in the man's name, even though the car would be jointly owned. But she gave Tony no choice as to who drove the car out of the garage. She took the exit through the narrow doorway like a demented kangaroo.

'Watch it – madam,' gulped Tony.

'Shut up, I've passed my test.'

'Yes, but only by using female wiles – madam.'

She cycles unsteadily, balancing the basket of washing on her handlebars. The Haricots Verts whistle and laugh as she approaches the checkpoint. She slides her skirt up her thighs. They signal that they want to search her, assuming she doesn't understand German. She leaps off the bike, bends down exhibiting her cleavage as she places the basket on the ground, and raises her arms, presenting her body for examination. The soldier lasciviously feels her all over, commenting lewdly to his colleague. When he has finished, she winks at him and puts the basket back on the bike, cycling away as fast as she can, lest he remember to look inside it. Back in the village she strips off and pours a bucket of cold water from the well over herself, before taking the radio out from the linen, and arranging for a parachute drop of weapons the next day.

The car made life much easier for Marguerite. On their *Good Food* jaunts, long journeys on a motorbike, especially in bad weather, could be miserable. Marguerite could hardly stand when they arrived at their destinations, and it was difficult to appear respectable at dinner in the more elegant dining rooms after her hair had been blown around and often rained on, and any frock crushed into the saddle bag had come out not looking its best.

They decided on a long first trip to run-in the car's engine. They ventured onto the terrifying new M1 motorway that led to the north of England. The windscreen became black with pulverised insects, confused by the invasion of their territories.

With the roof down, the weather having at last cheered up, singing away to Tony's state-of-the-art transistor wireless all the pop songs that poor Miss Fryer despised, they had the time of their lives, once they got over the size of the road.

The hotel they chose for the initiation of Gladys was on the edge of Lake Ullswater in the Lake District. It turned out to be a good choice. It had been opened by a young ex-Spitfire pilot Francis Coulson, who had used his demob pay to buy some saucepans, arriving in 1947 at a virtually derelict house. He set about turning it into what he called a Country House Hotel. Joined a few years later by a businessman, Brian Sack, who became his lover, they created a place to restore the soul. Marguerite and Tony sensed there was no need to perform their usual married-couple charade. Francis and Brian were indifferent to their status.

Marguerite had long since stopped thinking of Tony as a sexual partner, but the next morning, in the four-poster bed, gazing through the swagged curtains to the view beyond, supping on champagne provided by Francis, and with the memory of that desperate kiss on the CND march, she could not help but speculate about being there with a true lover. They chatted affectionately about the view and the sticky toffee pudding but soon ran out of small talk.

There was an uneasy silence, then Tony got out of the bed and stood looking down at her.

'You need a man. It should be easy enough for you to find one. You've got lovely lallies and gorgeous long willets.'

'I presume that's a compliment, is it?'

'Yes, you're beautiful. Any omi would give his eye teeth for you.'

'Well, I much prefer you to a man with missing teeth.'

'Don't be flippant. I mean it. It's not right.'

Tony sat on the window seat with his back to her.

After a long pause he said, 'We're weird. You know that, don't you?'

Marguerite laughed.

'What's brought this on?'

'Seeing those two old poofs together, so full of love. They have a proper relationship. We don't. I go off and have my sordid little adventures and you have nothing.'

She still did not mention Jimmy, as what had happened, or had not happened, on the march would be unlikely to satisfy Tony's ambition for her.

'I have you.'

'Which bit of me? Who the hell am I?'

'Oh don't go all existential on me.'

'No, truly, Mags. I'm such a phoney. Look at me. All my left-wing ranting about the working classes, and here I am, like all the middle-class Marxists that I despise, sitting in a luxury hotel, stuffing myself with gourmet food and drinking champagne for breakfast. And pretending to be married. When I am queer. And where does that leave you?'

'Oh shut up, Tony. We're fine.'

'No we're bloody not.'

Marguerite knew that when Tony got into one of his self-hating states of mind, there was little she could do to talk him out of it. She needed to be practical.

'Tony, I have an idea. It's not too much of a detour to go home via Oldham. Why not go there and let me meet your parents?'

'Are you mad?'

'You said you didn't know who you were. Why not go back and remind yourself? You know it cheers you up to see them. And I would love to meet them.'

'But they don't know—'

'Don't worry. I'll not tell any secrets. You can trust me. I'm just one of your colleagues at work.'

'They'll have a heart attack if we just turn up, especially in a car. I shouldn't think one's ever been down our road.'

'Let's stay another night here, and send them a telegram.'

'They'll think I've died when the telegraph boy turns up.'

'Well, it'll be a nice surprise to find out you haven't.'

Tony knelt back on the bed and kissed her on the forehead.

'Thank you, my darling. You're right. I would like them to meet the love of my life.'

'I suspect you haven't found him yet. But that's sweet of you.'

'I meant Gladys.'

When they left, Brian and Francis saw them off. They blushed with pride, and Francis babbled denials when Marguerite said how wonderful the hotel was.

Brian smiled at Francis.

'It's that man. He's a genius.'

'No no,' said Francis. 'It's him, the old fool.' And he kissed him on the cheek.

Brian drew away, looking around.

'Careful, my love.'

As they drove off, waving to Brian and Francis, Marguerite felt angry.

'They have achieved so much together. It's unfair that they should be made to feel ashamed.'

'Life is,' Tony muttered. 'Unfair, I mean. As you're about to see.'

Chapter 18

Tony was uncharacteristically quiet on the drive to Oldham. There was sweat on his upper lip and he gripped the steering wheel unnecessarily hard.

'Tony, let's stop and take the roof off then we can enjoy the scenery.'

The landscape of the Dales was eerie in the misty morning. Great sweeping curves, broken by drystone walls and the occasional, often ruined, grey building, although some of the old weavers' cottages with their long upper windows were still in use. Here and there was a large grand house created from the money made from wool, cotton and coal. 'Rich bastards,' was Tony's only comment. They drove through towns thrown up around mills and coalmines, where the workers lived far less luxuriously.

Marguerite had never seen a town like Oldham. Rows and rows of red-brick, tiny, back-to-back houses, black with the soot that belched from factory chimneys, and opening straight onto cobbled roads. No gardens, no colour, no cheer. No life.

'Where is everyone?' whispered Marguerite, as they stopped at the end of one of the identical streets on a steep hill, deserted apart from a woman on her knees scrubbing the narrow pavement in front of her house.

'At work,' answered Tony. 'That's all people do here. Work. Apart of course from drink and gamble. Every other corner is an illegal betting shop, or a pub serving drinks after hours. It's a great life, I tell you. You'd love it.'

'Did you?'

'I couldn't wait to bloody leave.'

'What are we doing sitting here?'

Tony explained that his parents wouldn't yet be home from the local cotton mill where they still worked long hours in their late fifties.

'He won't take a penny from me, the stubborn old fool. He'd rather starve. She won't want you to see her before she's had a chance to smarten up.'

As they sat in the car, the scene in front of them gradually changed. Children started running home from school or walking hand in hand with their grannies. They began playing in the streets; hopscotch, marbles, ball and, of course, football. One little girl started vigorously revolving a hula hoop around her skinny hips. Then, a crescending noise heralded the approach of a crowd of chattering men and women, clack-clacking up the road in wooden clogs. As they watched them Tony told her the footwear was not only cheap but suitable for the wet and oily floors in the mill, although some went barefoot, and some men shirtless, to help cope with the eighty-degree heat and humidity necessary for the weaving of the cotton. Few wore the masks provided to protect them from the clouds of dust and fluff, or the earmuffs to help lessen the horrendous rattle of the machinery.

'Everyone can lip-read. It would be a good place to come if you were deaf,' said Tony. 'Mind you, you might get cancer of the lung from the air in there.'

Despite this gloomy description, the scene now unfolding

was one of cheerful animation. People laughed, and gossiped, played with the children, and the grey setting was made colourful by the women's bright cotton overalls and headscarves. Some of the young women stood in groups, arms around each other, others sat on the doorsteps and kerbs smoking a cigarette and enjoying the late-day hazy sun.

'Poor sods, what a place,' muttered Tony.

'What do you mean?' said Marguerite. 'It looks beautiful now. It just needed the people.'

'OK,' said Tony. 'Hold tight. Here goes.' He started the engine and drove slowly out of the shadows.

As Gladys wove her way up the road, everyone stopped and stared. A couple of men cleared the way for the car, and the women shepherded the children onto the pavement, and held them protectively. Then an elderly woman, in a black dress with a shawl round her shoulders, shouted, 'Eeup, it's tha' li'l booger Tony Stansfield, ent it? In a bloody car.'

Now the fearful mood turned to one of incredulity. Eight or nine surrounded the car, bringing it to a halt. Children clambered into the back, and everyone cheered, and shook his hand. The royal family could not have had a more ecstatic welcome.

Several of the women gabbled happily to Marguerite, but she was finding it difficult to understand the accent. Tony was having no such difficulty, having lapsed into the vernacular.

'It's gradely ter see y'all.'

He parked Gladys at the kerb, warned the children not to touch the handbrake, and got out. Taking Marguerite's hand, he weaved his way through the excited little crowd, greeting most of the adults by name, and the children as 'flower' or 'sweetheart'. Marguerite was moved by their obvious affection for Tony, and their seeming delight that, as several patting him on his back acknowledged, he had become 'reet posh' or 'a proper swankpot' with 'a fancy car an' all'.

Tony led Marguerite to a house in front of which stood an awkward-looking couple, who in contrast to the overalls, aprons, flat caps and curlers of their neighbours, were very definitely in their Sunday Best. The man, tall, grey-haired, with Tony's good looks, in a shiny black suit, with waistcoat but no tie and laced-up boots, shook him formally by the hand.

'Ello, son, glad yer 'ere. Yer mam's been mithering me to death since yer telegram.'

Tony leant down and kissed his small, frail-looking mother on the forehead.

'Hello, Mam, you look a bobby dazzler in that frock.'

'It's only an old utility thing.' She cast an anxious glance at Marguerite.

'It's lovely, Mrs Stansfield. Really lovely.' Marguerite felt a ripple pass through the onlookers and was aware her voice sounded out of place.

'This is Marguerite. Marguerite, my mum and dad, Ethel and Bert.'

More handshaking.

'Reet, cum in t' house,' Bert said, before shouting, 'Oi you, gerroff that car or I'll gie yer a bunch of fives.'

The children squealed and after some banter he closed the front door on them.

It led directly into a small dark room with a sofa, and armchair with protective antimacassars. As she and Tony hesitated on the threshold, Marguerite noticed numerous pictures on the walls, and knick-knacks on the mantelpiece, photos of royalty, a studio photo of Tony as a child, religious icons, mementoes of Blackpool, a faded photo of his father in a uniform, a sepia wedding photo.

Tony's father was about to open a door when Ethel told him, 'Dad, we're in 'ere. I'll mash some tea and we'll sup it in t' parlour.'

'Oh la-di-da,' laughed Tony.

'Excuse me, could I use the toilet,' asked Marguerite.

There was an embarrassed pause.

'She means the lavvy, Mam. I'll take her.'

Tony led Marguerite through the adjoining room, which had a big black stove, and table and chairs, and then through a tiny room with an old-fashioned sink and mangle, and finally into a yard at the back.

'There it is, in all its glory,' said Tony.

He showed her to the corner of the cracked paving and lifted the latch on a wooden door. Inside, across the wall, was a wooden box-like fixture, topped by a well-scrubbed lid with a hole in the middle.

'I used to sit in here for hours as a kid. Only place I could get a bit of peace. The neighbours had to thump on the door. It's shared by four families. I give you fair warning, Mags. Don't ask for a bath. It'll be a tin thing in front of the stove.'

'Good Lord, Tony – in this day and age?'

'I know, I know,' and he shook his head in disgust. 'Bit different from Ullswater, eh?'

When they returned, Bert was seated uncomfortably in the stiff armchair, and Tony and Marguerite were told to 'perch on't couch'. Ethel brought in a tray of tea poured into pretty china cups.

'Blimey, Mam. We are privileged. I 'aven't seen those since Granddad's funeral. It's usually a pint pot.'

'Well, this is a special occasion. Meeting your lass for the first time. I'm sorry if the house is a bit of a midden, but I couldn't risk taking time off.'

Bert interrupted, 'There 'ent the demand for cotton no more. They're laying people off and the bastard owners are bringing in foreigners to work cheap. They'll do nights an' all. Mind you, they're good workers, them. And we have a laff. Pakis mainly.'

Tony went to protest but Marguerite nudged him. Instead he said, 'Do you meet outside the mill? At the pub?'

'No, son. They live up Glodwich way. Got their own religion and all that. And that funny food. Stinks, it does. Not for me, thank you. I prefer fish and chips.'

Turning to Marguerite Bert said, 'You know what Oldham's famous for, Marguerite?'

'Apart from your son – no.'

'Chips. We invented 'em, yer know. Aye, that's our claim to fame.'

Ethel interrupted, 'And weaving. We're good at that too, Dad. Or were. Don't think it'll last much longer.'

Bert pulled a face at her.

'Now, Mother, we mustn't be all mardy in front of this bonny lass. I'm sweating cobs here. I'm going to get out of these keks, now you've seen how posh I am, Margaret, and my lad and I'll go down to the pub and get kaylied, while you ladies get the tea ready. Eh, son?'

It didn't sound like the ideal outing for Tony, but he nodded bravely.

In their absence it was easier for Marguerite to get to know Ethel. The tea was a local speciality called Rag Pudding, minced meat and onions and potato inside a suet crust wrapped in a cotton rag. This was boiling happily in a large pot on top of the stove, so there was little to do. Marguerite resolved, without betraying Tony's secret, to somehow put a stop to any unrealistic expectations on Ethel's part.

When she said shyly, 'You are a really lovely lass. My boy is very lucky,' Marguerite replied, 'Yes. We get on very well. We have a lot in common.'

She was about to try and explain that they were only colleagues, when Ethel fetched a small box from the dresser in which, wrapped in tissue paper, was a pair of exquisite lace gloves.

'My nan made these. She worked in lace in Nottingham. I wore them at my wedding. I want you to have them for when—'

'Oh no – I couldn't.'

'Please, lass. You've made me so happy.'

Marguerite could not bring herself to hurt this gentle woman, so she took the gloves and said, 'Thank you. I love beautiful gloves. I'll treasure them.'

She hoped that thus she had told the truth to Ethel, without crushing her sweet hope.

Marguerite was relieved when Tony and his father returned, rather unsteadily, from the pub. As they ate their supper the conversation was stilted. Their life in leafy Kent seemed as alien as sub-Saharan Africa. Tony's parents' pride in their son's escape from the treadmill of factory work and want was obvious, although his father expressed it obliquely.

'I suppose it's all caviar and them hoity-toity cocktail parties now you're a smartarse down south.'

Ethel insisted that Marguerite had her and Bert's brass bed to herself, whilst they bundled into the back room that used to be Tony's. Tony slept on the couch in the parlour. It was still dark when Marguerite was woken by a banging on her window. Leaping out of bed she looked out to see a man in a muffler and flat cap, wielding a big cane with a ball on the end. He was almost as startled as she.

'Oh sorry, luv. Is Bert with you? Tell 'im to gerrup.'

Puzzled, she went back to bed. Shortly after, the silence was broken by the clatter of clogs on the cobbles, and the dismal howl of the mill's siren, bidding people to work.

Bert was chuffed that the knocker-up would be spreading the rumour that he had a luscious redhead in his bed.

Several of the neighbours joined Bert and Ethel to wave them goodbye. Bert shook his son's hand and said awkwardly, ' 'Ang on to her, son. She's a belter.'

Ethel started to shake Marguerite's hand then shyly kissed her instead.

She whispered, 'Thank you, luv.'

As they drove away Marguerite's mind was in a whirl. Had she misled these good folk by omission? Did it matter anyway? Having now seen his background, she realised the utter impossibility of Tony revealing his sexuality. The lace gloves were an emblem of the wedding that Ethel dreamed of. The community, the family were the elements that made these people's hard lives bearable. And to them, that meant a man, and a woman, and their children.

Tony thanked Marguerite for her tact.

'Sorry it was such an ordeal.'

'Not at all. I loved it.'

'Not going to get a rave in the *Good Food Guide* though, is it?'

'Nonsense. "Dinner of a regional dish using local ingredients, i.e. cotton to wrap pudding. Service first class. Ambience—"'

'A shithole,' rasped Tony.

'Not at all. "Historic architecture".'

'And sanitary arrangements?'

'"Warm welcome from hosts".'

Tony sighed.

'What a miserable bloody existence.'

'They don't seem miserable to me, Tony. OK, the conditions are shamefully primitive and they work damned hard but, forgive me if I seem sentimental, they seem happy. It feels like a close community.'

'Bloody suffocating. Thank Christ I fescaped.'

'And how did you escape? You told me. A teacher inspired you. That's us, Tony. It's up to us.'

'Well, I'm not doing a very good job for children like I was. Look at me, working in a posh grammar school increasingly packed with middle-class kids, whose parents get them privately tutored to make sure they pass the eleven-plus, and crowd out those without pushy parents.'

Marguerite was stunned.

'God, Tony. You're talking about me. That's what I do.'

'Sorry, sorry. I always get angry when I've been back home. I'm not blaming you. It's the system. I'm just as bad, making money teaching the privileged to swim.'

They sat in silence as they left Oldham behind them and headed towards London.

After about two hours they stopped for some tea from a Thermos flask that Ethel had put in the car.

'Have I upset you, Mags?'

'Not at all. I've been deliberating.'

Marguerite looked him in the eye.

'Oh Lord, you've got your "not do nothing" look. Deliberating about what?'

'Us. You're right, Tony. We've gone off track. We need a rethink.'

Chapter 19

The Oldham odyssey had a profound effect on Marguerite. She knew such living conditions existed and that there were inequalities in education, she had seen evidence of that several years ago at the secondary modern school; what shocked her was that she had allowed herself to forget about it.

For over a decade she had been a good, dedicated teacher but that wasn't really difficult in a well-run grammar school. In her time at Dartford several of the original staff had retired, including Miss Belcher, whom she had succeeded as deputy head of English. She sometimes, in the staff room, caught the newcomers looking bemused as she waxed lyrical about some pupil's work. They were much more confident and blasé than she had been when she started, having been to teaching colleges where they learnt child psychology and classroom technique. They were, in popular parlance, cool. She realised she had become Miss Belcher in their eyes, one of the old school. She had a career for life, on good money, in a pleasant environment, and was, it dawned on her, stagnating. Contentment had never been one of her goals. She had always thrived on challenge, adventure. Why had she changed? Her discontent, increased by her Oldham visit, culminated in an unpleasant row in the staff room.

About a dozen teachers were gathered in a self-congratulatory mood, having just heard that two girls had been accepted for Oxford and four others for top universities.

'Well done us,' shouted Miss Farringdon, beads and bangles rattling as she raised her teacup for a toast.

'Hear, hear, splendid,' echoed the others.

Marguerite hid her face in a book. One of the plaited ones, Miss Haynes, noticed.

'What's the matter, Marguerite? Aren't you proud? This is a lot to do with your coaching for the interviews.'

'Thank you. It's just – oh I don't know – it's all very well. For us. But even if our school is doing a great job with most of the girls, what about all the rest, in other words the vast majority? In secondary modern schools. Techs. The tips.'

Miss Farringdon, due to retire at the end of term, had abandoned any pretence of tact.

'Those children are as thick as pigshit.'

Marguerite was furious.

'Do you really believe that?'

'It's a proven fact. That's why they're at the secondary modern.'

'I beg to disagree. I don't believe there's a child in the world that hasn't got a talent for something. It's just a question of finding it and developing it. That's our job, for God's sake.'

Miss Farringdon was adamant.

'Not everyone can be clever. Someone's got to mend our bloomin' pipes and build our houses.'

'But should they be made to feel inferior?'

Miss Lewin sought to impose calm.

'Well, what's the answer?'

Tony, who had been silently listening, said, 'Well there's the new comprehensives. One's just opened in Kidbrooke.'

Miss Farringdon waded into the fray again.

'Oh heavens. They sound awful. Too big. Too soulless. We need the grammar schools for the clever ones. Let's face it, however altruistic you are, you've got to admit that some will always be cleverer than others.'

Marguerite said, 'You keep saying "clever". Define that. What in hell's name do you mean, "clever"?'

Tony put a calming hand on her shoulder.

'I think what Miss Farringdon means is some will be more academic, better at Latin and Greek. But surely the others can excel in different ways, Miss Farringdon? If they're all under the same roof, taking some of the same lessons and all doing sport together, but specialising in what they're good at, no one will feel inferior. The girl who is a good cook will reach cordon bleu standard, and be as respected as the Greek scholar. The dim-witted boy who is brilliant at football will be admired by the boy who gets a scholarship to Oxford.'

Even Miss Farringdon seemed impressed by Tony's advocacy.

'My goodness, this is a side of you we don't often see.'

Miss Haynes demurred, 'You'll have to abolish the public schools and grammars to make it work. Otherwise the mix will be unbalanced.'

'Yes, of course,' said Tony. 'It won't work otherwise.'

'But that would be tragic. You would lose some wonderful schools.'

Miss Farringdon let out one of her raucous laughs.

'Well, Mr Stansfield, they didn't do that – your lot – when they were in power, did they? And no wonder, even Atlee went to a public school.'

Tony rallied, 'But Rab Butler and Morrison, and Aneurin didn't. They are determined and the public will be behind it. Only five per cent go to public schools and eighty per cent don't get to grammar schools. My lot, as you put it, will get back and make it happen, you mark my words.'

Miss Farrington neighed with laughter again. 'Pity they didn't take the chance while they had it. Too late now. Can't see Macmillan abolishing Eton and Harrow.'

That night, as they did the washing-up together at Marguerite's flat, she said, 'How come you know so much about these comprehensives?'

Tony looked uneasy. He told her that he had contacted Miss Scott, the secondary modern head, whom he had heard was moving to a comprehensive opening in a rough area of Islington. She was to be deputy to an inspirational new headmaster.

'Good for her. I don't know how she has stuck it so long.'

'Mags. Let's sit on the sofa. I want to tell you something.'

'What? Is it something bad? You're frightening me. Please don't say you're leaving me—'

'You make it sound as though we're married. I told you in Ullswater. I'm worried about our relationship, and what it's doing to you. You need a man who can give you much more than I can. Who will treat you like the desirable woman you are.'

'I'm happy with you.'

'Well, you shouldn't be. Anyway that wasn't all I wanted to say. After our visit to Oldham and you saying we needed a rethink, I've felt really unsettled.'

'So have I.'

'For you Dartford is perfect. Getting bright girls to achieve their best is what you do brilliantly and I suspect that when Fryer retires you could well get a headship. I'm just an ageing PT teacher with no great career path ahead. I only have my ideals. Dartford is a great school, but I need to move on.'

'What do you mean?'

'Look, Mags, I've been intending to discuss this with you but I wanted to find out more about it before I did. I want to work with children from backgrounds like mine. That's why I came into teaching. I've lost my sense of purpose. The new headmaster of Miss Scott's school seems full of new ideas and he's looking for staff.'

That was when Marguerite realised that this odd relationship was absolutely indispensable to her. She could not imagine her life without Tony. She couldn't bear the thought of losing someone else that she truly loved.

He looks awkward, out of place in the bustling airport. She hands him a piece of paper.

'This is my hotel in London, Marcel. If you change your mind—'

'I won't. You must follow your dream. I don't belong in it.'

'You could, you could—'

'No. But, Marguerite—'

'Yes?'

'I will always love you. Till the day I die . . .'

'Well . . .'

But he turns, blows a kiss over his shoulder and is lost in the crowd.

Marguerite leapt to her feet.

'I'm coming too.'

'What?'

'It sounds exciting. I'm in a rut here. I want to "follow my dream". A fresh start. That's what I need.'

Yes, that was exactly what she needed. To move on. Move on. With Tony.

Her idealism came gushing back.

'Yes, Tony, a fresh start. Wonderful new things! We will change the rotten world after all!'

Tony stroked her hair and kissed the top of her head. He laughed, but he sounded solemn.

'Take it easy now, Lizzie Dripping. Take it easy.'

Chapter 20

Marguerite's walk, in the drizzling rain, from the Angel tube station to Risinghill Street for her interview at the new comprehensive, was not as uplifting as her approach to Dartford County Grammar School for Girls on her first day as a teacher eleven years ago. But her eager anticipation was, if anything, more fierce than it had been then. The grimy tenements, bomb sites still not cleared, the chaotic Chapel Street market with its rotting waste, starving dogs and raucous shouts were all grist to her renovated reforming mill. The queue outside the pie and mash and jellied eel shop was, to her, made up of salt-of-the-earth Londoners, and she laughed as they whistled when she clacked by on her high heels, thinking: With a bit of luck, I'll soon be one of you.

Standing in front of a ramshackle pub at the top of the market she looked across the busy road to Risinghill Street on the other side. It was not an imposing sight. There were several reeling winos outside the church on the corner, opposite which was a huge blackened wall of a decaying warehouse, and beyond a group of wretched slum houses. Dodging the heavy lorries, she crossed to look closer at her possible future workplace. A pinched face was staring out of a broken window in one of the houses. Marguerite smiled up at the woman.

'Piss off,' the face mouthed.

The short road terminated in a high wire fence, inside which was a building site. It did not look as if it would be ready to house two thousand children in six months' time, but Marguerite was moved to see this phoenix rising from the ashes of all the dereliction. A surly doorkeeper led her across the rubble to a hut near the entrance. A tap would not be heard over the banging and clanking of the builders, so Marguerite tentatively opened the door. Sitting at a desk, head in hands, a picture of despair, was Miss Scott, late of the secondary modern. Suddenly aware of Marguerite, she leapt to her feet, immaculate as ever, with her black hair now in a pageboy style and wearing a two-piece navy suit with a white blouse. She shook Marguerite's hand warmly.

'Oh heavens, am I glad to see you. Forgive me, you caught me off guard. I'm helping the headmaster with the staffing. I have had a dispiriting morning interviewing people who believe that "six of the best" is a "jolly good thing" and "never did me any harm". Or worse, men wearing grubby jeans, saying they took up teaching because they didn't know what else to do. Lord, there is some rubbish in our profession.'

Marguerite was startled. At Dartford some teachers were obviously more able than others but none could be categorised as 'rubbish'. As for the cane, though it was legal to thrash children, the subject had never even been discussed.

Miss Scott continued to pour out her frustration.

'We are going to need high-calibre teachers here. It's going to be a mighty struggle to make it work. We will be an unwilling amalgamation of four different, and I do mean different, schools, plus the intake from local primaries. We'll have one group in their final year, who are not going to feel any loyalty to the new school. Plus – and this is the saddest thing for me – there are good grammars and posh schools in the area which will have creamed off the top stream, therefore our share of high-flyers will be less than one per cent, so it is not truly a comprehensive. Most pupils will be ordinary working-class kids but we'll have ninety on probation, many on the books of the NSPCC, some deemed educationally subnormal and a third immigrants with little or no knowledge of English. Would you like to sit down?'

'Perhaps I'd better.'

'There's more.'

'Oh really?'

'The building is a disaster. Four exits for them to escape, seven playgrounds, several dining rooms, perfect in every way for bunking off and causing mischief. Michael Duane, our head, is doing his best to remedy some of this, which is why he's not here. He is giving them a belated input from someone who will actually use this architectural folly. We have been forced to take on two of the heads and a lot of the staff of the previous four schools, who will be reluctantly answerable to Mike, who doesn't believe in the cane or expelling people, whereas they have always ruled with a rod of iron – literally in some cases, except that the rod was made of wood. Several of the children have fathers in Pentonville Prison up the road, and a few of the mothers operate as prostitutes.'

'No competition to Cheltenham Ladies' College then?'

'Not really no. They're single sex.'

Marguerite laughed.

'Of course, silly me.'

'We're mixed. In every sense of the word. A thoroughly mixed bag. Two of the four schools have been single sex up to now, so imagine the fun and games when the boys and girls are let loose.'

Miss Scott looked anxiously at Marguerite.

'Well, what do you think?'

'I'm thinking that you personally seem to have jumped out of the frying pan into the fire.'

'No, there's one big advantage—'

'What's that?'

'A visionary, dedicated, remarkable headmaster.'

On cue a tall man in paint-bespattered corduroys and crew-necked sweater burst into the shed.

'Trying to get rid of some of the grey walls,' he said, indicating his stained yellow hands. 'Diana told me about you. I hope you'll join us. Please excuse me. I have to change into my respectable headmaster's suit and tie. I have a governor coming. I'll change in the builders' Elsan toilet. It's going to be thrilling. Has Diana asked you about being head of house? And about doing French as well as English? Do become part of our family. We – they – need you.'

Grabbing a crumpled dark suit from a hanger he rushed out.

'Is that—?'

'Yes, that's Michael Duane. He's apt to jump the gun, I'm afraid. I was going to build up to it tactfully.'

Marguerite raised an eyebrow.

'Well, no, I haven't actually made a very good job of that, have I? But you see I am passionate about what we're trying to do here, and I'm having trouble finding teachers who are prepared to rise to the challenge. We are dividing the school into houses so the pupils have a smaller group to relate to in this vast place. You would be ideal as a head of house.'

'Just a minute, just a minute. You know nothing about me—'

'I saw you handle my lost souls at the secondary modern. You cared, you listened, you reacted truthfully and spontaneously. That is the approach we need here. We have to throw away our teaching rule books and be in each scary moment. Mike needs people who are prepared to look at new ways of tackling the problems in an area like this. Maybe it is a consequence of the war, or government policies, but it's a changing world, and there are children that need our help. Whatever happens it will be an adventure, and believe me, we have an inspirational leader. Go on, Marguerite – you're not needed at that splendid grammar school. You are here.'

A pause.

'I'll hand in my notice on Monday.'

Miss Fryer expressed regret at Marguerite's decision.

'I had hoped you would apply for the headship here when I retire. I have already recommended you.'

Marguerite was taken aback. The conflicts they had had over the years had not led her to believe that Miss Fryer would entrust her beloved school to someone like her.

'I realise a new broom is necessary. But wielded by someone I can trust. Whose first concern is the girls, not some risky experiment. We live in dangerous times. This talk of a birth pill, the obsession with television and its casual violence and vulgarity, the lack of deference. I know you have a vision for the future of education, but please be careful, Miss Carter. Be careful with the young.'

'I will, Miss Fryer. I respect your approach. You have taught me so much.'

Miss Fryer smiled.

'That's kind of you. I realise I'm an old fuddy-duddy, but I seriously believe if inhibitions are broken down too suddenly, too drastically, it is very destructive for some, especially the children. Evolution is better than revolution in my book. I hope you enjoy your final term with us.'

She took Marguerite's hand and held it in both of hers.

'The school will miss you, Miss Carter. And so will I.'

Chapter 21

'What the hell have I done?'

Marguerite and Tony crouched, sharing a cigarette in the rabbitry.

'I could be a headmistress of a fine school, in a nice environment, with lovely pupils. Instead I'm going to work myself to death, in a slum, with two thousand juvenile delinquents.'

'Nonsense. You can't be headmistress of a grammar school. Not with your hair.'

'I could wear it in a bun.'

'It's the colour, you'll have to wait till it goes grey.'

'Which will be pretty soon when I'm teaching ninety kids on probation for heaven knows what crimes.'

'Then there's the boobs and the wiggle. Much more suitable for Islington. This is London we're talking about here. Think – you'll be living in the centre of where it's all happening.'

'All what?'

'Well, I'm not sure. But we'll find out.'

'In Islington? Didn't look like much happening, except poverty and misery.'

Tony said sharply, 'Marguerite, stop it. It's your decision to do this.' He put his arm round her. 'This is what we believe in. We made a vow "not to do nothing". Remember?'

Her voice sounded shaky.

'Oh yes. Sorry, for a moment I forgot I was going to change the world.'

'And we will. Or at least a little bit of it. Buck up, Marguerite, this isn't like you. I'm usually trying to control your blind optimism.'

'I'm scared, Tony. I may not be any good.'

'Nonsense. You're a brilliant teacher and I'll hold your hand, OK?'

'OK.'

'Right, let's put the fag out before we suffocate these bunnies. We'll go and look for digs tomorrow.'

'Together?'

He shook his head.

'No, pet. If we share, our gentleman callers would be put off, and we don't want that, do we?'

After much scanning of the small ads and traipsing around the area near the school, Marguerite found a room, a short walk away, in King's Cross Road. It was above a spit-and-sawdust pub called the Carpenter's Arms. The landlord and landlady, Bob and Florrie, with whom she would share the kitchen and bathroom, were a cheerful couple. Her room was light and airy and overlooked the back yard, under which ran the trains from King's Cross Station, making all the glasses in the bar rattle. To reach the door to the stairs leading to the flat she had to run the gauntlet of the tough guys and old regular soaks in the public bar; the few women customers went into the more respectable saloon bar, or the little nook at the back traditionally kept for ladies only, to sip their port-and-lemons and gossip in peace.

With its large speckled mirrors, colourful tiled walls, converted glass gas lamps and marble-topped tables, the pub was a picture of faded Edwardian splendour and Marguerite fell in love with it. That it was shabby was in its favour. It would not have seemed right to live in luxury while many of her future pupils lived in squalor. She gave the landlord Bob a retainer and he was happy to keep the room free till she needed it. People were not queuing up to occupy it anyway, he admitted.

Tony settled for the YMCA hostel in Great Russell Street. He said he needed the gym to keep fit, and doubtless the pool, where it was the rule to swim naked, was an added attraction.

'Naked?'

'Yes of course. It's to stop bits of cloth from the costumes getting into the filtration system.'

'Of course it is.'

'And it's very Christian and lovely so don't look at me like that. I'll be very happy there.'

'I'm sure you will.'

As their final term drew to an end Marguerite and Tony were made aware of how well liked they were. Even Miss Farringdon told them that they were insane to enter the savage territory of a comprehensive, but she wished them God speed on their voyage. There were farewell parties with staff and girls, and presents, and tears.

The last party was given by Mrs Schneider. A Sunday lunch of roast chicken, followed by apple crumble and custard, complemented by wine provided by Marguerite and Tony. Miss Allum wore the same special-occasion lace frock that had graced the Coronation party, there not having been another event in the subsequent seven years of her life to warrant a new purchase. Mr Humphreys, too, seemed to be sporting the same outfit, but

Marguerite noticed, with some relief, that either the trousers were new, or Mrs Schneider had persuaded him to have a zip inserted to replace the errant fly button. Moira was resplendent in a skin-tight crimson-silk dress created from a Vogue pattern, with nails and lips to match. Mr Humphreys had to sit down when she made her entrance.

'Darlings, sorry I'm late, lines to learn.' The stray pin in the hem of her frock suggested last-minute adjustments to her hard-won glamour as well.

The four of them were intrigued to hear about the new school. They thought it was an excellent decision, if not a safe career move.

Miss Allum, having imbibed quite a lot of Chardonnay, burst out, 'To hell with that. Go where your heart leads you. Don't do what's expected of you. Or else – look at me.'

They all did. With some alarm.

'I'm a lonely old maid who's achieved nothing. I was engaged to a beautiful boy . . .' She waved her left hand with the mysterious sapphire ring. 'He died at Ypres and we never even made love. I wanted to, but it wasn't done. I didn't follow my heart. And I'm still a bloody virgin. Then I became a secretary. That wasn't my heart's desire either, I can tell you. Do you know what was?'

They held their breath.

'This.' And she crossed to the piano in the corner. 'I was good – won competitions – I played for the troops during the last war – I loved it, but then my father died and my mother needed me at home.'

'Why, was she ill?'

'No, just lonely. Single girls were expected to look after their mothers. That was the done thing. I couldn't swan off doing concerts around the world. So I stayed at home and gave piano lessons to bored children. Then she died. Children don't want to learn the piano any more, it's all washboards and electric guitars now, so I had to sell the house to provide myself with an income. And here I am. And here I shall stay till I die.'

Tony said gently, 'Do you still play, Miss Allum?'

'No, I haven't touched a piano for years and years and years.'

Tony opened the lid of the piano and pulled out the stool.

'Please, Miss Allum. Marguerite and I would love to hear you. A farewell gift.'

Tentatively the old woman's hands explored the keys.

'It's out of tune. But here's some Chopin, if I can remember it.'

Everyone was transfixed as she grew in confidence until the room resonated with the clarity of her playing. The fragile woman was suddenly powerful, commanding the music and her audience. When she stopped there was an awestruck silence. She looked round as though coming out of a trance.

'Sorry, I'm out of practice.'

Mrs Schneider went over and hugged her.

'Please, Miss Allum, use the piano whenever you want to. I'll get it tuned. It will give me such pleasure to hear you.'

Mr Humphreys leapt to his feet.

'And I'm going to follow my heart's desire.'

Whereupon he fell to his knees in front of a startled Moira.

'Moira the divine, will you marry me?'

Marguerite prayed silently that Moira wouldn't laugh or be cruel. She needn't have worried. The actress rose to the occasion.

'Mr Humphreys, I love you far too much to marry you. You are a dear sweet man and I would eat you alive.'

Still on his knees, Mr Humphreys burbled, 'Well, I'd like that. I mean sorry – I didn't mean—'

Moira gently took his hands and helped him to stand.

'My profession will always come first, I'm afraid. I heard yesterday that I have an amazing job in the West End. It could be what I've been waiting for. So I'm afraid I have to focus on that. But thank you so much for asking me.'

And she kissed him gently on the cheek.

In the flurry of goodbyes, Marguerite managed to ask Moira what the 'amazing' West End job was.

'Understudy in the sodding *Mousetrap*. The actors' graveyard. But I need the money. I'm washed up, passé, a failure, but I'd rather he went on being deluded into thinking I'm wonderful – from a distance. He's the only person who does.'

'Moira, you handled that beautifully.'

'I'm a good actress.'

'You are.'

'But these tears are real. I'm very fond of you and Tony. Let's meet in the Salisbury for a drink one day?'

'Let's.'

They smiled at one another. Knowing they probably wouldn't.

'The end of an era,' sighed Moira.

'And the start of another,' said Marguerite.

'Yes.' Moira sounded bleak. Then she added wryly, 'This is like the last scene of *Uncle Vanya*, when everyone's left him alone with sad old Sonya.'

And suddenly, on the doorstep, Moira was a young girl:

'"We shall go on living, Uncle Vanya. We shall live through a long, long succession of days and tedious evenings . . . When our time comes, we shall die submissively, and over there, beyond the grave, we shall say that we've suffered, that we've wept, that we've had a bitter life, and God will take pity on us . . ."'

There was a burst of applause from Mr Humphreys, standing behind her, tears streaming down his face.

'Bravo, bravissimo.'

Whereupon Moira pivoted on her high heels, sashayed past him, and shouted back, 'Right. Off to learn Miss Christie's magic bloody text.'

As Mr Humphreys closed the door, strains of a Brahms sonata were heard under Moira's cry:

'Back to the real world, everyone.'

Chapter 22

The real world of Marguerite's first day at Risinghill School was daunting. There was a marked contrast between the pupils' arrival at the new Islington comprehensive and the lively scene that had delighted her at the grammar school in Dartford. Pushed around by the authorities into an uneasy alliance, the children from formerly separate schools showed resentment, bewilderment and some fear. Sartorially, too, they looked a mess.

Mainly to please the London County Council it was decided that they should wear uniforms. The colours chosen were grey and royal blue. It was obvious that the rule was unworkable. One of the four schools had had an uniform, so these pupils managed a motley mixture of the old and new. The rest did their best from scratch. Some of the boys had managed over-large shirts that looked as though they had belonged to their fathers, and a few girls were wearing their mothers' white blouses in satin or lace, similarly ill-fitting. There were quite a few new grey trousers and skirts, which was the most some could afford. There was not a hat in sight, Marguerite was pleased to see. The group of older pupils due to leave after one year had, not unnaturally, not bothered at all, and looked rather attractive, the boys in either Rocker gear of leather jacket and jeans, or Mod gear of sharp suit, and the girls in pretty dresses.

Consequently at the first assembly, taken in two parts to accommodate the size of the new school, Michael Duane took the pressure off, in view of the differing family circumstances, by declaring uniform optional. It was the start of many adaptations he made to deal with the circumstances as they presented themselves. This volte-face caused some concern in the staff room amongst those teachers who believed in making rules and keeping them.

It was a harrowing day of children getting lost in the vast building and becoming overexcited and unruly. The only time when silence reigned, apart from the sound of gulping and sighing, was when the skinny youngsters warmed their little bottles of free milk on the radiators, and then, holding them with both hands, eyes closed, slowly sucked on the straw, savouring the precious fluid as if it was the finest wine.

At the end of the exhausting day the head held a staff meeting in which he outlined his policy of making the school a place where the children were treated with the respect so many had been denied; where they felt no fear and had a refuge from the violence in the outside world.

'Schools should be for the less fortunate, what home is for the fortunate.'

'Sentimental claptrap,' snarled Mr Fletcher when Mr Duane had left. 'He doesn't know the dodgy little herberts round here. Give them an inch, and they'll take a mile. He won't last a minute.'

Mr Fletcher was an unsmiling man, with the ramrod back and stentorian voice of an ex-sergeant major. He was as disorientated as the pupils by the enforced change, and, in addition, aggrieved at being overlooked as headmaster, a job for which he considered himself eminently suited, with his war record and knowledge of the behavioural problems of some of the local children. He resented Mr Duane from day one. The atmosphere in the staff room had none of the warm friendliness of Dartford. The newcomers were ignored by the old guard of teachers from the previous schools, and even the sexes seemed to separate. Inspired by Mr Duane, Marguerite comforted herself that, when things settled down, they would all unite in the common cause of creating a successful comprehensive.

Marguerite's first English lesson the next day with the twelve-year-olds was a disaster. Although it was supposed to be the A stream, the class was mainly composed of less able kids that had to be incorporated to make the form a viable size. She made the bold decision to do the sonnet class that had always proved successful at Dartford. The format, with variations, was a good introductory lesson, in which she could learn a lot about the pupils' ability and background and they could relate to her.

This time nobody would offer to read out the sonnet and when she did so herself it was deemed 'a load of shit'. Trying to get the class to expand on this brought no response. Using every technique she knew she still could not get them to participate in the lesson. She panicked, and gradually lost control. Eventually the children were chatting, giggling, looking out of the windows, reading comics. They were bored by her and showed it.

Marguerite was desolate. She had never experienced failure like this as a teacher even at the beginning of her career. She happened to pass Michael Duane in the corridor and, as he had told the staff, and indeed the pupils, that his door was open at all times, she asked to speak to him.

'I'm sorry, Mr Duane. You may have to let me go. My training and experience have not equipped me for this job.'

'That's true of all of us, Miss Carter. We are all starting from scratch. Allow yourself time to get to know the children. Forget about the exams and syllabus. It's about educating them as opposed to just forcing them to learn.'

'But they won't respond. They won't talk to me.'

'That's no surprise. A lot of them have been told to shut up all their lives. In overcrowded homes it's "Belt up and watch the telly", "Don't answer back". At school they weren't allowed to talk in the corridors and certainly not in the classroom. They were given the cane for "talking" as if it were a crime. Is it any wonder they are inarticulate? So count that as your first task. Teaching them to talk.'

Easier said than done, she thought, but then sternly reminded herself that she had handled difficult pupils before. Irene and Elsie were the first of many. But one at a time. Not a whole classful.

On playground duty later she broke up a row between two groups. Each accused the other of being the cause.

'Well, he's a Bubble, ain't he, and they always pick on the Turks. They're worse than the Bacon Sarnies.'

Marguerite defused the row by asking for a translation.

They clamoured to instruct her:

'Bubble and Squeak – Greek. Bacon Sarni – Pakistani.'

'Four by Two – Jew.'

All these nomenclatures seemed to be used with no special rancour, it was just how people were categorised, whether in anger or friendship.

The next day she gritted her teeth and announced to the class that they were going to do poetry. She ignored the groans.

'I'm going to start with rhyming.'

They slumped in their desks until they saw what she was

writing on the blackboard. It was her newly learnt Cockney rhyming slang. She requested any more suggestions, and once they had got hold of the fact that their everyday language was a kind of poetry they joined in with zest. Some were difficult to unpick.

> My old china: china plate. Mate.
> Use your loaf: loaf of bread. Head.
> Would you Adam and Eve it: believe it.
> Apples and pears: stairs.
> Sweeney: Sweeney Todd. Flying Squad.

Without flinching she included Hymie Cohen's suggestion of, 'Apple: apple tart. Fart.'

Never having worked with boys before she assumed this was usual behaviour.

Then Rita Oshenado undermined her gender stereotyping with, 'Barclays: Barclays bank. Wank.'

As Marguerite wrote them on the blackboard she hoped no governors or LCC inspectors were around. Mary O'Shea came up with the curious, 'Brahms and Liszt: pissed. Drunk.' When questioned, she had no idea that it referred to composers. Marguerite saw an opportunity to open new doors at some later date.

As the lesson progressed they had begun to have fun with language, and the idea of poetry had become less frightening. They began to invent their own words. She was henceforth to be called Juicy.

Juicy tomater: Miss Carter. Because of your ginger hair, miss.'

Having got their interest, she ventured to read them 'Jabberwocky', the poem from *Alice's Adventures in Wonderland*, as an illustration of play with words. It seemed much more accessible to them at this stage than Shakespeare. In fact they all wanted to have a go at reading it out loud, and fell about laughing at one another.

Over the following weeks she was to supply them all with pocket dictionaries, and after laboriously teaching them how to use them, she had competitions to see who could find a word first. She found other accessible ways of teaching them, after a while, risking dictation. She solved the problem of involving the less able pupils by making them pretend to be the teacher, and mark the higher-flyers' spelling, using their trusty dictionaries, of course. Their margin notes of 'idyert' and 'boloks' were not perfect, but gradually their vocabulary and spelling improved, without them even knowing it.

After the first term, when Marguerite had gained their confidence, they began to write their own verse and stories, some of which were heartbreaking reflections of their home life. She even persuaded them, as she had her grammar-school girls, to learn a verse, or piece of prose, a week by heart. In the process they understood it, as well as felt rightly proud of their achievement when they were called upon to recite it to the class. And they were generous in their applause for classmates who could only manage a nursery rhyme, or the words of a popular song.

All this took time and trust. It was sometimes difficult to tolerate the disruptive elements, but by never raising her voice, and always being polite, she could control the troublemakers, who usually gave up for lack of attention. Those that didn't she would talk to separately, to try and get to the bottom of their problem. Arthur Smith who could not sit down, but rambled about the room during lessons, proved to have an unmarried mother and four brothers and sisters, two of whom had already been taken into care. When school finished for the day he roamed the streets before curling up to sleep on the stairs of the block of flats in which he lived.

It was not possible in this environment to follow Miss Fryer's stricture against engaging with the children's backgrounds. Mr Duane's study was frequently full of parents and children coming for advice. A Parents' Association started up, with participants impressed by how much the headmaster valued their opinions. Marguerite was appalled at how some of the children were living. On one visit to the home of a child she was concerned about, the elder brother came back with a young girl, and made love, loudly, in the next room, which distracted Marguerite, but left the mother and the child she was worried about completely unfazed.

One of the biggest culture shocks to Marguerite was the obscene language that poured out of some of the youngsters' mouths. Variations of 'cunt' and 'fuck' were used as nouns, adjectives, adverbs and Marguerite would have liked to ban them, like Miss Farringdon's 'nice' and 'lovely'. Freddie Marshall barely uttered a sentence without one of these words. Marguerite asked to see his mother to discuss it. She turned up in a black satin dress, perky hat with a little veil, and red high heels. On her best behaviour, she expressed dismay that her child should be so rude in front of a teacher.

'Jesus, the little bugger. I don't know where he gets his fucking language from. You tan his arse, the little sod.'

Duane's reaction was to start giving talks on sex to teach them the correct etymology.

Tony and Marguerite's admiration for the headmaster grew as he gradually gained the confidence of even the most wayward children, but some of the staff were deeply unhappy about the way the school was being run. The school council, for instance, made up of a mixture of staff and pupils, was set up to resolve problems. To begin with it went well; gang battles were talked through, punishments jointly decided. But when one of the boys complained that teachers kept not turning up for playground duty, leaving it to prefects to supervise sometimes difficult situations, some of the staff complained later to Mr Duane that he had allowed them to be humiliated. They found it impossible to change their belief that they were always right, and that the pupils had to be tamed by unquestioned discipline; the ultimate sanctions being the cane and expulsion.

When Marguerite discovered that Sammy Bream couldn't hold his pen properly, because of the three welts on his hands inflicted by Mr Fletcher's cane, she stormed into the staff room to confront him.

'Well, he's a thieving little bastard. He stole cash out of the dinner-money tin. And it's the second time.'

'Oh, and did you cane him the first time?'

'Yes, he's got to learn a lesson.'

'Well, it doesn't seem to have worked. If he did it again. Do you know about his family?'

'No, and I don't care. I'm not a bloody social worker.'

Echoes of Miss Fryer.

'Well, for your information, his father is in Pentonville for thieving, and his brother is in Borstal. So he's had better teachers in robbery than he's had here in other subjects. And what is more, being beaten is an everyday occurrence for him when his dad's not in prison. The only thing that might stop him in his tracks would be kindness.'

For once the whole staff room became involved in an intense discussion about the pros and cons of corporal punishment. The new intake were vehement in their condemnation of using violence on children, and the old guard seemed to take notice. Marguerite could see that for many of them it was the first time they had questioned the casual cruelty that had become normal.

The clip round the ear, the rapped knuckles with a ruler, the throwing of a book or chalk, the shaking and shouting into a youngster's face. Tony told them that he was puzzled that some of the children looked behind them before jumping over the horse in the gym, until he discovered that, in their previous school, the teacher had walloped them on the bottom with a plimsoll to make them jump higher. For once a feeling of unity was apparent, and an uneasy agreement was reached to abolish the use of corporal punishment – at least for a trial period. A grateful Duane announced the decision to an astonished school in assembly. He caused even more amazement when he told them that henceforth no one would be expelled either, pointing out the responsibility this gave them for their own good behaviour, which should be adopted for its own sake, rather than out of fear.

These assemblies were enjoyable occasions. There were no prayers or hymns, just discussion of various topics. When the school was uneasy on the day a young man of twenty-one, Edwin Bush, was to be hanged up the road in Pentonville, Duane opened up a discussion on capital punishment, which ended in some of the pupils getting up a petition to abolish hanging, and taking it to No. 10 Downing Street. Sometimes there was music from the new orchestras and choirs. Following up her promise to tell her pupils more about Brahms and Liszt, Marguerite had the risky idea of getting Miss Allum to come and play for them. Thus it was that a sniggering school watched a little old lady in a lace frock come onto the platform, bow to them, and sit down at the piano, adjust the stool, and transform herself into a magician. She chose a piece of dazzling virtuosity by Liszt, and Marguerite was delighted to see them all open-mouthed and wide-eyed at the dramatic performance. They cheered Miss Allum to the rafters, and Mr Duane asked if any of them would like to play like that. A roar of approval resulted in Miss Allum being appointed to teach the piano. Her heart's desire was achieved. Her shining talent had found a meaning.

After a couple of years, Marguerite and Tony were in their element. Every day was a challenge, each tiny success a triumph. Tony's task was easier than Marguerite's, as most of the children loved sport, and the facilities were good, especially for those more used to playing games in the street. He had a good relationship with the boys, whose background he empathised with, and the girls, as usual, all had crushes on him.

Marguerite started to take some of the older pupils to the theatre, an alien world to most of them, and Tony came along to help keep them under control. Stratford East was a favourite destination. *Oh, What a Lovely War!* caused a heated debate, and led easily into study of the war poets. Eventually she risked some Shakespeare. When she told them that they were going to see one of Britain's greatest actors, Laurence Olivier, as Othello they were unimpressed. 'Is he on the telly?'

As she and Tony shepherded this multicoloured, rowdy bunch of youngsters into the hallowed plush and gilt of the Old Vic Theatre, Marguerite sensed that the middle-class audience, reverently anticipating the monumental performance they had read about, were not best pleased.

There was quite a bit of fidgeting and whispering to begin with.

'You didn't say this Oliver bloke was black, miss.'

'He's not.'

'Well, he walks like he is and talks like he is.'

'That's great acting, Joshua.'

'But poor taste,' muttered Tony.

She had outlined the plot beforehand, so even though the language was strange to them, they began to get involved. When Othello smothered Desdemona, Rita Oshenada shouted out, 'Stop it, you bastard.'

There was a lot of shushing, and tutting, but the children had become too absorbed to care. At the end some of the girls were weeping audibly.

As they left one woman said loudly, 'Guttersnipes.'

John Fernandez said, 'Does she mean us?'

Marguerite reassured him.

'Don't worry, John, she's just a silly prig.'

He looked shocked.

'That's not very nice language for a teacher. I don't think you should talk like that, miss. You should set an example.'

She was bewildered. Tony was laughing behind the boy. She decided to let it pass and do some dictionary work the next day with the lad about the word 'prig'.

That night over a drink in the saloon bar in the Carpenter's Arms, she brought up the incident with Tony.

'He thought you said "prick".'

'What are you talking about?'

'He misheard you, and thought you said "prick".'

'Well, even if he did, what's wrong with that?'

'Don't you know what it means?'

'Yes of course. I can't give the exact dictionary definition but it's roughly to pierce, make a small hole.'

'And a cock.'

'I beg your pardon?'

'A cock.'

'A what?'

'A man's penis.'

A pause.

'Don't be ridiculous.'

Tony shook his head and roared with laughter.

'You amaze me sometimes, Mags. After the life you've led, you still manage to be totally innocent, verging on naïve. You need to get out more. We have to do something about your love life, Lizzie Dripping, if only to improve your vocabulary.'

Chapter 23

Tony had the accusatory tone of the priests of her childhood.

'Marguerite, listen, this is serious. Mark well my words. You are on the rocky road to forty.'

'I know, yes, I confess. I'm sorry. So?'

His voice rang with righteous indignation.

'So? So? Isn't it obvious? You have to find a man.'

'Amen,' said Bob the landlord of the Carpenter's Arms, getting into the spirit of the inquisition.

Marguerite retaliated, 'That's easy to say, but where? And when? All I meet are the teachers at school.'

'Well, what about one of them?' said Bob.

'The only ones I could fall in love with are Tony and the headmaster, and they are both unavailable.'

'You don't have to be "in love".' Tony was exasperated. 'Not nowadays. This is the Swinging '60s. Sex is fun. Everything's changed. Get with-it.'

'I'm no good at that. I have to be in love.'

'What about the one-night stand you told me about?'

'That was different. It was wartime and we both thought we

would die. And anyway, I did love him. For that one night. Very much.'

They were eating bread and cheese and pickled onions and gherkins. After Bob had rung the hand bell and bellowed, 'Time, gentlemen, please,' and chivvied the stragglers out with 'Come on, you lot, let's be 'avin' you', he joined them at the table for a beer.

Tony entreated him and his wife Florrie, 'Don't you think Mags should have a boyfriend?'

Florrie shouted across, 'Of course she should – lovely girl like her. She works too bloody hard, that's the trouble. She never gets to meet anyone. Like me. That's why I'm stuck with him. One day I'll go off with old Len.'

Len came in at the afternoon opening hour and stayed till 'time' every day, nursing a stout and speaking to no one.

Marguerite said, 'You'll have to fight me for him. He's my only hope.'

With good publicans' tact, neither of them ever broached the subject of the relationship between Marguerite and Tony. Florrie was now vigorously wiping down the counter. She stopped in her task when Marguerite said, 'It's no good. I'm destined to be an old maid.'

Florrie came over to the table. 'Oh don't say that, duck. You need love in your life. Everyone does. And what about kiddies?'

She looked genuinely upset, so Marguerite reassured her, 'Don't worry, Florrie. I have had love in the past. Great love. That's why it's difficult to find anyone. Nobody matches up. And I have never longed for my own children. Some women don't, you know.'

'What happened to him? The great love.'

'I don't know. He's probably married with lots of children now. I had to leave. Long story.'

'You must follow your dream. I don't belong in it. I will always love you till the day I die.'

Bob gave his wife an admonitory look to stop her pursuing the subject. He said, 'You've got to get out more and meet more people. What about those sit-in things you go to? That Vietnam one you went to last week. Didn't you get chatting to any fellow weirdos while you were waiting to be arrested?'

The cosiness of the closed pub and friendly concern of her friends tempted Marguerite to confide in them.

'Well, as it happens—'

'What?' all three snapped in unison.

'I did meet someone on the first CND march six years ago—'

'Six years ago?' Tony couldn't believe his ears. 'And you've never said anything about it? What happened?'

Marguerite asked Bob for a whisky chaser to follow her beer before she launched into the story of meeting Jimmy. Even, after several gulps of the whisky, telling them about the kiss.

'You had a kiss! Six years ago!' Tony exclaimed. 'And here's me thinking you had no love life.'

'I've been busy.'

Tony was suddenly resolute.

'Right, go upstairs, find that telephone number. Now. It's Saturday tomorrow. In the morning, you will phone him. If you don't – I will.'

True to his word the next morning Tony, who had moved into a basement flat in nearby Myddelton Square, came round and stood over her in the corridor as she phoned the number she found in the pocket of her knapsack. The man who answered said that Jimmy had moved, but gave her another number. Marguerite would have given up but Tony wouldn't let her.

After going through two more numbers she recognised the voice at the other end. It was Jimmy's friend Stan, who was delighted to hear from her. He said he didn't have a number for Jimmy, but he would find him, and give him her number.

That same evening she was doing some marking in her room while the pub downstairs was having its Saturday-night sing-song, with Florrie plonking out the tunes on the tinny piano. Usually, she quite liked the sounds of life below, and would occasionally go down and join the locals for a game of darts or cribbage. Tonight it made her feel left out. The conversation the night before had unsettled her. Thus, when she heard Bob shouting up to her, 'Mags – phone – I think it's him,' she felt a rush of pleasure. She had dreamed up a story, which was nearly true, about losing his phone number, and then surprise, surprise, coming across it when throwing out her old knapsack. Jimmy seemed so pleased to hear from her that he didn't care. He was coming round to take her out for lunch the next day, in case she disappeared again.

Marguerite, according to Flo, had let herself go. It was so long since she had dressed to be attractive rather than comfortable and professional that she had become, Tony agreed, 'dowdy'. She dithered for a long time between the slacks that she remembered Jimmy had liked and a dress that made her look younger than the threat of forty made her feel, after Tony's sombre warn-ing. Florrie, who was almost as nervous as she was, advised the dress, with a cardigan over her shoulders 'in case it turns nippy'. Bob said she looked 'a regular treacle tart', and she waited in the saloon bar, where, thanks to Florrie, all the customers were agog to see the teacher's new fancy man.

His arrival went down very well. A roaring, dark blue MG, with the roof off, screeched to a halt and out scrambled the windblown Dish, who was even more handsome than she remembered. Ancient Agnes, who had spent most of her long life in the ladies' bar at the back, staggered out to give her opinion, which was expressed with a startlingly loud wolf whistle. Florrie hugged her and said, 'Blimey, he was worth waiting for.' Jimmy took all the attention in his stride. He greeted the gaping neighbours charmingly and then offered Marguerite his arm. 'Your carriage awaits, madam.' This got a round of applause.

'Sorry about all that,' she said as they zoomed off. 'They – we – don't get much excitement.'

'Well, I'd better live up to expectations. As it's such a lovely day, I thought we'd drive down to Brighton, and have a picnic on the way. How does that sound to you?'

Frightening, thought Marguerite. 'Lovely,' she said. She shouted above the engine, 'The last time I was asked to go to Brighton was by Mr Worms.'

He looked at her quizzically.

'My driving instructor,' she added.

He looked again.

'I didn't go,' she said feebly. 'So it's nice to go now.'

She felt like an awkward schoolgirl rather than a mature teacher, and gave up any attempt at conversation. Gradually she relaxed and took in the scenery. It was good to get out of the city and feel the wind on her face. She occasionally exchanged smiles with Jimmy who seemed quite content not to talk. After about an hour, he drove down a side road and pulled the car into a field overlooking a sweeping view of lush Sussex countryside.

'This is perfect. How did you know this place?'

'I've been here before. Champagne?'

He opened the bottle, and poured the drink into two glasses he took from a picnic basket.

Raising his glass he said, 'To CND.'

Surprised, Marguerite clinked his glass. The champagne bubbles tickled the back of her nose pleasantly.

'Are you still a supporter?' she asked.

'Not really. Are you?'

'Yes, I march and petition and go to meetings, but I fear that after the Cuban missile crisis it's difficult to persuade people to take a moral stance. Although in my opinion . . .' She trailed off, aware that a political argument was not appropriate to the situation.

Jimmy was laying out a white linen tablecloth on the ground, with china plates, and salad and ham in Perspex boxes.

'Sorry, I'm boring myself, let alone you. This is lovely — you've gone to a lot of trouble.'

He stood up and brushed a wisp of hair from her face.

'You are worth it. I toasted CND because it led me to you.'

She was about to respond with some quip about that not, perhaps, being Bertrand Russell's prime objective, but she bit her tongue, and decided to enjoy the compliment.

She smiled and said, 'Thank you.'

They sat on the grass, on opposite sides of the cloth, and ate the food and drank champagne.

'There's no pudding,' said Jimmy. 'You must wait for that.'

In her nervous state, Marguerite wondered about the possible sexual implication of this remark, although the champagne was beginning to take the edge off any concern. Jimmy took some cups and saucers and a Thermos flask out of the basket. He cleared the dirty crockery, and suggested they sit on the tablecloth, and sip their very good coffee. It flashed into her mind how pleased all the regulars at the Carpenter's Arms would be to see her now. And, of course Tony. She would not allow herself to think of how much more relaxed and fun it would have been with him. Fun, yes. But this stirring in her body, almost a shudder, when Jimmy's

shoulder touched hers as he drank his coffee? No, this was different. And exciting. When his hand brushed hers as he took her
cup, it was like an electric shock.

'Are you all right?' he asked.

She wasn't sure, but she nodded. She needed to lie down. She
was wonderfully aware of the sun on her face, the hum of insects
in the grass and then soaring, breathtaking birdsong.

She whispered, 'That's a skylark.'

'Really?' He lay down beside her and she pointed to the
hovering bird, then gently she recited:

> '"Up with me! up with me into the clouds!
> For thy song, Lark, is strong;
> Up with me, up with me into the clouds!
> Singing, singing,
> With clouds and sky about thee ringing,
> Lift me, guide me till I find
> That spot which seems so to thy mind!"'

'What's that?'

'First verse of "To a Skylark" by Wordsworth.'

'Very sexy.'

'How do you mean?'

He put his hands either side of her head, and leant over her.

'Sometime I'll show you.'

Her throbbing body wanted her to say, 'Go on then – now,'
but due to her years of abstinence, and a Catholic childhood, it
came out as an embarrassed laugh and, 'Maybe – sometime.'

He grinned, kissed her briefly on the forehead, leapt to his
feet, and pulled her up to stand, for a moment, slightly too close
to him, before returning to the car.

Chapter 24

As Jimmy drove, she looked at his confident hands controlling the gears and steering wheel, and bare feet on the pedals. His profile, she decided, helped by the champagne, was that of an ancient Roman bust, strong nose and chin, sculpted curly hair. Under his thin shirt, his body looked firm and, as far as she could see through the open collar, smooth and probably hairless. She found herself longing to put her hand inside and find out. The vibration of the car accentuated the feverish pulses in her body. She was grateful for the bracing sea air when they arrived in Brighton. She very definitely needed to cool down.

'Let's go for a swim,' he said.

'I haven't got a costume.'

'I've got one for you.'

'How do you know my size?'

'I remembered exactly what you looked like.'

Jimmy had the key to a beach hut belonging to a friend. He stood outside while she changed and blew a kiss of approval when she appeared in the costume. It turned out that it wasn't just the head that was Roman. When he emerged wearing his brief swimming trunks, with a towel draped casually over his shoulders, he was the epitome of a Roman statue. As he turned to close the door of the beach hut the towel swung aside to reveal the burn scars on his back that Stan had spoken of. He picked her up and carried her over the pebbles, and when they got to the sand pulled her into the sea. They fell and rolled about in the waves. Marguerite had the surreal feeling that she could be in the sexy beach scene in *From Here to Eternity*, had they not been watched by sedate holidaymakers, sitting in deck chairs, the women fully dressed, the men in rolled-up shirt-sleeves, with knotted hankies on their heads.

After their swim, in the intimate darkness of the hut, Jimmy held a towel around her as she slipped out of her costume, then wrapped her in it and slowly, oh so slowly, patted and stroked her dry. Holding the towel as a screen, he turned his head away as she dressed. As she left the hut discreetly while he changed, she could not help glimpsing, as he removed his trunks, yes, oh joy, his buttocks were Roman too. Still tingling from her elemental thrashing in the sea, she felt excited. Her body was awakened by the challenging cold and the feel of Jimmy's hands in the hut. She yearned for more.

'Right,' he whispered in her ear. 'Now for dessert.'

'Yes!' she said, ready for anything.

Dessert turned out to be a dainty tea of slender cucumber sandwiches, strawberries and cream and a three-tiered cake stand of luxury gateaux, in the nearby elegant Royal Crescent Hotel.

'Well, you're full of surprises,' she exclaimed as he poured the Darjeeling tea.

'You're a classy French bird. And I've got ideas au dessus de ma gare. I like a good tea.'

'So do I. It makes a lovely change. Merci.'

She did indeed appreciate the plush elegance of the hotel lounge, after the stark reality of Islington. She sank into an armchair and it dawned on her that this strange feeling she had was relaxation, something she had not felt for a long time.

'Eat your tea, there's a good girl.' Jimmy was holding out a cream éclair. 'Open your lips.'

She did so, and he put it into her mouth. She bit into it. 'Mmm, delicious,' she murmured. The cream spurted onto her chin. He took a serviette and wiped it.

Oh God, thought Marguerite. Now we're doing *Tom Jones*.

But she didn't stop him feeding her with a tiny iced bun. The conversation in the hotel lounge had gone quiet. The other clients seemed to be ladies in hats and chiffon, and gentlemen in hacking jackets with moustaches. They were staring at Marguerite and Jimmy.

When Marguerite pointed this out to Jimmy he said, 'They're just jealous. We are young and alive, and they are old and past it.'

'Not that young,' said Marguerite.

'You're by far the most beautiful woman in the room. The old colonels would give their eye teeth to be where I am sitting now. And thanks to the *Lady Chatterley* trial, all the old girls realise what they've been missing.'

So do I, thought Marguerite, noticing anew Jimmy's mouth sometimes pursed in a sideways grin like a naughty little boy. She picked up a remaining solitary strawberry, dipped it in cream and put it between his bewitching lips.

'Shame to waste it,' she said, stretching luxuriously in the chair. Her foot touched his under the table.

'Yes. I hate waste. We've wasted six years, Marguerite. Let's not waste any more time, eh?'

'No. Today has been lovely, Jimmy. You planned it so perfectly. An antidote to my daily grind.'

'I thought when I met you you were wonderful. But perhaps you took life too seriously.'

'I have a friend who tells me that.'

'Really? A boyfriend?'

'Sort of.'

'Oh. Is it serious?'

'Yes, but not in the way you mean.'

The little-boy grin.

'So, will you see me again?'

'Of course. You are a joy to be with. "Happy happy Liver".'

'I beg your pardon?'

'It's what Wordsworth calls the skylark. And that's what you seem to be. You relish life. You do it so well. It makes me feel very dull.'

'That's the last thing you are.'

'I've so liked being with you, Jimmy. I don't want to go back. I understand the last couplet so well now.'

'How does it go?'

'"I, with my fate contented, will plod on,
And hope for higher raptures, when life's day is done."'

Jimmy frowned. 'That's very sad. I don't want you to feel like that.'

He took both her hands in his.

'Let's go for a walk.'

He paid the waiter and, as they left, he gave a regal wave to the still-transfixed clientele. He led her round the corner to the eighteenth-century crescent with its restored black-tiled façades.

'That's where Laurence Olivier lives,' he said. 'And this is where my friend lives. They're away. I have the key.'

He looked searchingly at her. 'Shall we go in?'

She nodded.

Once they were inside the door, all the pent-up passion

exploded. He led her, or rather dragged her, up the two flights of stairs to a lush bedroom with a four-poster bed. There they ripped off each other's clothes, and spent the next two hours doing what they both admitted in gasps was what they had lusted to do since the picnic several hours ago. They groaned, they panted, they laughed uproariously, as they explored each other's bodies. Jimmy was an expert lover and guided her to new experiences. At one point it crossed her mind it was like an orgasmic gymnastic display. Of Olympic standard.

When at last they lay, breathing heavily, side by side on the bed, Jimmy asked, 'What was that bit "lift me, guide me" in "our poem" – for that's what it is from now on.' Marguerite managed to recite:

> '"Lift me, guide me, till I find
> That spot which seems so to thy mind!"'

He rose on one elbow and looked at her shyly.

'Well, did I lift you to the spot?'

'Yes, yes, you did. Oh boy, you did. It was very much "to my mind". Thank you, you clever little skylark.'

'Good.' He looked pleased with himself. 'I think champagne is called for.'

In a corner of the bedroom was a fridge from which he took a bottle of champagne and poured it into two beautiful glasses.

'Lalique,' he said, as he gave one to her.

'Wow, your friend must be very rich.'

'Yes. Stinking.'

Marguerite looked around the room that she had scarcely registered until now. It was luxurious. Voluminous silk curtains in the windows overlooking the sea, as well as draped around the ornate bed, deep pile carpet, adjoining marble bathroom with gold fittings. They put on their crumpled clothes and, carrying their glasses, Jimmy showed her round the rest of the house with its library, replete with first editions, stylish all-white lounge and dining room, with a massive table for serious entertaining.

'Won't he mind you bringing me here?'

'It's a she. No, she won't mind. We're related, distantly. Anyway, she's in America at the moment. Can you stay the night?'

'No, I have school tomorrow.'

'Phone and say you're ill.'

'It's tempting but no, sorry. I have to be there. Do you mind if we go back now? It's getting late. Shall we clear up here?'

'No need. There's a housekeeper who comes in every day. I'll leave a note and a couple of quid. She'll be very happy with that. Come here.'

He pulled her to him and looked into her eyes.

'Don't leave me again, Marguerite. I need you and I think that you need me.'

Being needed she was familiar with, but apart from Tony, her needing someone was a puzzling concept for Marguerite. Everyone knew good old Marguerite was strong, she was inde-pendent, she was reliable, and she was, she realised, often lonely. With Jimmy today she had felt an overwhelming physical close-ness that even with Tony, whom she did love, she could not experience. She had adored being cosseted, wooed and pos-sessed. And yes, she needed that.

She kissed him and said, 'When shall we meet again?'

They agreed on the following weekend and drowsily drove back to London. The pub was closed when he dropped her off at King's Cross Road. She let herself in, crossed the bar with its smell of stale beer and climbed the stairs, thinking how much had changed since she descended them that morning.

Florrie poked her head round her door.

'How d'it go, lovey?'

'Bliss,' replied Marguerite.

'Oh wonderful. The punters will be thrilled. You go for it, girl.'

Yes, she thought, as she lay in her too-large bed. I will. Why not? I've got nothing to lose.

Chapter 25

Duane had called an urgent staff meeting. Whilst they waited for the headmaster Tony cut to the chase.

'Did you have it off?'

'We made love, yes.'

He hugged her.

'Welcome to the Permissive Society. Better late than never.'

Michael Duane bounced into the staff room with his usual energy.

'I've called you together to discuss the rumours that I know are going around about our school. We have achieved much in our first four years. We have already had some good O level results. Our probationers are down to nine from more than ninety, which is remarkable, and I hope you all agree that the ever-increasing cooperation of the families means that we have become a true community school.'

There was a murmur of agreement from most of the staff, although Marguerite noticed that Mr Fletcher and his gang of naysayers were pursed-lipped. Duane continued, 'However, some of our governors and a couple of the councillors on the LCC are not altogether happy with us.' He laughed. 'I have even heard absurd false rumours that they may close us down. Some of our methods are difficult for people to understand at first, but the results speak for themselves. We will continue to care for and respect our young people in the way we believe is right. I warn you there will be some inspection visits by these sceptics, but I urge you not to be put off by them. You are doing a great job. Thank you.'

Marguerite was dumbfounded. She and Tony were a hundred per cent behind the ethos of the school and proud to be part of it. Duane was one of the most inspirational teachers Marguerite had ever encountered, and she could not believe that the powers that be were not impressed and grateful for the success of his work. She knew nothing of the rumours, but Miss Scott had told her that it was increasingly difficult to find good teachers, which was why class sizes were becoming unwieldy. Marguerite knew there were some who would not apply because they found the school's unorthodox approach alien, but she now wondered whether the talk of closure was putting people off. Where were these rumours coming from?

The staff room was even more divided now. Duane had engaged foreign teachers to help the diverse nationalities of the intake, and they were not welcomed by the diehards. There were frightened supply teachers covering for regular staff who were treated with contempt by some. Mr Fletcher's dislike of the headmaster and constant undermining mockery of his approach had several more sympathisers now. As a teacher of long-standing, he probably knew councillors and governors well enough to report his version of what went on in the school.

It was true that some of it would not look good to outsiders. For instance, when the headmaster discovered that Mickey O'Sullivan, a constant truant, was frightened of maths and history, he made a deal with the boy that he could skip them and do carpentry instead, a lesson he enjoyed. It worked. He turned up for all his other lessons. Duane said, 'He may never be a mathematician or a historian, but at least he'll be able to spell, and write his name, and make a table.'

The school council was also likely to be frowned upon by those who believed that children should do as they are told, and if not be punished as a matter of course. But Marguerite thought it a wonderful way to make children think seriously about justice and living in a community. On one occasion, a school cleaner reported that her shopping basket had been stolen. Duane reported this in assembly, and asked the culprits to come and talk to him in his study. To their credit and his, two boys did. When he told them that they must give the basket back and apologise they admitted they had already eaten most of the contents. The school council was called upon to adjudicate. One child immediately suggested, as she always did, that the boys should be caned.

Duane countered, 'Well, that wouldn't bring back the food, would it?'

'No, but they'd be punished for doing such a rotten thing.'

Duane pointed to the two boys sitting hunched in front of them all, one near to tears.

'I think being here with you all cross with them is a fairly awful punishment. Look at them. They don't look very happy, do they?'

One of the girls said that they should pay Ada the cleaner back what her shopping cost.

'Right, good idea. Let's do the sums. How much was it? And how much do Alan and Jack have?'

After some intense calculations, it came to light that even if they put aside a percentage of their money from paper rounds and Saturday work in the market, it was going to take the boys several weeks to repay Ada.

Then Kenneth White, who was good at art, had an idea.

'Why don't we sell some of our work in the market to raise the money? And if we make more, then we can give her a present to say sorry.'

One of the girls, whose father had a vegetable stall, persuaded him to give them some space, and they not only achieved their objective, but also showed the public how excellent was the work done in the art and handicraft classes.

'How much better a school council,' said Marguerite to Tony, 'than a caning, surely?'

Tony agreed. 'That sort of thing goes on at Bedales, Summerhill and Dartington all the time. But they're middle class, so that's considered OK.'

Mr Fletcher, who overheard them, interrupted.

'Those parents have chosen to send their kids to an experimental school, and paid through the nose for the privilege. Ours thought they were going to a perfectly normal school.'

Marguerite was riled.

'Are you saying it would be more normal if we beat the children?'

Mr Fletcher smiled.

'Well, let's see what the inspectors think.'

The one that walked into the middle of Marguerite's English lesson was a cadaverous man, wearing metal-rimmed glasses and a grey three-piece suit. Councillor Jackson stood at the door, looming over the class, saying nothing, until Marguerite invited him to sit down, and listen to the poems that four of her pupils had chosen to learn. It was an eclectic mix of a brave attempt at a Shakespeare sonnet, a few words from the Beatles song, 'Love Me Do', and Timothy Barker, who was mentally slow, managed 'Old Macdonald Had A Farm', encouraged by animal noises from the class, who knew what a mighty effort it was for him to participate. It was hard to believe, when she remembered what they were like in the early days, how they now loved these performances. There was much laughter and enthusiastic chatter. Marguerite sneaked a look at the inspector to see if he too was having fun. He was not. His only comment as he left was an incredulous, 'You did say that was an English lesson, didn't you, Miss Carter?'

After Councillor Jackson's frosty reaction, it was no surprise to hear from Duane that the overall report was bad. He had been given a list of criticisms. 'The children do not hold authority in awe, and friendliness often degenerates into informality' being one of them. Were it not for the word 'degenerate' Marguerite would have considered the comment was meant as a compliment. The inspector was particularly offended by the CND symbol painted on the playground wall. Mr Duane pointed out that all school-children wrote on walls; he even understood that carving names on wood was not unknown at Eton, but of course they were sometimes famous and successful names, so that was all right.

Duane was doing his best to put on a brave face in public. Staying late one night with a troubled student, Marguerite had passed his open door as she left, and saw him slumped at his desk, a glass of whisky in his hand.

She went in.

'Mike, its serious, isn't it? Are we really in danger of being closed down?'

He looked bewildered.

'No, I can't believe that. It's absurd. Surely no enlightened education authority could be influenced by the predilection of one or two officials. Because that's what it is. Most of them have never been near the school. They couldn't close it on the evidence of a lot of tittle-tattle, could they?'

'We must stand up to them.'

Duane looked exhausted.

'I'll try. But the opposers are as fanatical as I am. They are deeply religious and puritanical, and I am anathema to them, with my humanist assemblies, and sex-education lessons, and, in their eyes, lack of discipline. They mean well. They think I am dangerous. Perhaps I am. People with a mission often are.' He looked at her. 'I recognise the same reforming zeal in you, Marguerite.'

'Tony calls it my Messiah complex.'

'It's a sort of conceit, really. We think we are right, and want to change things to our way. That can lead to terrible things. Hitler thought he was right. So did Stalin.'

'I don't think we are quite in their class.'

He poured her a glass of whisky, and topped up his own.

'Do you know what drives me?'

'No, I sometimes wonder how you keep going, though.'

'I'll tell you something. I was amongst the first troops into Buchenwald concentration camp. It was not just the horror of what we found there – Jesus Christ, such horror – but my own behaviour. Such was my rage I stood by and allowed – watched – relished further atrocities, carried out by my troops in retribution.'

The man hung by his neck from one lamp-post, the woman by her feet from another, her skirt falling back mercifully to hide her tortured face, but much to the delight of the children, displaying her soiled underwear. Marguerite recognises the bloated purple face as Marc, the member of the Milice who had hit Antoine with his gun as he sent him to his death. And she is glad he has suffered.

'It was the depth of human degradation all round. The worst of what we are capable of. So I wanted to cultivate the best in our young. I crave a better, gentler world.'

Marguerite thought it best to stay silent. There was a long pause.

'Forgive me, Marguerite. I have never talked about this before. Even to my wife. But I believe you will understand, from things Tony has hinted at in your past.'

'I do,' said Marguerite, continuing quickly. 'We will fight back. Make them realise how good the school has become. You said a lot of them haven't even visited. I have an idea that I would like to pursue. I have been wanting to do a school play for some time. As part of our propaganda offensive, let's invite all the critical bastards and show them what we can do.'

He smiled.

'You're right. I have been being too defensive. We need to make them see what it's really like here. A school play would be a good start. Thank you. "We shall overcome", eh?'

Marguerite felt her old optimism flooding back.

'Yes. We shall. We bloody well shall.'

Chapter 26

The atmosphere at school was uncomfortable. The staff were keeping a low profile lest supporting Duane should jeopardise future employment were the school really to close. At work Marguerite leant on Tony, who was as determined as she to see off the backstabbers. What little free time she had, she now spent with Jimmy.

Tony was not upset by this.

'I'm delighted for you, Mags. I was so worried that I was in the way of your having a relationship.'

That relationship continued to be a delight and distraction to Marguerite. Jimmy expressed little interest in her work, allowing her to forget about it whilst she was with him, which was a blessed relief. They had good times together. He was not as amusing as Tony, but he was attentive, and the sex was wonderful. Finding places to make love was sometimes a problem. Jimmy had just given up a flat, and not found another, so he was staying with various friends, and occasionally stayed overnight with Marguerite. He was welcomed at the pub, and would often drink with the locals, but her room was not a perfect setting for romance. The owner of the sumptuous house in Brighton had a second in Eaton Square, which they occasionally visited.

Marguerite always felt slightly uneasy about using the house of someone she'd never met, as, putting it politely, a love nest, but Jimmy was very relaxed about it.

'She likes me to enjoy the houses. Don't worry your pretty little head about it.'

'But would she mind you bringing a girlfriend here?'

'She'd be delighted that I had found someone as wonderful as you.'

'But would she—?'

'Shut up about her and give us a kiss.'

Which was how Jimmy always successfully diverted her from conversations that annoyed or bored him. Such was Marguerite's hunger for his lovemaking, it was a successful strategy.

She discussed her affaire de coeur with Tony.

'We don't talk about anything very important. Although he is so passionate in bed, he doesn't show much emotion about other things. It's odd.'

'Give it time, Mags. Men are not so heart-on-sleeve as you girlies.'

'You are.'

'Yes, but I'm gay. Oh. That's the new word for us, by the way.'

'Gay? How strange. Why?'

'Well, some people think it stands for "good as you", but I prefer to think it's because we are rather jolly.'

'You are, my darling, you are. But you are also serious sometimes. He isn't. Except when we first met. He got drunk, and was genuinely upset about his wartime experience then, but he's never talked about it since.'

'Well, neither do you, Mags. Nor do a lot of people. We prefer to forget it, and move on.'

She thought of Duane.

'True. But I don't know what he believes in, or what he wants out of life.'

Tony gave her a hug.

'Don't be so intense. Just relax and enjoy it. He sounds a nice enough bloke, and he's obviously besotted with you. As well he might be, lucky chap. Have a bit of fun, Mags. God knows it's grim at work.'

Actually, despite all the anxiety about the future, Marguerite was enjoying herself devising the school play. It was loosely based on the Nativity story, as it was to be performed at Christmas, and Marguerite thought it might be a good idea to counterbalance Duane's humanism that so disturbed some of the school board. The theme was the bringing of gifts to the infant Jesus. There were two babies due to be born to parents about that time, one Muslim Indian, the other Chinese, and whichever arrived in time would be the real live Christ child. The gifts would be performances of songs, dances, poems from the country of origin of all the various ethnic groups in the school.

For weeks the children made props and rehearsed in corners. Afro-Caribbean parents supervised the making of steel drums in craft lessons. The art department constructed and painted sets, Tony was arranging an acrobatic display, and for safety's sake, the children had to be restrained from cartwheeling in the corridors. Anything the children suggested was considered. Timothy, after his triumph in recitation class, wanted, with the help of his kindly classmates, to give Baby Jesus all the animals in Old Macdonald's Farm, which Marguerite agreed was a lovely present for a baby in a stable. She suggested they could get the whole audience to join in the singing, hoping against hope that it would include the sniffy inspector. The only idea she rejected was Ahmed's proposal of a performing elephant.

The play's organisation took up all her breaks and evenings. Jimmy began to be fretful at her neglect of him. In the pub one night after hours, he suggested they went to spend the night at Eaton Square, as it was Saturday the next day.

'Sorry, no, I've got a rehearsal.'

'On Saturday? I never bloody see you. You care more about those snotty-nosed kids than you do about me. Sorry. I'm just jealous, because I want you to myself.'

'Well, that's sweet of you but it's just not possible at the moment. This is important.'

'And I'm not?'

Florrie and Bob had stopped chattering as they cleared up behind the bar.

'You're being silly.'

'I'm not one of your sodding kids. Don't patronise me.'

Jimmy downed his whisky.

'I'm off. I'm sure you have marking, or making costumes, or something else to do. I don't want to be in your way. Night, Bob – Flo.'

And he was gone.

Florrie came over to where Marguerite was sitting, carrying a brandy.

'Here, get this down you. Mind if I say something?'

'No.'

'Be careful. I know you love your job, but you should look after your man. That's what women do. They have to come first. You don't want to be an old maid, duckie, do you?'

Marguerite didn't see much point in quoting Simone de Beauvoir to Florrie. Anyway, the author's battle-cry about women's rights hadn't seemed to bring Sartre's mistress much joy; just an unfaithful, sometimes cruel, lover, and dodgy relationships with underage girls. Perhaps Florrie and the majority of women, all of whom thought the same, were cleverer than that revered intellectual. Not that Jimmy had talked about marriage, indeed not even about love, but the possibility was there, which was more than she'd had before she met him.

Florrie persisted, 'I don't want to intrude, duckie, but what about kids of your own? I know you love your pupils but it's not the same. My two boys have been the joy of my life and now I'm looking forward to being a grandma. You'll miss out on all of that if you're not careful.'

'I think I already have, Flo. But honestly it doesn't worry me. There's probably something wrong with me that I don't yearn for babies but I made the choice a long time ago to focus on other things.'

'That's sad. It's not too late to change your mind.'

'Yes it is. I told you before, I loved a man once with all my heart. He was the only one I could have imagined creating a family with but I had this crazy vision of being part of something bigger.'

'Bigger than love?'

'Another form of love, I suppose. Love of humanity. Oh God! That sounds so pretentious, I'm sorry.'

Florrie wouldn't give up.

'OK, but let's get down to brass tacks. What about sex? Even you need a bit of that now and again. But you have to make an effort. You don't want to lose him, do you, pet?'

Marguerite thought of his grin, his hands, above all his expert Skylarking.

'No,' she said. 'I don't.'

'Well, get on that phone, and say sorry, there's a good girl.'

'I can't.'

'All right. Don't say sorry but just talk to him. You would if he was one of your stroppy kids.'

'Touché.'

Marguerite gave Jimmy time to get somewhere, and then phoned Stan to see if he knew which friend he might be staying with that night.

'Sorry, miss. We've had a bit of a falling-out over something.'

'No, Stan. That's awful. What?'

'I think it's partly to do with me having found a girl. We're going to get married. Jimmy and me have been muckers since the war, and maybe I've left him out a bit since I found Alison. I feel bad about it. But there are other things too – and I'm afraid my girlfriend doesn't approve of him.'

Suddenly Marguerite understood. No wonder Jimmy was so upset. His best friend had deserted him and then her. She felt guilty. She resolved to track him down even though it was now the small hours of the morning. Starting at Eaton Square.

She rang the bell several times on the shiny black door. Then she nervously tried using the big lion's head knocker, which she thought might be only for decoration. She was about to leave when the door slowly opened and a bedraggled Jimmy peered out.

Squinting, he said, 'Christ, it's you.'

'No, only me, I'm afraid.'

He stared at her through red-rimmed eyes. He was wearing only underpants. and a gaping woman's kimono-style dressing gown.

'Can I come in?'

He clung to the door as he opened it.

'What time is it?' he asked.

'Ten past two.'

He looked puzzled.

'In the afternoon?'

'No, morning.'

'I've had a bit of a skinful.'

'You surprise me.'

'It's your fault. I thought I'd lost you.'

'Well, here I am.'

'Oh I'm so glad. I want to make love to you but I know I stink.'

Without his customary panache he looked pathetic. She felt truly sorry for him.

'Well, how about a shower?'

She stumbles into the bar in Sault. Marcel rushes towards her. 'You got away. Thank God.' She collapses, sobbing, shuddering. He lifts her into his arms and carries her upstairs. He lays her on the bed. As she sinks into the feather mattress, trembling, eyes wide, remembering, speechless, he fetches a basin of warm water and, gently, oh so gently, bathes the blood and filth from her face.

She guided Jimmy up to the bathroom and, as he stood limp and helpless, she disrobed him of his ridiculous pink satin dressing gown and grubby pants. She turned on the shower, took off her own clothes and got in with him. She washed him all over in the perfumed gel hanging on the tap.

I'll give her 'Look after your man', she thought. She continued the ministrations on the bed, insisting on him lying back and leaving things to her. He did. It perked him up no end.

'Thank you, my angel. I feel a lot better now. How about a drink? Champers, old girl?'

The grin had returned.

'I think coffee would be better. I'll go down and make some.'

She enjoyed using the splendid kitchen with all its mod cons. Jimmy's relative had installed the newest machines. One fully automatic monster for washing and drying clothes, even one for washing the dirty dishes. There was an electric coffee-bean grinder. As she used it the nostalgic aroma filled the kitchen. While she was waiting for the kettle to boil, she noticed that, when she had filled it, she had splashed water on a cheque lying beside it. Thinking to dry it out, she saw that it was made out to Jimmy and signed by Daphne Goldstein. It was for £100.

'Good old auntie.' Jimmy was standing in the doorway with a tumbler in one hand and a bottle of whisky in the other, which he indicated. 'Hair of the dog. Getting a beastly hangover.'

'She seems very generous. This auntie of yours.'

'It's a loan, sweetie. Bit short of the readies at the moment.' He gulped back the whisky.

'You don't want coffee then?'

'Yes. I'll have that as well. And there's some Fernet Branca in the cupboard. I'll have a swig of that. Bit of an expert at hangovers.'

As he poured some of the liqueur into a small glass his hands shook.

'How will you pay her back? Have you found a job?'

He swigged back the glass of brown, evil-looking liquid in one.

'Ugh. It looks promising, yes.'

'Doing what?'

He tapped his finger on the side of his nose.

'Don't want to talk about it till it's all signed and sealed.'

'You can tell me, surely?'

'Why so serious? We're together again. Let's talk about that.'

He sat on a stool by the breakfast counter and gazed at her blearily.

'Show us your knickers – go on.'

Marguerite was not to be diverted this time.

'If we are to be together, we have to be honest with one another.'

'Well, I honestly want to see your knickers.' He moved towards her. She pushed him away.

'No. we have to talk. I don't understand what's going on here. It makes me uneasy. Is your aunt supporting you? Is that how you manage to wear mohair suits and silk shirts, to run a car, to take me to smart restaurants and buy me presents? With the money she gives to you?'

'No!' He was now shouting. 'She doesn't give it to me. I bloody well earn it.'

He looked desperate.

'OK. I'll tell you. She pays me. She pays me a salary for taking care of the houses. I'm a glorified houseboy. Or I suppose, at forty years old, that should be house-man. Or servant. How's that for a brave war hero?'

'Is that why you haven't got a place of your own? You can't afford it?'

'Oh I could afford something. I don't just do housekeeping, you know. I've got other talents. I could get a grotty room somewhere, but I prefer to stay most of the time in luxury here or in Brighton. But I earn money all right. Haven't you noticed in the pub? I can pull a nifty pint. Oh yes, I'm the toast of all the sordid dives in Soho. As a barman. And I occasionally do a turn as a waiter.' He looked at her. 'So now you know. Not in your class at all, I'm afraid.'

He stopped, hid his face in his hands and said quietly, 'And that's why I didn't want you to know.'

'Do you seriously consider I would think like that? You really don't know me at all, do you?'

'I know you're clever and too good for me. And brave.'

'So are you.'

'You think so?' His voice was mocking.

'I know so. You got a medal for it.'

He poured himself another whisky.

She continued, 'More importantly, this last year I have had a wonderful time with you. But looking at you now, in that ridiculous dressing gown, shaking and wretched, and hearing you tell the truth about yourself, now' – she kissed his forehead – 'now I love you.'

'Really?' His face lit up. Then the little-boy grin. 'Prove it. Come upstairs.'

She ruffled his hair.

'You're hopeless.'

She loved his sudden changes of mood. She would have preferred him to make some verbal commitment, but she nevertheless felt they had moved into a deeper stage of their relationship.

'I am now really in love with him,' she told Tony at rehearsal the next day. 'He's vulnerable and needy, and I want to help him.'

Tony looked quizzical.

'Not sure that's a perfect formula for falling in love, is it?'

'Maybe it is for me.'

Chapter 27

The last week of rehearsals was a challenge. Even Tony was worried.

'Some of the kids are getting very edgy about the play. It's going to be tricky controlling them. They're very overexcited.'

'As Mr Fletcher and his cronies never cease telling me.'

Marguerite feigned a confidence she did not feel.

'I've got all of them together for the first time this afternoon. I'll talk to them.'

Tony was right. As the youngsters crowded into the hall for the rehearsal it was bedlam.

Marguerite used a loudhailer to get their attention.

'OK, calm down, all of you. We have a lot of work to do, so you're going to have to shut up and concentrate. Neither one of your favourite things, I know, but there is a lot hanging on this performance of yours. It's no secret that our school is in danger. We want to show them how good we can be, and what a splendid school this is. That means behaving courteously to our visitors, and towards each other, and doing your parts as well as you possibly can. OK?'

There were cheers and shouts of 'Yea!'.

'Right, school. We'll show 'em, won't we?'

Even louder shouts and cheers.

'OK, you have been given the order you appear in, so be ready to come on when it's your turn.'

The rehearsal was a shambles with Marguerite yelling orders through her megaphone and Tony and the supporting staff trying to herd the confused children into place. Throughout the week intensive rehearsals continued until everyone was exhausted, but gradually the play was taking shape.

On the night of the performance the children were terrified but determined not to let the school down. Marguerite was backstage helping them dress in the wonderful costumes made by the needlework group, which included some boys, surely destined for a great future in tailoring. The hall was packed with people standing round the sides. It seemed the whole of Islington had turned up, some of them doubtless to see what the teara-ways from this comprehensive of ill repute would get up to. Marguerite thought that the governors and LCC representatives would have to admit that it was a true community school.

The school orchestra played an overture, composed by the pupils and guided by Mr Davis, the head of music. Those who took conventional instrument classes were augmented by others with musical saws, mouth organs and washboards. The result was triumphantly tuneful and witty. The curtain drew across to reveal an Irish Virgin Mary, holding an Indian baby and standing beside them an Afro-Caribbean Joseph. Mary explained that she was expecting guests, and there followed a succession of extraor-dinary performances. The children had responded to the idea of trying to cheer up a poor family, who were tired and uncom-fortable and had a new baby to take care of. An experience not unknown to many of them.

The Greek children, arms around each other's shoulders,

swayed gracefully in circles and lines, the Turkish girls did a rather wriggly belly dance. The Irish contingent, led by a no-longer truanting Mickey O'Sullivan, did a wondrous jig, bodies erect, and small feet going like the clappers. The steel band had everyone jiving in the aisles, and the audience also, as hoped, joined in with Timothy's farm noises. A surprise item for Marguerite in this sequence was Ahmed entering astride two of his friends in an elephant skin.

The music was beautiful. The choir sang 'Greensleeves' and some African chants, and an English boy and an Indian girl gave a poignant performance of the duet, 'Somewhere' from *West Side Story*. Miss Allum, now a much-loved member of staff, had transcribed a piece of Mozart to be played by four of her star pupils on two pianos. Five of the juniors played Bob Dylan's 'Blowin' In The Wind' on combs wrapped in lavatory paper; the result was surprisingly haunting. There was poetry, jiving, acrobatics, a stage full of youngsters doing the new twist, and audience and children doing a spirited rendering of a song by their favourite group the Beatle's, 'She Loves You'. Even Marguerite, her sweaty hand clasped by Tony, was astounded by their confidence. They did what they had practised but with added zest. When Hymie Cohen's Elvis Presley split his pants, his giggling backing singers spontaneously created a circle round him as he shimmied off the stage.

The children gave everything they had got, and what they had got was joyful high spirits. Tony told them afterwards that he betted Joseph, Mary and Jesus would much have preferred their concert to a load of old frankincense and myrrh. Looking at the audience, Marguerite could see that they were uplifted and moved by the beauty of the children's fervour, and she knew that the critics could not help but be swept up in this great surge of youthful energy.

At the end, all the performers took their bows, and stood in wonderment as the audience raised the roof with their cheers. Tony and Marguerite hugged each other and jumped up and down.

'We've won, Tony, we've won. They'll never close us now.'

Duane came up and congratulated them and the children.

'What did they say? Did they like it?'

He hesitated.

'I'll tell you tomorrow.'

Marguerite was appalled.

'They didn't! You're joking. How could they possibly not have?'

'I'm sorry, Marguerite.' He put his hand on her shoulder.

'What? What did they say?'

'They didn't come.'

'What? None of them?'

'Not one.'

Marguerite shook her head in disbelief.

'Bastards. What unutterable bastards.'

'I fear their minds are made up. They couldn't face us, although apparently we're having one more inspection next week, so there's still hope. I'm so sorry, Marguerite, it was a wonderful play and, whatever the outcome, all of us will be able to cherish this memory.'

When the news got about of the continued, every-growing threat to the school, the parents and local community, fired by the magnificent play, were incensed. People not used to political action, or indeed standing up to authority in any way, were galvanised into protest. A public meeting was held in which feelings ran high.

'Why is nobody talking to us parents about this?'

'Our kids have been mucked about. They've already changed schools once. Nobody cares about them.'

'We're not going to be shat on by a load of toffee-nosed gits in some office up West.'

'Mr Duane's a good man and a wonderful headmaster. It's awful that they are being so insulting to him.'

The official reasons given for the proposed closure was that people didn't want to send their children to the school, so the rolls were falling, and another institution needed the premises.

'Of course the bloody rolls are falling,' raved Tony, 'with all the rumours of closure and the campaign of undermining by that arsehole Fletcher and his council cronies.

When the visiting inspector, Councillor Jackson, came again into Marguerite's class he was openly hostile. Marguerite tried her best to be polite when he constantly interrupted with asinine comments. The children had been warned to be on their best behaviour and she could see the usually outspoken Sammy Bream actually physically biting his lip.

It was a senior class and the topic was contemporary playwrights, about which they were extremely knowledgeable after frequent theatre visits. It was obvious from the harrumphing that came from Councillor Jackson that he was not altogether happy about them discussing Pinter and Wesker, although Marguerite doubted he knew much about them. When it came to Shelagh Delaney's *A Taste of Honey* he could contain himself no longer. He had heard about this one from the scandalised reaction in the tabloid press.

'Really, Miss Carter, I do not think this is suitable material for young people.'

Sammy Bream had had enough.

'Oh shut up, you stupid old prick,' he shouted.

Councillor Jackson flushed bright red and responded, 'Listen to me, young man, I do not think the fact that I consider a play about homosexuality, illegitimacy and mixed marriage unsuitable for children, makes me a prig.'

To prevent Sammy landing himself in more trouble, Marguerite intervened politely.

'Excuse me, Councillor Jackson. I think you misheard Sammy. What he actually called you was "a stupid old prick". It's an easy mistake. I've made it myself. "Prick" is slang for a man's genitals, "cock", "penis". It's in the dictionary. Ursula, give the gentleman yours, will you?'

The girl gave it to him and, in her determination to be courteous, curtsied as she did so.

'You can look it up. I feel inclined to congratulate Sammy on an apposite use of language. Don't you agree, class?'

They were a few mumbled 'Yes, miss'es amongst the giggles.

'Maybe one could question the choice of the word "old". Perhaps "middle-aged" would be better, do you think?'

The children were now falling about with laughter.

'Yes, I think so too. So— ' She crossed to write on the blackboard. 'We now have' – the chalk squeaked as she wrote – '"you stupid middle-aged prick". Excellent. Descriptive, vivid, and above all accurate. Congratulations, class.'

Councillor Jackson turned on his heel and stormed out of the room. The pupils stamped and cheered. Marguerite was shaking. She had allowed her pent-up fury to make her behave rashly. But at least she had shown the children that you can stand up to destructive and ignorant authority figures. Speak truth to power. Albeit ideally less rudely than she had. Anyway it had made them all feel a lot better and she knew, in her heart of hearts, that the stupid middle-aged prick was going to condemn them anyway.

Chapter 28

The future of the school remained uncertain. Duane and the staff that supported him did their best to keep things as normal as possible for the children's sake, as, for many of them, the school was the only stability in their lives. Mr Fletcher and his gang slunk around looking furtive. Marguerite did her best, after her outburst with the inspector, to restrain the fury she felt towards them for the harm they were doing to the youngsters she loved and admired. She forced herself to write an abject apology to Councillor Jackson for her behaviour, pleading that it was her 'time of the month'. She judged that, inhibited puritan that he was, he would be too embarrassed to take the matter further if it involved discussing female functions. It irked her to be so craven but the well-being of the school was paramount.

This preoccupation came at a cost to her private life. Especially in respect of Jimmy. Whereas she knew she had given many of her pupils the confidence that comes from self-respect, the teacher in Marguerite felt she had not addressed Jimmy's feeling of inferiority. She wanted him to realise that he did not have to impress her with smart restaurants and champagne. Having made a crack in the veneer of his glamorous lifestyle, she wanted to delve into his real world, the world he had opted to keep secret from her. It was not easy. How to suggest they choose less expensive amusements without highlighting his lack of money? Such was his view of how a man should behave, it was difficult to suggest that she pay her way, let alone his, although she was better off than him. It boosted his ego to invent enjoyable distractions from her woes at work. When she raged at the neglect of the governing body to acknowledge the children's massive efforts to make the play such a triumph she would have liked him to discuss it with her, but he merely came up with, 'Let's go for a slap-up meal at the Savoy. That'll cheer you up, old girl.'

Rather than say, 'You can't afford it,' she said, 'There are some lovely little cafés in Soho, I believe. I'd love to go to one of those and then maybe visit where you work.'

He said at once, 'Soho is not your scene, Marguerite. You wouldn't like it.'

'You're so wrong about me, Jimmy. Stop thinking about me as some stuck-up teacher. I love Soho. I often shop there.'

'That's different. Not the Italian delis and nice restaurants. We're talking serious sleaze here. I want to take you to nice places.'

Marguerite was determined not to let go of the opportunity that his honesty over his earnings had presented. As with the children at school, she needed an all-round picture if she was to help him out of the corner which he seemed to have got himself trapped. For such an accomplished lover he was lamentably lacking in confidence, and that limited his ambition to make something of himself.

When she shared those thoughts with Tony he said, 'Blimey, you sound like his mother.'

'Oh sod off. I've got Florrie lecturing me on not taking care of my man, then you mock me for doing so.'

'Sweetie, don't take any notice of me. I'm just an ageing poof.

What do I know? Let's face it – neither of us is going to get a job with the Marriage Guidance Council.'

Her persistence paid off, and Jimmy was persuaded that a guided tour of his Soho haunts would be diverting fun for her. She arranged to meet him in a restaurant he had chosen in Greek Street. Meandering from Piccadilly Circus tube station to the back streets of Soho, Marguerite realised Jimmy was right. She had not been to Soho for several years and was astounded by the change. The village atmosphere of quaint shops run by all nationalities had been spoilt by the sex trade. The narrow alleys and roads were disfigured by myriad signs advertising so-called clubs, and frighteningly young girls stood in halls and at the bottom of filthy stairs, offering membership, entitling men to see 'live kinky sex show' or some such delight. There were dozens of new bookshops, which did not look as though they stocked Jane Austen, and other premises that sold objects and clothing that spoke of more complex sexual adventures than she had ever encountered. Yet again, thought Marguerite furiously, the powers that be had sought to impose their wrong-headed order on a situation of which they were completely ignorant. The women selling 'a good time' on the streets of Soho in the 1950s had been part of the community. By passing a law to ban them, did they imagine the whole thing would go away? Be restricted to lords and government ministers like Profumo cavorting with naked girls in stately homes? Which was perfectly all right, unless the minister in question told a lie in their sacred House of Commons. Then, blame the man who organised the parties, and drive him, Stephen Ward, to suicide and forget all about it. That's the way to deal with it, they thought. Banish it from sight. Get rid of the prostitutes. Close down difficult schools, and banish their trouble-making headmasters.

It was a relief to walk into the cosy atmosphere of Bianchi's restaurant, where she had arranged to meet Jimmy, and be greeted by a gracious Italian-looking plump middle-aged woman with a London accent.

'Jimmy has told me about you. Welcome.' And she led Marguerite to a table in the corner where he rose to greet her.

'She's lovely. I approve,' said the woman. 'You will have the risotto as always, and I suggest my special ravioli for the lady.' And she disappeared into the back kitchen. It was apparently not up for discussion.

Marguerite was surprised.

'She knows you.'

'Yes, I'm a regular here. Have some wine. It's a very good little Pinot Grigio.'

She looked around at the tables laid with immaculate white cloths and shining cutlery and glass and at the photos of famous diners on the walls.

'I was thinking more of a little café, when I suggested Soho. This seems quite posh.'

He raised his eyes to the sky.

'Don't worry, I can afford it.'

It was a delicious lunch, and Marguerite enjoyed it, despite Jimmy's strange discomfort. The owner herself looked after them, whilst a waiter served the rest of the quite small room. Out of the corner of her eye Marguerite saw him give Jimmy a thumbs-up sign. Which Jimmy ignored.

The proprietor came to the table.

'Did you enjoy your meal?'

'Very much. Thank you. It was delicious.'

'I'll have the bill, please,' said Jimmy.

'Don't be ridiculous,' said the woman. 'It's on me. And you needn't come in tonight. We're not very busy.'

Marguerite was stunned.

When they got outside she said, 'You work there.'

Jimmy's eyes darted as if searching for an answer.

'What's up with you, Jimmy? I was bound to find out. And what does it matter? It's a lovely place, the owner is fond of you. Why pretend?'

He looked genuinely bewildered.

'I don't know. I suppose I just can't face—'

'What?'

'What I am.'

'As far as I can see you are someone these people are very fond of. What's wrong with that?'

'I want you to respect me.'

'Well, I won't if you keep lying to me.'

She was angry and unsettled about this strange behaviour, but mindful of the fact that some children behave badly to draw attention to themselves, she decided to ignore her inclination to leave. Besides, he looked so forlorn.

It started to rain.

'Let's get inside somewhere.'

He brightened at once.

'OK, let's go for a drink.'

'We can't. The pubs are closed till 5.30.'

'Come with me. Anything is possible if you are in the know. You want the truth? I'll show you somewhere else that I work.'

Jimmy took her arm protectively as they walked to the next street. They passed a group of reeling football fans regaled in red-and-white scarves and rosettes, whirling their wooden rattles and shouting. Their chanting was brought to a halt by a Brylcreemed, silk-suited man stepping from a filthy doorway, followed by a dazed-looking, near-naked, nubile girl. Above him was a crudely hand-painted board with the stark promise of 'A live double-act show on bed'. Some negotiation went on and the football fans stepped sniggering inside.

'Poor sods,' muttered Jimmy.

After edging past smelly dustbins, they groped their way down the dark stairway that led to their next port of call. At the bottom was a battered door. As Jimmy pushed it open, a voice from inside bellowed, 'If you're not a member – fuck off.'

Jimmy shouted back, as he went in, 'No one's a member, you silly moo, and watch your language. I'm bringing a lady to meet you.'

The room was small, dimly lit and smoky, with little more than a threadbare carpet, a piano, some sagging armchairs and sofas, and a wilting cheese plant. Seated majestically on a high stool at the bamboo bar was a woman with black hair scraped back from her face, and pencilled eyebrows over hooded eyes that missed nothing.

'A lady? This place is full of ladies, duckie. Look at her over there and her in the corner.' She pointed to a respectable-looking man in a suit, and a policeman in uniform.

'I'm Mavis.' She scrutinised Marguerite's face. 'Do you want a drinkette then, my pretty pedigree ginger pussycat?'

Marguerite asked for a gin and tonic. Mavis clambered off her stool and went behind the bar to pour the drinks. Marguerite noticed she drew a double whisky for Jimmy from the optic without even asking.

Marguerite whispered, 'Is this a gay club?'

Jimmy explained, 'It's anything you like. Those two are perfectly normal, but Mavis calls everyone "miss" and "lady". This is the Dominion Club – a dive where people come to drink when the pubs are closed. You're supposed to be a member, but the membership is a question of whether Mavis likes the look of you or not. She's very choosy.'

That was proven as a man with glasses tentatively came in the door and she bellowed, 'Piss off – you're not pretty enough to be a member of my clubette, four-eyes.'

Sitting on her bar stool again, she chain-smoked, adding to the choking fug. The cigarette in a long ivory holder, held in elegant blood-red-nailed fingers, was used to languidly point to the subjects of her savage wit. To a woman whom Marguerite recognised as the star of a current West End show, who was talking loudly about her latest triumph, she directed her cigarette accusingly. 'If you don't belt up, Gertie, you'll be barred. You're boring the arse off all of us.'

To which the victim replied, 'You won't bar me, Madam Muck. You need my money. I'm the only bugger who pays for my drinks.'

Mavis thought for a bit.

'Yes, that's true. You can stay.'

Turning to look at Marguerite, she asked Jimmy, 'Does it talk, this one? Or is it just for decoration?'

Jimmy replied, 'You're frightening her to death, you awful woman.'

'How dare you. I'm a sweet little lambikins. Well, she can stay because I love you. Give your mother a kiss.' He did and she turned to Marguerite. 'I adore him because he stood up to that naughty Mrs Hitler.'

A willowy young man appeared behind the bar.

'Oh there you are, Amadeus. Get to bloody work. What do I pay you for, or rather what does the toast of the West End over there pay you for?'

She slapped the pianist on the backside as he made his way to the piano.

'Classically trained. And he's ended up in this shithole. Where did it all go wrong, Ludwig?'

Marguerite sat next to Jimmy on a lumpy sofa and looked

around. It was the oddest social venue she had ever been to. It was as though a bizarre party was being given for people that one didn't notice in the daylight outside, if it was still daylight – there was no way of telling. Time was suspended in this basement. They were creatures of the underworld.

Everyone seemed to know one another, and Jimmy. One Hogarthian old woman, who looked and smelled as if her clothes had not been washed for a long time, staggered towards them and leant over him. 'Get us a drink, Jim,' she slurred, giving a toothless smile.

'Don't you dare,' Mavis intervened. 'They won't let her in the hostel if she gets any more pissed.'

She crossed to put her arm round the old woman and, with surprising tenderness, led her to the door and up the stairs. Jimmy told a shocked Marguerite that when she was young the woman had been a great beauty and modelled for several major artists, two of whom still came to the club.

The habitués of this closeted world seemed to have little in common but their devotion to alcohol. Each new arrival was greeted warmly by the clientele and insultingly by Mavis. The laughter became raucous as the drinks flowed. One ignored woman in the corner wept continuously.

When Marguerite pointed her out to Jimmy he said, 'Don't worry, she enjoys it. She can let it all hang out here and nobody cares.'

Jimmy was proudly introducing Marguerite to one strange character after another, some of whom expressed exaggerated pleasure in welcoming a new person to their bibulous fold, and some of whom ignored her completely. She was trying to understand a rambling tale of woe told by a man in a floral dress, about an outrageous arrest for being drunk and disorderly, when she was conscious of a hush descending on the room.

Two aliens had descended from the real world outside. A young woman, tall, with blonde hair in an upswept beehive hairdo revealing diamond earrings, and wearing a white dress, low-cut to set off a string of pearls, stood in the doorway. Behind her was a short middle-aged man, immaculate in bowtie and dinner suit.

As everyone stared at the couple, Mavis drawled, 'Hello, darlings, doing a bit of slumming, are we? OK, animals, don't just stare – perform for the two ladies. Do louche, do bohemian, do the scum of the earth. Give them their money's worth.'

The young woman strode to the counter.

'Two double whiskies, please.'

Mavis didn't budge.

'I don't think so. I think it's champagne all round, don't you, petal?' She looked across to the man cowering in the doorway. 'The party's on you, you lucky lady. Open your handbag, Lottie, and let's party. Do the honours, Jimmy.'

The little man was hauled into the club, and everyone beamed as they told him what a fine chap he was. Jimmy meanwhile opened several bottles of champagne and handed out glasses to the grabbing hands.

Marguerite noticed that the young woman was talking to Mavis, who went to the till and handed her several £5 notes. She turned round to put them in her satin pochette. Peering through the gloom, Marguerite gasped. As Jimmy had taken his working stance behind the now-busy bar, Marguerite left her seat in the shadowy corner and walked towards the young woman.

Her face lit up as she caught sight of Marguerite.

'Miss Carter. Bloody hell. What on earth are you doing here?'

'It is Elsie, is it? I wasn't sure. You've changed so much.'

'I knew you at once. I'd recognise your lovely hair anywhere, Miss Carter. What are you doing in this dump?'

'I'm here with a friend. There, behind the bar.'

Elsie looked surprised.

'Jimmy?'

'You know him?'

'Only by repute. From coming here. I thought . . .' She trailed off.

'Are you here often then?'

The noise from the champagne-drinking clientele was becoming deafening.

Marguerite said, 'Let's go outside. I can't hear myself think in here.'

They retreated up the stairs and stood by the dustbins.

'Fag?' Elsie took out a cigarette from a silver case and, in cupped hands, lit one for each of them. Then she took a pill from a small box and gulped it down without water.

'Have you got a headache?'

'No, it's a magic pill. I've got a long night ahead with that boring old git. Do you want one? They give you a real high. Purple hearts, they're called.'

'No, thank you.'

'They're harmless. You get them from the doctor.'

'So, Elsie. Who is the boring old git?'

'A customer. I work for an escort agency. High-class one. He's down from Manchester and I'm showing him the sights and keeping him company.'

'And this club is one of the sights?'

'Yes, they love it. They think it's really cool.'

'And what do you think, Elsie?'

'I don't think anything. It's my job. And I get extra from Mavis and others for bringing them customers.' Her eyes were bright. 'I'm doing really well, Miss Carter. I'm making a bomb.'

Unlike Jimmy, there was a refreshing honesty about the girl's attitude to the way she earned a living that made it possible for Marguerite to ask, 'And do you sleep with these men?'

'Not unless I want to. Most are quite happy to just talk and be with someone who knows her way around. Someone attractive, that they can show off about.' She looked diffidently at Marguerite. 'Do you think I'm attractive, Miss Carter? Bit different from when you last saw me, eh?'

'You look very glamorous, Elsie.'

'I bought these earrings myself. They're real diamonds. Only little, but real. What about that?'

Faced with this slightly frantic enthusiasm, which Marguerite supposed might be related to the pill, she could only reply, 'Congratulations, Elsie. They're lovely earrings. But—'

'No. No buts, miss, please. I know you would rather I was a teacher or something but I bet I earn a lot more than you. And anyway it wasn't possible.'

'I know, Elsie. I'm sorry. How is your child?'

'He's fine. Well looked after,' she continued quickly. 'You probably think the trouble you took with me was wasted, but it wasn't. Especially the acting. I use it all the time. The old git thinks I find him fascinating, funny, clever, handsome. *Saint Joan* was a piece of cake compared to this.'

They laughed together. Marguerite hugged the girl and said, 'Oh Elsie, take good care of yourself, please. Go easy on those pills.'

'I'm fine, Miss Carter. Unlike that lot downstairs, I hardly drink at all. Well, better get back and rescue my client from those vultures or he won't have enough money left to pay me. Have a dab of perfume, take away the dustbin smell.'

She took a small bejewelled phial from her bag and dabbed the fragrance behind Marguerite's ears.

'Thank you. It's lovely. Joy, isn't it?'

'Yes. Do you use it?'

'No. I knew someone who did. Years ago.'

'Don't leave me, Maman. I don't want you to go. Who will look after me? I'm frightened.'

'I like the smell. It cheers me up.'

'I wish you joy, Elsie my dear.'

'And you, Miss Carter.'

Elsie scrutinised her face in the mirror of a gold powder compact.

Colonel Buckmaster looks embarrassed. 'I always give the blokes ciga-rette cases before they go into action. I thought this was more fitting for you. Don't worry, it's French-made so quite safe to take with you. Must keep that pretty nose powdered, eh?'

He shakes her hand. 'Good luck, my dear.' He smiles but his eyes look troubled.

'Are the scars showing?' Elsie asked Marguerite.

'Hardly at all.'

Marguerite followed Elsie down the basement stairs and saw that the unfortunate git was handing over wads of notes to Mavis. Then he and Elsie left, ignored by the revellers, who with the champagne drained dry were back to their usual gossiping.

Jimmy came over and hissed, 'Where the hell have you been?'

'Talking to Elsie. Why?'

'You're here with me. You should stay with me. They see you disappearing with that slag it makes me look a fool.'

'She is not a slag, as you put it. She is an ex-pupil of mine of whom I am very fond.'

'She's a buddy of Mavis, who's a dyke, so if you disappear with her, the bitchery starts. What did you talk about?'

'Jimmy, you're drunk. Stop this. I told you, she was a pupil of mine.'

'I'm sick to death of your pupils. You're here to meet my friends. Did she talk about me?'

'No.'

'Right. Here's your coat.' He threw it at her and got into his trench coat and hat.

Mavis was watching this scene like a hawk watching its prey. She clapped her hands.

'Oh look, everybody, a lovers' tiff. We like those, don't we? Breaks the monotony of the sweetness and light we usually have down here.'

They hadn't gone more than a hundred yards up the road in stony silence before Jimmy doubled up dramatically, and started moaning, 'I'm sorry, I'm sorry, I'm so sorry.'

Marguerite said nothing.

With his head hanging down over his knees he howled, 'I'm jealous of anyone who takes you from me, even for a minute. You're so beautiful I can't believe that every man, and even every woman, doesn't want to steal you from me. Especially in that place.'

Marguerite was rooted to the spot. He grabbed a lamp-post, lit a cigarette and leaned against it, looking at her piteously.

'Don't leave me alone, Marguerite.'

She started to giggle.

Jimmy looked affronted.

'What are you laughing at?'

Marguerite, who had had a few glasses of champagne herself, spluttered, 'Don't worry, Jimmy, "you're never alone with a Strand".'

In a trice, despair abandoned, there it was again. The lopsided grin.

Chapter 29

'It's the end of an era,' said Marguerite.

She and Tony were standing on London Bridge in the pouring rain, surrounded by mourning men and women, and wide-eyed children. Sir Winston Churchill's coffin, covered in the Union Jack, with some of his many decorations on top, was piped on board a boat that was to take it upriver to Waterloo, and thence to the grave in his country home. Bagpipes played a melancholy dirge and a military band struck up with 'Rule, Britannia!' as the boat set sail. Planes swooped by in a fly-past, but most moving of all, the cranes in the dockyards all slowly lowered their huge arms in unison like a herd of weeping pre-historic beasts. The crowd was still and silent, but there was much dabbing of tears with hankies, and a child was crying his eyes out, bewildered by the adults' grief.

It was a while since Marguerite and Tony had spent time together. This melancholy occasion could not be classified as one of their treats, but Marguerite was glad to be sharing it with Tony. Jimmy had flatly refused to even watch the momentous event on television, having never forgiven Churchill for order-ing the Bomber Command operations during the war, and then ignoring any reference to the participants in the victory tributes, when the justification for the annihilating raids was in question.

'He was a great man,' said Marguerite.

'You can say that? When the old bugger destroyed your fleet? And you were on our side?'

'It was war, Tony. The Nazis were on the other side of the Channel and we didn't stand a chance, but he got us through it. By sheer force of his personality. When you listen to the likes of mealy-mouthed Wilson, you wonder how a man could be so brutally honest as Churchill was. "Blood, sweat and tears", "fighting them on the beaches" and "never surrendering". All that.'

'Yes, he certainly had the gift of the gab.'

'He was a great orator. The present lot are non-entities in comparison.'

Despite the rain they decided to walk along the South Bank and have lunch at a café they knew near the Royal Festival Hall, all that was left of the Festival of Britain. The desolation of the empty muddy landscape around the hall was especially poignant when they remembered the optimism of their younger selves on that heady day in 1951.

'I've got a bit jaded since then,' said Marguerite. 'Especially at the moment. The end of Churchill is in the natural course of things. His time has passed. But I can't believe that we are seeing the destruction of the future, because that is what Duane is. Or should be.'

The situation at Risinghill was desperate. It seemed incredible to both of them that one or two retrograde councillors and a handful of teachers could bring an end to such an imaginative way forward, before it had had a chance to prove itself. The parents and children were fighting back hard, but learning that, when it came to the crunch, democracy did not work in their favour. The absence of any of their critics at the school play proved that the powers that be were not listening to them. The pupils even organised a march to Downing Street with home-made banners and steel band accompaniment, but no one heeded them. The insecurity of their futures unsettled the children and it was difficult to control their anger. Mickey, the serial truant, disappeared again, and Marguerite saw no point in trying to persuade him to return to such instability.

Over a Welsh rarebit, Tony questioned Marguerite about Jimmy.

'Is he a comfort to you while all this is going on?'

'He certainly takes my mind off it when I'm with him.'

'Do you love him, Mags?'

'I think I do. He's feckless. I get furious with him, but he wins me round. He's irresistible. You know I like to collect lame ducks, so yes, I do love him.'

Tony put down his knife and fork and looked at her.

'Good. Because I've got something to tell you.'

Marguerite felt a pang of fear.

'I, too, have fallen in love.'

She stared at him.

'I know. Hard to believe. Sad old queen that I am, but I've found a bono homi and I think this is it. So he's moving into my flat.'

Her mouth was dry.

'Why didn't you tell me before?'

'Why didn't you tell me about Jimmy straight away?'

'Fair enough.'

Theirs was a curious relationship. The rules were not clear. Each had thought the other would be upset about a serious commitment to someone else, although they had no claim on any conventional sort of loyalty. Marguerite was shocked at how devastated she felt about Tony's news. She managed a smile, but found it difficult to know what to say.

'Why, that's wonderful, Tony. What's he like?'

'He's a hoofer with the Royal Ballet. Far too beautiful and clever and young for me. Can't think what he sees in me.'

'He's lucky to have you.' And she meant it.

'Why don't you and Jimmy come to supper and meet him?'

'No – no, not Jimmy. One thing at a time.'

Marguerite did not want to introduce Jimmy to Tony, partly because she didn't think they would have much in common, but also because they belonged in separate compartments of her life. It was less complicated that way.

Normally when she was going to meet Tony she felt her spirits rise, but when a couple of evenings later she walked round the terraces of Myddelton Square, she felt disorientated. The ground was shifting under her feet at work, and in her private life. The front door had been newly painted in shiny dark blue. Before she could ring the bell, the door opened. 'Marguerite. I'm so pleased to meet you at last.' His voice was soft. 'I'm Donald. Welcome.'

Whatever she had expected of 'a hoofer from the Royal Ballet' it was not this. Donald was tall and slender, yes, and his dancer's feet turned out, but he was quietly courteous with no trace of flamboyance.

'Come into our humble abode.'

It was anything but humble. Tony's flat was transformed from its usual messy state. It shouted baroque style. The walls were covered, floor to ceiling, in paintings and photos, some of which were of Donald in dance pose. The sofas and cushions were upholstered in rich velvets and brocades and the curtains were silken. In the corner a table was bedecked with exquisite china and lit with candles. She could see Tony watching her from the kitchen.

She said, 'Tony, this is beautiful.'

'Oh it's all him. As you know, I've always lived in a slum from childhood onwards. But he's got taste. That's the only reason I've shacked up with him.'

'Get back into the kitchen, slave,' said Donald. Marguerite noticed the look that passed between them. She felt like an outsider.

The meal was delicious but Marguerite could not settle into her changed role in Tony's life. The proud smiles, the gentle mockery, the touching, the ease with one another bespoke a closeness between the two men that she was not part of. They both made every effort to include her, but she was a visiting friend. Donald had taken over her role, and she could not find a new one. It was an awkward evening. When it ended, Donald took her to the door.

In the hall he said, 'Marguerite, I know how close you and Tony are. That won't change. I promise you.' And he kissed her on the forehead. Marguerite could see why Tony felt as he did. It didn't help her to think that Donald was a thoroughly nice man.

As she walked back to King's Cross Road, her throat and jaw were stiff with held-back sobs. It was absurd, she knew that. She had been having an affaire de coeur, and Tony had never objected, in fact he had been delighted for her. She had no claim on him, but the thought of someone else taking first place in his life was unbearably painful to her. She was ashamed of her selfishness. She passed a telephone box and considered calling Jimmy at the club, to come and comfort her, but she knew that he would not comprehend why she felt as she did and it would probably trigger a jealous outburst. Instead she had a brandy in the saloon bar and poured her heart out to Flo, as she cleared up the pub after closing time.

'Well, lovey, perhaps it's all for the good. He's a nice man, Tony, but now you can concentrate on Jimmy. There's more future in that for you.'

Marguerite was not keen on contemplating the future. Surviving the present was taking all her energy.

The final decision about the school had been taken. It was to be closed in its present form, and reopened under a new headmaster, charged with changing the liberal, 'unruly' ethos created by Duane. Duane and Miss Scott would be 'let go', a euphemism, Marguerite learned, for being sacked. Her instinct was to resign in protest, but Duane, ever concerned for his pupils, persuaded her to stay as a much-loved teacher and give the children some sense of continuity. Tony too would stay on as sports master. It was a wretched outcome and Marguerite was in despair.

On the final day of term, when the five-year journey that they had all been on was terminated, there was an overall sense of disbelief. The children, especially the seniors, were distraught. Tough boys, whose lives had made them ready for anything, were yet crying in the toilets. Long after the rest of the school had gone home, Duane's study was full of troubled youngsters. Never had Marguerite admired this exceptional man more than on that last day. He focused entirely on building up the confidence of his children and their parents. He restrained a gang intent on destroying the school – 'If we can't have it, no one else can' – explaining that nothing was gained by harming others because you had been harmed. His behaviour demonstrated what a terrible injustice had been done to him.

The young man is squealing for mercy. François laughs. 'You showed none when you betrayed that woman. She was murdered in front of her child, you bastard, now it's your turn.' A shot. The pleading stops.

'François, what have you done? The girl in the flowery dress was the traitor.'

'No, it was him. She was just his girlfriend. She knew nothing apparently. Pity, but C'est la guerre.'

Once the school was empty, Duane flopped into a chair in his study and shared a bottle of whisky given to him by the market traders with Marguerite and Tony and Miss Scott. He thanked them for being his most loyal supporters. He was calm and controlled as he talked of his dreams for the future.

'I suppose what I want above all is to teach not Maths or spelling, but kindness and wisdom. They are what the world needs.'

Marguerite had got Kenneth White to copy, in his best calligraphy, a speech by Winston Churchill. A girl in the carpentry class had carved a frame for it. They gave it to Duane. He read it in silence.

'The only guide to man is his conscience; the only shield to his memory is the rectitude and sincerity of his actions. It is very imprudent to walk through life without this shield, because we are so often mocked by the failure of our hopes and the upsetting of our calculations; but with this shield, however the fates may play, we march always in the ranks of honour.'

As he carefully put the gift back in its wrapping, only then did the tears flow.

Chapter 30

The next few months in Marguerite's life were a period of transition. The new headmaster, Mr Pryor, was a good, if unimaginative man, and apart from insisting on more focus on exams and adhering to a curriculum, left her alone. Marguerite endeavoured to maintain the techniques of teaching she had developed under Duane's regime, and her dedication to, and delight in, her pupils. She was able to continue to treat them with respect and concern. But her pride in her work had gone.

At school her relationship with Tony was unchanged. Their support of one another was a safety valve for their frustration at the new regime. They helped each other cope with the loss of an ideal, a dream.

'Oh Mags, why do the petty bureaucrats always win?'

'Illegitimi non carborundum.'

'OK, smartarse. What does that mean?'

'Don't let the bastards get you down.'

She wished that Jimmy was more understanding of her distress. On their sporadic dates he was intent on having a good time to cheer her up.

'Don't be gloomy, Skylark. It's only a job.'

As time went on, Donald and Tony did all they could to include Marguerite in their social life. There were parties at their flat, which Jimmy didn't want to attend, full of exquisite men and women from the ballet company. Marguerite marvelled at their capacity to drink and smoke until the small hours of the morning, despite having an early start for class the next day, which continued with rehearsals and performances until eleven o'clock at night. After which they would party again. She went to the Royal Opera House with Tony when Donald had a role and marvelled with him at his lover's dark beauty and breathtaking agility. She joined them, after the show, at a nearby café, full of theatre people letting their hair down. It fascinated her to hear these other-worldly creatures she had seen magically leaping and twirling an hour or so before reducing their artistry to the mundane.

'You've got to lose some weight. I nearly got a rupture doing that last lift.'

'You're supposed to grip my leg, not my fanny, on that arabesque, you know.'

She enjoyed herself with both of them but she could not stop the stab of pain when she had to go away and leave them alone together. When she tried to explain how she felt to Jimmy he was, as she thought he might be, unsympathetic.

'Why do you want to be some sort of fag hag when you've got me?'

Sometimes, observing Donald and Tony's obvious devotion, she wondered what exactly she had 'got' with Jimmy. Sex. No gainsaying that. 'Joy and jollity be with us both', as Wordsworth had it. She would think back to Jimmy's wooing of her on that first trip to Brighton. It had such grace and thoughtfulness. But Wordsworth also said of his skylark, 'There is madness about thee.' Jimmy's jealous moods could be disturbing but she had learned to handle them, more often than not with a bit of 'joy and jollity'. She uneasily wondered whether she actually enjoyed the drama and subsequent passion.

'Marguerite, move. The bastards are dead.' She stares at him blankly. It is as if she is deep, deep underwater. He kicks her to her feet, dragging her behind him by the hand, running and weaving through olives and aspens, jumping over rocks and bushes, the dry pine and rosemary scent tickling her nose and the dust flying round their feet. They get to the safety of Marcel's home where the ancient oak stands. She leans panting with her back against the huge girth, hands outstretched behind her feeling its strength. Clinging to reality.

'Oh Christ. Oh Christ.'

Suddenly Marcel is thrusting against her. Laughing and crying she grips him to her, digging in her grimy fingernails; they are ripping, tearing, clawing at each other's clothes and bodies in orgasmic triumph.

Because of their jobs, Jimmy and she could not meet as often as Marguerite would have liked, and they were limited by the uncertain availability of his boss's two houses. There was tension between them about the time Marguerite spent with Tony and Donald.

Tony suggested, 'He'll feel a lot better about it if we get to know him. Why don't you bring him round to dinner? Is he a homophobe or something?'

It was not something they had discussed, but considering his relationship with the sexually ambiguous habitués of the Dominion Club, Marguerite thought it unlikely. To eliminate any doubt in her friends' minds, she agreed with Tony that they should have a cosy dinner for four in his and Donald's flat.

She held Jimmy's hand as they waited at the blue front door. It was clammy.

'You look so dishy,' she said reassuringly. He was in an immaculate grey mohair suit, with a blue-silk open-necked shirt that enhanced the colour of his eyes. She wondered if he had spent all his earnings on making a good impression on her friends.

They welcomed him warmly and Donald thrust a glass of champagne into his hand.

'You probably need this. It must be like meeting the in-laws. We're pretty nervous ourselves.'

Jimmy was surveying the room.

'What a lovely place you have,' he said politely.

He wandered over to the wall of pictures.

'Smashing paintings. Is that you?'

He pointed to a picture of a dancer.

'Yes.'

Jimmy looked closely at it.

'*Le Corsaire*?'

'Well spotted.'

Jimmy squinted at a sketch of a ballerina squatting, tying her shoes.

'She did a lot of ballet paintings, didn't she? Dame Laura Knight.'

'How did you know? It's not signed.'

'I recognised her style.' Jimmy peered at a photo.

'That's a Cartier-Bresson, isn't it?'

'Right again.'

Jimmy moved along the wall, entranced.

'You've got some fabulous watercolours.'

Tony took Marguerite into the kitchen.

'Come and be my commis chef, like the old days. We won't get any help from Madam once she starts talking Art.'

He stood and put his hands on her shoulders.

'I'm doing your mother's cassoulet. I thought it's what she

might have cooked when she met your new boyfriend. I know a couple of poofs are no substitute for her, but we care about you very much, Mags. Is that all right?'

He looked at her anxiously.

'It's perfect. It's all falling into place. Look at them.'

As she busied around cleaning up after Tony while he cooked, they watched Jimmy and Donald talking animatedly to one another. She took some home-made bread in to the table and listened as Donald said, 'I spend all my hard-earned cash on pictures. It's almost worth my poor deformed feet. Most of them are worth nothing but let me show you my prize possession.'

He went into the bedroom and came back with a small painting of a cornfield lit by moonlight.

'My God,' said Jimmy. 'It's a Samuel Palmer.'

'It is. Here, hold it and look closely.'

Jimmy held it delicately and stared in wonder.

'He's used pen and ink as well as paint. Genius. Look at the light. It's real but somehow magical.'

'I know – brilliant, isn't it?'

'It's Shoreham. The work he did there is the best, I think.'

Marguerite was transfixed as Jimmy went on, almost to himself, 'You won't believe this. But when I was twelve I went camping in Shoreham with the Scouts. We visited his house and gallery. It blew my mind. I asked if I could buy one out of my pocket money, I had no idea what they were worth. I'd never seen anything so lovely. It changed my life in a way. Isn't that an extraordinary coincidence? Thank you for letting me hold it.'

Donald received it carefully.

'I love it too. It took a tour of America and Russia to buy that and it was worth every lousy hotel and splintering stage.'

Jimmy was communicating with Donald in a way that

surprised her. She didn't know he was so affected by art. They had never gone to galleries together, yet she had seldom seen him discuss anything with such intensity.

Tony and Donald were entranced by Jimmy. The conversation flowed easily. Jimmy was witty and knowledgeable about wine and fashion, and Marguerite was amazed to hear him putting forward vigorous views on education that he had obviously heard from her, though she thought that he had never listened to her rants. Even when the subject turned to ballet Jimmy seemed well informed, questioning Donald on what effect Nureyev had had on the company when he arrived after his defection from Russia. It helped, thought Marguerite, for two men not unaware of male beauty, that in the candlelight Jimmy looked devastatingly handsome.

The evening was a triumph.

As they were leaving Tony said, 'We are so glad to have met you at last. In future when Marguerite comes to see us, or we go out together, you must come too. Don't be a stranger.'

Jimmy gave his irresistible grin to seal the bond.

'I didn't know you were an art connoisseur,' said Marguerite, taking his arm as they walked to his car.

'There's a lot you don't know about me.'

Jimmy seemed suddenly drained of the energy he had had during the evening.

Marguerite laughed.

'Like what? Tell me.'

He stopped walking and turned to look searchingly at her. He hesitated for a moment. Then his head fell back and his eyes closed and he gave an agonised groan.

'Some other time.'

Marguerite did not pursue it. She was used to his dramatic scenes when he was drunk.

'Oh shut up, Jimmy. Get in the car and I'll show you my knickers.'

He didn't respond. He drove the short distance to the pub and pulled up outside. He turned off the engine and, looking straight ahead, he said quietly, 'You're a fine person, Marguerite. And so are your friends.'

'Glad you like them. Are you coming in?'

He still did not look at her.

'No, I have to drive down to Brighton. Get the house ready for Madam. She's arriving tomorrow.'

Then he turned his head and looked at her intensely.

'I'm so sorry.'

He leant across to open the car door.

'Goodnight.' He kissed her gently. 'My Skylark.'

And he drove off.

Chapter 31

Marguerite was used to Jimmy disappearing for long periods on various jobs. He still had no place of his own and such was the peripatetic nature of his work there was no way of contacting him. She did not have the telephone number of the Brighton or Eaton Square house as, although Jimmy assured her that the owner would not mind him using the phone, it was not deemed tactful for him to receive calls from friends. All this she accepted and waited for him as she always did to contact her when he was back in circulation. This time, the days of absence became weeks, and because of his strange behaviour when she had last left him, Marguerite became increasingly anxious.

Tony suggested they all have an outing to an exhibition of watercolours to follow up the success of their first meeting. He was surprised when Marguerite told him that she hadn't heard from Jimmy for nearly a month.

'Bloody hell, we must have scared him to death.'

Marguerite was disconsolate the next day so Tony came up with his usual remedy of a treat.

He said, 'When we first came to the big city we were going to get "with-it". Well, you've been so busy changing the world that, if you don't mind me saying, you've become a bit without-it.'

'What are you talking about? I go to Donald's parties. They're with-it.'

'I mean the look. There's a fashion revolution going on out there.'

'Aren't I a bit old hat for all that? Old and jaded.'

'Well, maybe you are, but there's no need to look it. You can be a glamorous pussy when you try, you've just become a bit passé, darling.'

'Oh thank you very much. I've had other things on my mind.'

'Your English part seems to have taken over, with your Gor-Ray skirts and nice blouses. We need to get back a bit of that French chic.'

'I wouldn't know where to start. All this new stuff. I'm happy with Jaeger.'

'Well, fortunately I have cradle-snatched Donald and he knows all about these things. He buys all my clothes which is why I am such a sartorial vision. So he has planned a day out for us. He's got a matinée but he'll join us in the evening and he's given me my orders.'

The outing started with a lunch at the Casserole on Chelsea's King's Road. It was packed with overexcited young people, the girls in minuscule skirts, exposing variously shaped bare legs or white fitted boots, and young men in jeans and T-shirts or shirts open to the waist so as to exhibit the medallions round their necks. Music was blaring out from loudspeakers that made it difficult for her to hear what Tony was saying. Marguerite cowered in the booth that Donald had booked for them, feeling old and frumpy.

'Don't worry,' said Tony. 'We're going to fix that.'

A walk down the King's Road, where Vespas whizzed up and

down amongst the open-topped cars, everyone shouting to one another, seemed like being at a glamorous club to which Marguerite didn't belong. Halfway down was Bazaar, the shop she had read about opened by Mary Quant. One frock stood on display in the window. It was starkly simple. Sleeveless, in salmon pink with a beige panel in the front either side of a visible zip. It looked quite demure with its straight, unwaisted line. Tony coaxed Marguerite inside, despite her protests that nowadays she would be happier up the road in Peter Jones.

'This is my revenge for when you made me buy that awful suit in Dartford.'

Looking at the scraps of cloth displayed on hangers, calling themselves skirts, Marguerite protested that it was a shop for young girls not middle-aged teachers. She was about to drag him outside when a pretty girl asked in an upper-class voice,

'Hi. there. Need help?'

Gripping Marguerite's arm firmly, Tony said, 'We're interested in the dress in the window. That is, she is, not me. It's not for me.'

'Oh, goodie. The colour will be better on her,' drawled the girl. She turned to look at Marguerite. 'It'd look super with your hair.'

'But the length. It's too—'

'How are your knees?' The girl asked.

'All right thank you, how are yours?'

The girl ignored this and lifted Marguerite's skirt.

'Oh, they're super. I suggest you wear it just above. We have it in several lengths.'

Tony grabbed the dress the girl brought, and bundled Marguerite behind a flimsy curtain to try it on. When she came out, vigorously tugging the hem down, the girl said, 'Super.'

'It's too short.' Marguerite protested.

Tony took her by the hand and twirled her round.

'Truly, Mags, you look – super.'

It had reached a point where it was impossible to say no. When she went to get her handbag Tony said, 'It's a present from Donald and me. Keep it on.'

So they wrapped up her skirt, cream blouse and nylons and she launched her knees into Swinging London. A gnarled builder working in the forecourt of the shop gave her a wolf whistle, which – grasping at straws – gave her some confidence. When she got used to it – her bare legs striding free – it felt good.

Tony hailed a taxi, which sped to Bond Street. Alighting and seeing the name over the glass-fronted building, she quailed. Vidal Sassoon was the toast of the town with his new geometric bobbed hairstyles.

'He's much too groovy for me. I keep trying to tell you, I'm just a frowsy teacher.'

'May I remind you,' said Tony, pulling her into the salon, 'you told me that you were the girl that turned up for her graduation in the New Look.'

'Yes, but that was to make a point. I've never really cared all that much about my appearance.'

'No. You've had it easy. You are a natural beauty, but, sweetie, we have to make a bit of an effort as the bloom fades.'

'Charming.'

As she stood at the reception desk, she looked at the willowy models and other women that she seemed to recognise milling around.

'I think you may be Marguerite, yes? Auburn, curly, unmistakable. Wow, can't wait to get my scissors on that mane.'

Coming towards her, hand outstretched, was a small dapper man in black trousers, tight-fitting white shirt and grey kipper tie.

'Hello. I'm Vidal. Donald's told me all about you,' and he took hold of her chin, rotating her head with one hand and tousling her hair with the other. Then he shouted, 'Trevor, shampoo this lady.'

Marguerite stuttered, 'Wait a minute, I—' but Vidal had already gone.

Tony waved goodbye as she was whisked into the bustling mayhem of the salon. Confused by being told to lie full-length on her back on a black leather contraption with her head backwards over a basin, she was stiff with fear. Gradually the deep massaging of her scalp by the young boy with blond hair sticking up in spikes soothed her and she could see the reason for the bed. She was nearly asleep when he sat her up, wrapped her head in a towel and told her to wait for 'the master'.

He and his trainees approached like a flight of chattering starlings, settling at Marguerite's chair, where the young acolytes gathered round in sudden silence as Vidal whipped the towel off her head, like a conjuror revealing a rabbit. He walked up and down looking first at her, then at her reflection in the mirror. Marguerite felt as Marie-Antoinette must have, as they cut her hair before the guillotine.

'It's beautiful hair,' he addressed his apprentices, 'but it's doing nothing for her face. We need to balance the chin, emphasise the cheekbones, and take the weight out to give it lift.'

For the next hour he crouched, he jumped, he danced, he pushed her head into different angles and snipped and tugged at her hair, which gradually formed a heap by her chair. Marguerite had given up any hope of protest. So intent was he on his creation that she honestly believed he would have held her there by force if she had attempted to leave. Gradually the shape he was aiming for emerged.

'Spray,' he demanded of a minion, who doused her hair with

water. He put some lotion on his hands, ran it through her hair. Then another passed him a hand-dryer. He ordered Marguerite to stand and put her head down. Then he blow-dried her hair upside down. Marguerite thought longingly of restful times spent under an old-fashioned hairdryer reading an out-of-date magazine. Abruptly he pushed her to sit again and went hither and thither with his free hand flicking and pinching the curls into shape.

When he eventually stepped back, breathing heavily from the exertion, and said, with a flourish, 'There you are. The new you,' everyone applauded.

She was transformed. Shaped into a V at the nape of her neck, her hair was a mass of short tousled curls that shook as she moved. The auburn colour was enhanced by the shine and different angles. She looked ten years younger and ten times more stylish.

'Thank you. It's lovely.'

Vidal gave it another pat.

'Not bad for an East End Jewish crimper, eh?'

Tony was waiting for her at the door.

'Here I am,' she said. She felt rather marvellous.

'Who is this woman accosting me?' he asked. 'Surely not that teacher from King's Cross.'

'Bien sûr, c'est moi.'

Tony said, 'Well, look at you. When that bastard gets back he won't believe his eyes. You're going to stun them tonight.'

The last part of the treat was to have cocktails at the Ritz and then go on to dine at a recently opened restaurant in Chelsea, Le Gavroche.

'They're a couple of Froggie brothers, the Roux, so you should feel at home. It is *the* place to be,' said Tony as they walked from the tube station down Lower Sloane Street. Marguerite was astonished at how her liberated limbs and bouncing unlacquered hair altered her frame of mind. She felt free, light-hearted, and attractive. They were welcomed by the maître d', who led them to the corner table where Donald was waiting.

He rose to greet them with a cry of delight.

'Wow, what a stunner.'

All traces of the depressing insecurity caused by Jimmy's absence disappeared as they ate their way through the gourmet delights of the menu. The melting cheese soufflé, the langoustine and pigs' trotters in mustard sauce, the raw tuna with spicy ginger and sesame dressing, the venison and cranberry sauce were the food of the gods and they relished and swooned over every flavour-filled mouthful. These delicacies, combined with the different wines that complemented each course, sent them into a state of hedonistic delight.

They were pausing to digest the main feast before embarking on the dessert when the quiet of the restaurant was disturbed by a group of four people in evening dress who, from their over-loud conversation, had obviously been to a First Night. The maître d' was fawning over a woman whose age it was difficult to assess.

'She's about fifty,' whispered Tony.

'Nah, sixty if she's a day. She's had her face done,' contradicted Donald.

'Vada the Aunt Nelly danglers,' said Tony.

The woman's earrings were spectacular diamond drops. In addition she had a three-string pearl necklace that looked real. Her black hair was swept back in a bouffant style that Vidal would have chopped to pieces, but with her pale make-up and flashing green eyes, she was a spectacular sight.

She took off a sable stole, revealing a black-satin décolleté frock, which made Marguerite, in her simple little Mary Quant, feel underdressed. The woman handed the stole to a man in a dinner suit with his back to them, kissing him lightly on the mouth as she did so.

'Get rid of this, sweetheart.' The man turned to give the fur to the maître d' and Marguerite saw his face for the first time.

'Christ,' said Tony. 'It's Jimmy.'

'Dear God. The arsehole,' said Donald with disbelief.

'I'm going to be sick,' said Marguerite.

'Please don't, darling,' said Tony. 'It would be a terrible waste of money.'

The three of them slumped down in their chairs in the mercifully dark corner as the woman put a proprietary arm around Jimmy's waist and, chatting and chuckling, led him through the tables. From the furtive glances the woman gave, to see if people were watching, which indeed they were, she wanted her companions and the world to know that the handsome younger man was hers. Just as the earrings and the pearls and the sable were.

'Who the hell is she?' said Tony.

'I recognise her,' replied Donald. 'I've seen her photo.'

'Yes, come to think of it, so have I,' said Tony. 'In that bloody awful "Jennifer's Diary" in your *Queen* magazine. All those old-hat High-Society idiots.'

'Who is she though?' asked Donald.

Marguerite hesitated.

'His auntie.'

At that moment the woman was holding her champagne glass for Jimmy to drink from, whilst caressing his hair.

'Oh really?' drawled Tony, and despite the grotesquery of the situation all three let out a burst of laughter. The noise made Jimmy look across the room over the rim of the glass from

which he was sipping. He squinted in the dim light, then spluttered the champagne, a look of stark terror crossing his face.
Choking, he left his worried companions and made for the
toilet. Before Marguerite could stop him, Tony had followed
him out.

'There's probably some simple explanation, Mags.'

'Let's go, Donald. Do you mind?'

Donald summoned the waiter who was unctuously expressing
dismay that they were missing the superb dessert selection when
Tony nearly knocked him flying returning from the Gents.

'Good, I see we're leaving. Let's pay the bill and go.'

As they made their exit, Marguerite saw Jimmy had returned
to his table where the woman was fussing over him anxiously.

Outside the restaurant Tony said, 'OK, Mags. He'll be at the
pub at eleven tomorrow morning.'

'I don't want to see him.'

'You must. Do you want me to be there with you?'

'No. I'll be all right,' she said wearily. 'I usually am.'

Chapter 32

'Love the hair, old girl.' The grin was uncertain.

'Don't, Jimmy, please.'

'No. All right.'

As they stood facing one another in Marguerite's room, a train went under the building.

Jimmy laughed.

'The house is shaking as well.'

He did look terrified. She said nothing.

'I suppose you want an explanation.'

'That would be nice.'

He moved to the window.

With his back to her he said, 'Right. No more bullshit. I'm not her nephew. I'm her lover. She gives me lavish presents, keeps me in a style to which I am unaccustomed, in return for boosting her ego with her friends and the odd fuck.'

She flinched as if he had struck her.

'How long has it been going on?'

He took a deep breath before answering.

'All the time I've known you.'

Marguerite was too stunned to speak.

Jimmy was shaking.

'You may ask yourself why I behaved like this. The answer is – that's what I do. I lie. I cheat. I dissemble. I con my way through life. Usually I'm very good at it, but you have been my Achilles heel. I made the worst mistake for a conman. I cared about you.'

Marguerite laughed,

'I can't believe this. You're conning me now.'

He turned to face her. He was ashen.

'I swear not. Please sit down, Marguerite. I need to try and explain. To myself as much as you.'

Marguerite reluctantly sat on the bed.

'All right but it had better be good.'

'That night at Tony and Donald's, I prepared in my usual way. I know a bit about art from her collection. I read up on ballet and Donald's career. I dressed as I thought they might find attractive, and did my full charm offensive.'

Marguerite was appalled.

'Is that what you did with me? That trip to Brighton, was it all coldly calculated? The picnic? The hotel?'

He shouted, 'Yes. Don't you understand? That's what I do. I please people. I make them happy. I do it well. As I've often heard you say, "All youngsters are good at something." Well, I'm good at understanding what people want and giving it to them. Being it. Whatever they need.'

'Even when you make love?'

'Usually, yes. I've got it down to a fine art. Haven't I? I'm good at it, aren't I. Aren't I?'

She closed her eyes to shut out the image of his beseeching little boy's face and murmured, 'Yes.'

'Well, it all went wrong that night. It was the painting.'

'The painting?'

'Yes, the Samuel Palmer. When I asked to buy it, as a child, the

man laughed at me. "You won't ever be able to afford that, sonny."
Sod you, I thought. I made a vow there and then to prove him
wrong. I wanted lovely things like that painting in my life and I'd
damn well get them. But when I listened to Donald, I realised
that man in Shoreham was right. Donald's got real talent. I hav-
en't. I'm just good at pouring drinks and fucking. He worked for
that painting and deserved it. I looked at all three of you that night
and I felt jealous. You've made something of yourselves, you do
something worthwhile. I liked them both so much. How kind
they were to you and welcoming me like that. And you' – he
turned to look at her – 'you're a good woman, Marguerite.
Dedicated, loving, clever. But I'm sorry – I can't live up to you.'

*'You're special, Marguerite. You have a mission. A vision of a better
world. I fought because I had to. Now I want peace. You must obey
your voices, my brave little Jeanne d'Arc. I am just a peasant farmer. I
only want to hear the sound of the birds, and the wind in the trees. I
can't be part of your quest.'*

Marguerite put out her hand and pulled him to sit next to her.
  'It's not too late for you, Jimmy. You obviously have a talent
for art. I could find a course in art history that you could do—'
  'Could but wouldn't. I'd give up when it got difficult. And
what would I be in the end? Some old bloke working in a
museum. It's too late for me. Why do you suppose I've not done
anything serious in the twenty-odd years since the war? You
think education is the answer to everything but for some of us
it isn't. I don't want to work hard. I can't stick at anything for
long. The only time I was really happy was in the RAF when I
was told what to do and everyone thought I was a hero.'
  'You were.'
  'For a while. Not later. After the war no one wanted to know.

I wasn't one of the famous Few. I was Bomber Command. We destroyed Dresden, Cologne, Hamburg, killed thousands of civilians. We lost more men, half of us in fact, than any other set up, including my navigator. He got hit by flak in the rear turret and when we limped back to base, I scraped him off the bloody walls of the plane. We thought he'd died for his country, but then we found out he was a war criminal.'

'You won a DFC, Jimmy. That's more than Donald or Tony ever did.'

He stood up suddenly and started pacing round the room.

'Right, now I'm spewing it all out. Let me tell you the truth about that. Let me tell you about that valiant event. The true version, not Stan's. When the plane was hit I knew I was badly injured. I managed to ditch the plane. Two of them had got out and were in the drink. I thought the other two, still inside, had gone for a Burton. Mind you, I didn't spend a lot of time checking their pulses, I was too busy trying to get the dinghy out, because I knew – I, you understand me, I, me, I didn't care about the others – I knew I was too knocked about to do much swimming. I managed to release the dinghy just before the plane went under the waves. Then, I helped Chalky heave Stan into it, and I fell into it myself.'

'Yes, that's what Stan told me. You saved his life.'

'Actually he saved mine. There I was flopped on the bottom of the boat like a dead fish, with my face in 6 inches of water, drowning, and, as usual, I gave up. But he lifted my nose out of the water with his foot. I managed to sit up. And then – then, I could hear this voice calling for help. One of the other lads was in the drink somewhere. He wasn't dead.' Jimmy's face contorted with grief.

'What happened then?'

Jimmy started pacing again.

'This is the funny bit. Get ready to laugh. I organised a sing-song to drown out the noise. The sound of him dying – drowning – begging for help. It went on for fifteen minutes. And, guess what? They gave me a medal for keeping up the morale of my crew until we were rescued. You're not laughing. Don't you think it's funny?'

'Jimmy, listen to me. I know from Stan you were badly wounded. You couldn't have reached the other man.'

'You would have. Someone like you would have. But not me. I just got the lads singing "Roll Out The Barrel" to stifle the noise of a drowning comrade. So there you are, Marguerite. That's me. Phoney war hero, without a pot to piss in. I bum around, and truth to tell, I like it that way. I get the lovely pictures, the Lalique glasses, the silk shirts and the luxurious houses. Second-hand, but better than a bedsit in Pimlico. You think they're deadbeats, but I even like my friends at the Dominion. I feel at home with all those failures. Yes, it works for me. But it wouldn't for you, my dearest, dearest Skylark.'

He looked intensely at her face, as if he were drinking in its features.

'Thank you. Knowing you has been a Samuel Palmer painting for me. Something truly wonderful that is out of my reach.'

He kissed the palm of his hand and laid it on her lips. Then he turned abruptly, and picked up his jacket from the chair.

He held it up,

'Best chamois leather,' he chortled. It was back. The lopsided grin.

And then he was gone.

Five minutes later Tony arrived, presumably tipped off by Flo. Marguerite had not moved from the bed. He sat next to her. She no longer felt any anger at Jimmy's betrayal, just a terrible despair that she could see no way to help him.

'Has it occurred to you, petal, he actually doesn't want or need help? He's surviving in the best way he knows. Your way is not his. Beware the Messiah complex.'

Marguerite murmured:

> '"And, though little troubled with sloth,
> Drunken Lark! Thou would'st be loth
> To be such a traveller as I."'

'What's that?'

'A poem we liked. Or I liked. And he probably pretended to like. Who knows? My judgement is not very reliable. Is it?'

'Listen, it's not the end of the world, Mags. So a romance has failed. It happens. You should hear my track record. You've had some fun, and a lot of sex. Count yourself lucky.'

'But I thought it was something more than that. Oh Tony, everything's gone so hideously wrong. I keep letting people down. I want the world to be a better place and it gets worse. That sodding war is still affecting everything. Jimmy's youth was squandered killing people, when he should have been building his life. The damage is never-ending.'

Tony put his arm round her shoulders.

'Nonsense, Mags, the world's a much kinder place than it was. Think of these last few years. We've stopped hanging people "by the neck until dead", women don't have to bleed to death having illegal abortions, people can divorce without reviling one another in public, and Donald and I can have it off in private without being nicked.'

'I'll probably never have it off again.'

'Nonsense, with that hair and your lovely knees they'll be flocking round you.'

'But what will happen to Jimmy?'

'Frankly, my dear, I don't give a damn. And neither should you.'

'I feel weary, Tony. I keep being disappointed.'

'Cheer up, honey. The future's bright. We've got a man onto the moon. If all else fails we can go and live there. But if, as looks possible, Wilson gets thrown out and even if the dreaded Tories get back we may be all right. Two of my early protégés are emerging on the political scene. Heath and that Thatcher woman. She looks like a "not do nothing" sort of gal. If they were listening to my heckles all those years ago, they won't be so bad as their predecessors. Anything is possible. Hold on a minute. I can't believe I'm saying this. That should be your line, surely? I seem to have taken over your role.'

'Well, you play it well. I almost believe you. Fingers crossed for the future, eh?'

'That's better. That's the Lizzie Dripping I know and love. Fingers crossed, my darling.'

Chapter 33

Tony's 'protégés' were to dominate the next two decades to an extent neither he nor Marguerite could have predicted from seeing the humble start of their political careers in Kent in the 1950s. Margaret Thatcher in particular had changed beyond recognition. As Education Secretary she had evolved miraculously into a bouffant-haired, elegant-suited, slightly old-fashioned Galatea to the Saachi PR agency's Pygmalion.

While watching her purring on television one night a growling Tony quoted his idol Aneurin Bevan:

"'No amount of cajolery, and no attempts at ethical or social seduction, can eradicate from my heart a deep burning hatred for the Tory Party. So far as I am concerned they are lower than vermin.'"

Heath, who had amazed them both by becoming Prime Minister in 1970, was less adaptive to the new image-making. He remained obdurately gauche and remote, apart from spasms of grumpiness, interspersed with sudden bouts of alarming shoulder-shaking laughter. It was difficult to like this odd man but, because of the continuing sniping at Heath's single state, Tony did his best. Marguerite, in her turn, felt honour-bound to defend Margaret Thatcher, the first woman, against mammoth odds, to gain a foothold on the political power ladder.

Marguerite had never really been as politically committed as Tony. Now, in her mid-forties, she was even less so. In fact, since Jimmy's disappearance from her life she had found it difficult to engage in much at all apart from her work. Her severance from him had been painful. She grieved his absence continually. It left a chasm in her life. Sometimes she was tempted to find him and beg to continue their relationship on any terms he wished. Sitting in her room, marking books to the sounds of humanity from the pub below, made her ache for his laughter, his moods, the closeness of his body. She didn't care if it was all pretence, it was better than this nothingness.

She lies on the narrow bed, listening to the chatter and laughter in the corridor. Why is she not excited like them? This is what she wants. A student at Cambridge. A brilliant future. No. All she wants is Marcel lying beside her, their legs and arms entwined.

Tony, as so often in her life, rode to her rescue.

'The flat below us has become free, Mags. It's got a garden and two poofs living above who adore you. Why not leave that grotty pub and make a nest for yourself? It's the done thing now to have a mortgage and become one of the property-owning class.'

If someone had suggested joining a religious sect, living in tents in the Sahara Desert, she would have probably grabbed their hands off, so needful was she of change, but she opted for a very nice garden flat in Myddelton Square. There was a rowdy knees-up at the Carpenter's Arms to wish her goodbye. After closing time the customers, under the direction of Bob and Florrie, heaved her possessions onto wheelbarrows and market stalls and trundled them through the streets to her new abode,

Marguerite had never had a real home. She was surprised how much she enjoyed creating a place of her own, where she intended to live for the foreseeable future. With Donald and Tony's help she stripped off the fading wallpaper and crumbling plaster, revealing the bare brick walls, which they painted white. They peeled back the cracked lino and hired a terrifying electric sander to clean off the old pine floorboards.

The move was the catalyst she needed to get back her joie de vivre. To help pay for the refurbishment of the flat she took on extra work as a tutor for the newly formed Open University – a job she enjoyed; working with mainly older students who were avid for study, sometimes to improve their job prospects, but often for the sheer joy of learning. It was a relief, after struggling with increasingly indifferent youngsters at school, to work with people who slaved away in the privacy of their own homes and listened greedily to the lectures and her advice.

One of her students, a middle-aged vicar's wife, mentally bullied by her husband for years, was so emboldened by the discovery that she had a good brain that, on her return from a week's summer school, at a dinner party she was obliged to give for her husband's stiff-necked colleagues, and after a slighting remark he made about her, she poured a bowl of soup over his head, packed her bag and left him before serving the dessert. Marguerite, delighted, helped her find a job as a social worker, for which, with her life experience and subsequent first-class degree, she was amply qualified.

Aware of the emerging strength of women who had been suppressed by lack of opportunity, she became passionate about improving their lot in society. This attracted her more than party political dogma. When, with the publication of Germaine Greer's *The Female Eunuch*, there was an upsurge of feminist militancy, she, campaigner that she had always been, was keen to participate. She took part in women's consciousness-raising groups, formed in workplaces and hideous tower blocks where women were trapped by low expectations and poverty. She supported some striking cleaners.

More fun was an escapade at the Albert Hall, when she joined a few women who interrupted a petulant Bob Hope compèring the annual cattle market of the Miss World Competition. She sat, rigid with fear, in the stalls, listening to the glib comic tell a string of sexist jokes.

'I don't want you to think I'm a dirty old man. I never give women a second thought. The first thought covers it all.'

Then, at the signal of a football rattle whirled by a woman in the front row, she joined the others scattered around the auditorium mooing and blowing whistles. The paper bag of flour she threw landed and burst into a white cloud at Bob Hope's feet, causing him to scuttle off the stage in terror.

As Marguerite ran round the corridors of the hall, dodging irate attendants, she heard him return, doubtless having quickly consulted his gag-writers, and say, 'Ladies and gentlemen, this is a nice conditioning course for Vietnam,' which, considering that that appalling war had already cost millions of lives including those of American troops, was perhaps not in the best of taste.

When she poked her head round a door to shout the slogan 'We're not beautiful, we're not ugly, we're angry', she heard him further demonstrate his lack of judgement by saying solemnly, 'Anyone who wants to interrupt an event as beautiful as this must be on some kind of dope.'

Running from the police waiting outside the Albert Hall, her heart pounding with fear and excitement, Marguerite hoped that, if nothing else, they had exposed Bob Hope for the berk that he was. Translation learnt at Risinghill that would not have been approved of by her more militant colleagues: Berk: Berkshire Hunt. Cunt.

Marguerite narrowly escaped arrest, whisked, or rather juddered, away by Tony, who was waiting in a side road in the ancient Gladys, now grandly regarded as a vintage car.

The whole country seemed to be campaigning about something. There were sit-ins, standoffs, marches, strikes, and Tony and Marguerite were in the thick of a lot of them. Afterwards she would retreat thankfully to her comfortable home, which she continued to embellish.

She made forays with Tony and Donald to Habitat for stylish furniture, Casa Pupo for highly coloured rugs, Biba for mulberry satin sheets and huge decorative feathers in jars for her bedroom.

'A proper tart's parlour,' said Tony. 'You can't fail to pull in this.'

'No way, Tony, I've finished with all that. I've decided I'm no good at it. I had the love of my life when I was young. I'll never match him. And I'm not going to try any more. I'm middle-aged, I've got my pupils, I've got you two dear friends, all my good causes, and now a lovely home. What more could a girl need?'

'There you are, my lovely,' Donald said, hugging her and grinning at Tony. 'Never mind our bolshie friend there. As the Tories told us, "We've never had it so good."'

Chapter 34

But what Harold Macmillan had actually said was, 'Most of our people have never had it so good.' Marguerite and Tony knew from their school that there was a whole swathe of the population that was not benefiting from this affluence. The people left out were able to see on their new tellies how the other half lived. The underclass that Miss Scott had warned about, coming out of the secondary moderns, disappointed and ill-educated, were now in their thirties and forties. The subsequent chaos brought about by half-heartedly converting to the comprehensive system had produced yet another generation of the inadequately educated. Those who had suffered and fought in a vicious war and then worked for a better more equal world were in their fifties and older, exhausted and disillusioned; whilst some were acquiring houses, cars, holidays abroad, others were left behind. Many of them were angry. This was not how life was meant to be.

Suddenly the era of kaftans and beads and peace and love seemed to have evaporated and in its place was a period of wanting more, and to hell with anyone who stood in the way of getting it. Poor besieged Heath tried to put an end to a succession of strikes by awkward appearances on television where he appealed to the nation's public spirit to agree to a pay freeze.

Whilst juggling all that, he managed to get Britain in as part of the European Economic Community. Marguerite insisted on them toasting the event in the best champagne, consumed with titbits of English Stilton cheese, German sausage and Italian bread dipped in Spanish olive oil.

'No more wars, boys. That's it. We're united.'

Tony snorted, 'Well, apart from the odd skirmish in Vietnam, Korea and Israel and troops on the street in Ireland.'

'I'm talking about with our neighbours across the Channel. There will be no more European wars; and best of all, I'm no longer part French, part English. I'm European and I love it.'

She served Chicken Kiev as a main course. 'A gesture of peace to our Communist friends.'

Donald and Tony were full of admiration for her cooking as they dug their knives into the chicken and released the garlic butter wrapped inside.

'Brilliant. You clever little Delia Smith.'

Marguerite went into the kitchen and brought out an empty carton.

'Tah rah. Frozen!'

'You're kidding.'

'I'm not. It's a whole new wonderful world. More champagne?'

After a few celebratory glasses Tony went into one of his periodic working-class angsts.

'Mmm, it's all right for some. While we are quaffing champagne what about the miners?'

Donald groaned.

'Oh God, here we go. He's going to tell us about the Battle of Saltley Gate – again.'

'You two wouldn't understand. You have to be working class. It was one of the most moving moments of my life, seeing those

Yorkshire miners marching over the hill to join the picket. Twenty-five thousand men, women and children crowding the streets chanting, "We are the people." We had to close the bloody gate against the blackleg lorry drivers, didn't we?'

Donald prompted quietly, 'And Arthur Scargill—'

'And young Arthur Scargill in his donkey jacket, red scarf and baseball cap climbed up on the urinal and said it was a victory for the working class. Wonderful. I wept with pride.'

'Well you've always been partial to brick shithouses,' said Donald.

Tony gave him a withering look.

'This is not funny, Donald. These are my people. Their communities and their whole way of life are threatened.'

Marguerite calmed him down.

'Well, they got their way. Heath's gave in. So all's well that ends well.'

She, as did Tony, despite all his triumphalism, knew that was not so.

The stark truth of the tightening of the country's purse strings was brought home to them by its effect on the elderly Ethel and Bert. They had been made redundant fifteen years earlier, not long after Marguerite and Tony's visit to Oldham.

'Fancy word, ent it, son? I looked it up. It means no longer needed or useful.'

Tony had been up several times to offer financial help but it was resolutely refused.

On his last visit Tony reported that Bert particularly seemed very low. Marguerite suggested that Tony invite them to have a little holiday in London. Ethel was too daunted by the idea of the big city, but Bert accepted the invitation. It was agreed that he would stay in Marguerite's flat to avoid any discussion of sleeping arrangements, the subject of Tony's sexuality still being taboo. Donald would be described as a pal sharing Tony's flat to help with the mortgage payments.

Having never been further than Manchester, Bert was gobsmacked by London, especially their flats. The ornate, camp opulence of Tony and Donald's home and the spare modern elegance of Marguerite's had him shaking his head in wonder.

'Dearie me, look at you smartarses. It's what you see in't pictures. Hollywood an' all that. Ye've dun reet well, son. Ye 'ave an' all.'

Whilst Marguerite and Tony were at work, Donald took Bert to see the sights. They made an odd couple. Bert in his flat cap and muffler, with his ancient three-piece suit a little tighter now, and Donald also in a suit, but his had bottom-hugging bell-bottom trousers and was worn with a fitted silk shirt and tie. They visited all the places that Bert had read about. Buckingham Palace of course, where they watched the changing of the guard. The clattering horses, the immaculate uniforms moved the old man to tears.

'It makes yer proud, lad. Proud to be British.'

Knowing that an IRA bomb had recently gone off outside the Houses of Parliament made Bert a bit shaky as he adjusted the time on his waistcoat pocket watch to that of Big Ben. He nevertheless insisted on wandering up to Downing Street to have his photo taken on the steps of No. 10 to show to Ethel. The policeman on duty outside the door smiled when Bert muttered, 'Bastard, yer bastard,' as he looked at the Prime Minister's front door. Donald assured Bert that Londoners were not in the least fazed by the threat of terrorist bombs, but even he was disconcerted when they saw on the news that night that one person had been killed and forty-one injured in an explosion at the Tower of London, half an hour after they left it.

When Donald suggested he should go to the Royal Opera House to see him dance, Bert looked embarrassed.

'Oh nah, not fer me, lad.'

Tony snapped, 'Don't be bloody ridiculous, Dad. How do you know it's not for you? You've never been.'

Bert looked shamefaced at Donald.

'No offence, lad – sorry. But I don't want to let you all down. It's posh, is't ballet. I've got owt to wear and I'll feel like a spare prick at a wedding.' His hand shot to his mouth. 'Oh beg pardon, luv – no offence.'

Marguerite chuckled.

'Don't worry, Bert. It's a word I'm familiar with.'

'But yer see what I mean. I don't know how to behave in company.'

Marguerite thought that Bert could have learned a lesson in bravado from Jimmy, but there was an honesty about the man who could not pretend to be other than he was.

Donald persisted, 'I would really love you to see me work, Bert. You can wear what you like. I'd be very happy to have you there to see me doing my job.'

'Oh well – if you put it like that, I better give it a go.'

Marguerite contemplated offering to take him shopping for a new suit but decided that that would make him more uncomfortable. Instead she washed and ironed his shirt and surreptitiously cleaned some stains off his waistcoat with Thawpit, hanging it in the garden to get rid of the pungent smell.

On the day of their outing Bert was very nervous. He was obsessed with cleaning his boots properly, rejecting Marguerite's white all-purpose shoe cream as useless. Eventually he became so anxious that Marguerite went out and bought the two brushes, a yellow duster and black Cherry Blossom shoe polish he said were essential for the operation. Marguerite watched as he laid some newspaper on the floor and, removing the laces from his boots, sat in his darned woollen socks in the armchair. He opened the wing-nut of the polish tin, and with one of the brushes applied dabs of it in small circular movements into every nook and cranny of the gnarled boots. This operation took about five minutes. Then he picked up the first boot and with the other brush used strong sweeping movements to bring up the shine, aided by an occasional delicate spit. Finally he applied the yellow duster with light, caress-ing swirls, to bring the radiance to perfection. There was sweat on his upper lip and his cheeks were red with the effort when he came out of his trance-like concentration to beam at Marguerite.

'There, lass. See yer face in 'em now.'

'Beautiful,' she said. And meant it.

There was one more ritual he needed to enact before he had the confidence to venture into the alien territory of the Royal Opera House. To 'perform his ablutions'. He rejected completely any idea of taking a newfangled shower, preferring 'a good wash down' at the sink. Accustomed to the lack of privacy when using the scullery at home, he left he door of the bathroom open so Marguerite was able to watch when he got to his shaving regime.

First he attached a leather strop to a towel hook. Then he took a cut-throat razor from a satin-lined box. 'It were my father's,' he shouted through the door. Holding the leather belt outstretched with his left hand, he slashed the razor up and down on either side of the blade to sharpen it. Then, from a wash bag, he took out a well-worn round brush and a box of shaving soap and smothered his lower face thoroughly with the foam. He picked up the razor and, holding it elegantly in his right hand, his little finger crooked like a duchess with a teacup, he stretched his skin with the fingers of his left hand and oh so delicately ran the blade down, flicking the foam he gathered into the sink. His elbows raised, his stance was that of a conductor feeling his way through a Mozart symphony. The foam removed, he rinsed, then re-lathered and went through the whole performance again, only this time lifting his nose and earlobes to get into the corners.

The spell was broken only once when he nicked his skin and whispered, 'Shite.' After splashing his face with water, spluttering and gasping, he took a bottle of some potion and patted it on, whooping and hopping up and down as it stung. 'Bloody hellfire.' A dab on the nick with some sort of pencil was applied, and he turned, shining, to Marguerite.

'Will ah do, lass?'

'I'll say, Bert. You're a real – what was that phrase? – bobby dazzler.'

'Hold me hand tonight, will yer, luvvy? I'm a bit feert. I've on'y been in't theatre once. To see panto at Oldham Empire when I were a lad, an' I didn't think much to it. All them men dressed as women and girls pretending to be lads.'

When the three of them entered the Opera House Foyer, Bert was gripping Marguerite's hand, but it gradually slackened when he realised everybody was much too preoccupied to bother with him, and anyway, they were such a motley crowd he had no reason to feel out of place. They ranged from a bearded man in a red satin-lined opera cloak, to an orange-haired boy wearing garish make-up and attired in what looked like a diamanté dress over billowing trousers. She had to pull Bert along, so fascinated was he by the babbling mêlée. As they walked into the auditorium he stood stock-still with his mouth gaping open. Marguerite had been there many times but now, seeing it through his eyes, which had been starved of wonderment, she too was awed by its magnificence.

'Come on, you two. You're holding everyone up.' Tony was touched to see his father so transfixed. And thus he remained throughout the performance of *La Fille mal gardée*.

When Donald made his first entrance with a display of dazzling pirouettes and leaps, Bert turned to Marguerite.

'That's norr our Donald, is it?'

And after one particularly fine series of turns he muttered, ''Ow the bloody hell does 'e do that?'

When he realised he was permitted to clap during the performance, and even cheer, no one was more vociferous than he. All inhibition gone, he stood up and putting two fingers in his mouth gave piercing whistles after the famous clog dance, beside himself with joy that this homely footwear, that meant drudgery to him, could be made to be so funny and clever.

After the umpteenth curtain call and the throwing of flowers, hoarse with cheering Bert flopped back in his seat. He shut his eyes.

'Ah didn't know suchlike existed.'

When Donald joined them at the café after the show, Bert stared at him wide-eyed saying nothing.

'Well, Bert. What's the verdict?'

After several attempts to find the right words, he said, 'Er – er – them kecks were a bit saucy.'

Donald looked disappointed. Chin quivering, Bert suddenly stood and folded him in his arms. Patting his back as if he were a baby, he murmured, 'Bloody brilliant. I was proud, son, proud that you and our lad—'

They all looked at him. He sat down abruptly and began toying with his fish and chips.

'I'm not a bloody fool, you know.'

'Dad?'

'Leave it, son. Nuff said, leave it there.'

Chapter 35

As they were all is such high spirits Marguerite suggested they take Bert to Piccadilly Circus to see the lights. They got the cabby to drive round a few times so Bert could take in the flashing signs.

'That in the middle is Eros, Dad.'

'Very nice.'

Donald pointed out, 'Actually it's not Eros. It was put there to remember a great philanthropist, Lord Shaftesbury. It's Eros's brother Anteros. He was the god of selfless love.'

'A bit scarce these days, eh?' said Marguerite.

Tony put his arm around her.

'Not while you're about, it isn't, pet.'

Bert pointed out of the window.

'Look, that chemist is still open. It's late, en't it? And people are queuing to get in.'

Marguerite suddenly shouted to the driver, 'Stop, please stop a minute. By that Boots. Here. Here.'

'I can't stop here, madam.'

Ignoring him, Marguerite wound down the window and, over the traffic noise, shouted, 'Elsie, Elsie!'

A wraithlike shivering woman turned to look fearfully at the taxi. After staring at Marguerite for a minute, she held out her hand as if to ward off a blow, shook her head and shuffled backwards, disappearing into the crowd on the pavement.

'Sorry, madam, I must move on. There's a copper coming.'

'Christ. Christ. What's happened to her? It's Elsie, Tony. From Dartford. Remember? She's obviously ill.'

Tony scanned the pavement.

'Are you sure it was her?'

Donald shut the window.

'Who is she?'

'She was one of my first pupils.'

Donald told the driver to take them home to Myddelton Square.

'No. Please, can we go and look for her?'

Tony pulled her back into her seat.

'Mags, sit down. You'll never find her in that crowd.'

'But what was she doing there? She looked awful.'

Donald explained.

'The people queuing there are addicted to drugs. They get them on prescription. That Boots is open all night so the more desperate can get their new prescriptions after midnight.'

Marguerite was appalled.

'What sort of drugs?'

'The hard stuff, I'm afraid.'

Bert looked baffled.

'Drugs? What do you mean, son? Like medicine, is it? Are they poorly, then?'

Tony changed the subject.

'Let's all have a nightcap in our flat.'

Marguerite stifled her panic about Elsie as it was Bert's last night with them and she didn't want to spoil it. After a couple of glasses of champagne, his boots off and the waistcoat undone, he sat in the crimson velvet armchair waxing lyrical about his visit.

'It's been a reet eye-opener, I can tell yer. How you live down here. I've seen some wonderful sights. I'm in no hurry to go home, I can tell you. Reet hole, Oldham is now.'

'Come on, Dad, you've got all your mates there. You like it.'

'Not any more, son. It's changed. No work for the likes of us. It's all Pakis and wogs. They're taking over whole bits of the town. Can't go there any more. Not that I want to. The stink is awful.'

The three of them stared at him, too shocked to speak.

'They don't know what a hanky is. Spitting and snotting in the streets. And they get free everything. Us white folks don't get a look in. They're taking all our jobs—'

'Dad, stop this. I remember you saying you liked the people you worked with.'

'Aye, in them days it was just a few menfolk come to do shift work. They were supposed to be going home. But then they brought all their families and crowded out our hospitals and schools and that. I tell you that Enoch Powell was right. We are swamped by them now. We should send them back where they've come from.'

'Dad, you're talking rubbish.'

'Oh, aye, it's all right for you down here. They're ruining my town with their funny churches and their curries and not speaking Queen's English. They're taking over. The only people standing up to them are the National Front.'

'Dad, for Christ's sake, they're thugs.'

'No, they're not. Not all of them. They talk sense. I don't agree with violence, but something's got to be done. And they're the only ones doing anything. I'm voting for them next election.'

'*Why did they take Rachel away, Maman?*'

'*Because she is Jewish, and they are silly people who don't like Jews, or anyone who is not like them.*'

'*Will they hurt her?*'

'*No, we are going to stop them. Papa and I and our friends.*'

'*Can I stop them too?*'

Tony stood up and shouted, 'For Christ's sake, Dad. Listen to yourself. This isn't you speaking. They've been feeding you all this rubbish. I'm telling you—'

Marguerite stood up and clapped her hands and in her best schoolmistressy voice said, 'Right, that's enough, kids. Bedtime. Come on, Bert, put your boots on and I'll take you down to bed.'

Marguerite put her arm round him and led him out. As she opened the front door she heard Donald gasp, 'Jesus – where did that spring from?'

Having settled Bert, she was about to leave the room when he said, 'I'm sorry if I spoke out of turn, lovey. I'm just feeling a bit nesh. I've worked hard all my life, but there's nothing to show for it. They've even taken away threepenny bits, and half-crowns, and farthings. I haven't got much brass, and I can't understand what I have got. Bloody decimals or whatever. I don't recognise me own home. I don't seem to belong any more. I want things to be like they used to be.'

'Me too, Bert. I often feel like that.'

'Then, there's our Tony. I want him to be happy. But it's all strange to me – how he is, I mean. The wife dreams of grand-children. The women round our way, they love all that. It gives them a fresh start. And a nice daughter-in-law. Like you – we had hopes we'd have you—'

'You do have me, Bert. As a friend. And Donald too, who is a kind, loving man.'

'I know, I know, lass. I'm a silly bugger – pardon my French. I know I'm stupid but I'm not a bad man. Am I?'

Marguerite kissed him on the forehead.

'Of course not, Bert. Things are changing so fast. It's sometimes difficult to keep up.'

Chapter 36

Marguerite left it to Donald to talk Tony out of the depression he went into after his father's departure. His working-class roots were the bedrock of Tony's life and Bert's outburst had made him question their strength. The neighbourliness, the kindness, the generosity in spite of need seemed to have been eroded, leaving him doubting something he had cherished – maybe sentimentally. Marguerite was relieved that he now had Donald with whom to build a more firm foundation.

Any jealousy she had felt when Donald first appeared had completely dissipated. Their threesome worked perfectly. She enjoyed the privacy of her flat at the same time as knowing that the two people she loved most were one flight of stairs away. They consoled, amused, delighted one another. The only element missing for her in the relationship was sex, and now, approaching her fifties, she decided she could do without that. Unlike some of the present generation for whom sex had become a flippant pastime, she had always found it profound and disturbing. She wondered what her pupils would make of the fact that in all her life she had only had three lovers. Apart from the blissful one-night stand, the other two had caused her pain of which she now decided enough was enough, a sacrilegious stance in this frenzied post-Pill era of sexual freedom. Sexual intercourse was now almost obligatory. Chastity was the new frigidity. Delighted that the ignorance and inhibitions of the past were being eradicated, Marguerite was nevertheless fearful for the casualties of this revolution.

Leaving Donald and Tony to have a quiet evening, Marguerite ventured back to Piccadilly to search for the woman she was sure was Elsie. Despite the rain, a bedraggled queue was huddled outside the chemist. Marguerite stood on the kerb scanning their faces. Late-night revellers passed, disdainfully pushing aside a dazed girl who had wandered into their path. A young man shouted obscenities at no one in particular, then lapsed back into vacant silence. Marguerite could not spot amongst these desperate faces the one that she had seen that night.

She approached a shivering woman.

'Excuse me. I wonder if you know someone called Elsie Miller?'

The woman drew back.

'Why?'

'She's a friend of mine.'

'Are you the filth?'

'No, I'm just a friend, I promise you.'

'She's not here anyway.'

Marguerite looked across the street to Swan & Edgar's. Outside were two young boys leaning on the railings, sharing an umbrella. Sheltering in the doorway of the department store she could see a woman in Salvation Army uniform with her arm around another lad.

Marguerite splashed across the street to talk to her.

'Excuse me. I wonder if you could help me.'

'I will if I can.'

'I'm looking for a woman I know that I thought I saw the other day in the queue outside Boots. Late thirties. Blonde, I think.'

'What's her name?'

'Elsie Miller.'

'Just a minute.' She turned to the boy. 'Alan, I have to talk to this lady. Excuse me. I'll see you later.'

The boy left them and joined the two under the umbrella.

'Why do you want to find Elsie? Who are you?'

'I was her teacher many years ago. I'm worried about her. She looked ill. You know her then?'

'Yes. I know most of the lost souls who come here at night. I think I know where she might be.' She looked at Marguerite, her round face smiling beneath her bonnet. She held out her hand. 'Major Lily James.'

'Marguerite Carter. Forgive me asking, but what are you doing here?'

Matter-of-factly she said, 'Saving souls for Jesus. And you?'

'I'm looking for Elsie. I'm afraid she's in trouble.'

'Most of the people hanging around the Circus at night are in trouble. This is our Gomorrah.'

'Is that boy you were talking to in trouble?'

'Oh yes. The devil has him in his clutches. The devil in the shape of predatory men who prey on children. That railing is known as the meat rack. And those dear children are the flesh on sale.'

Marguerite was mystified as to how the woman could be so cheerful as she said this, her eyes shining.

'But Jesus is watching over them and will lead them back to his path. He loves them as much as I do and with his help we will fight the good fight.'

'Well – let's hope.'

'No, let's pray.'

Marguerite fervently hoped that the woman didn't mean here on the wet pavement with people watching. When she saw a small group of men and women in Salvation Army uniforms approaching, she was terrified they would hand her a tambourine and start singing 'Who Is On The Lord's Side?'. To Marguerite's relief they merely informed Major Lily that the soup van had arrived.

She put her arm round Marguerite.

'Come with me, dear, we may find Elsie.'

To Marguerite's horror, they did. In an alcove in Jermyn Street under a sign saying, 'Criterion Stage Door', there were three people lying on the pavement, wrapped in newspaper and filthy blankets.

Major Lily knelt on the wet ground and gently touched a matted head.

'Elsie, here's some soup, darling.'

There was no response.

'Elsie – it's Lily. Look at me. Have something to eat.'

'Not hungry. Go away.'

Lily lifted the blanket to reveal a hypodermic syringe embedded in the woman's arm. Calmly she removed it, got a box out of her satchel and, dabbing disinfectant from a bottle onto some lint, wiped the angry wound and put on an Elastoplast. The arm was covered in scabs, cuts and bruises. Elsie barely stirred.

Lily stood up and said to Marguerite, 'She must have collected her script earlier. We must try and make her eat.'

Marguerite was struck dumb with horror; she could not move.

Major Lily stood and put a hand on her arm.

'Don't cry, my dear. I know it's shocking when you first see the ravages wrought by these evil drugs that are polluting our fellow creatures, but God will prevail.'

She knelt again and pulled the blanket away from the white

sunken face. She lifted Elsie's head with both hands to speak close up to her.

'Now Elsie, come on. Wake up, wake up.'

Trembling, Marguerite knelt the other side and spoke softly into Elsie's ear.

'Elsie my dear, look at me. Please.'

Elsie's eyes flickered.

'It's me, Elsie. Miss Carter.'

The girl turned her face away.

'No no no. You mustn't see me. Please don't.'

Marguerite sat on the ground and pulled her into her arms.

'Now listen to me, Elsie. You need help. I'll get you help.'

'Too late, too late.' The girl clung to Marguerite, shivering and retching. 'I've tried and I can't stop.'

Major Lily handed Marguerite the soup and she held it as Elsie took sips and struggled to swallow them.

The major was watching closely.

'Elsie – I think Jesus has sent you a guardian angel.'

Elsie's eyes were closing and she leant against Marguerite.

'Major – what can we do? How can we help her?'

'I'm afraid the sad truth is that no one can help her. We can only make suggestions and hope she will listen.'

She produced a slip of paper from her pocket with a name and address printed on it. A Dr Peter Chapple.

'He is a miracle worker. If she decides she wants to change, this is the man.'

Marguerite took the piece of paper.

'OK, I'll get a taxi now and take her home with me.'

'Forgive me, my dear, but you mustn't. This is her rock bottom. She has to want to get out of this hell by herself. She knows we have a hostel if she decides to change, but so far she has chosen not to. If you make her comfortable she will have no reason to. Come back here tomorrow to see her. Sadly she will still be around – and see if you can be more successful in persuading her than I. It may take some time. Patience is a necessary virtue in this battle.'

'But I can't leave her like this.'

'You must if you want to help her.'

Marguerite looked down at Elsie. She supposed she had fallen asleep but she looked like a corpse. She knelt and kissed her on her icy forehead. Major Lily helped her up and led her away.

Marguerite went back and poured her heart out to Tony and Donald.

'I told you when I saw her in that club in Soho I was worried about her. I should have done something then. I should have done something when she got pregnant. I've let her down all along the line.'

Tony handed her a brandy.

'She is not now and never was your responsibility.'

Marguerite shouted, 'Oh shut up, Tony. My pupils are all I've got. I've got no children of my own. They are my children. I should have looked after her.'

The brandy spilled as she fell back sobbing into the armchair.

Donald took it gently and knelt in front of her.

'Listen, Mags. The Sally Army woman is right. One of the corps de ballet got hooked on heroin. When we all faffed around making a fuss of her she got worse, but when we were told not to support her she eventually went to get help and now is better. It's called tough love. Like Alcoholics Anonymous. Your Elsie will only get better when she is desperate to do so herself.'

Major Lily and Donald were right. Over the months Marguerite tracked Elsie down to various of her squalid haunts, trying to persuade her that there was a way out of this vortex of degradation into which she had plunged. But it had no effect. As well as Jermyn Street, Elsie would sleep in shop doorways in the Strand, in the grubby park alongside an all-night portable snack bar on the Embankment, in the crypt or graveyard of St John's Church in Waterloo, which ironically had been the Festival of Britain church. She eventually graduated to the nearby underpass, refuge to a number of homeless people. Marguerite helped her construct a room from cardboard packing boxes that Major Lily provided and brought her some cushions, a camp bed and a set of shelves for her growing collection of books. Helping her to arrange them she came across the book of war poems that she had given to Irene who had handed it on to Elsie. It reminded Marguerite of the sensitivity of her response to these and other poems as a young girl. Marguerite was appalled at the way she was now living, but Elsie assured her that the Bull Ring dwellers were a family and took care of one another.

At first, the 'family' terrified Marguerite. There were alcoholics and drug addicts and those who were obviously mentally ill. One man, whose enclosure was unusually neat, left each morning in a creased pinstriped suit to a maybe mythical job 'in the City'. She occasionally joined them round a brazier that they lit on freezing nights and heard their stories of decline, and soon her fear was replaced by profound pity. Having lost all connection, by choice or misfortune, with their previous lives, they had good reason to cling together in this bleak underworld, lit only by candles, and stinking of rot and urine. The police were tolerant of their encampment, preferring to have these outcasts where they could keep an eye on them. They even turned a blind eye to a group of small children who congregated in an archway up the road, living off petty thieving and late-night soup runs. One despairing policeman pointed out that this was preferable to abusive parents, or some uncaring care home.

This insight into the Dickensian underclass existing beneath the hurly-burly of increasing affluence in the streets above filled Marguerite with disgust. And that Elsie, her beautiful Saint Joan, should be part of it broke her heart. It took all her self-control not to weep and somehow force Elsie to get treatment for her addiction, to rid herself of the octopus that was strangling the life out of her. When Elsie went into a rambling eulogy about the benefits of heroin, saying how she could manage perfectly well to live a normal life on drugs, Marguerite wanted to shake her and drag her by her hair to Dr Chapple's esteemed day centre, but Major Lily always insisted that it would not help Elsie. She pointed out that it was an improvement that Elsie had moved from sleeping in doorways to creating some sort of home for herself in the underpass. She had even taken on the responsibility of a puppy that along with the rest of the dogs that roamed there was considerably more healthy than its owner. It, like her, was washed in Waterloo Station's public lavatories.

'Let us rejoice in small mercies.'

Major Lily managed to find joy in everything. Whereas Marguerite would rage to Donald and Tony about her impotence to save Elsie – 'Beware the Messiah complex, Mags' – Major Lily James faced horrors with radiant confidence in her God. A God who was, Marguerite thought, at the very least, inefficient.

Marguerite had almost given up hope that Elsie would ever propel herself out of the twilight world of living from one drug hit to the next, risking death through overdose, when she received a phone call from her. This time it was not to ask for money.

'I've lost that piece of paper. I need to see that doctor.'

'Elsie, he won't give you a script unless you opt for treatment, so don't even try. You are getting enough to sustain you. For heaven's sake stop trying to get more.'

'Honestly, Miss Carter, this is not a trick. If I want more gear I can get it on the street. I've decided I want to stop. Please help me.'

Marguerite was used to Elsie using any lie or subterfuge to feed her habit but this time there was a new tone to her pleading.

Marguerite phoned Major Lily.

When she arrived at the Bull Ring Major Lily was already there.

'Our lost sheep is returning to Jesus. She's ready.'

'But why, what happened?'

Elsie was sitting on the edge of her filthy camp bed, trembling and staring ahead in a daze. The cardboard walls were down and folded in a pile and her books were in a bundle tied with string, her few clothes stuffed into a pillowcase. Marguerite sat next to Elsie and took her fidgeting hands in hers.

'What happened, Elsie?'

Elsie didn't look at her.

'It was my son.'

'Your son? But you told me you didn't know where he was.'

'Well I do now.'

Elsie tried to continue and couldn't. She said to Major Lily, 'You tell her.'

Major Lily put an arm round Elsie and spoke to Marguerite.

'Well, Elsie OD-ed yesterday and they took her to St Thomas's Accident and Emergency. It was apparently chaotic because there had been a bomb at the Ideal Home Exhibition and there were so many casualties they needed to use lots of hospitals. So

I'm afraid they shoved poor Elsie into a corridor on a trolley with an oxygen mask and left her.'

Elsie took up the story in an expressionless drone.

'The nurse said, "People like you are not a priority." I could hear groaning and weeping. Then two doctors came rushing by and the younger one knocked over my oxygen canister. He said, "What the hell is this? Why is this patient out here?" And then—'

Elsie turned her head away from Marguerite.

'The older one said, "Oh she's a junkie. A regular. Bloody nuisance. Let her die. We've got people with limbs blown off who want to live. There's a girl with shrapnel in her eyes who is going to be blind. Don't waste time with this useless bitch." And then he said, "Come on, Dr Miller, leave her. Don't waste your time. You're going to have to learn to prioritise."'

Marguerite put her arm around Elsie.

'They didn't mean it, Elsie. They were in the middle of an emergency.'

'As they ran off I heard the older one say, "How's the new baby, by the way?" and Dr Miller said, "A joy."'

Marguerite looked at Major Lily who smiled and said, 'A miracle.'

Elsie was mumbling, 'Dr Miller. My son. Dr Miller.'

'Your son?'

'Yes. He was my son.'

'But Elsie, Miller is a common name—'

'No, I knew when I looked at him. He is exactly like his father. The bastard. His father, I mean – not him. Although that's what he was. My baby. A bastard. Get rid of that bastard, he said.'

'Who said, Elsie?'

'My father – the bastard. Sorry, that's a lot of bastards. So I

302

did. It was just until I made good. Just until I could manage. But I couldn't, could I? "Useless bitch," he said.'

'Well, you're doing something now, Elsie. You're going to make good now.'

'And a baby, Miss Carter. A joy, he said. A grandchild. I can't see the baby – like this. I could love that baby properly – start again.'

Marguerite thought of Bert's description of Ethel's loss.

Elsie was rocking backwards and forwards.

'I've lost touch with everyone – everything. Too busy enjoying the good life.'

She looked around. A rat was scrabbling in a pile of rubbish. And then she started to laugh. Marguerite and Major Lily joined in, as did two drunks in the next-door box. As the three of them walked out, carrying Elsie's books and bag of clothes, Elsie trailing her dog on a piece of string, maniacal laughter echoed round the hell they were leaving behind.

Chapter 37

Major Lily suggested Marguerite delay visiting Elsie whilst Dr Chapple grappled with her withdrawal from the various drugs she was on. He had offered her the chance of the gentler system of taking an oral version of heroin, methadone, with gradual reduction in the dose over a longer period, but he preferred, and she opted for, cold turkey 'to get it over with'. At last, after four anxious weeks, Major Lily phoned Marguerite to tell her that Elsie wanted to see her. Both Tony and Donald offered to accompany her but she felt it was better for Elsie if she went alone.

The clinic was in a blighted area of Chelsea, at the unglamorous end of the modish King's Road, called, appropriately, World's End after a local pub. It was a desolate place. Marguerite's walk from the bus stop did nothing to quell the anxiety she felt. Badly bombed during the war, it was now a building site. Old terraced houses were being pulled down and replaced with high-rise blocks; side roads of derelict, once grand houses, were now inhabited by squatters. She noticed a poster on the side of a half-demolished building, advertising a car with the slogan, 'If this car were a lady it'd get its bottom pinched.' Marguerite was delighted to see someone had scribbled on it, 'If this lady was a car, she'd run you down.' On the main road there was an eclectic mix of shops. Dotted amongst the tacky local butcher, green-grocer, and fish and chips shop, were oddities like a cheap-dress boutique called Quick Nicker and one for antique clothing, named Granny Takes a Trip. As she was passing a furniture shop called Sophisticat, with what she thought was a stuffed lion in the window, she jumped out of her skin when the beast turned to look at her and opened its mouth in a toothy yawn.

Another boutique called SEX was crowded with grotesque apparitions. Men and women, regardless of sexual orientation, wearing maxi- and mini-skirts, or trousers, made of leather and rubber, bedecked with chains, their hair shaved or dyed in vivid colours and glued into elaborate shapes, their faces made up like works of art. Others, wearing layers of ripped clothing, and a superabundance of safety pins in their garments and alarmingly their flesh, looked like ornamental paupers. She was troubled by the swastikas displayed on T-shirts and jewellery.

Her ears were assaulted by the pounding beat of the music blaring out from one café she passed, where she had to step into the road to circumvent the pavement crowded with smoking, shouting, heedless youngsters. From the smell of the smoke and their hyperenergy, she suspected that they were boosting their excitement with something other than the milkshakes or coffees of the 1950s. She felt like Miss Fryer as she suppressed the urge to warn them of the risks they were taking of drifting into more dangerous waters. Or maybe it was too late. How far had the plague affecting Elsie already spread?

On the shabby door of what looked like a warehouse was a hand-painted sign reading, 'Care Understanding Research Education'. Fearful of what lay behind it, she could feel her heart pounding as she rang the bell. Major Lily let her in. Inside, people were drifting around or sitting on ancient chairs and sofas talking quietly. In a side room, she could hear someone crying and groaning and vomiting, and looking in, she saw a young man, covered in sweat, writhing on a bed, with someone sitting by his side, stroking him and talking calmly.

Marguerite was worried.

'Don't you have nurses and doctors here?"

Major Lily pointed.

'They are all medical staff. Peter insists on no uniforms or white coats, as our members often have a horror of hospitals. They all look after one another. This floor is used solely for consultations and treatment. Nobody goes upstairs until they are clean.'

They went up some ramshackle wooden steps and entered a large room, where a frail-looking girl was working on a potter's wheel. Several others were sitting on the floor or on wooden chairs sketching. A rangy, long-haired young man with a beard and a sweet smile was walking around discussing their work. On one side of the room was a big table around which some were eating soup, apparently made by the woman with shaking hands who was ladling it inaccurately into bowls.

No one leapt up to help her, they just watched patiently.

One of them said, 'Well done, Stella. You're doing fine.'

They all looked badly in need of sustenance but seemed relaxed and comfortable with one another. People were coming in and out and it was difficult to see who, if anyone, was in charge.

Major Lily stopped by one door with a glass window. Inside were about six sitting in a circle talking.

'That's a group therapy session – afraid we can't interrupt that.'

A door at the end of the big central room was open, and inside Marguerite could see a man perched on a desk, and talking to Elsie on an armchair in front of him. Unlike everyone else, with their sloppy jeans and T-shirts, he was smartly dressed in a grey suit and what Marguerite recognised as a Rugby School tie, her father's old school. His hair was cut into a neat short, back and sides revealing a large broad forehead. With his glasses and small mouth he was not a handsome man, but had the same all-seeing, compassionate eyes as Michael Duane. He certainly seemed to be enthralling Elsie, who was listening to him intently.

Seeing Major Lily and Marguerite hovering in the doorway, he beckoned them in.

'Welcome – welcome. I'm Peter Chapple. Join our conversation. We were expecting you, Miss Carter. Elsie and I were just discussing her next commitment.'

'Commitment?'

Marguerite hugged Elsie then sat on the chair he set down next to her.

'Yes. We work here on making commitments to the group. Elsie, are you comfortable talking in front of Miss Carter?'

'Yes. She's my friend.' She took Marguerite's hand.

'We are a self-governing therapeutic community, Miss Carter. When people come here their only distinguishing feature is their sex. All have an addiction problem. Everyone is equal. We support one another. We make commitments to our group. Starting with what seem like easy things to most. Getting here on time in the morning, which is a big step if your life is as chaotic as Elsie's has been. Then we gradually add different things to aim for. Having a bath, helping cook the meals, helping the others withdraw. Elsie has made amazing progress. As you can see.'

Marguerite said, 'You look so much better, Elsie.'

'Thank you. Yes, I feel it. Thanks to Peter.'

And indeed Elsie was transformed from the woman who a month ago had staggered out of the Waterloo Bull Ring. She was clean and neatly dressed. Her face was deathly pale but her eyes were clear and steady. Her bare arms and legs were scarred but not bleeding and oozing pus. Even her dog looked more perky.

'You know Elsie well, I understand, Miss Carter. I'd like your opinion. It strikes me she has a very good brain.'

'She has.'

'Maybe. But I left school at sixteen. I've only got O Levels. I should have—'

Dr Chapple held up his hand.

'Should – that's a forbidden word, remember, Elsie. Never mind the past. I'm not interested in that. What about the here and now? We're not interested in why you lost your way, how hard done by you are, we're only interested in what you're going to do about it. So, Elsie, what are you going to do next?'

'God knows.'

'Maybe, but do you? We're agreed it would be good to get away from London for a bit. Away from temptation until you feel really strong. The question is where?'

Marguerite said suddenly, 'What about university?'

'I'm forty, for heaven's sake. They wouldn't have me.'

'Ruskin College in Oxford would. I was there a few months ago at a huge conference on the Women's Liberation Movement. It's a great place. You don't have to be qualified. It's for people who want a second chance in education. Any age.'

'I've got no money.'

'You can get grants and scholarships. The trade unions support people.'

Major Lily clapped her hands.

'That sounds perfect for you, Elsie. You're always reading. Even when you lost everything else you hung on to your books.'

Marguerite could see that Elsie was interested but before she could continue to persuade her Dr Chapple stopped the conversation.

'Elsie, I suggest you go to your counselling session now and raise it with them. See if you feel able to make some kind of commitment to the group.'

When Elsie had left the room Dr Chapple shook Marguerite's hand.

'Thank you. That could work for Elsie.'

'And thank you, Dr Chapple, for what work you are doing here.'

'I'm just holding back a bit of the tide. I'm afraid I can't make the powers that be understand that this problem is going to grow. That drugs could undermine the whole of society.'

'Do you really believe that? I'm a teacher and it's not a big problem at my school. Not like alcohol. I passed some youngsters coming here who may have been smoking cannabis and I know we hear about pop stars behaving badly but the habit doesn't seem to me to be widespread. I've never thought reefers were particularly dangerous.'

'It's what they lead to. Organised crime is moving in on supplying illegal hard drugs on the street in a big way. Soon it will be out of control and not enough is being done to stop it. Even I may have to close. The Salvation Army through Lily here is wonderful, but our needs are growing and the money isn't. Anyway, I live in hope. We are asking for government funding. We have an inspection due and, if they approve of us, they will cough up.'

Despite a flutter of fear at the word 'inspection' Marguerite said, 'I'm sure they will.'

She offered to get information about Ruskin to Elsie but Dr Chapple insisted that any further action must be undertaken by Elsie herself without help.

★   ★   ★

On her return walk to the bus stop Marguerite felt much better. She was exhilarated by her meeting with Dr Chapple, but disturbed by what he had to say. She resolved to delve closer into the habits of her pupils and suggest the school start educating them into the danger of drugs. She needed to find out more herself and try to understand what was happening to youngsters outside the schoolroom.

She decided to start right away. Outside the café, instead of skirting round the alarming-looking crowd she went into the middle of the throng, smiling and nodding. Some of the youngsters looked suspicious, but others smiled back. One lad with blue hair stuck up like a cockatoo's, and a nail through his nose, nudged his friend and pointed at her.

'Diddle-oh – look.'

Seizing the opportunity, Marguerite stopped and asked, 'What does that mean exactly?'

'Er – nutter.'

'Really? Diddle-oh. It's a word I've not come across.'

The boy took a nervous step back.

'While we are at it, can you tell me the words of the song they're playing in the café? I'm finding them difficult to decipher.'

'Are you taking the piss?'

'Not at all. I teach English and I love poetry.'

Haltingly, with the help of one or two others, the boy recited, '"Hey ho let's go/Hey ho let's go". You do that three times.'

'No, four,' someone shouted.

'All right. Four.'

As the boy got into his stride others joined in, clapping and chanting:

'"They're forming in a straight line
They're going through a tight wind
The kids are losing their minds
The Blitzkrieg Bop"'

Now the whole crowd were singing, or rather shouting, the song. Marguerite had some difficulty hearing what the words were. One line, 'Shoot 'em in the back now', shocked her but when the performance petered out, she applauded them.

'Thank you, that's very kind. It has great energy, and a strange dark edge. I'm not sure what it means though. For instance "why Blitzkrieg"?'

'Dunno. It's just a word.'

'Just a word?'

'Yeah. don't mean anything. It's just a sound.'

A boy in a Japanese kimono, with green hair and white make-up, said, 'I think it's something to do with the war. I've heard my mum say it.'

'They never stop talking about the fucking war. Oh sorry.' It was a girl with a painted face, wearing a bridal veil and a sack fastened with nappy pins.

In preparation for the ambush she wears a Breton beret pulled down concealing her hair, Marcel's leather jacket and peasant blue trousers. She covers her face and hands with camouflage mud. Maman would not be pleased at her ensemble, but she feels fully alive.

The girl continued, 'I suppose you remember it an' all, but it's so boring. Boring, boring.'

'Yes, I do remember it, dear. But it was a long time ago. It's been so nice meeting you all today. Thank you.'

She left to a chorus of goodbyes and giggles, aware that they thought her weirder than she them. She was glad that 'Blitzkrieg' was just a meaningless word in a song to them. All the lyric was, as far as she could understand, vicious, but the young people were not. They probably got into office clothes and school uniforms when they went home. She found herself singing, 'Hey ho let's go' four, five, six times, only stopping when a convertible Bentley drew up alongside her at a traffic light with the lion from the shop in the back seat. One of the two young men escorting the animal shouted, in a broad Australian accent, 'Good day, madam. Meet Christian. He is going for a walk in the graveyard. Say hello to the lady, Christian,' and the lion roared.

Marguerite roared back.

The world is full of strange, wonderful 'diddle-ohs', she thought.

Chapter 38

The good work being done by Chapple inspired Marguerite to renew her 'not do nothing' vow. Her teaching job was not as all-consuming as it had been under the Duane regime. She had some leeway in her own classes, but the new strict syllabus requirements, and the worthy, but unadventurous, headmaster did not inspire her. She sought out new causes to support. An incident that happened not long after her visit to CURE reminded her of her earlier feminist interests which had somewhat dwindled.

One morning Marguerite went into a newsagent's for her *Guardian*. Behind the shelves of confectionery, she discovered a girl crouching on the floor, with a pile of magazines on which she was methodically sticking labels.

When she saw Marguerite she stopped and put a finger in front of her mouth.

'Shush. Don't say anything, please.'

Marguerite crouched down beside her. She saw that the magazine-cover photo was of a young woman kneeling on all fours wearing only a pair of knickers, her face turned coyly to the camera. The label went over the woman's breasts and read, 'this picture degrades women.' The girl hastily gathered up the labels and started putting the marked magazines back on the top shelf.

Marguerite took her wrist and whispered, 'Let me help.'

The two of them sat on the floor in amicable silence, grinning at each other as they defaced the Penthouse Pets. When the shopkeeper appeared and threatened to call the police, they ran out of the door, the girl darting down a side road shouting, 'Thank you, sister, whoever you are.'

Marguerite shouted back, 'Deeds, not words, sister.' She outpaced the pursuing shopkeeper.

Giving up, he bellowed, 'You should know better at your age.'

Incensed, Marguerite vowed forthwith to seek out further protest activity. She was delighted to find that the activist in her was still alive and kicking.

She read of a group involved in a long-drawn-out strike by Asian women, many of whom were refugees from Idi Amin's Uganda, who worked long hours for minuscule wages at Grunwick, a film-developing business in Willesden. For over a year the women had been striking for the right to belong to a union, a demand that was resolutely opposed by their boss, backed by the right-wing press and a posse of like-minded public figures and MPs. Coming in the wake of the shock of his father's racialist attitudes, and because of its union focus, the campaign ticked all Tony's boxes, so she had no trouble in persuading him to join her at a mass picket being organised in support of the women. On the day of the picket Donald was not well enough to accompany them. He had been suffering from flu for some time and Tony insisted that he take it easy. Donald was not too upset as he was not a born militant.

The event started well. Tony and Marguerite were enjoying themselves. Thousands of members of various unions, universities, women's groups and families thronged the streets round the factory. The multicolour trade-union banners, the bands, the chants were a splendid display of unity. They were moved by the sight of the tiny Jayaben Desai and her valiant band of strikers, resplendent in saris, leading the parade. Tony and Marguerite mingled with a contingent from the Teachers' Union.

Tony pointed out to Marguerite that the group of burly men behind them were the London dockers.

'Those bastards marched in support of Enoch Powell. They seem to have changed their minds. Perhaps I should get them to go and talk to Dad.'

The huge crowd was trying to stop the bus carrying the non-striking workers into the building, so that they could put their side of the argument. But the police would not let the pickets get near enough to talk.

At first there was friendly banter with some of the police, who were also fighting for a wage increase. But their friendliness cooled when Arthur Scargill arrived with his miners. A policeman with a loudhailer started ordering people to clear the road.

'They'll never forgive them for winning at Saltley Gate,' said Tony.

A very large man grabbed the megaphone from the policeman and said, 'Me and my comrades built the bloody roads. I'm not going to be ordered off 'em by you, matey.'

He was backed by an aggressively shouting group with a banner declaring themselves the Workers' Revolutionary Party.

'They're just here to make trouble,' snarled Tony. 'Middle-class wankers, the lot of them.'

Marguerite joined the women in the front when she saw one being roughly dragged away by a policeman.

'We have a legal right to picket,' she protested.

'But not to obstruct the highway.'

The policeman pushed Marguerite away so violently that she fell to the ground. The mood was changing. The police were manhandling the women strikers, which incited their male supporters to attack them. Suddenly the pent-up fury of the last eighteen months' battle exploded in a vicious fight between the police and the pickets. Men were shouting, women screaming. Marguerite instinctively started to defend the women, using techniques she had learnt long ago.

Grabbing her round the waist Tony shouted, 'For God's sake, Marguerite. You'll kill somebody.'

Appalled, she let go of a shocked policeman whom she had in a choke-hold and gasped, 'Sorry,' as Tony thrust her away through the battling crowd. They passed a policeman lying on the ground with blood streaming from his head and a broken bottle beside him.

A boy in jeans stood by the unconscious man yelling, 'Serves you right, you fucking pig,' before being dragged away by his hair into a waiting police van. The police were now wielding batons and seemed intent on injuring people.

Marguerite and Tony joined a huddle clinging to each other in one of the small front gardens of the street.

Marguerite was bewildered.

'What's going on? Why are the police being like this?'

A man in a pinstriped suit said, 'This is out of order. The police are definitely using undue force.'

A grey-haired woman, her coat-sleeve torn in the scrum, said, 'These are not your usual coppers. They're a squad called the Special Patrol Group formed to control public order. They're thugs.'

Tony was incensed.

'But we're not bloody terrorists.'

The woman replied, 'You don't have to be. Trust me . . .'

Marguerite shouted, hoping the police would hear, 'But they're our fellow countrymen. Why behave with such venom?'

Tony took her hand and said quietly, 'Why did you?'

Jacob and she are amongst the next four to be herded out by the Milice to be shot. Jacob hurls her in front of him through the barn door.

'Vite. Tu t'enfuis. Je te suivrai. Merde, ma chérie.'

She runs. The shots, the shouts, she turns her head to see Jacob weaving from side to side behind her, deliberately taking the bullets to shield her. She reaches the trees, turns to see him writhing, juddering on the ground. One hand indicating 'Go'. If she goes back his absurd bravery will be in vain. So she stumbles on, gasping, sobbing, cursing, down into the ravine and up the other side, eventually losing her pursuers and collapsing under a tree in a paroxysm of rage and hatred. Never again would she run away. She would confront brutality with all her might to avenge the deaths of her comrades and Jacob's sacrifice for her.

The police were arresting numerous people, but the situation seemed out of control.

'They look as if they're going to seal the road off,' Tony said. 'Let's get out or we'll be trapped in this.'

They managed to force their way through a phalanx of police and reach the tube along with other shocked protesters.

When they got home a frail Donald poured them brandies, as they sat trying to make sense of what had happened.

Tony said, 'Remember it was only a small minority making trouble. The vast majority were supporting some Asian women in a just cause. That's got to be good.'

'Yes, but that small minority of hotheads in the police and the crowd were violent and out of control enough to destroy the whole thing, Tony.'

He caught her eye.

'Yes, I know, me too. I don't exclude myself. I hate how I reacted. But I was so angry. Something's changed, Tony. I remember you telling me that society was kinder. Not any more. Not today.'

Donald refilled their glasses.

'Look at you two. You'll be saying "Young people are not like they used to be in my day" in a minute.'

They were silent. Then almost in unison Marguerite and Tony said, 'Well, they're not.'

Donald roared with laughter.

Tony continued, 'They have no values. They don't care.'

'What about Rock against Racism? Thousands of kids standing up to racist bullies.'

Tony stared into his glass. 'They're just going to a lot of free concerts.'

'Oh, you miserable old git. Drink your brandy and cheer up. This was obviously a horrid experience for you both, but people are basically lovely. It's not the end of society as we know it just because a few hooligans had a punch-up.'

Tony stood up and hugged Donald.

'What would I do without you, my little Mary Sunshine?'

Back in her flat, Marguerite wished she had someone to comfort her. She lay in bed, rigid and open-eyed, trying to understand the violence in herself, and others. Like Miss Fryer and poor lost Bert, she was finding some changes difficult to comprehend. That hatred today, the hell of the Bull Ring. Thirty years ago the girls at Dartford County Grammar had been avid to learn, they wanted to excel, to do something with their lives, despite, or perhaps because of, all the odds being against them; her present pupils seemed to regard being clever and working hard as 'uncool'. But so had Elsie.

Thinking of Elsie's ability to rise above disaster uplifted Marguerite and restored her faith. She had respected Chapple's insistence on not assisting Elsie to chart her future, but she hoped she would pursue the possibility of attending Ruskin College and belatedly enjoy the development of her excellent brain. She had heard nothing from her for several weeks. Maybe this was a good sign, that, with the support of her group, she was sorting out her life. But the next morning there came a phone call.

'Miss Carter, you've got to help.'

Elsie's voice on the phone was hysterical.

'Elsie, I was thinking of you last night. I was happy for you. Please, please don't tell me you've relapsed.'

'No, it's the Centre. They're closing it down.'

'What are you talking about?'

'That inspection. Those two arseholes that came round and asked stupid, snotty questions. They've told a lot of lies and refused the funding, so we have to close.'

When Marguerite arrived the whole community of CURE were gathered in the main hall, some on chairs, some on the floor. They were listening desperately to Peter, believing that he could solve this problem, as he always did, with reason and calm. Peter was doing his best to reassure them that they could keep in touch with him and the rest of the staff but the terror in their eyes at the thought of being abandoned by the those who had given them hope and security was devastating. The word 'why' filled the room.

Marguerite read the report with growing disbelief. It was Risinghill School all over again. The two men who conducted the inspection were insultingly dismissive of Peter, using the word 'charismatic' as an insult, suggesting that it blinded people to his manifold supposed crimes. One of the inspectors ran a residential clinic along strict conventional psychiatric lines, and was obviously appalled by CURE's lack of discipline and conformity.

'It didn't help when they discovered I'd once been a member of the Communist Party,' Dr Chapple laughed. 'That frightened them to death, then when I said I'd ceased to be a member after the tanks went into Budapest, they seemed to regard me as some sort of deserter, which was worse.'

Peter tried to make them laugh when he read out one passage.

'Listen to how they describe you. It will make you proud. "The group presented as being articulate, pseudo-intellectual, cohesive, anti-establishment, anti-psychiatry, anti-everything except each other." I think we can safely say they got that right. We are out of the norm, it's true. But if we are judged unorthodox, so what. What matters is that our treatment is successful. Looking round at you all I can see that it has been. And promise me that you will continue to be there for each other and anti-bullshit when you leave this place.'

Several of the patients were openly weeping. Elsie had her arms tightly folded. Chapple's mouth was set in a fixed grin but his eyes were angry as he comforted them. Several started wrecking the place, breaking windows and kicking down doors, and no one stopped them. Marguerite watched in disbelief as another visionary project was falling apart, thanks to two hidebound, blind idiots, who had, judging by the report, set out to destroy something they could not begin to understand. She marvelled that the narrow-minded bigots always seemed to win.

Elsie came towards her.

'I'm off, Miss Carter, I can't bear this.'

Marguerite gripped her by the shoulders.

'Yes, you can, Elsie. You must. You must prove that Peter's work was worthwhile. Please don't betray him. Don't fall back.'

'I'll be all right. I've just got to get out of here. It's doing my head in.'

'Elsie, come and stay with me.'

'No. I've got to do this on my own. Don't worry about me. I'm a survivor. I'll show the bastards. Oh, Miss Carter, look at him.'

They both looked over to where Dr Chapple was embracing and talking intently to a succession of patients.

'It's so unjust. He saved my life.'

They watched in silence for a while.

'I could do that line better now,' Elsie said.

'What do you mean, Elsie?'

'That line at the end of *Saint Joan*. "O God, that madest this beautiful earth, when will it be ready to receive Thy saints? How long, O Lord, how long?"'

Elsie's ravaged face was momentarily that of the radiant fifteen-year old girl. But a second later it faded as she snarled,

'Shits, all of them shits.'

She kissed Marguerite, and kicked her way out of the front door, swinging on its broken hinges.

Chapter 39

For several months Marguerite made regular tours of Elsie's old haunts, terrified that, despite her reassurances, she may have sunk back into her drug-ridden existence. She found no trace of her.

The winter of 1978–9 was the coldest for many years. Thick snow turned to filthy slush in the streets of London. In January, crossing Leicester Square on another fruitless search for Elsie, she found it piled high with rubbish, dumped there because of a strike by dustmen. Rats ran among the garbage. Britain was grinding to a halt as more and more people competed for increasingly high wage increases: factories were closed, transport was at a standstill, there was no fuel for cars or heating, supermarket shelves were bare, even grave diggers were refusing to bury the dead. Marguerite was saddened by the brutal disregard for others that seemed to have gripped the country. Tony tried to defend his beloved unions until he himself was confronted by their intransigence.

For several months Donald had suffered recurrent illnesses. Because of the strikes he had caught a bad chill from doing class in a bitterly cold, unheated rehearsal room, after having struggled through deep snow at seven o'clock in the morning from

Myddelton Square to Covent Garden. For several days he lay in bed alternating between shivering and sweating. In the middle of one night he had an attack of violent vomiting and diarrhoea, eventually passing out. Tony phoned for an ambulance, but they would not come out when he told them that Donald had regained consciousness. They were on strike and would only come for what they considered emergencies. Tony took Donald, who was by this time feeling slightly better, to the hospital by car, where he sat forlornly in the back seat, holding a basin in case he was sick again. After a cursory look at him, the pickets would not let them into the hospital. An attempt to reason with them fell on deaf ears.

Tony was furious. He jettisoned his working-class allegiance.

'Who are you to decide? You are not doctors. You're bloody cleaners and boiler men. We need a medical opinion.'

'We're in charge now. Emergencies only. He looks all right to us.'

Tony gave Donald an incredulous look.

'The world's gone bloody mad.'

By the time they got back to Myddelton Square Donald was still feeling a bit better. Marguerite had prepared some chicken soup and, after he had managed to eat a little, she helped him to bed where he fell asleep, exhausted by his pointless journey.

When she came down to sit with Tony he was growling at the television, squirming in frustration.

'Stupid bastards. They're destroying the Party.'

After a fierce exchange between some MPs and union men, Margaret Thatcher, perfectly coiffed, perfectly elocuted, voiced her response to the crisis.

'Some of the unions are confronting the British people; they are confronting the sick, they are confronting the old, they are confronting the children. I am prepared to take on anyone who is confronting those and who is confronting the law of the land . . . If someone is confronting our essential liberties, if someone is inflicting injury, harm and damage on the sick, my God, I will confront them.'

Marguerite and Tony were silent for a while.

Then Marguerite said, 'I'm sorry, Tony. I'm going to vote for her. Not just because she's a woman, but she sounds resolute. Things have got to change. What about you?'

'I can't, Mags. I can't. I just can't. I hate my lot as well. Their weakness, their incompetence, but I can't vote for those bastards. It would be a betrayal.'

His eyes brimmed with tears.

'Oh Tony, darling, please don't. It's not that important, it's just politics.'

He blew his nose.

'It's not just politics to me, Mags. Ever since I first heard Bevan speak, it's been a driving force in my life. The Labour Party, the working class have been my gods. They are what I believe in. But now – it's all crumbling. Just before he died, in 1960, Nye said we'd become a vulgar society, a meretricious society where all our priorities had gone wrong. God, what would he make of us now? Greedy, selfish, ignorant.'

So great was Tony's despair that Marguerite could not openly celebrate the advent of a woman prime minister when the Tories predictably won the election with a thumping majority. She was worried about him. He was drinking too much and was often morose and uncommunicative. She knew he was distressed by his parents' unhappiness. Despite his father's reluctant acceptance of his relationship with Donald, the rift between them had deepened, and on rare visits to Oldham he came back visibly saddened by the fading of his rose-tinted memories of his working-class childhood.

'The future is scary, the present a nightmare, and the past a fantasy.'

One night, after an uneasy supper, Donald went to bed because Tony had snapped at him for daring to suggest that at least Margaret Thatcher had good legs.

Marguerite said, 'You seem to have lost your sense of humour, Tony. What's up?'

'I know. I'm sorry, Mags. I'm going to tell you something that you mustn't tell Donald. It's something that started way back in 1963. You remember when there was all that stuff about Kim Philby disappearing? Well, I was interviewed by MI5.'

'You? Why on earth—?'

'Because they knew Philby had worked with Guy Burgess, who'd scarpered to Russia in the '50s. And I knew him. Oh don't worry. I'm not a traitor. I was just a pretty boy who went to the same parties as Guy. Everyone was questioned. All the queers. We didn't take it very seriously. We were used to be being blamed for everything. Then Philby turned up in Moscow and it all calmed down.'

'Then why is it still troubling you?'

'Then I met Donald, who has never been promiscuous like me. I was terrified of losing him. We agreed to forget about my past. Not even discuss it. Start afresh. We poofs became legal in 1967 and everything was hunky-dory. Till now.'

'Why till now?'

'Some of the parties I went to were given by Anthony Blunt.'

'What? The Queen's pictures bloke? Who's been in the papers?'

'Yes, I didn't know he was a spy. I've only just read about it now. They kept it quiet all this time. Giving him a knighthood, letting him work for the Queen. Some kind of fucking gentlemen's agreement, I suppose.'

'And now Thatcher's let the cat out of the bag.'

'Yes. And now my fear has come flooding back. Like when I was young. I'm terrified the press will come nosing about. They've probably got all the names from his address book, the same as MI5. I'm frightened to death every time the phone rings or someone comes to the door.'

Marguerite put her arms round Tony.

'Of course they won't, my love. You're getting it all out of proportion. They're not going to be interested in a nice PT teacher.'

'There's something else, Mags.' His voice broke. 'I'm so worried about Donald.'

'Don't be silly. Donald wouldn't care about your past.'

'I meant his health. He keeps being ill.'

'Well, he's run down.'

'Two of our friends died recently. They kept getting sick. Then they became riddled with disease. One went blind. They just wasted away and died. The doctors couldn't explain it. They pumped them both full of antibiotics and other drugs but nothing worked. Someone told me that in America several gay men have died of a mysterious illness.'

'But that's nonsense, Tony. Just malign gossip. Why on earth would some illness be confined to gay men? You've got to get a grip. You keep looking on the black side. You're depressed.'

'Well, everything is bloody depressing. The country's going to the dogs.'

Marguerite seized on an opportunity to change to a subject that always invigorated Tony.

'Nonsense. I know she's anathema to you, but I think Maggie's doing a good job. You've got to admit she's got guts.'

Tony rose to the bait.

'I hate her. She's caused mayhem. I'll never get over that

326

sick-making entry into No. 10. What a joke that turned out to be. Where there is discord let there be fucking harmony? Some hopes. The destruction of our industry. Race riots. The Troubles. It's bloody civil war, I tell you.'

'That's my boy. Now stop worrying about nothing.'

Whereas in the past, with the Queen's Coronation and Churchill's funeral, they had felt part of the patriotic unity in the country, Marguerite and Tony did not join the rest of the confused British public as they went from cheering the meek girl submerged in billows of crumpled ivory silk, nervously eyeing her husband, the future King, to half-heartedly waving their flags in the victory parade, not attended by the royals, to celebrate the defence of some islands few even knew existed.

Apart from one visit to Greenham Common to support the removal of American missiles, Marguerite's radicalism again faded. Tony did not actively support the miners either in their struggle for existence. Activity generally seemed to be too much of an effort for him. Sport at school was limited as they had no playing fields, since they were sold off by the government.

Tony was surprisingly pleased.

'I can't run up and down a football pitch any more. Blowing my whistle for a gentle game of girls' netball in the playground is about my limit nowadays. Bugger the health of the nation's youth. What about mine?'

Over the years Tony's face had matured into craggy good looks but Marguerite had to reassure him.

'You're still devastatingly handsome. You look like Paul Scofield. Much more interesting than that Greek God blandness you used to have.'

But Tony was inconsolable. Being in his early sixties troubled him deeply.

'I hate being old. My body doesn't do what I want it to, and I don't want an interesting face. I want to be young and beautiful again.'

'I'm the one who should be saying that. I'm a woman. It's supposed to be worse for us to lose our looks.'

'Well, it's not. I'm turning into a decaying old queen and it horrifies me. You're an attractive mature woman. That's much nicer.'

'Well, I love you. And so does Donald. So shut up and count your blessings.'

Marguerite frequently found herself boosting Tony's ebbing confidence and joking him out of depression. Usually these grey moods engulfed him for no apparent reason, but as time went on and Donald seemed often to be sick, Marguerite too began to be worried about his health.

After several years' respite from the repeated illnesses that he had suffered at the end of the 1970s, he was ailing again. One of his feet had a painful spur, which made every leap torture, and there were signs of early arthritis in his overstressed knees. He missed several scheduled performances because of various maladies. Due to this unreliability in the age-averse world of ballet, at forty he was deemed too old for romantic leads. He was now less in demand, even for smaller character parts. There was talk of him becoming ballet master, which involved teaching the newcomers roles that he had danced.

Donald and Tony began to discuss their future. The talks included Marguerite as their lives were so entwined. Tony, frustrated as he was at teaching sport with no facilities and his reluctant physique, planned to retire in four or five years' time and what with Donald being less involved with the ballet company, they looked forward to travelling and generally enjoying themselves. Marguerite was not so happy at the idea of retirement but considered leaving the grind of school to do more part-time tutoring with the Open University. The prospect of more travel, more fun, had great appeal. Having spent all her working life controlled by timetables, she felt cautiously excited about the idea of more freedom from responsibility. The three of them made lists of countries they wished to visit, journeys they would make. When Tony suggested they go to France and see her old haunts in Paris and the Vaucluse, she agreed to Paris but demurred at the Vaucluse.

'I'm not ready.'

'After forty-odd years?'

'I don't want to open old wounds.'

'You'd prefer to cover them up and let them fester?'

'Yes.'

Since his disenchantment with the cosy memories of his own past, Tony was understanding of Marguerite's fear of revisiting hers.

'OK, fair enough.'

'He's probably dead or married. I'd rather not know. I prefer to hang on to my memories, carpe the diem, and look forward to lovely new adventures with you two.'

Chapter 40

A few weeks after the night when they began planning their futures Tony and Marguerite were watching television in her flat, waiting for Donald to join them for supper after a performance. He was very late, and when he eventually arrived he looked wild-eyed and had obviously been drinking. Tony, ever worried that Donald would leave him for someone younger, upbraided him for being rude to Marguerite.

To their alarm Donald burst into tears.

'I've been having a drink with Rudi and some of the boys. He was telling us how many people have died in America. There has been some research done and they have found this thing called GRID. Gay Related Immune Deficiency. There's no cure. You can be tested to see if you've got it. Rudi said we should be. He has, but he wouldn't tell us the result. I'm terrified. All those illnesses I've been having. I think I've got it.'

Tony was silent.

Marguerite said, 'Why on earth do you think that? How do you get it? Is it infectious or contagious?'

'They don't know for sure. It seems to be through sex. Gay sex. No one seems to know anything for sure. But people are dying. More and more people. And nearly all gay.'

Tony was poleaxed by fear for Donald, but Marguerite decided to find out all she could about this secret scourge. Few seemed to either know or care about what was happening to the increasingly ostracised gay community. Soon the news began to filter into the papers, as deaths were reported in England. The tabloids made a meal of this 'gay plague'. Little was done about it, whilst it was thought the illness only attacked homosexual men.

She didn't want Donald to know that she was scrabbling around for help until she had some good news to report, so she only talked confidentially to his best friend in the company who recommended she talk to a ballerina, now retired, whom Donald had partnered in leading roles. Still exquisite, hair swept back in a bun, erect and graceful with her tortured, turned-out feet now in comfortable furry slippers, Isabella told Marguerite all she had found out in an effort to help her former colleagues.

'It's no longer called GRID because they realised it's not just gays who get it. It's now Human Immunodeficiency Virus. That's the first stage, which can last for years. That develops into Acquired Immunodeficiency Syndrome. If you get that, you've had it.

'Surely not. There must be some cure?'

'Nope. And what's more, nobody's really trying to find one. Did you hear what that charmer in Manchester said?'

'Who?'

'Oh the Chief Constable of Police, no less, James Anderton by name. He waxed poetic, saying homosexuals were swirling around in a cesspool of their own making. Nice, eh?'

Although Isabella gave Marguerite little hope for a good out-come, she recommended a visit to a doctor they all knew.

Dr Patrick Woodcock lived in Pimlico, where various actors, dancers and singers picked their way through the street market to his elegant house for supplies of purple hearts, pep-up Vitamin B12 injections, beta-blockers for stage fright and advice on plastic surgery. He understood and was deeply fond of his colourful talented patients and was distraught at this catastrophe that was engulfing them. He had known Donald since he was a pupil at the Royal Ballet School and had kept him dancing through injuries and the wear and tear on his body of the brutal regime of a dancer. When Marguerite took Donald to see him he gave Donald a physical examination, checking his glands and lingering over a raised black patch that had recently appeared on his back. His hand was trembling as he took a sample of blood. When Donald went behind the screen to put on his clothes Dr Woodcock looked at Marguerite and slowly shook his head. Then Donald reappeared and he assumed his usual jolly demeanour.

'Well, lovey, I'll let you have the results in a few days. In the meantime take it easy. No lifting those girlies. Take some time off. Let Tony and Marguerite here make a fuss of you.'

The results of the test confirmed their worst fears. Donald was HIV-positive and had already started the terrifying descent into full-blown AIDS.

Tony seemed unable to comprehend what was happening. He wandered around the flat in a state of shock, sometimes sitting by Donald's bed or chair, holding his hand and muttering, 'I love you. Please, please, get better.'

It was left to Marguerite to do what she could to nurse Donald through the horror of the illness. She was pleased to do it as it gave her no time to think.

Donald's suffering was appalling. Over a few months his perfect body wasted away to a skeleton, and was further desecrated by the purplish black pustules. He could not swallow or talk properly, because a vile fungal infection blackened his mouth. His sight began to fail. He was dying before their eyes, and they were helpless.

She wants to go back. She doesn't want him to die convulsing, bleeding on his own. He writhes in agony but she runs on. Jacob wants her to escape. That's why he is dying. She has no choice but to run on.

As she sat with Tony by Donald's bedside watching the sweet man they both loved trapped inside his rotting body, yet still struggling to comfort them with word or gesture, she could hardly bear her pain, but for Tony's sake she had to simulate calm. The outside world was seething with hatred towards these grotesquely suffering men. More and more of their friends were dying and nothing was being done to help them. It was confirmed that drug addicts too were falling victim to the scourge and nobody cared about them either. Marguerite was terrified that wherever she was Elsie too might succumb.

Despite some drugs from Dr Woodcock it was obvious to Marguerite she lacked the expertise to ease what was clearly becoming the final stage of Donald's life, so that he could die with the same grace with which he had lived. She tried desperately to get him into a hospice, but none would take patients with AIDS. He eventually died an appalling death on a trolley pushed into a corner of a hospital emergency ward, with one doctor, masked, gloved and gowned, looking nervously on. Marguerite and Tony each held one of his hands, as his cracked, bleeding lips tried to smile, before his lids at last, mercifully, closed over his gentle brown sightless eyes.

Then ensued the horror of finding an undertaker that would handle his body. Eventually Donald was cremated in a bleak chapel, with a rudimentary service, conducted by a vicar who did not know him. They were both too consumed by despair to arrange the funeral. His family had disowned him years ago and it seemed unfair to ask the beleaguered members of the company to put their minds to the funeral of someone who had died of the disease of which they were all living in dread, so they left it to the vicar.

It proved a challenge to the poor man. Coming from the James Anderton religious standpoint, his chosen readings tended towards ominous warnings about sin and the difficulty of entering the kingdom of heaven. As Marguerite and Tony and a few members of the ballet company were the only people there, none of them was particularly worried about that likelihood.

The vicar did make one misguided attempt to be tolerant with a passage from the Gospel of St Matthew, '"Jesus said not everyone can accept this word, but only those to whom it has been given. For there are eunuchs, who are born that way, and there are eunuchs who have been made eunuchs by others, and there are those that choose to live like eunuchs for the sake of the kingdom of heaven. The one who can accept this should accept it."'

Marguerite and Tony listened open-mouthed. Their exhaustion got the better of them, and they collapsed into helpless giggles as the coffin slid bumpily through a grubby purple curtain, accompanied by some unidentifiable organ musak. The vicar strode out without a word, and they were left clinging to one another sobbing and laughing.

'Donald would have loved that. What a farce.'

Then as suddenly as it had started the laughter died. Tony gripped her shoulder, wiping her tears with his other hand.

'I killed him you know, Mags, I killed him.'

Judging them both to be in no state to talk seriously Marguerite decided to wait until they were home before she asked Tony what he meant. They went into her flat, neither of them able to deal with Donald's gaping absence upstairs. Marguerite cooked Welsh rarebit. They finished a bottle of wine and then settled in front of the fire with large brandies.

For a long while they were silent staring into the flames, trying to comprehend the finality of Donald's death and not daring to articulate the horror that had preceded it. As she poured more brandy into their glasses Marguerite remarked, 'Thank Christ that's over,' meaning the funeral.

Tony stared at the flickering light of the fire on his glass.

'No, it isn't. It never will be. Even if one day I get over this wrenching loss, which I doubt, the guilt will never leave me.'

'What are you talking about, Tony? You were his life. You gave him love and support. He adored you.'

'But I killed him.'

'Stop it, Tony. This is nonsense.'

'How do you suppose he contracted HIV?'

'Nobody knows why people get it.'

'They are pretty certain now that one way is promiscuous sex. Now which of us, Donald or me, fitted that category?'

'But not recently.'

'The virus can be undetected for years and years, but you're still a carrier. Besides—'

'Tony, I don't want to hear this, do I?'

'And I don't want to admit it. But I need to. When Donald was away on that tour of America, God forgive me, one night I went cottaging. Force of habit. It didn't mean a thing. Only once. I was ashamed of betraying him, but could never have imagined what the consequences would be. A mindless, empty adventure, and I killed our beautiful boy.'

It was pointless trying to argue with Tony. He would not even agree to be tested to see if he was actually carrying the virus.

'What's the point? If it wasn't me, then it opens other unthinkable possibilities, and what would I personally gain by knowing? There's no cure, and I'm not likely to infect anyone else. There will never be anyone else. Anyway, I want to get it. I want to die. Who knows, that vicar and his gang may be right. There may be an afterlife. Donald will be in paradise but he'll put in a word for me and we'll be together again. Or there will be nothing. Nothing would be good. Better than this.'

'Come to bed, Tony. Let's have a cuddle.'

'Aren't you afraid—? Remember the advert, "There's a new danger that's a threat to us all."'

'Listen, I've tried for years to seduce you, I'm not likely to succeed now.'

All night they clung together as they used to do, gently kissing, stroking, comforting, sincerely loving.

Chapter 41

A few days after the funeral Marguerite forced Tony to go with her to work. The febrile atmosphere caused by the leaflets warning against AIDS delivered to every household, and the doom-laden adverts on the television, as well as ignorance as to the cause and means of transmission, made it dangerous to reveal that their friend had died of the disease. Feeling like traitors, they did not mention the cause of his death, merely that they had attended the funeral of a mutual friend. Neither had ever become close to other staff members at the school so no one was particularly interested anyway. An assumption had been made that Marguerite and Tony were in some sort of relationship, which successfully covered any questions about Tony's sexuality. Thanks to the innuendoes of some outrageously camp comics on television, people were more aware of homosexuality; as a joke though, not, certainly since the AIDS scare, with much more tolerance. Such was the public confusion, linking homosexuality with paedophilia, that it would have been impossible for Tony to work as a sports master if it had been known that he was gay.

Over the next few months they struggled to come to terms with their loss of Donald. It felt as if all the joy had gone from their lives. His exquisite taste, his gentle concern for them both, and his indefatigable sense of fun had brought enjoyment to the everyday. He supervised what they wore, what they ate, and had taken over from Tony as 'treats' organiser. It was impossible to be bored with him around. He made the ordinary exciting: a walk on Hampstead Heath, a visit to the Zoo, shopping in the food hall at Harrods, a Gilbert & George exhibition at the Whitechapel Gallery, old-time music hall at the Players' Theatre, ham, egg and chips at Pellicci's Café in the East End.

'Hurry up, you slowcoaches, you've just got to see/hear/do this.' Donald's eyes aglow as he danced ahead of them. His chortle of pleasure when they shared his relish.

That someone who cherished all that was lovely should have died such an ugly death erased for ever any possibility of a benign God. Marguerite could not be bothered to try and reconcile her Catholic conditioning, which still lurked in the recesses of her mind, with the unutterable cruelty of what had happened to Donald.

The incense, the candles, the soaring choir, knees on hairy hassocks, I believe in God, the Father Almighty, creator of heaven and earth and my lovely new dress and shoes, my Sunday best. Forgive me, Father, for I have sinned.

She was sure some priest, or the funeral vicar, or years ago, her mother, would have come up with a platitude about suffering or free will but she just wasn't interested. Better to veto any possibility of help from above, and get on with it yourself. She was relieved.

'Tony, I want you to know. I am now a fully paid-up atheist.'

'Welcome to the club, petal.'

As the months went by, she tried to restore in Tony his old

zest for life, but any enquiry as to what he would like to do in their spare time was greeted by a shrug.

'Whatever you like.'

There were so many places that were out of bounds because of their association with Donald, practically the whole of London in fact, and some more, like Soho and Brighton, because of the scars from her relationship with Jimmy.

'This is ridiculous, Tony. We can't spend the rest of our lives avoiding.'

'You're a fine one to talk.'

'Touché. But we are lucky to be alive. So let's try and live, Tony. We've still got each other. We were blessed to have Donald. He was so completely and joyously alive. It's a betrayal of all he was if we allow this loss to make us sad for evermore.'

The first year passed agonisingly slowly for them both. To mark the first anniversary of Donald's death, with Tony's reluctant agreement, Marguerite organised a trip to Venice. Neither of them had ever been there. Marguerite hoped that they could recapture the pleasure of their *Good Food Guide* expeditions, before Donald came into their lives.

Although it was February, and cold, the trip in the water taxi from the airport to their hotel was exhilarating. They stood at the back as the boat roared and crashed through the waves of the grey lagoon, the wind and spray lashing their faces. When it turned into a small inlet between decaying houses with their doors facing the canal, Tony shouted, 'Good heavens, the streets really are full of water.'

Both of them cried out when they turned into the Grand Canal. The faded colours, the crumbling grandeur of the palaces lining the water, the gondoliers actually wearing boaters and striped shirts were like all the pictures, but animated and quite noisy and ten times more beautiful than they had ever imagined. Like nothing, anywhere, either of them had ever seen before. Unique. Glorious. The taxi turned into another narrow canal; all was silent apart from the slowing engine. They drew up at the steps of their small hotel.

They had decided to share a room as they had in the past. Their bedroom was the bridal suite. Frescoes on the ceiling, peachy ochred walls, a four-poster bed and terracotta-tiled floor, with a balcony, from where they could see people in the opposite windows sitting down to supper. They hugged each other with delight.

'It's as good as they say.'

'Better.'

Armed with their Links guide, which mapped out walks that took them into backwaters away from the tourists, Tony and Marguerite greedily devoured Venice. It seemed that every corner they turned offered new delights. Marguerite would barely allow Tony to stop for a coffee.

'Hold on, Mags. I'm not as young as I used to be, you know. Venice may be sinking but it won't go before we leave.'

In her new role as militant atheist, Marguerite was unsettled by the plethora of Madonnas and dying Jesuses the artists had been obliged to paint.

Tony was fascinated.

'They were sort of interior decorators, weren't they? It must have been fiendishly competitive. I bet they were well pissed off when Tintoretto got the whole of that scuola to do.'

Marguerite could not help wondering what they would have painted had they not been forced to earn a living pleasing doges and rich merchants. They both began to notice what they decided were jokes in the paintings. Carpaccio managed to get a cheeky white pet dog in the centre of several of his pictures, even in one supposed to be a holy miracle by the Rialto Bridge. Cherubs were often quite larky, one even exposing his bum in the corner of a very solemn crucifixion scene.

Their favourite angels were in the Frari at the foot of a breathtaking triptych by Giovanni Bellini of the Madonna and Child. Marguerite allowed Tony to sit with her in the chapel for a while and look at it. They were alone. It was breathtaking. So real was it, Marguerite would not have been surprised if Mary had stood up and handed her the naked baby to hold. Or the two cherub musicians had danced a jig.

She risked saying out loud what both had been privately thinking.

'How Donald would have loved her.'

'Yes. But we're loving her for him.'

A change had happened. The picture had rid them of their fear of talking about their pain. They went to a nearby café and shared a shift in perception; an awareness that Donald lived on through the way he had taught them to see the world. They doubted if before they met him they would have sat looking at the Bellini for so long, or found the fun in the sacred art. He was there in their eyes and they welcomed him back.

For the rest of their trip their conversation was peppered with 'Donald would have's.' A running joke was that Tony was Dirk Bogarde in *Death in Venice* and Donald would have pirouetted around being that beautiful object of his desire. Marguerite was uneasy that Tony still harboured this image of himself as a sad raddled homosexual who was losing his looks, but she laughed on cue, and claimed the role of the red-coated dwarf in *Don't Look Now*.

On their last night, in high spirits, they went to a nearby campo, and had Venetian spritzers, a delicious ruby-red concoction of Campari and Prosecco, with a slice of orange and an olive. They sat watching the locals, out for an evening stroll, and only then did Marguerite dare to raise her glass.

'To our absent friend.'

Tony took her hand, and kissed the palm.

'And to my dear, dear present one.'

Chapter 42

Returning to their separate flats, after Venice, was not easy. Tony insisted on keeping his exactly as it had been when Donald died. Marguerite had cleaned out the medicines and oxygen cylinders, but Donald's clothes, pictures and books had to be left exactly as if he were still there. Nevertheless, Tony seemed in a more accepting frame of mind. He also appeared less concerned that his sexuality would be revealed.

Trying to make something positive out of the anguish of Donald's suffering, they involved themselves in the setting up, in the face of vitriolic opposition, of London Lighthouse, a hospice for people dying of AIDS. They were there when Princess Diana, now blossomed into a glamorous, vital young woman, challenged the prevailing fear by striding into the hospice in a brilliant red suit and sexy black stockings, and posing for press and television, sitting on beds, holding hands, and kissing the patients. The public, and particularly the press in view of Diana's popularity, became a bit less antagonistic towards the gay community after that.

Then Parliament brought in Clause 28 of the Local Government Act that decreed that it was wrong for local authorities to 'intentionally promote homosexuality, or publish material with the intention of promoting homosexuality, or promote the teaching in any maintained school of the acceptability of homosexuality as a pretended family relationship'.

Tony was incensed.

'Well, thank you very much, Mrs sodding Thatcher. We're right back in the 1950s. We can join the miners as "the enemy within". Who else is going to be deemed "not one of us"? Not acceptable. They couldn't have chosen their words better to show the contempt they feel. Another group to hate in this fractured fucking country.'

Marguerite was pleased to see the return of Tony's old political fury.

'So, in the pitiful sex education classes we have, are we to ignore the poor kids cowering at their desks, who already realise they are "unacceptable"? That they mustn't "pretend" they are ever entitled to a family life? They have to be like me, do they? Spending their whole lives trying to be something they're not. Living a lie. My love for Donald was central to my existence yet I can't even tell my own mother. My father died not really reconciled to who I was. I can't join in when the people I work with are gossiping about their bloody wives and girlfriends. Yet our relationship, our family, which includes you, Mags, our "pretended family", is every bit as good as theirs.'

Marguerite shared his anger, knowing that Tony and Donald's relationship was as genuine as any heterosexual marriage. Had they adopted a child, as two of their gay friends in America had done, there was no doubt in her mind that they would have been better parents than those of some of her damaged pupils.

'Well, that's it,' Tony continued, 'I've had enough. There's a march happening against the Clause. I'm bloody well going on it.'

'Tony, be careful. This is going to get a lot of press attention. We're teachers. We could be in serious trouble if the school governors find out.'

'That's not like you, Mags. It's time to stand up and be counted.'

'I'm not worried about me. But it's more risky for you.'

'We have to go. You know that.'

She smiled.

'Of course I do.'

With a group of their colleagues from London Lighthouse they joined the 30,000 people converging on Whitehall. They were on the march once more. Despite its seriousness the event was fun; the anger was expressed with humour. Marguerite particularly liked a chant that didn't greatly amuse the dour, accompanying police: '2,4,6,8, is that copper really straight?'

There were silken banners, men in drag, girls defiantly kissing girls and men kissing men. There was music and dancing. The crowd was not just made up of lesbian women and homosexual men; there was support from many families and people from all walks of life including politics.

Tony, who was helping to organise the march, yelled through his megaphone, showing his rather ungracious prejudice, 'Will the fucking SWP get to the back?'

After the excitement of the day, Tony and Marguerite put their feet up in her flat.

Marguerite congratulated Tony on his part in the organisation.

'Although the Clause is awful, it's certainly united the gay community, hasn't it?'

Tony agreed.

'There were people marching who'd never been politically active before, and some who hadn't even come out of the closet.'

'Like you have, you mean.'

'Yes, at last. Pity I left it so late. It's easier for the youngsters. They haven't got the history. But Donald would be proud of me, wouldn't he?'

'He would, my darling, he would.'

'I'll try and make up for lost time.'

There was a reckless quality about Tony's new honesty that concerned Marguerite. Once, in the staff room at school, a homophobic diatribe by the deputy headmaster had him standing in front of the man and saying through gritted teeth, 'I think you should know, mate, that I am gay, and if you don't stop this bigoted claptrap, one of those "fairies", as you call us, may well punch you on the jaw, and if what you have been ignorantly saying is true, you'll probably catch AIDS.'

Marguerite warned him to be careful. But he wasn't. Sometime later he was summoned to the same deputy headmaster's study. He had been seen in a café, talking to one of the boys, who then told the other boys that Mr Stansfield was queer. When he pointed out that, even if he was 'promoting homosexuality', it was not on school premises, he was reluctantly let off with a stern warning.

Tony explained to Marguerite what had happened. Cycling back from school, he came across a group of pupils standing round a weeping boy, laughing and pushing him violently from one to the other. He dismounted and walked towards them. Seeing him, they all ran off, leaving the crying boy to pick up his scattered books and torn jacket.

'What's that all about, Geoffrey?'

'I can't say, sir.' The boy looked terrified.

'I tell you what, come into this caff and we'll straighten you out and have a cup of tea.'

After the boy had calmed down, Tony got him sufficiently relaxed to admit that the boys thought he was queer.

'And I suspect he is. I recognised myself at his age. And said so. What could I do, Mags, tell him he was a dirty little sod and must stop having wicked thoughts?'

'But then he went back and betrayed you to the others.'

'He was scared stiff. I expect he hoped they'd stop bullying him if he snitched on me.'

His laugh was rueful.

Afraid that his depression would engulf him again, Marguerite said uncertainly, 'It'll probably all blow over. The kids are very fond of you.'

'What a nasty world it's become, Mags. For all our campaigning and shouting nothing seems to get much better.'

'Nonsense. This is a tiny setback. They'll repeal that stupid Clause with all this uproar against it. People power. That's the thing. Look at the people pulling down the Berlin Wall. And the first missile has gone from Greenham. All those keening women made it happen. We've got to keep fighting.'

'You're right. That's my girl. How I love you, my Half-Full Lizzie Dripping.'

Chapter 43

The incident did not blow over. It lit a fuse that was to burn uncontrollably. The rumour of Tony's homosexuality spread through the school. Whereas, when Tony was on playground duty he was usually surrounded by youngsters wanting to talk and joke with him, they began to avoid him, and stand and stare from a distance, whispering and giggling. This behaviour culminated in Tony being asked to see the headmaster.

That night he told Marguerite about their conversation.

'He's a good man. I felt sorry for him. He looked really embarrassed. He told me there has been a complaint. One of the boys said I touched him inappropriately.'

Marguerite was aghast.

'What are you talking about?'

'James Matthews' father went to see her and said his son told him I interfered with him whilst teaching him to swim.'

'In the public baths? In front of dozens of other kids?'

'James said I held him in my arms.'

'Of course you did. You were teaching him to swim. If you hadn't, he'd have drowned.'

'Anyway, he explained he had to be extra cautious because of

Clause 28. He was obliged to suspend me, pending an inquiry by the council. He asked me to stay away from the school.'

'What did you say?'

Tony laughed.

'I asked if I should wear a pink triangle.'

She arrives in England and opens her father's letter as he had instructed.

Read this and understand why we have to stay and fight. It was written by Joseph Goebbels:

There are differences between people just as there are differences between animals. Some people are good, others bad. The same is true of animals. The fact that the Jew still lives among us is no proof that he belongs among us, just as a flea is not a household pet simply because it lives in a house. If someone wears the Jewish star, he is an enemy of the people. The Jews have no right to claim equality with us. If they wish to speak on the streets, in lines outside shops or in public transportation, they should be ignored because they are Jews who have no right to a voice in the community.

Marguerite, my darling daughter, we have to stay and rid your world of this hatred because we love you so very much.

Papa

For several months, Tony was not allowed in the school. Marguerite did her best to keep his spirits up and convince him that the case would be dropped. He began to drink heavily and she could not even persuade him to go to the cinema. He shut himself in his flat, reluctant to see her. On her sixty-fifth birthday, however, he invited her for a meal. He cooked her mother's cassoulet and opened a bottle of very good wine. After a dessert of crème brûlée she felt relieved that he had made an effort, even though he seemed abstracted.

'That was lovely, Tony. Can I stay for a bit? Let's talk. I miss you.'

'I know, I have not been very good company lately, I'm afraid.'

'Tell me what's happening. Have you been told what the inquiry will consist of?'

'Well, actually—'

'Go on.'

'I had a letter yesterday. The father is not happy with the delay, and has threatened to involve the police.'

'God, Tony. He can't.'

'Yes, that'll be fun, I must say. Like the old days. They'll probably look up my record. Homosexual, paedophile, what's the difference?'

'You must see a solicitor.'

'Yes, yes, I will. But first I need a little break to get my head straight. And I have some business to sort out. I'm going away for a couple of days.'

'Where? I'll come with you.'

Tony was adamant he needed some time on his own to get things in perspective. He would not tell her where he was going. He evaded her questions. In fact he seemed to want her to leave.

As she got to the door, he said, 'You do know I love you, don't you?'

'Don't look at me like that, Tony. You're frightening me to death.'

'You – frightened? You're the most courageous person I've ever met, my darling Lizzie Dripping. Give us a smile. Go on. Your lovely, lovely smile.'

He kissed her on the lips and they looked long and hard into one another's eyes.

'No, Tony. Please.'

'Hush, my love.' He kissed her hand and gently pushed her through the door.

She knew something terrible was about to happen, but for once she felt powerless to stop it.

Three days later she received a letter:

My dearest dear (thank you, Ivor, cue music)
When I said goodbye to you, I think you knew it was over. Thanks for not trying to stop me. I am weary. I haven't any fight left. I can't inflict the shame of a police inquiry on my mother. Especially now she is so old and on her own. I can't live with the guilt about Donald. I had the test, by the way, I'm positive. I can't put you through that inevitable nightmare again. I have some very good pills from a sympathetic gay doctor and will be found in one of those hotels in King's Cross. A note will tell the police to inform you. Please sell the flat and give the money to my mother. You can have the contents. I can't imagine all that campery working in Oldham. You'll find a will on my desk and hopefully I've left debts paid, and everything in order. I've written to my mother.

How can I do this to you? You, who I love with all my heart? Because it's better than the alternative. All that hatred flying around. A clean break, rather than a long-drawn-out agony. By the way, I went to the French Embassy and checked their census and found out that a Marcel Boyer, Croix de Guerre, is still living in Les Galets. On his own. Take the risk, my darling. Don't be a coward like me.

Thank you for a lifetime of love and support, especially since our beautiful boy died. I've tried, but it has all become unbearable. I want it to stop.

If there is another life, I will be watching over you and

one day we will all be together again. What on earth will poor St Peter make of us three? Our 'pretended family'. Oh, but it was wonderful. Thank you, thank you and forgive me. Tony.

Marguerite doubled up, moaning, 'You bastard, you bastard, you bastard, you bastard.' She collapsed onto the floor, writhing and howling, trying to black out the image of Tony alone in some squalid hotel. She found herself on her knees, praying that he had changed his mind, that his suicide attempt had failed. But the God she had rejected ignored her. The next day two policemen came to tell her of his death. They doubted if the coroner would want a public inquest. It seemed 'an open and shut case'. Mr Stansfield had made it clear that it was suicide in his note. They were blunt with Marguerite, assuming, as she was not a relative, that the usual sensitivity was unnecessary. She was glad. She just wanted to get rid of them.

After they left she went up to Tony's flat insanely looking for him. It was immaculate. She opened the wardrobe and inhaled the smell of him on his clothes. She sobbed, 'Where are you, where are you?'

Then she felt numb, exhausted. She felt nothing. She tried to bring some order to her mind. All it contained were questions:

> Could I have stopped him?
> Why didn't I talk to him?
> Why didn't he tell me he was HIV-positive?
> How can I bear this?
> How can I bear this?
> Dear God, how can I bear this?

Chapter 44

Marguerite stayed at home the following day, not even phoning the school. But the day after, she got herself up and, like a robot, washed, dressed and went to work.

As she walked into the staff room, it was obvious they all knew. They stopped talking and stared at her, unable to gauge what tone to take. Were condolences in order? She wasn't a wife or lover, the man was gay, they all knew that now, so how to behave towards this woman with the drawn grey face and dead red eyes? And anyway, suicide? What can one say about that? Apart from a few mumbled 'sad's and 'sorry's they opted to settle for breezy attempts to cheer her up with cups of tea and staffroom chit-chat.

The children were more forthcoming. Her first lesson of the day happened to be in a class with Geoffrey Wilkins, the lad Tony had tried to help, who had been questioned about that encounter, and James Matthews, who had accused Tony of molestation. When she walked into the room they were all in a state of high excitement, passing around a copy of last night's *London Evening Standard*. She asked to see it.

'Look, miss, there. It's Mr Stansfield.'

It was just a few lines on page four. 'Teacher found dead in hotel room.' Her hands shook as she read it. It was so inadequate. Such a meaningless, throwaway summing-up of the death of the man she knew. The class stared expectantly at her as she sat at her desk.

'And how does that make you feel, class?'

They were not expecting that. Silence.

'He was a queer, miss.' Giggles.

'Yes. I know.'

'My dad said, "Good riddance." That all of them should be done away with.' More giggles.

'Why did he say that?'

'Because they spread disease.'

'It's wicked being queer.'

'And suicide too. That's a sin. He committed suicide, miss.'

Marguerite looked around the room.

'So that is what your parents feel. What about you?'

Nothing.

'Did you like Mr Stansfield?'

After a long pause one of the girls raised her hand, blushing.

'I did, miss. He was nice.'

'Me too.'

'And me.'

A few muffled murmurs of agreement.

'And what about you, Geoffrey? How do you feel?'

The boy put his head down on his folded arms saying, 'Sad, miss. I feel so sad.'

'Oh he feels sad. Poor old Wilkins. Bloody pansy.'

James Matthews stood looking round at the class for approval.

'What about what he did to me?'

'And what exactly did he do to you, James?'

'You ask my dad.'

'I'm asking you.'

'He interfered with me.'

'Come here, James.'

The boy swaggered up to her desk.

'Show me what he did.'

'Don't be disgusting.'

Marguerite shouted, 'Show me. Richard Hopkins, come here, please.'

The boy moved to the front of the class nervously.

'Thank you, Richard. You be James. Now, James, you are Mr Stansfield. Do to Richard what Mr Stansfield did to you.'

For a moment the boy stood looking defiant. Then suddenly, shockingly, he started to cry.

'It's not fair. It's not my fault. I didn't mean it. I didn't want him to die.'

Marguerite took him in her arms.

'Don't worry. You're right. It's not your fault, James. Your father didn't understand. Mr Stansfield wouldn't have harmed you. Look, I'm holding you now. I'm embracing you. There's nothing wrong with that, is there?'

The boy was not used to hugs. He clung to her awkwardly.

'No, miss. It's nice.'

'Yes, Mr Stansfield was gay. Just as one or two of you may be.' Gasps. 'But he was a good man. He was my friend, you know, and I loved him very much. And he loved me. And all of you. There are all sorts of love. There are no rules. Apart from not damaging others. Mr Stansfield has left us, because the world finds it difficult to accept difference. And everyone's confused and frightened about AIDS. When we are frightened, we turn on those people who are not like us, but we must be careful because that's what causes wars. I beg of you to learn from this sad thing that has happened. Remember that Mr Stansfield was kind, and fun, and wanted to make the world a better place. Not just queer. That was only a tiny part of him.'

Only then did Marguerite realise that the door was open and that the headmaster was standing listening. Marguerite picked up her books and handbag.

'Don't worry, Mr Pryor. I'm leaving. Goodbye, class. Don't be upset by my tears. Or yours. There's nothing wrong with tears.'

Mr Pryor followed her down the corridor. Marguerite felt sorry for the man, as had Tony.

'There's bound to be a reaction from poor little Matthews's father when he tells him what I've said. Don't worry. I'm leaving for good. You can say you sacked me. That will make him happy.'

Mr Pryor put his hand on Marguerite's arm.

'The profession will be the poorer, Miss Carter. You are a wonderful teacher.'

Marguerite could not yet allow herself to contemplate a future without her lifetime dedication to teaching, so she threw herself into a frenzied organisation of Tony's funeral. She would not let it be a debacle like Donald's. She called upon Miss Scott, who had remained a friend, and was now head of a successful comprehensive, to conduct the ceremony in place of a token indifferent priest. Marguerite vetoed the crematorium's canned organ music and substituted recordings of the exquisite Beethoven string quartet No. 14, Op. 131, and for the departure of the coffin, it had to be Judy and 'Over The Rainbow'. In place of a eulogy Marguerite chose a poem. She thought how Tony would have loved Moira to read it. She had lost touch with her but thought someone at the St Martin's Theatre, where *The Mousetrap*, having moved from the

Ambassadors, was still ploughing on, might know her whereabouts.

She was amazed to find Moira was still in the cast. When they met Moira explained that, after her stint as an understudy in the play, she had left. Then, in desperation, after enduring years of unemployment, apart from occasional engagements in tatty repertory or depressing third-rate tours, augmented by stints serving in Harrods, she had returned to the play to perform one of the parts. 'My last gasp before I'm carted off to the actors' rest home. It's a boring old crone who gets bumped off in the first act. Sic transit bloody gloria, darling.'

The actress in her was gratified to be asked to do something well written for her old friend, despite her devastation upon learning of the circumstances of Tony's death.

On the day of the funeral, Marguerite filled the bleak little crematorium chapel with sweet-smelling spring flowers, and dressed herself in a bright red frock, which was the last one that Donald had chosen for her. She wore the lace gloves that Ethel had given her all those years ago. Not long after Bert's death of a heart attack Tony had organised Ethel's move to an old people's home in Oldham. Marguerite contacted them and arranged for a carer to accompany the old woman to London in a hire car. As Marguerite led her into the chapel Ethel looked around her, smiling broadly and stroking the gloves. She mercifully did not seem to understand what had happened to her son, or even that it was him in the coffin.

The chapel began to fill up. There were a few members of the ballet company, who had known Tony through Donald, Mr Duane and some of the old staff from his time at Risinghill, as well as a dozen or so men with thinning hair and chatting women that she recognised as pupils they had taught there. Looking even older were Pauline and Hazel from their Dartford days. She searched the faces to see if Elsie was among the crowd. Elsie would surely have been there if she could. Her absence reawakened Marguerite's fears that she might be one of the drug addicts who had contracted AIDS. Miss Allum had given up teaching music some time before but still lived with Mrs Schneider. They arrived together, Miss Allum in a wheelchair pushed by a bent, gnome-like Mr Humphreys.

Just as the service was about to begin there was a disturbance at the door. Led by Geoffrey Wilkins, at least twenty pupils from 4b crept in and sat at the back. An unexpected moment of magic was created when the children, delighted to recognise 'Morning Has Broken', embellished it with the harmonies they knew from the Cat Stevens recording.

The poem she had chosen for Moira to read was by Primo Levi. The part that resonated agonisingly for Marguerite was,

> I speak for you, companions of a crowded
> Road, not without its difficulties,
> And for you too, who have lost
> Soul, courage, the desire to live . . .

As Moira joined her in the pew after her reading, Marguerite kissed her on the cheek.

'That was beautiful. As Tony would have said, "Not a dry eye in the house."'

When the service was over Marguerite thanked all the children for coming and gave Geoffrey a special hug, mindful that he probably faced a battle against prejudice similar to Tony's, but comforted to see, as they walked down the path to the gates, that he was the centre of the group, rather than trailing on his own.

The mourners repaired to a nearby pub, and reminisced about

their friendship with Tony. There was laughter and some tears, but everyone avoided discussing the nature of his death. Ethel held tight to Marguerite's hand, occasionally looking at the lace gloves with a puzzled expression.

When eventually Marguerite and the carer settled her into the car she said happily, 'I'm glad you wore my gloves.'

'That's right, Ethel. They are the ones you gave me, remember?'

Ethel nodded.

'Yes, I remember.'

Marguerite smiled. Delighted that Ethel's confused mind had grasped something.

Then Ethel shook her hand formally.

'Thank you so much. It was a lovely wedding.'

Marguerite thought how much Tony and Donald would have enjoyed that.

Back at home, Marguerite collapsed into the armchair with a large brandy. After the frantic preparations for the funeral, putting the flat on the market, tying up loose ends, she had nothing to do. She went over the events of the day in her mind. In the silent flat, she felt an agonising ache in her throat and chest. All the words that would have poured out when she shared experiences with Tony and Donald were choking her. They had nowhere to go. This was how it would be from now on. She went into the toilet, knelt on the floor and vomited.

Chapter 45

Marguerite had never known true loneliness. She had always had people to confide in, to share with, to love and be loved by. As a child she had had her parents and best friend Rachel, in the Resistance loyal comrades and Marcel, and during her teaching career, her colleagues, pupils, and fellow campaigners. Above all, for forty-odd years she had had Tony and for more than twenty Donald. Because of the all-consuming nature of their relationship, she had had no need for other close friends. Even when she was on her own she had not felt lonely. She was too busy thinking, planning. In fact, she had enjoyed solitude, an occasional pause in the symphony of conversation, argument, laughter. There had always been the knowledge that communication was a staircase or a phone call away. Now, in the space of three wrenching weeks, she found herself excluded from the companionship of work, and had no one at home to care how frightened she was.

She had no reason to get up in the morning. So she didn't. For days she lay in bed, convulsively weeping or blankly staring at the ceiling, rising only to shuffle to the bathroom where she stared uncomprehendingly at the reflection in the mirror of an old woman, swigging a large glass of brandy. She didn't eat. Or look out of the window. She could hear that life was going on in the outside world, and she wondered how that was possible. She couldn't bear to think of the past, even less the future, so she tried to sleep away the present. That was worse, because inevitably she woke up, and agonisingly realised anew that everything she cared about had been swept away.

After several days in this stupefied state, she heard rain thrashing against the curtained windowpane, and had an overwhelming urge to go outside. She threw on the clothes that lay on the floor beside the bed, her funeral garb, the red frock that Donald had bought her, high-heeled shoes, lace gloves, and teetered out into the deluge. Outside the house, she stood, arms outstretched, face turned to the sky, and embraced the rain, allowing it to soak into her clothes and run down her face, arms and legs, in an attempt to wash away the pain. She automatically began walking towards school. The rain mingled with her tears and no one seemed to notice that she was unsuitably dressed and weeping. If they did, she was just a weirdo caught in a storm. And London is full of them. Weirdos and people caught in storms.

The gates of the school were locked. There was barbed wire on top of the fence. It kept marauders out and pupils in. That's the way it was nowadays. As she stood, staring through the gate, rain dripping from her skirt and hands and chin, she remembered how it had been with Duane, when people came and went as they pleased, a community school, and she felt angry and guilty that she had gone along with the compromise of his vision. She wanted no more of it. The sterile approach to education. The kowtowing to the mindless law that had defeated Tony.

'Fuck you all!' she screamed through the gate.

I'm going mad, she thought, as she made her way home via the Carpenter's Arms, only remembering when she saw its new blinds and pavement tables that Bob and Florrie had retired to run a bed–and–breakfast place in Devon. So they were happy. She tried to be pleased for them and the young couple that passed her, cuddling under an umbrella, but she just felt jealous. And even more alone.

When she got home, she stripped off her sodden clothes and sat, naked, eating a slice of stale bread and Marmite. Shivering, she ran a bath and lay in it, gulping a glass of wine. As her body thawed, she felt a flicker of life, the need to do something; she had no idea what. She got out of the bath and stood bewildered, muttering, 'Pull yourself together.' She examined in the mirror her hunched, skinny body, she tried to touch her toes, and couldn't. Tony had always insisted that exercise was better for depression than pills, hadn't he? He attributed Donald's high spirits to his daily dance and practice regime.

'OK, darling, I'll try that,' she said out loud.

She rushed into the bedroom, grabbed a pair of old slacks and a T-shirt. It had stopped raining so she just wore a cardigan and plimsolls. Wrapping her old bathing costume in a towel, she made for the local sports centre.

At the desk, she was about to ask for her ticket when the blonde receptionist shrieked over her head, 'Benedict, Peter, how lovely to see you. Where have you been all my life?'

Mouth caught open, ready to speak, Marguerite turned to see two young men ambling through the door, swinging squash racquets, the personification of the young upwardly mobile breed that had been gentrifying her area. Marguerite hated both of them on sight on Tony's behalf. Their vulgar offices were replacing the docks where men had done proper work, he would have said. She would have too, if she could have made herself heard, but now one of them was talking loudly into a huge, just-about portable, phone about some deal he was broking, whilst the other drawled over Marguerite's head about his 'out of this world trip to Ibiza with ecstasy of every sort'; this was accompanied by a discreet pantomime of swallowing a pill and reaching orgasm.

The mime was the first indication that either of them were aware of Marguerite's presence, so she said, 'Oh, don't worry about me. I may look old, but I know all about drugs and fucking. Now, my dear, do you think you could possibly spare a moment to give me a ticket for a swim?' The silence was palpable as Marguerite marched through the barrier.

She decided to have a sauna to sweat out some of the poison of grief. A man was already sitting in the room, pouring with perspiration. His eyes flicked in her direction as she entered, but he did not acknowledge her. Indeed, after that cursory first glance, she seemed to disappear off his radar. She didn't exist for him. How else to explain his uninhibited groping and scratching of his genitals? She did not flatter herself that he was being sexual. Surely it would have been a more appealing gesture if so? No, he had deemed her not worth noticing. Even when she coughed, he continued ministering to his crotch.

She could think of nothing to say. 'Will you stop that?' could well make him angry, or worse, surprised and embarrassed that there was actually someone there, who had feelings, was once a woman, a category into which, to him, she no longer fitted. So she held her tongue, whilst he held his balls. With as much dignity as she could muster from her shattered ego, she left the room, showered and dived into the pool.

As she glided through the water, she tried to imagine it was washing through her body. There was no one else in the pool, so she could close her eyes, sigh and groan, as her body stretched and relaxed in turn. She was actually beginning to enjoy the feeling, when her reverie was disturbed by a noisy splash and large waves raised by the man from the steam room, who was throwing his sweaty body into the water, ignoring the notices requesting people to shower first.

Marguerite tried to continue her sedate breaststroke, despite the turbulence caused by his ungainly crawl. Her training in the Scottish lochs for the SOE had made her an elegant swimmer. She had not had much practice other than occasional forays to the pool with Tony, but she found a rhythm that despite her age propelled her smoothly forward. She was conscious of the man accelerating his speed. Some of the old aggression stirred in Marguerite and she changed to her stylish crawl, easily gaining half a length on him. Splashing and coughing, Thatcher's competitive child desperately tried to catch her up, but she pulled out all the stops, and, using every ounce of her strength, did a few strokes of dazzling butterfly, leaving him standing in the shallow end, trying to look nonchalant. Marguerite leapt out of the pool and stood, panting, legs astride, hands on hips, staring down, willing him to meet her gaze. And he did. For the first time. With something akin to awe. Marguerite glowed.

'Hello,' she said and waited expectantly, until eventually he muttered a confused, 'Hello.' He stood gawping, his errant hands now scratching his head, as she turned on her heel and strode triumphantly into the changing room.

She walked back to Myddelton Square with a new spring in her step, despite having exhausted herself at the pool. She felt as if she had won a major victory, not only over the itchy man – he was irrelevant – but over herself. Her old fighting spirit was seeping back. Half-Full Lizzie Dripping was still in there somewhere. As she went down Pentonville Road she saw several people standing outside a newsagent's reading papers and talking to one another. The headline read, 'Maggie Resigns'.

Back home, she opened a tin of baked beans, toasted the stale bread, brewed a cup of tea and settled in front of the television. She watched Margaret Thatcher leaving 10 Downing Street, having seemingly been stabbed in the back by her own party. After her smooth smiling speech of farewell, the camera peered into the car as it drove off, revealing an unsettling image of the Iron Lady, red-eyed and tearful. 'Good bloody riddance,' she said on Tony's behalf, but could not help remembering, with something like affection, the dowdy young woman with blazing blue eyes standing next to Anthony Eden at Dartford football ground. Marguerite's early admiration of the woman had gradually disintegrated, egged on of course by Tony, starting with her disquiet at Thatcher's chilling intransigence in the face of the deaths of ten young IRA hunger strikers. This relentless hard determination to do what she considered right continued, no matter what the cost, making the country a meaner and more selfish place, but as the television repeatedly showed the devastated, ousted woman, Marguerite wondered why things always seemed to end sadly.

When she was younger she, and certainly Tony, would have seen Thatcher's demise as a golden opportunity to prepare to rid the country of the Tories at the next election, but Marguerite had lost all interest in politics. The days of passionate meetings in football grounds were over; it was all carefully orchestrated televised spectaculars, with obligatory standing ovations, pop groups, and a new breed called 'celebrities'. She did not fit in any more. The same was true of her work for the Open University. She continued to do some tutoring, but the object was now preparing people for jobs rather than encouraging learning for the sheer love of it and her supervisor subtly made her aware that her emotional approach to literature was out of step with the current postmodernist thinking. Miss Fryer's phrase 'I am no longer relevant' kept crawling, uninvited, into her brain.

Chapter 46

As various aspects of her life closed down, Marguerite was hideously aware of time. Whereas in the past she was always rushing about, trying to do several things at once, now the days were limitless deserts. Over the interminable weeks that stretched into endless months, she drifted around trying to find a reason for existing. She forced herself to go to galleries, concerts and the theatre but could not master the art of enjoying things for herself. She ached to share everything with Tony, to discuss a new film into the small hours, to relish Donald's rapturous reaction to a picture, a performance, a soufflé, a flower, to help a pupil open their heart to a poem. Encountering beauty, her first reaction had always been: Must show Tony, or Donald, or Class 3; she realised she was only fully alive through and for other people. It was a fatal flaw when age or circumstance left one alone.

She tried to make friends with the yuppie couple that had bought Tony's flat, but the only communication they managed was her banging on the ceiling with a broom when their thumping music and squawking voices went on way after midnight, and she heard herself referred to, through the open windows, as 'that miserable old cow downstairs'.

She realised her isolation was not unique when, treating

herself one day to tea in Fortnum and Mason's, she became fascinated by an elderly woman, wearing a heavy brown tweed cloak, a head-hugging cloche hat and pearl earrings, and with crimson lipstick bleeding into the lines around her mouth, sitting majestically erect, one hand clutching a silver-topped walking stick. She picked up her bill, and squinted at it through a pair of pince-nez on a gold chain round her neck. She repeatedly tried to get the attention of the waiter with fluttering waves of her gloved hand. He obsequiously continued to attend to everyone but her, so she vigorously struck the sugar bowl, and sent it crashing to the floor. For one glorious moment, she commanded everyone's attention. It mattered not that her audience were disapproving, because for the two minutes it took to pay the bill and sweep out the world was aware of her existence. Something of the woman she once was coloured her exit. Marguerite wanted to applaud. As the woman wove her way out of sight through the shop, Marguerite saw her shoulders drop, and her pace hesitate, as she shrank back into her wizened shell.

The waiter ignored Marguerite too. He, in fact, treated her with disdain bordering on disgust. Walking down Piccadilly she caught sight of herself reflected in Hatchard's shop window, and felt some sympathy for him. She looked a freak. There was no reason of person or occasion for her to dress up, so she habitually chose comfort over elegance. This involved a pair of well-worn trainers, tracksuit bottoms for their comfy, loose waist, and either a voluminous Sloppy Joe jumper that had belonged to Tony or, if it was very cold, her smelly thirty-year-old Afghan coat. She dragged her grey curls back with an elastic band and didn't bother with make-up. She was not a pretty sight. She didn't give a damn.

After the night in each other's arms on the earth floor of the borie, she
strips off and washes under the waterfall. Marcel watches as she puts on
her crumpled, grubby frock and wooden shoes. He places a wild rose in
her tangled hair. 'Comme tu es belle,' he says.

People edged away from her as she continued her walk down
Piccadilly, chuckling to herself, wondering whether to alarm
them further by following the example of Tony in his cruising
days, by asking someone for a light, even though she no longer
smoked. She could use it to set on fire the sleazy cinema
showing dirty films that defiled the hitherto pleasant street.
She lingered, as she always did, at Piccadilly Circus, dreading
seeing Elsie there, although she longed to know how she had
fared since she last saw her over a decade ago. Occasionally she
went to the Bull Ring. This was now packed full of homeless
people. It had been dubbed Cardboard City. Not many people
ventured in but Marguerite wandered among the tragic outcasts in a futile quest for information. She had almost accepted
that Elsie was probably dead yet clung to the faint hope that
she was, as she had said at their last meeting, a survivor.
Looking down Shaftesbury Avenue towards Soho she wondered too about Jimmy. She had never rid herself of the regret
that she could not help him out of the morass into which he
had sunk. She thought how pleased Tony would be to know
that her Messiah complex was a thing of the past. She had no
lame ducks or great causes in her life now, and pace Tony, she
felt lost without them.

After the funeral, she had kept in touch with Tony's mother for
a while, until, her link with Ethel being mainly because of Tony,
she let it go. When she received a phone call from the carer who
had come to London telling her that Ethel had been moved to

a hospital, she felt duty bound, for Tony's sake, to go up and visit her.

At the main reception of the huge hospital they looked up the name and directed her across the concourse to 'our new wing, we are very proud of it'. She had to ring the front doorbell and when, eventually, somebody unlocked the door and let her in, she could hear screaming in what sounded like terror. The nurse said, 'Take no notice. It's only Keith.' A woman passed by, walking unnaturally slowly, looking straight ahead with no acknowledgement of Marguerite and the nurse, who ignored her and said, 'We are the most state of the art dementia ward in Britain. Isn't it lovely? Let me show you around.'

As they went down the wide corridor Marguerite could not but agree. Big ensuite rooms, pot plants, paintings, and pleasant relaxed staff but, oh God, the patients. Did they notice the brightly coloured curtains, the sunny yellow walls? One lay on the floor, howling like a wolf, lashing out at any kindly hand that reached towards him. He had a beard and wore a cardigan. An academic like her perhaps? Reduced to writhing rage at his disappearing mind?

In another room, a woman sat ashen-faced, frightened eyes looking at the television screen. Every now and then, her face crumpled into a grimace of tears, like a tiny child, and just as quickly it reverted to fearful staring.

'Julie likes Elvis Presley, don't you, darling?' said the nurse.

And the sunken frame rose and momentarily gyrated as she cackled, '"You're nothing but a hound dog,"' then the Greek mask of grief returned and she fell back into her seat. To and fro her mind careered at terrifying speed, taking her on a nightmare ghost train.

When they eventually came across Ethel she was sitting in her cheerful room, staring blankly out of the window. Her feet were bare and her usual tight perm had grown out, leaving wisps of white hair on a pink scalp.

'Do you know me, Ethel?'

'Why, of course. You're . . .'

'I'm Marguerite.'

'Yes, how did . . . I'm sorry . . . What was I? She's a lovely . . .'

Ethel would start a sentence quite normally then trail off, bewildered. Since their last meeting her mind had completely fractured. She muttered meaningless fragments that Marguerite could make no sense of. It was impossible to converse with her. All communication had broken down. Marguerite resorted to a monologue about Bert and Tony. Suddenly Ethel stood up and started pacing round the room gabbling to herself, then shouting, snarling, fists clenched, face contorted with some elemental fury. Then, abruptly she stood dead still, whimpering.

'I'm sorry, dear. She's having a bad day,' said the nurse cheerily.

On the train back to London, Marguerite was appalled that Ethel's life should end this way. It frightened her. She was grateful that her body was still healthy, but what about her mind? How long before she got like that? She was already a bit odd; the talking to herself, the bizarre clothes. Maybe it stemmed from not having to bother what other people thought? She must communicate more. That's what animals, especially humans, do. She must reach out. Exercise her brain. Why hadn't she spoken to that woman in Fortnum's, for instance? She must make an effort. She looked around the compartment.

A man was typing on one of the new fangled portable computers.

'You look busy,' she said.

He seemed alarmed.

'Yes, I am – very,' fingers flying over the keys.

She tried again.

'Not long ago only women typed and it was considered a rather lowly occupation. Now men do it on their wonderful new gadgets and it's considered very smart. Interesting that, isn't it?'

The man sighed.

'Madam, I am afraid I am too busy to engage in a debate about feminism at the moment.'

'No, no, that wasn't meant as a criticism. It's rather wonderful that—'

'Please, madam, I have to finish this report before we get to London.' And he twisted his body sideways to present his back to Marguerite.

Not to be defeated, Marguerite addressed a young man seated on the opposite side, wearing earphones, his head nodding in rhythm to the 'tsk-tsk' sound that came from them.

'What are you listening to?'

He ignored her.

She tried again, this time waving to attract his attention.

'Is it good?'

Seeing her hand the man lifted one earphone from his ear.

'Er?' he said.

'It must be lovely to take your music with you wherever you go. I'm thinking of getting one of those things. What are they called?'

'Sony Walkman.'

He looked her up and down fearfully, picked up his bag, and moved swiftly to sit several seats away, as though fleeing the plague.

It was not an encouraging start, machines being preferable to her conversation, but she resolved to make further efforts to make new friends and perhaps seek out some from the past. To keep herself sane.

Chapter 47

As Marguerite was leafing unenthusiastically through *Time Out*, an event caught her attention: the Queen Mother was to unveil a statue of Sir Arthur Harris, chief of Bomber Command, to which Jimmy had belonged. It seemed possible that he would attend – if he was still alive – and Marguerite could maybe catch a glimpse of him and even, after all this time, when the blood had cooled, have a conversation as friends.

Out of respect for an occasion to be attended by the Queen Mother, Marguerite made more of an effort with her toilette, donning one of her old schoolmistress frocks that hung loosely over her diminished frame. She put her hair up with combs and essayed some lipstick, but wiped it off again, remembering the incongruity of the woman in Fortnum's. She carefully wrapped a gift, on the off chance that Jimmy would be there.

Marguerite had visited St Clement Danes before, on one of the long walks she sometimes took to pass the time. Lapsed Catholic that she was, she enjoyed sitting in the quiet of these ancient places of worship, savouring their calm amidst the turmoil of the city. This one was particularly affecting, marooned as it was on an island in the middle of the Strand, encircled by the distant roar of traffic. She relished the bitter irony of this new statue. Built by Christopher Wren, the church was almost completely burnt down in the Blitz, and then was restored by the RAF to be a memorial to the dead, and now it was to be home to a statue of the man whose strategy of mass bombing had caused decimating firestorms that laid waste to much of Germany.

By the time Marguerite arrived, a crowd of protesters had gathered on the pavement opposite the church where dignitaries and ex-RAF personnel were attending a service. One home-made placard proclaimed, 'Bomber Harris is a war criminal and a mass-murderer.' Another, held aloft by a child, said, 'War is not healthy for children and other living things.' Supporting their large wooden model of a dove, standing peacefully behind the barriers in the warm sunshine, were several grey-haired people, and Marguerite wished she were one of them. Had she not met Jimmy, paradoxically on a CND peace march, and heard his story, she might have been.

The service over, Marguerite searched the faces of the small congregation in their best clothes emerging from the church. Jimmy would doubtless have changed, as had she, in twenty-odd years, but she was sure she would recognise him. Especially if he were smiling. Her eye fell upon one distinguished bald-headed man who seemed to be looking for someone. It took her some time to realise it was Stan, no longer shambolic and humble but exuding an aura of success. Marguerite watched as the neatly dressed woman with him, sharply tapped his arm to stop him peering round and pointed to the Queen Mother, plump and pretty, wearing a pale blue floral dress and wide straw hat, her white-gloved hand resting on the arm of a medal-and-gold-braid-bedecked RAF officer.

Her gracious smile froze as the crowd round Marguerite started to boo and throw eggs. The demonstrators were some distance away so their missiles landed in the road, but a policeman in shirtsleeves sauntered over to the most vociferous group and said mildly, 'Now now, ladies and gentlemen. I think that's enough, don't you? You've made your point.' A young man with a beard, wearing jeans, shouted, 'OK, people, let's be silent and remember all those who died. On both sides.' Heads were bowed, and over the traffic could be heard the Queen Mother's piping voice as she remembered with 'pride and gratitude the men in Bomber Command' adding loudly, glancing across the road at the egg throwers, 'Let us remember, too, those of every nation and background, who suffered as victims of the Second World War.' This was greeted with a smattering of polite applause.

Then Marguerite saw him. A man wearing a leather sheepskin-lined flying jacket walked unsteadily across the road, weaving between the traffic, and when he got to the island, opened a shooting stick and, sitting with his back to the now unveiled statue, took a swig from a hipflask, before training a pair of binoculars at the porch of Australia House opposite. Two policemen rushed to his side, but hesitated. They chatted briefly and then, following his pointed finger, and using the proffered glasses, looked up at the sculpture of a very explicitly naked man, with four horses curiously lying down with their front hooves waving in the air. Jimmy, his thick hair greying and with a bit of a paunch, but still dashingly handsome, had the policemen roaring with laughter, until a superior officer rushed up to them, and barked an order. The policemen quickly grabbed Jimmy and were frogmarching him away, when Stan broke from the astonished onlookers and, after a brief chat with the constables, led a laughing Jimmy across the road, to cheers from the crowd.

Marguerite caught up with them, and watched as Stan angrily pushed Jimmy into a doorway.

'You stupid bastard. What did you think you were doing?'

'Well, it's a more amusing work of art than a statue of Butcher Harris.'

'You were insulting the Queen Mother and all our comrades.'

Jimmy shouted, 'No, they were insulting us. By paying tribute to a man who misled and destroyed 50,000 of us, and untold thousands of Germans. If they want to give us a statue, I'd rather it was that bollock-naked man and his daft horses than that bastard.'

'Jimmy, you're drunk.'

Jimmy drew back his fist as if to punch Stan, and Marguerite stepped forward.

'Jimmy, don't.'

Both men wheeled round. Jimmy, clinging to Stan, turned his head away and muttered, 'No, no, not you. Go away.'

Pushing him off, Stan said, 'Miss Carter—'

'Marguerite, Stan – please.'

'Marguerite, I'm sorry to do this to you, but my wife will kill me if I don't get back   will you take over here?'

Jimmy roared with laughter.

'God yes, she'll have your guts for garters for being with me, the cow.'

Stan ignored him.

'Will you take care of him, Marguerite? I seem to remember I asked you that once before.'

He kissed her on the cheek, gave a despairing look to Jimmy, now swaying, moaning, with his face covered by both hands, and rushed off up the Strand.

'There he goes – back to Mummy. He used to be free like me, now he's a bloody accountant with a detached house in Tunbridge Wells.'

'Right, Jimmy. Let's get some coffee down you.'

'I'd rather have a drink.'

'I'm sure you would.'

She found a quiet café in one of the back streets.

'Have you eaten?'

'Not today. I don't do a lot of eating.'

Marguerite ordered him some fish and chips and a pot of black coffee. After a while, he put down his knife and fork and stared at her. There it was – the crooked smile.

'I can't believe it's you. Still as beautiful as ever. Sexy—' He reached to take her hand. She snatched it away.

'Jimmy, stop it. Don't be a fool. It's me, remember.'

'Sorry, old girl. Old habits die hard.'

Marguerite looked at his shaking hands.

'How are you keeping?'

'Oh I'm fine. Busy – you know.'

'Doing what?'

'Oh the usual. Ducking and diving. Make a bit on the horses. Thus the gear.' He indicated the shooting stick and binoculars.

'Sounds chancy.'

'Oh, some you win, some you lose.'

She looked at the frayed cuffs on his shirt, which she had first noticed when she took off his flying jacket.

'Yes, sorry about the shirt. I put this old one on because I thought I might be arrested. No point in dressing up for jankers.'

'Why did you do that, Jimmy?'

'Oh I don't know. Bit nutty really. It was for my muckers. All the stuff that's come out since the war. The top brass, the politicians, Churchill, all that "let them reap the whirlwind" stuff. And we believed them. That it was necessary. Then I saw an exhibition of photos of Dresden after the raids. I'd imagined it in my nightmares but it was worse. The total desolation, the burnt bodies, the women, the children. We created hell on earth. I did.'

Now she took his hand.

'It's war, Jimmy. It's filthy.'

'Yes, there's not many of us left who remember just how filthy. The "We won the war" shit. It started again with the Falklands. "Gotcha". Obscene. At what cost? Eh, Marguerite, who are the heroes, eh?'

'Jimmy, you have to move on. It's over.'

'Yes, but they keep trying to mythologise it all with statues and ceremonies. Turning it into a time of glory. The British at their best. "War criminals. Mass murderers". That's what those people in the street said. I used to think it was unfair to say that, but not any more. It's no excuse really, but I was only a lad, doing what I thought was right, but the men in charge, including Harris, were adults and should have known better. Anyway, enough about me. What about you? Tony? Donald?'

When Marguerite told him about their deaths, Jimmy was aghast.

'How come I'm still living and they're dead? Natural selection doesn't seem to be working. I'm afraid I have to have another drink. Can we find a pub? I'm a bit of an alkie, you see.'

'Apart from your betting, how do you pay for your drinks, Jimmy?'

'Oh you know, a bit of this, a bit of that. Bar work.'

'No rich girlfriends?'

'Not rich, no. 'Fraid not. I've gone a bit downmarket. I work for an escort agency occasionally. Old girls from the sticks who've lost their husbands one way or another and need someone to accompany them to the theatre or a meal. They're lonely, poor old things. No hanky-panky, I'm afraid. I'm game, but they're usually not.'

'And where do you live?'

'I've got a nice house in – No, shut up, Jim. I don't have to pretend to you, do I, Skylark? Truth is, I've ended up in that bedsit in Pimlico I was so afraid of. Between you and me and the gatepost it's pretty bloody depressing.'

'Maybe I can help there.'

Marguerite took the parcel she had been carrying and gave it to Jimmy.

'A present.'

He put the parcel on the table and undid the brown paper and then the tissue beneath. For a long time he sat completely still, no movement bar a tear that appeared in the corner of his eye and ran down his cheek.

'I don't understand. Is this for me?'

'I'm pretty sure Donald would rather you had the Palmer than anyone else.'

Jimmy was now holding his trembling hands above the painting, moving them gently from side to side as if stroking it or casting a spell.

'It's worth a lot of money, Jimmy. You can sell it and get somewhere decent to live.'

'I don't need to. With this on the wall, anywhere is paradise. I will never, never, never part with it. I don't deserve it, but no one in the world, apart from Donald, would cherish it as much as I will. I don't know what to say.'

'That's a first for you.'

He looked at her.

'What I'll give you is to get out of your life again. Oh and maybe this.' He dug into the pocket of his flying jacket and brought out a battered tobacco tin. 'I was going to throw it at the bloody statue, then it seemed a futile gesture.'

Marguerite opened the tin. Inside was his DFC medal.

'It's a bit grimy and it smells of tobacco but it's the only thing I've ever achieved in my life – even if under false pretences – which is fitting really. I'd like you to have it.'

'Thank you, Jimmy. I'm very honoured.'

'Now, Skylark, please go, or I'll start trying to con you into thinking we can start again and, even though I can tell you are lonely, I am a disaster area. Alcoholic. A dedicated failure, a foolish man, I would break your heart all over again.'

'I know you would, Jimmy. Goodbye, my dear.'

She walked to the door of the café. When she turned back to wave, Jimmy did not notice; he was too engrossed in gazing at his painting with simple, unfeigned wonderment.

Chapter 48

Marguerite could scarcely believe that it was fifty years since the end of the war. Her wounds though superficially healed still ran deep. Three years had passed since her farewell to Jimmy but she still thought of him. Not only was she saddened by the husk of the ebullient man she had known, but his abhorrence of his participation in the war had stirred up her own disquiet about hers. Now there was to be a public hullabaloo to mark the anniversary. Since most of the country didn't even bother to be silent for one minute, let alone the traditional three on the eleventh hour of the eleventh day, she was cynical about the value of that.

As she watched on television an event taking place on Horse Guards Parade, she yearned for Tony to send it up, to counterbalance her abhorrence of the triumphalism of the marching bands, and swirling bagpipes and the sentimentality of the celestial choirs, interspersed with distinguished thespians giving their all with Kipling and Blake. No Sassoon or Owen, needless to say. She wondered what the 1990s children made of the staged street parties, with their grandparents creakily demonstrating an embarrassing dance called the jitterbug, and crying over an old lady called Vera Lynn, singing an uncool song about Dover, when to them the war was just a boring part of their History syllabus.

She made up her mind to make an effort to participate out of respect for the dwindling numbers of fellow survivors. She stood in the Mall and watched a curious ramshackle little parade of restored Army vehicles, tanks, Red Cross ambulances, and jeeps carrying Chelsea Pensioners. They were all immaculate; not a sign of mud, bullet holes or blood. A Lancaster bomber flew over and dropped a million poppies, which created a somewhat prettier picture than the one that haunted Jimmy. The event was to raise money for victims of the war. It was a pity Jimmy, Moira, Mrs Schneider, and a generation of damaged wartime children like Elsie and Irene, couldn't have benefited. But their injuries were not manifest.

As Marguerite wandered the streets, trying to enter into the party spirit, she felt more and more wretched. She thought there was nowhere lonelier than London when everyone, except you, is enjoying one of its periodic knees-ups. But then her memories of the end of the war were not of the rejoicing taking place in England that she had read about and heard on the radio in France. The final battle to oust the Nazi regime in the Vaucluse was grim but necessary. The aftermath bore no resemblance to these jolly, warm-hearted celebrations.

For a while the man's hand tries to catch hold of the lamp-post, but his body swings away and eventually he hangs limp and his screams stop.

Sitting in her flat on the night of May the 8th, listening to the drunken revelry going on in Tony's flat above, Marguerite felt enraged that they were using something that they knew nothing about as an excuse for a party. With their cushy lives how could they understand what it had been like? She hated their happiness. She wanted to go up there and tell these carefree youngsters about the images gouged into her brain. About Ruby Eisenberg who, after the liberation of Auschwitz, made her way, with millions of other displaced persons wandering around Europe, to Apt, where she hoped to find her nephew, Jacob, all her other relatives having been killed by the Nazis. It fell to Marguerite to break the news that he was dead too, having sacrificed his life to save hers.

He writhes in agony, the blood he sheds for her saturates his clothing and the ground where he stumbles, still trying to deflect the bullets from her.

She would tell these baying members of the consumer society upstairs about her friend Rachel, who ended up in a camp where for days she lay on a wooden bunk next to a rotting corpse so that she could fool the bestial guard into giving her its ration of stale bread. Where the fashion of the day was rags that could be seen to move because of the lice feeding on your body. Where the coiffure was a shaved head and pubic hair, and the only ornamentation a tattoo reducing you to a number rather than a human being with a name. Where the ubiquitous perfume was the stench of putrefying bodies and if, like Rachel, your tenuous luck ran out, Zyclon B gas. Enjoying their nice jobs in an affluent society, did they know, had they been taught, that just over fifty years ago, during this war that the pretty parades and jolly parties were celebrating, a whole army of people were involved in the industry of methodically, effectively, murdering en masse anyone who differed from their twisted ideology?

Marguerite tried to restrain her frantic rage. Her mind was running out of control. She was pacing dementedly round the room, fists clenched, muttering to herself. Like poor Ethel. What on earth was she thinking? She didn't know these young people. Was it not good that they had no concept of these horrors? Wasn't that what she had spent her life doing, trying to build a better world? Trying 'not to do nothing'?

You have a mission. A vision of a better world.

Marcel, Marcel. Her shrivelled, unloved body longed for his arms to enfold it. To hear him laugh at her, to reason, to comfort, to calm, as he had when her skin was firm and aware. How was he feeling on this fiftieth anniversary? Was he celebrating with grandchildren, content, or was the census right and he was alone, like her, wondering where her life had gone? What he had achieved? Whether it had been worth it?

'I will always love you. Till the day I die.'

As the noise level of the party above rose, she could not be bothered to rap on the ceiling with the broom. She sat remembering the utter silence of the nights in Les Galets once the crickets had stopped and the shutters were closed. Was it still like that? Did she dare to find out?

What had she to lose? A few years before death, becoming increasingly batty, roaming around the streets of London talking to herself, feeling hatred for young people who had done no harm other than to have a party? The nightmare of the dementia ward lurking.

'Don't be a coward like me.'

'No, Tony, you weren't, but I am. I have things to confront and I bloody well will.'

The next day she went to a travel agent and booked a flight to Marseilles.

Chapter 49

Thus it was that Marguerite found herself going through security at Gatwick with nary a glance from the staff towards her or her suitcase. They were too busy searching the nubile girl behind her in the queue to worry about the old crone that she had become. Marguerite stood for a while enjoying the girl's insouciance. This needless procedure was an insignificant hold-up in the headlong race of her burgeoning life. She did hesitate momentarily when a funny old lady touched her arm and muttered, 'Carpe diem, carpe diem.'

Accustomed to compliments, the girl flashed an automatic smile. 'Thank you so much, that's very kind,' and rushed towards her future. Resisting her teacher's instinct to correct the misinterpretation, Marguerite steeled herself to fly to Marseilles and face her past.

As she got onto the plane amidst the chattering holidaymakers and was welcomed aboard by a chirpy air hostess Marguerite found herself remembering a very different departure. On the pitch-black airstrip, the Lysander's propeller whirring, Major Buckmaster awkwardly wished her luck as he gave her the badly wrapped powder compact. She noticed his hand was shaking. Poor man. He had not wanted to recruit her. She was too young, too redheaded, too female. He was of the generation that thought young women should be protected rather than exposed to the danger of possible torture and death. However, she had persuaded him that her skill in getting out of France and making her way to England, plus her profound wish to avenge the deaths of her parents and a schoolfriend at the hands of the Nazis, made her a good candidate. He chose her for an assignment in the Vaucluse area where she explained that she had spent a lot of time at her parents' country residence in Gordes. Thus she became part of Operation Jedburgh, its objective being to unite all the disparate groups of the Maquis into a fighting unit, in preparation for the Allied invasion of the South of France.

Marguerite sat in her seat and looked around her. She found modern aircraft claustrophobic with their sealed windows and doors. The old Lysander rattled and shook but at least you could jump out in an emergency and float down to terra firma on your parachute.

Since the war Marguerite had done her best to suppress memories of that time but now, on this journey to confront her disquiet, she made a determined effort to bring them to mind. She recalled how, despite her commando-type training in Scotland for the SOE, she had never mastered the art of an elegant parachute-landing. Her first meeting with Marcel had therefore not been a great way to start their relationship. Grovelling on the ground at his feet she could see in the torch-light that he was appalled that headquarters in Britain had sent him a woman. He was even more appalled when he discovered she had hurt her ankle in her inept touchdown so that she could not ride the bike they had brought for her to get away from the landing field. It was the only available transport other than horses, or noisy cars fuelled by wood-burning stoves towed behind.

As the plane took off Marguerite looked out of the window at the disappearing runway and forced herself to remember how after her ungainly arrival in a field near the village of Lagarde, three shadows had quickly dowsed the lanterns marking out the runway, burnt and buried her parachute suit, and gathered up the canisters of weapons and ammunition, and an unhappy carrier pigeon. She put on a headscarf to hide her hair and, with as much dignity as she could muster, hitched up her skirt to ride on the handlebars of Marcel's bike, the pillion having been loaded with supplies. Luckily the safe house where she was to meet some of the other résistants wasn't far away but it was not an impressive entrance.

The motley crew waiting in a darkened yard behind the house had at first thought that the agent from England had not arrived, but when she was introduced by Marcel they gaped in disbelief. She had had the foresight to fill her pockets with cigarettes and some coffee beans with which she broke the ice, handing them round as though at a cocktail party. The men laughed at the incongruity of her behaviour – this strange English miss, who spoke perfect French. She then asked them to turn away whilst she pulled up her blouse to extract the money she had strapped to her waist. That went down very well. More even than her bosom. Marcel explained that they had not been paid for a long time and were dependent on local support, which was far from unanimous, for food and occasional shelter, although most of the time they slept rough on the Plateau de Vaucluse or Mont Ventoux as she was often later to do herself. They were hungry and Marguerite's first show of authority was to stop them eating the pigeon.

Looking around at the disparate collection of men she wondered whether she was up to her assigned task of forming them into a cohesive whole in time for the planned invasion. Gathered to greet her were representatives from several different groups operating in the Vaucluse area. Like wild gypsies, long-haired, unshaven, weather-beaten, dirty and smelly, they were an odd lot. Marcel introduced her to some of them that night but it took a few weeks for her to discover that the Maquisards were an eclectic mixture, made up of fiery Communists, extreme right-wing nationalists, deserters from the French Army who refused to do the forced labour the Germans were demanding of them, veterans of the Spanish Civil War, intellectuals like her parents, who were fighting the Nazis, as were the two Jewish members of the group that had escaped the purges. In addition there were several lads who just liked making trouble.

It pained her to recall that that was the first time she had seen Jacob. She had been warned by headquarters, he needed controlling. No wonder, considering his story. Being Jews, he and his family had been taken to Les Milles, near Marseilles, where a converted factory was used as a holding pen before transit to the death camps. Some Quakers and a valiant pasteur, Manen, had managed to persuade the French commanders to let fifty children be rescued and sent to safety abroad. Jacob's wife could not bear to let their two children be taken away for ever, so the night before their proposed departure, she jumped with them from the roof to their deaths. Jacob escaped before the transport to Drancy from whence it would have been to Auschwitz, vowing revenge. When Buckmaster told her what Jacob had endured and stressed the need to rein in his desire for vengeance, she knew he was warning her as well.

As she sat in the plane sipping a glass of wine Marguerite dared to do what she had avoided for fifty years – think deeply about Marcel, the man with the bike. He was tall, with penetrating brown eyes in a sun-burnished face. Despite wearing a battered old leather jacket, well-worn Basque beret and heavy boots, he had a grace and quiet dignity about him that appeared to command the respect of the others. After the meeting in the farmhouse he helped her onto his pillion and as they rode through the night he told her he had organised a safe house for her in the hamlet in which he lived, and her cover was to be that of a cousin who had, with thousands of others, fled Paris in the occupied north of France to live in the south under the Vichy government. She recalled being pleased that she would be living near Marcel.

As the plane landed in Marseilles Marguerite was swamped by a wave of anxiety. Her recollections of her arrival in France as a young woman had not distressed her as much as she had feared. But what lay ahead?

Chapter 50

She had booked into a hotel in Sault for her first night back in the Vaucluse after half a century. This town had been the centre of the Le Maquis de Ventoux. Because it was perched on a rocky hill it was easy to see anyone approaching from below and the residents, apart from those that joined the much-hated Milice, a French police force formed by the Germans to quell opposition, closed their eyes to what was happening, or actively helped, which bravery had earned the town the Croix de Guerre after the war.

As Marguerite drove in her hired car up the winding climb to the town, she felt something of the excitement of her youth. The buildings were the same, but the streets were now thronged with laughing, chatting people, not deserted and fearful as they had been during the occupation. She parked her car and wandered towards the hotel.

She found herself looking at the names on a memorial to the dead of the Second World War. She knew most of them; roistering, bawdy, brave men. Nearby was a group of old fellows absorbed in a game of boules, while at a concrete table several others were playing cards, shouting as they slapped them down, laughing and jokily punching one another, enjoying the pleasurable old age of which Antoine, Jacob, Jean, Georges, Roget

389

and Philippe had been deprived. They died to make possible for others this comradely fun in the dappled shade. She continued on her way to the Hotel du Louvre.

It was so changed since it had been a vital meeting place during the war that she had difficulty recognising it. Where there had been a bleak courtyard there was now an outdoor restaurant, all gaily coloured tablecloths and parasols. Inside, the café, which had been nothing but the habitual zinc bar smelling of garlic and the foul tobacco substitute herbs, was now part of a large hotel, walls having been knocked through and buildings either side incorporated.

She registered at the reception desk. Upstairs not much had altered. The landlord showed her to the very room to which Marcel had carried her, traumatised after the massacre and her escape. She sat on the bed and put her head in her hands.

Jacob hurls her in front of him through the barn door.

'Vite. Tu'enfuis. Je te suivrai. Merde, ma chérie.'

She runs. The shots, the shouts, she turns her head to see him weaving from side to side behind her, deliberately taking the bullets to shield her. She reaches the trees, turns to see him writhing, juddering on the ground.

Marguerite took her toilet bag from her case and put it on the modern sink. After gently removing her filthy clothes, Marcel had brought hot water in a jug which he poured into a china basin, and using the corner of a threadbare towel wiped away the dust and sweat from her face and body. As she had then, she looked at the Provençal tiled roofs through the window and in the distance the white crest of Mont Ventoux, shale not snow. For a sacred hour they had escaped the turmoil and she had blanked out the image of the dying Jacob as Marcel stroked her as though she were a wounded animal. She had looked at the clock on the church tower as they sank into the feather bed and lay on their backs, hand in hand.

'Lovely,' she had whispered, meaning his gentleness.

He misunderstood.

'Yes, it used to chime every hour. The enemy took away its voice along with ours. But it will come back. As will ours.'

And there it was now.

She sluiced her face in cold water and went outside into the square. As she sat at a table among the dining holidaymakers a man with a clown's white face and wearing a flat cap over a red wig, waistcoat and oversized checked trousers started to do a strange mime. Oh Lord, thought Marguerite, he's going to do the window or mirror routine. But no, it looked as though he was walking an imaginary tightrope. He was absorbed in his own world. His movements were delicate and mesmeric. He didn't appear to want money. He was on his own. The diners smiled, embarrassed, those that noticed him. Most didn't, involved in their conversations. It was incomprehensible but beautiful to watch. No one reacted except a mangy cat who stared at him. The clown was now climbing onto a chair and making an imaginary noose. He mimed putting it round his neck. Marguerite felt a chill in the sunlight. With a sad gesture of bending his fingers in a tiny wave, he jumped from the chair and fell in a heap on the floor.

The crowd cheers as the Milice's body is cut down from the lamp-post. A man that Marguerite recognises as an informer kicks the corpse to more cheers. She says nothing.

Those at the tables near the clown mumbled their disapproval, pulling their children close. He leapt to his feet, came over to

Marguerite and performed an elaborate bow. She alone applauded and he blew her a kiss over his shoulder as he left, exactly as Marcel used to do.

As she sat there in the sunny square, the cat now settled at her feet, her life during the war seemed as fantastic as the clown's portrayal of a brutal reality. Did those things that scarred her mind really happen? She doubted if anyone laughing around her knew or cared. When no one remembers a thing does it cease to exist? Does that matter? Is it in fact a blessing? She had tried to forget some things, to obliterate them from the record, to make amends by the way she lived her life, so that, like the people at the tables, she could just enjoy the sun and feed the sweet little pussycat. Some things are best forgotten, so why did she now want to risk delving into them? Maybe it was a natural process of taking an inventory before death to try and justify one's existence. Was it Descartes who said 'We hold nothing entirely within our power except our thoughts'? It was within her power to find peace. Forget the past, enjoy the present. That corner on the way down from Sault would be a good test. Could she go there and just enjoy the view of the ravine and Mont Ventoux in the distance?

The drive down the winding route was as beautiful as she remembered. When she got to the spot, she parked her car and stood on the edge of the road. Silence, apart from a light breeze rustling the leaves. She looked up at the cliff where she had lain in wait, the sun on her back, her lover by her side. That day she was fully alive. Heart beating fast, excited, happy. Yes, she was happy. Her older self looked back in disbelief.

As the car comes into focus she sees the German soldier has blue eyes. He is sternly handsome. Attractive. Aryan. Bastard. They round the last curve until they are nearly level. As she pulls the pin from the grenade he looks up and stares into her eyes in wonderment like a beautiful child. Then his head bursts open and splatters all over the other men in the car. Marcel fires at the cars with his Sten. From the other side of the road grenades and bullets are flying through the air.

In an instant, with one throw of a grenade, there had been rivulets of blood running into the flowery verge, bits of body strewn at random, jagged lumps of metal, screams and shouts and explosions. She looked for any clue that this peaceful place had witnessed such a dreadful scene but there was nothing but a plaque on the wall of the cliff, half hidden by ivy. Seven were killed, it said. Seven of the enemy. One had blue eyes. Let the ivy grow and obliterate the remaining evidence. Move on now, as nature had.

It was market day in Saint Saturnin-les-Apt. Pungent smells of rôtisserie chicken, Arab spices, lavender. The market was packed with people of all nationalities. In one corner a strident German was rallying his party to return to their tour bus, oblivious of the bullet holes in the wall marked now with the names of the slaughtered. Marguerite looked up at the window of the Hotel de Voyager where she had secretly watched the young woman refuse to be shot in the back, facing her assassins with blazing eyes.

'Shoot me as I face you. I die for France.'

Another name on the wall, a woman who had been shot in her home for refusing to give away the whereabouts of her Maquisard husband. They had left her seven-year-old son alone in the house with his mother's body. Marguerite forced herself to recollect how the cycle of violence continued further.

She stands holding the small boy's hand, watching the man shoot the girl in the flowery dress. Then he shows the boy how to hold the gun and helps him pull the trigger, 'Good,' he smiles and pats the boy's head. 'That's for your mother,' he says, as he pokes the body with his boot to check that it is properly dead.

And she did nothing. She should not have done nothing. Later the girl was proved innocent.

Vengeance was truly served by the rampage after the Liberation. L'épuration sauvage. Who could imagine this savagery on a colourful market day? Obese people wandering around, tasting, smelling this plentiful feast, could not conceive that some had starved in this town. They could not know what it was like.

One person could. He would surely bear the scars of the war like her. They were a dwindling generation. She needed to share this burden. Say it aloud, give it credence.

As a child she had paddled on the shingly beach and got caught in an undertow, the pebbles pulling her legs from under her, swirling her backwards, until she was thrashing about underwater, with nowhere firm to put her feet. Her father had carried her to safety. Now she felt the desperation of having no one to rescue her from this maelstrom. She remembered Marcel's hand in hers or gently soothing her. Her tired old body yearned for him. He may very possibly be dead or married or senile but she could not leave without finding out.

To not look for him would leave unfinished business and tying up loose ends was a necessary task before she died.

Chapter 51

Saignon, perched on the side of the Luberon Mountains, was now a centre for artists, and chambres d'hôtes for grey-haired ramblers. Alongside the winding lanes and alleys, the medieval houses sported multicoloured shutters. Marguerite took a room in the Hotel du Presbytère whose labyrinthine layout had proved useful during the war. Now it had a smart restaurant and the obligatory tables and parasols grouped around an encrusted stone fountain outside. Several houses had become cafés and for two mornings she sat outside Chez Christine with an old-fashioned bowl of chocolate and baguette with apricot jam, enjoying the gleaming white simplicity of the village church with its deafening half-hourly chimes. While tourists stopped their ears, she rejoiced that the bells rang out again.

The old man across the lane from the café was cashing in on the upturn in fortune of the town. Whilst he reclined in a dirty deck chair his dog sat on a cushion beside him with a notice propped up behind forbidding photos without a payment of 15 francs. He was also selling grubby leaking sachets of lavender. As she sat there he sold nothing, possibly because he was continually talking angrily to himself and anyone in his vicinity. He must have been here during the war. Marguerite looked hard to see if she recognised him, but old age had dried up any semblance of the boy he was then. Was he one of her team or could he have been in the Milice? Or just trying to exist? So many secrets, so many wrong decisions made in one's youth, so many regrets.

After a few days she steeled herself to visit Les Galets where Marcel had lived with his family. It was a hamlet of five houses at the end of a dirt track surrounded, during the war, by neglected cherry orchards and vineyards. They seemed well tended now. Stones and trees along the path were marked with blue and orange paint laying out routes for hikers; this path that they had tried to conceal. And there it was. The oak tree – it was still there. Even more massive than when she lay against it with Marcel.

She climbed the last remaining hill to the hamlet. She could hear voices and laughter and the familiar clicking of a boules game in progress. They were on the rough patch behind the barn, the men of the hameau. She hid behind a wall, heart pounding, trying to see if she recognised anyone. Was Marcel there or any of the brave souls who had hidden her identity and given her cover; had accepted that she was a cousin of Marcel's family from Paris? That bent sunburnt man was surely Pierre, she recognised his laugh, full-blooded and loud. The tiny man giving a running commentary as he tossed his boule was surely Patrice. She knew the battered peaked cap he wore. Was it the same one after all these years? There were two other men but she could not identify them as Marcel.

Then she looked across the field below the hamlet. Beyond it was an area of newly ploughed land. There were three lines of shallow trenches into which a man was studiously placing potatoes. There was something about the delicacy of his fingers as opposed to the solidity of his astride stance and Marguerite knew at once. She walked slowly across the field.

She called his name.

'Marcel.'

He stood up, still straight and tall. The long hair was grey now. He looked at her.

'Tu es venu.'

'Oui.'

'Enfin.'

He held out his hand. She took it silently and, hand in outstretched hand, they stared into one another's lined faces. Eventually he pulled her to him and they stood on the pebbly earth, his arms holding her in a motionless embrace. The ground felt firm beneath her, his body strong. For a long while they did not move or utter. Eventually they walked back across the field, his arm tight around her shoulders.

He still lived in the same cottage in which he had been born and grown up and it was little changed. He cooked his food in an ancient oven or slowly on the top of a log-burning black stove, the only source of warmth apart from an evil-smelling kerosene heater in the depths of the winter. He made her an omelette from the eggs that they gathered from the chicken run and they drank some local wine. Come nightfall she sat with him on a bench outside his house, marvelling at the myriad stars, invisible in London, and telling him something of her life, which sounded sadly ineffectual for one who had left him in order to change the world.

'And what about you, Marcel?'

There was not a great deal to tell. As she knew, his father had died when he was a boy so it fell to him to look after his mother till she had died in her eighty-eighth year. It had been his duty, as his two brothers and one sister were married with their own families, to care for her.

'Did you not have a family of your own?'

'No.'

'But did you not fall in love?'

'Yes.'

'With whom?'

'You. There could be no one else after you.'

It was said in such a way as to brook no question.

As when he stated, 'And now you'll stay.'

She could see no reason not to. What had she to go back for? Lonely teas in Fortnum's? Sitting in parks hoping to find someone to talk to? A two-roomed flat in King's Cross where she knew none of her busy neighbours, and was constantly reminded of the painful absence in the flat above? In London it was probably raining, whereas here the spring was starting.

By the door of the cottage was a tree that looked naked apart from a sprout of leaves at the top of each branch along which were tiny brown balls, which promised later in the year to be lush black figs with a pink succulent interior. They were surely worth waiting for?

In Marcel's garden was an ancient quince tree that had still managed to produce bouquets of the palest pink flower cups from its dying trunk. Later there would be sweet-smelling fruit to perfume the kitchen and make into a jelly. Could this aged tree really produce such riches? It looked too fragile. Should she wait and see? With its delicate blossom it was a happy tree, despite its failing strength. It was facing death with a radiant smile.

Yes. Yes, she would stay. And take care of it. For a while.

Chapter 52

Living with Marcel in Les Galets wasn't easy for her. After London, life there was so slow and uneventful. She tried her best to confine her Messiah complex to looking after Marcel and the land. When she got involved with a campaign to rid the area of a nuclear warhead stored on a plateau in the mountains, Marcel tried to calm her feverish efforts.

'Relax. Let me look after you, instead of you looking after the whole world all the time. Allow me that joy. Please.'

Several Resistance fighters had killed themselves over the years since the war so Marcel was wary of Marguerite's volatile moods. He succumbed to her pleas for a television to keep in touch with events in Britain, but did his best to leaven her disquiet about IRA bombs and riots and injustices, with his belief in the soothing power of nature.

'Look,' he said, gripping her shoulders and turning her to face a radiant sunset.

'I am looking,' she laughed.

'No, really look. Really, really look,' and he held her still with her back leaning against him, until she felt herself dissolve, merged into the orange and red and purple of the sky and the strength of his body.

At length he said, 'Well?'

'It's better than Piccadilly Circus.'

In truth, she was reluctant to acknowledge the beauty of the landscape and the gentle devotion being offered by Marcel, for it made her painfully aware of what she had sacrificed for her absurd mission to change the world. She could have had a lifetime of peace here with a man who loved her. When the hamlet gathered on Sundays to play boules, her grandchildren could have joined those of their neighbours. Instead, she was a barren woman, who had loved thousands of children who would not even remember her, and had strived for an impossible goal, wasting her life in the process. The world had indeed changed, but it was nothing to do with her.

When she watched on her television the rejoicing at the election of Tony Blair and, at last, a Labour government, she was glad, but she could not pretend that this success was in any way due to her campaigning with Tony. Or indeed that it was socialist. The party was now a brand called New Labour, unrecognisable from the one they had believed in. The death of the ebullient Princess Diana hounded by a new breed of voracious press upset her, and she was astonished that Londoners expressed their grief with cascades of flowers and extrovert weeping in the streets, and even a revolutionary zeal to make the royal establishment give this sad, damaged woman a fitting farewell. She marvelled how much behaviour had changed since Churchill's solemn funeral. In this part of France, her other native country, change was not so drastic. The pace was perhaps more suitable for a woman in her seventies. She made up her mind to embrace a rural life with Marcel. But she did not sell her London flat.

It was, after all, a pleasurable existence. They grew their own vegetables – aubergines, tomatoes, courgettes, asparagus, frisée lettuce. Marguerite enjoyed cooking fragrant meals, with herbs that grew wild, on the creaky old stove. She worked alongside Marcel on the land, learning the seasonal tasks. She sometimes wondered what Tony would have made of this peasant woman tilling the soil. She thanked him in her heart for guiding her back to Marcel. When the vines began to spread tiny green buds on their wizened black hands reaching out of the soil towards the life-giving sun, Marcel taught her to prune them in preparation for another season of wine, the quality of which he was labouring to improve. It was slow work with time to relish the view and listen to the birdsong.

Marcel showed her that this place she had thought dull was seething with life, most of it friendly, apart from the odd scorpion and viper. When some ants invaded the house Marguerite stamped on them and put down poison. The next day she was distressed to see a few survivors staggering around, carrying their dead back to a hole in the wall.

When they had all gone Marcel filled the hole with cement. 'No need to kill them, eh? They live here, too. C'est la campagne.'

If she tried to discuss the killings of the past, Marcel shrugged and in the same tone he would say, 'C'est la guerre.' He had joined the conspiracy of silence that prevailed in the area. How else would they all live on together? The secrets were known but not discussed. The anguish was buried and forgotten. Only his love for her had remained burning bright for all those years.

He showed little interest in what she had been doing before she came back to him, as he told her he always knew she would. He was intent on living fully the time they had left together. He wanted her constantly by his side. As long as she was there the rest of the world did not interest him. He seldom read a paper or watched the news on television. She missed the intellectual discourse she had had with Tony and her friends and colleagues, yet Marcel was wise and knowledgeable about the land and the seasons. He tended his chickens lovingly but did not hesitate to wring one's neck when it ceased laying and was ready for the pot. His dogs were kept in an outside kennel and cage, well fed but guarding and hunting was their function, they were not pets. He was unsentimental but she sometimes caught him gazing at her with a kind of wonder. He would stroke her faded red-and-grey hair and say tenderly, 'You've gone rusty.'

Each spring turned into summer. The cherries ripened and were picked by visiting Romany workers, the grapes were taken in the tractor to be processed into improving wine. Next came the melons and the lavender filling the air with sweet perfume. Marcel and Marguerite went into the nearest town, Apt, on market day to sell any produce they had as well as sit in a café and watch the world go by.

Apt seemed to be stuck in a timewarp. Clothes and hairstyles were from the 1950s, mobile phones a rare sight, canned music non-existent, and when a McDonald's opened on the outskirts of the town it was as if something had arrived from outer space. The only sound was that of chattering voices, people who had known each other all their lives giving three kisses on alternate cheeks and then standing to talk for minutes before moving on to the next encounter.

This busy existence continued through summer until the hunting season in the autumn. Then the guns were cleaned and prepared and the dogs released to search for wild boar to stock up the freezer for winter. When in the first year a group of men gathered at Marcel's house at dawn for la chasse several of them turned out to be gnomic members of the Maquis. They greeted Marguerite with emotion but there was no reminiscence, just meaningful nods and shrugging of shoulders. Marcel produced

Marguerite's sixty-year-old revolver with bullets. She loaded it and demonstrated her old skill by shooting at apples on a tree. She saw in their faces the admiration she eventually won from them during the war. But she did not join them on the hunt. For her the killing was over.

One spring she stood in a field ablaze with poppies, laughing with Marcel at the cacophony of mating frogs and toads in the nearby stream, when a feeling flushed through her body, taking her breath away and bringing tears to her eyes, that she could only define as ecstasy. Or at the very least happiness.

Kissing her, Marcel said, 'That's it. You're beginning to understand.'

This way of life: being in tune with nature, absorbed into the earth and the sky, loved, gave Marguerite a foothold again; over the years it calmed her troubled mind. The nightmares no longer haunted her. Until an event sent her and the rest of the world whirling into chaos. As she sat in the cosy parlour in front of the wood stove, watching with Marcel the endless repeats of the falling twin towers in New York and the splayed figures of people leaping to their deaths, the old terror swept over her again. The hatred, the fanaticism, it was still there.

As the car comes into focus she sees the German soldier has blue eyes. He is sternly handsome. Attractive. Aryan. Bastard. They round the last curve until they are nearly level. She pulls the pin from the grenade.

The cycle of violence would start again. Marcel reassured her that Bush and Blair would be cautious.

'No, Marcel. They have never lived through a war, they don't know what it is like. They will want to show how strong they are. Seek out someone to blame and punish.'

Her fears were justified when Britain joined with the United States and other countries to invade Afghanistan. Marcel tried to console her, but as they watched the situation getting out of hand she lapsed back into depression at her futility. She avidly scanned the newspapers and sat white-faced in front of the television watching the chaotic developments. When a non-smiling Tony Blair spoke of lethal weapons of mass destruction in Iraq, Marguerite was horrified at the implications: a gadarene rush towards further war.

Then a letter arrived from her campaigning pupil from Dartford County Grammar, Pauline, with whom she had kept up a sporadic correspondence over the years, telling her of a big demonstration happening in London against further military intervention. Marguerite tried to explain to Marcel why she felt impelled to return to England and take part. She liked her life here with him but she was still driven to be a participator; she could no longer just stand on the side-lines and watch.

Marcel reluctantly agreed, on condition that he accompany her.

Chapter 53

Although he had never travelled abroad, Marcel took it all in his stride. If the prospect of leaving his familiar surroundings alarmed him it did not show, but then he had faced more daunting challenges in the past. He was a man devoid of vanity so he did not care that his one and only old suit and indispensable beret were not the height of London fashion. He was bemused by the security procedure at the airport, and thrilled at the flight itself.

The flat was musty and sad after its years of neglect but Marguerite spent a day hoovering and polishing to bring it back to life. She did not restrain Marcel from tackling the overgrown garden; after the journey from the airport, the tube, the crowds, the concrete under his feet, she knew he needed to make contact with the earth. During the few days they had before the march, Marguerite showed Marcel the obligatory sights, noticing several new buildings. She was reminded of how much she loved this ever-evolving city. What she most enjoyed was sharing it with Marcel, his hand in hers as they walked the streets, in contrast to her loneliness before she had left for France.

The day of the march was freezing cold. In Marguerite's wardrobe still hung her old Afghan coat as well as Tony's duffel, which she could not bring herself to part with; it fitted Marcel perfectly and he declared himself honoured to wear it, so they set off to the rallying point on the Embankment looking much as she and Tony had in all their previous demos over the years. But this one was very different.

It was on a scale that Marguerite had never seen before. They sought out the CND contingent and were told by the excited leader that it was reckoned that nearly two million people were congregating in London and about thirty million worldwide. It was the biggest demonstration in history, making the disorganised little march to Aldermaston in 1958 to rid the world of these same weapons look tame.

Marguerite did think to herself:

I shouldn't be doing this again. Forty-five years later. We should have learned by now. Surely we should?

But this was different. The magnitude of this protest could not be ignored. Surely?

Even Marguerite was overawed by the size of the crowd as they started to walk towards Parliament Square, so she was concerned for Marcel for whom Apt market on a Saturday was too crowded. But he was having the time of his life. He had palled up with some French students who had handed him a saucepan, which he was vigorously banging with a wooden spoon, in time to the group's drums and whistles.

The column was very slow-moving as it was over three miles long, winding its way past Parliament, 10 Downing Street, Trafalgar Square, Piccadilly Circus and along Piccadilly to Hyde Park. Marcel was having a splendid guided tour of some of Marguerite's favourite haunts, accompanied by British people of all colours, classes, and ages. He asked Marguerite to translate the slogans for him. There was a big contingent with a banner declaring, 'Eton College Orwell Society, people not profit, peace not war'.

When Marguerite pointed out they were from one of England's top public schools Marcel was very impressed that a kingdom could be so egalitarian.

'They won't be once they leave and become the ruling class,' she snarled on Tony's behalf.

Marcel admired the many largely home-made banners and chortled with delight at their absurdity: 'Boring middle-aged men against war'; 'Make tea not war'.

One very big banner had a long message which Marcel judged must be a worthy quotation. He loved it when Marguerite told him it meant, 'Notts County supporters say make love not war (and a home win against Bristol would be nice).'

His favourite and Marguerite's was held by two small children and a middle-aged woman. Written in crayon it read, 'Auntie Jane says no to war'.

Pauline was very solicitous. Marguerite was touched that, despite her being one of the organisers of the march, she kept darting back to see if they were all right. She found time to explain that she worked for the Quaker Peace and Social Witness, a job that had taken her all over the world putting her childhood campaigning zeal into practical use.

After the speeches were over in Hyde Park and people began to light fires and get down to some partying, Marguerite and Marcel decided it was time to leave. Pauline came running after them suggesting that they could meet up for lunch the following day.

Marguerite was delighted.

'That would be lovely, Pauline. But where? I'm a bit out of touch. It's eight years since I was last in London and it's changed so much.'

'It certainly has. Have you seen the Millennium Wheel?'

'Only from a distance.'

When Pauline suggested they meet there Marguerite hesitated. Over the years she had avoided going to the site of the magnificent Festival of Britain. Its savage annihilation for political reasons came to symbolise to her the destruction of visionary ideas by mindless authority. She had seen too much of that in her life. The last time she went there was with Tony after Churchill's funeral when he told her that he had fallen in love with Donald. That led to another ending she preferred not to dwell on.

She was about to suggest they went somewhere else when Pauline said, 'I love that place, Miss Carter. It has such wonderful memories for me. Do you remember when we all went to the Festival?'

Pauline was suddenly the ardent young teenager and Marguerite could not crush her enthusiasm.

'Lovely idea, Pauline. Where shall we meet?'

'There is a plaque in the pavement not far from the Wheel that marks where the Skylon was. Let's meet there.'

The next day Marguerite and Marcel crossed the new bridge that had replaced the dingy old Hungerford Bridge footpath over the Thames to the South Bank. It looked as though it was suspended by lots of giant umbrellas that had lost their covering fabric. Marcel was transfixed by the views up and downstream of the river. Although she was impressed by the gigantic Wheel Marguerite was saddened when she saw the area that had been packed with the wonders of science and art was now bland stretches of grass and pavement. Nevertheless the crowds of people queuing for a trip on the Wheel or enjoying some winter sunshine on the grass seemed to be having fun.

Pauline seemed very excited to see them. She was dressed in a smart coat and her hair looked fresh from the hairdresser's.

'My goodness, you're very soignée, Pauline. I feel a real country bumpkin.'

'You're still as beautiful as ever, Miss Carter.'

Marcel, who had been introduced as 'a good friend', Marguerite not being sure how to designate his role, smiled when she translated what Pauline had said and nodded vigorously.

Pauline pointed out where the Skylon had been and, taking them to an area of rough ground being used as a car park, she indicated some broken-down steps which she told them had been those leading to the Dome of Discovery.

'That's the only thing left of the Festival, I'm afraid.'

Marguerite did her best to conceal the anguish she felt at the sight of all that remained of the time when she, everyone, had been so full of hope; so determined not to do nothing, to change the world. A few shattered steps leading nowhere.

Marcel put a comforting arm around her waist as they followed Pauline towards the Royal Festival Hall. People huddled in gloves and scarves were picnicking on tables outside. Marguerite laughed remembering Tony's prediction.

'It did take on then. Alfresco eating.'

As they went inside Marguerite was astonished. The place was buzzing with life. Hordes of children were pouring up the stairs to attend a matinee performance given by some school choirs, another group of youngsters were playing gamelan instruments in the foyer.

'There seems to be a lot going on, Pauline.'

'Yes. It's open all day and not just for concerts. And they have lots of festivals and free events. I want to show you something. There is a poetry library. Every book ever written.'

'How do you know so much about the place, Pauline?'

'Oh . . . well . . . just . . . I know someone who works here. Will you excuse me, I have to make a quick phone call.'

Pauline walked ahead and spoke briefly on her mobile.

'Sorry about that. Follow me, we have to take the lift.'

On the fifth floor they crossed a large room towards stacks full of books, where people were sitting in comfortable chairs reading or at desks writing. It was very quiet. Pauline introduced her to a woman whose face seemed familiar.

'This is Mrs Heydon, our librarian. She is a poet herself.'

'It's so lovely to see you, Miss Carter. Come round this corner. We have a room where we do performances and lectures. We call it the Voice Box.'

Marguerite was startled to see the room was full of people standing strangely still and silent. As she entered they started to cheer and clap. A small girl stepped forward clutching a bunch of flowers.

She said hesitantly, 'This is to say thank you, Miss Carter.'

'Elsie? I'm going mad. You can't be Elsie?'

'No, I'm Elsie.'

A smart, white-haired woman with tears in her eyes stepped forward.

'This is Margaret, my great-granddaughter, named after you. Except we couldn't cope with the French version.'

Marguerite was clinging to Marcel's arm.

'I'm sorry. Is this really happening? What's going on?'

Pauline explained.

'A few months ago I came to organise a conference in one of the rooms here and my contact turned out to be Elsie. When I told her you were coming on the march she said she'd arrange a get-together.'

Elsie was smiling now.

'I work here on the creative team. Been here for two years now.'

'I was terrified you were dead, Elsie.'

'Well, it's been touch and go. But I got my degree at Ruskin and despite everything I have ended up in my ideal job. With my friend. My true friend.'

Elsie pushed forward the blushing librarian.

'Here is the woman you made me look after at school, who has spent the rest of her life looking after me.'

Marguerite clasped them both by the hand.

'Irene?'

'Yes, Miss Carter. I know I disappointed you and I so much wanted you to know it all turned out all right.'

Elsie took up the story, explaining that Irene had taken in her baby and brought him up as part of her family, so that his mother could keep in touch with him. Although he did not know until he was an adult he was Elsie's son he already loved her as a close friend of his mother. When her life was out of control she lost touch with him but he was safe with Irene. The baby Elsie had heard her son, Dr Phillip Miller, mention in St Thomas's Accident and Emergency was introduced as Matthew, now a handsome young man of twenty-seven who had inherited Elsie's talent and was a budding actor. His daughter Margaret was this little replica of Elsie now holding Marguerite's trembling hand as she met these ghosts from her past.

Irene introduced two daughters and a son, the daughters' husbands and the son's wife, or in modern parlance their 'partners', and their offspring. Marguerite was delighted to see they were a microcosm of the multicultural Britain she had seen thronging the rest of the building.

'They all went to university, Miss Carter. So you see although I couldn't make it I made damn sure they did.'

Looking out of the window, with their arms round Marguerite, at the chunky brutalist buildings clustered by the panorama of the Thames, Elsie and Irene talked of the ambitious plans to develop further the Southbank area with its art gallery, concert halls, film centre, and National Theatre into a place worthy of the legacy of the 1951 Festival.

'Arts for everyone, not just the posh,' said Elsie. 'A place to discover, create and have fun. We're even planning a garden on the roof of the Queen Elizabeth Hall over there, so people with no gardens can sunbathe and picnic or make love if they like.'

'Well, I'm your man for that. Sorry, don't misunderstand me. I mean you'll need to construct some raised beds. A speciality of mine.'

A flashily dressed middle-aged man introduced himself as, 'Mick O' Sullivan, the truant from Risinghill, now a successful builder and cabinet-maker.' He handed each of them a card along with some wine in a plastic cup.

Helping him take round the wine Marguerite recognised Geoffrey Wilkins, who proudly told her he had been battling to get clause 28 repealed and it looked as if it was about to happen this year.

'Wouldn't Mr Stansfield be pleased?'

Marguerite hugged him.

'He would, Geoffrey. He would.'

Before Marguerite could put names to any of the other faces Elsie clapped her hands and shouted, 'Right. Shut up everyone for a minute. I want to propose a toast.'

Marguerite held Marcel's hand very tight, fearful of losing control of her emotions. He put his arm around her as Elsie said, 'Miss Carter, we got you here today because we want you to know how you influenced our lives. Most teachers never find out what they have meant to pupils and we thought we'd tell you before you pop your clogs.'

Now Irene stepped forward.

'We are just a handful of the thousands of people that you

have inspired. All going round amazing, or maybe boring, everyone by quoting those wonderful poems you made us learn. And here is a little present for you. My first published collection of poetry dedicated to you who told me I could do it. Better late than never.'

Elsie continued, 'You gave us something to treasure for the rest of our lives. I came across a quote when I was working in the archives here. It's from a speech made by some bloke called Lord Latham who was trying to persuade the establishment that the wonderful festival we went to fifty-two years ago was important. They thought it was a waste of money. There was a war going on then, the Korean War, just as we are threatened by another one now, so what he said is still true. This is it: "In view of the terrifying possibilities of the atomic bomb, the common bonds of culture will be the greatest insurance against future wars."

'That's what you taught all of us here today, Miss Carter. And we, and hopefully our children, will continue to spread your message. But above all you believed in us, you fought for us, you're bloody wonderful and we are deeply, deeply grateful.'

There was applause and cheers.

'Speech, speech.'

Marguerite was moved beyond words but managed to say, 'My dears, you've reminded me of something I sometimes forget. When we were here in 1951, I was down there by that wall and I said it to someone I loved very much, as I do all of you.'

She looked around at them all.

'"Oh, wonder! How many goodly creatures are there here! How beauteous mankind is! O brave new world, That has such people in't."'

413

Chapter 54

It was icy cold when Marcel and Marguerite returned to France. For three days the mistral whirled the naked trees and long grass into a turmoil. Torrential rain sent streams and waterfalls cascading through the fields and lightning turned night to day, thunder rumbling towards them, shaking the shutters with its overhead ear-splitting blasts.

Marcel had been very quiet since they came back, then one night, sitting in front of the stove, with the storm howling outside, he said, 'I can't keep you here. I understand if you want to go.'

'What are you talking about?'

'Now I've seen your life back there, I realise this place and I have nothing to offer you to compare.'

'And what do you think my life back there has to offer me?'

'Marguerite, I saw that you are a highly esteemed person and London is an exciting city.'

'But that was exceptional. It was extraordinary and wonderful and I was so moved and relieved to find my life hadn't been completely wasted and the march was thrilling, but real everyday life is not like that. What I remember most of our visit is your hand in mine and your arm round my shoulder when I needed it. Seeing your enjoyment.'

'Really?'

'Yes, really. It is a terrible weakness, but I need to share my pleasures, to look after people, to be a busybody. It was lovely to find my busy-bodying had been useful in the past, but that is over now. They have all moved on. People have died. My loneliness and idleness was driving me insane. Now I have found you again. I too am moving on. Into an old age spent here with you. If you will have me?'

'Oh, my dearest,' he whispered and he led her upstairs where they made love gently, kindly, safe in each other's arms.

'Tomorrow the storm will end and soon spring will arrive,' promised Marcel.

The next morning Marguerite set in motion the legal gifting of her flat to Elsie and Irene. She had discovered that Irene's husband was dead and she and Elsie were living together in a rented bedsit, neither of them ever having had the money to invest in property. After their hard lives she hoped the flat would make them comfortable in their old age.

As for herself, Marguerite thought that nowhere in the world was spring more beautiful than in the Vaucluse. In the course of one week she watched the brown landscape burst into colour. The bare branches of the cherry trees covered themselves in a white froth of blossom. The vista gradually revealed every shade of green that exists. A group of silvery trees quivered constantly even when there seemed to be no breeze. And the sun, oh the sacred sun. It lit the mountains, woods and fields as it rose in the morning making them radiant, iridescent. Soon the ground was carpeted with buttercups, primroses and violets, and narcissi that made her swoon with delight at their perfume as she carefully walked through them, marvelling at the occasional rare orchid.

Wandering on her own one day down the path she was intrigued to see that someone had tucked some small sculptures into the roots of the oak tree; an artist had chosen to pay tribute to this venerable work of nature with his or her own works of art. Marguerite too would leave an offering.

She went back to the house and lifted down from the top of the wardrobe the leather hat box that had belonged to her mother. From it she took her Croix de Guerre, and the tobacco tin that contained Jimmy's DFC. When she told Marcel what she planned to do he gave her his Croix de Guerre too, which he had some difficulty finding. She dug a hole beneath the oak tree, and buried all three medals, putting on top an ancient Roman roof tile that she had found in a freshly ploughed field. Maybe someone in a future generation would find these relics and wonder about some long-past, long-forgotten war. Or maybe they would disintegrate and disappear. The oak would outlive them. She embraced the tree but her arms did not even reach across the front. She dug her fingers into the 2-inch-deep crevices of the bark and looked up at its massive boughs stretching out around and above her and contemplated the miracle of its hundreds of years of existence. There were many birds in the tree but none had been impertinent enough to build a nest in it. She could hear a cuckoo in the distance mocking her strange ritual. She was alarmed that two of the huge lower limbs had no leaves and appeared dead. The tree had survived generations, observing the seasonal routine, and it was unthinkable that some disease should kill this giant witness to time. It was rooted deep in the world, it was more important than anyone or anything, more noble, more steadfast, more blameless. It deserved to be eternal. Then she noticed the mass of seedlings and young trees around it and realised it would be.

This continuity of nature would be her new mission. Instead

of cultivating the lives of children she resolved to improve the land. She set about it with vigour. She gathered information about installing a wind turbine and solar panels to generate their own electricity and she pored over books on gardening and viticulture.

That winter a local farmer started to uproot trees in the forest to open up land for crops.

Marguerite was incensed.

'That forest is full of wildlife and rare plants. It will upset the balance of nature to change it. It should be protected.'

She confronted the man in his tractor but he dismissed her with contempt as a meddler who should stay at home and gossip with the other old biddies. Marcel dissuaded her from threatening the man with her revolver.

'Right. I'm going to the mairie. We must fight this. It's not right.'

Marcel walked with her to the top of the track where he stopped and said, 'I have to plant the potatoes for the winter. Good luck, ma chérie.'

'Aren't you coming with me? Do you disapprove?'

'No, of course not. You are right, and you can win this. I am just relieved you have stopped trying to save the whole world.'

'Well, I don't have to. The world is in good hands. There will be no war in Iraq after that huge protest. They have got to listen. People Power works.'

Marcel looked at her with much the same expression as Tony had at Half-Full Lizzie Dripping.

She hesitated for a moment.

Then she stomped purposefully up the hill.

ACKNOWLEDGEMENTS

This book would not have been started without the enthusiasm of Alexandra Pringle, nor continued without her unfailing support. Her guidance and that of my editor Gillian Stern have been crucial to my journey on this new adventure of writing a novel. For forcing me to pay attention to detail I am grateful to Mary Tomlinson. And for boosting my confidence, to everybody at Bloomsbury, led by Alexa von Hirschberg. And my wise agent Paul Stevens. And the ever-calm Clare Eden.

My own memory of the period this story covers has been supplemented by the books of Dominic Sandbrook and David Kynaston among many others, mostly borrowed from the London Library. The staff there have led me to newspaper reports, diaries and illustrations, as well as relevant books.

For information about Risinghill School I am grateful to ex-pupils Isabel Sheridan and the Risinghill Research Group, who will be publishing a factual version of the school's history. I was also helped by the builders working on the site of the school, little of the original of which remains, it having been replaced by a fine comprehensive, the Elizabeth Garrett Anderson School. I think Duane would have been pleased. I am indebted to Leila Berg's version of what happened there in her book *Risinghill: Death of a Comprehensive School*.

For insight into attitudes towards education, among other sources I used the Black Papers by Cox and Dyson.

For help in the difficult task of researching events in the Vaucluse area during the war, I am grateful to my friend Elizabeth Evans, who also accompanied me in locating the frequently forgotten places where they happened.

Roddy Maude Roxby was invaluable in recalling Dr Chapple's CURE organisation.

The Imperial War Museum has endless potent, sometimes deeply moving, artefacts and reports of events during the war.

For research into the history of the South Bank I am grateful to Judy Kelly and Siân McLennan.

I am grateful to Kate Marsh for her patience in typing out my handwritten copy with all its numerous rewrites.

The poem attributed to the character Irene on pages 55–56 was actually written by the then thirteen-year-old Gemma Currens from the Lochend Community High School during a writing retreat led by their inspirational teacher Gordon Fisher, which was organised by the Arvon Foundation and funded by the John Thaw Foundation. The poem is called 'Midnight's Child'. Gemma has now left school but is still writing and performing.

I have learnt so much over the four years of writing this book. I am deeply grateful to all my teachers.

The author and publishers express their thanks for permission to use the following material:

Extract from *Two Cheers for Democracy* by E.M. Forster reproduced by kind permission of The Provost and Scholars of King's College, Cambridge and The Society of Authors as the E.M. Forster Estate

'There'll Always Be An England'. Words & Music by Ross Parker & Hughie Charles © 1939 Chester Music Limited